"OKAY, HERE IT IS, GOD. I'M SCARED."

Casssidy relaxed her shoulders and grew still, more reverent. "Trevor is a man who adores his children. What will he think of a woman who kept such a terrible secret from him?" She swallowed emotion. "I've already lost so many people. I don't want to lose Trevor and the children, too. I don't want them to leave me."

I'll never leave you.

"I know that, God." She opened her eyes, focusing on His sky. "You've already proved it." The times in her life when she'd pulled away from God, He remained and waited for her return. "So what do I do now?"

Trust me.

Cassidy sighed, tired of running from God's will. "I choose to stand still and trust You. I don't understand all of Your ways, but I believe You want what's best for me. My hope is in You and . . . there are things You want me to learn, things You want me to do . . ."

forgivin' ain't forgettin'

mata elliott

West Bloomfield, Michigan

WARNER BOOKS

NEW YORK   BOSTON

Published by Warner Books with Walk Worthy Press™

Warner Books
Hachette Book Group USA
1271 Avenue of the Americas, New York, NY 10020

Walk Worthy Press
33290 West Fourteen Mile Road, #482, West Bloomfield, MI 48322

Printed in the United States of America

Time Warner Books name and logo are trademarks of Time, Inc. used under license

ISBN: 978-0-7394-6965-1

Book design and text composition by L&G McRee

To my husband, David, because you love me just as I am.
And to my sisters everywhere who suffer in silence;
you are not alone.

acknowledgments

This book exists because of You, Heavenly Father. Without You, I could not have written one word. Thank You for choosing me to be a pen for You and for pulling me out of my comfort zone. Thank You for loving me when I did not love myself and did not love You. You are my Everything.

David Elliott, my husband and friend, thank you for giving me the opportunity to write full-time. You accepted the vision when I had only one page, so these few words here hardly measure the appreciation I feel.

To Lamont, my son, you have taught me a lot. Thank you for accepting me into your life and for being patient while I learned to be a mother.

To my father and mother, Wyman and Lillian Taylor. Although you are gone from this life, I can still feel your hugs and hear your many, many words of encouragement. Thank you for your daily example of what it meant to love God with all your heart, mind, and soul. I always smile when I think of you.

Aunt Eunice Tucker, you've lovingly supported every major event in my life. I'm so glad you're here for this one, too. Cousins Maria Watson, Michelle Harris, Stephanie Watson, and Alex Morgan, a special thank-you for cheering me on. And to all my family, Watsons and Taylors, I could not have come this far without you.

To my mother-in-law, Mary Elliott, thank you for praying for me. To my sister-in-law, Mary Franklin, thank you for answering every question I had about anything. To each member of the Elliott family, I love you.

Elder and Mrs. Harold B. Hayes, Sr., thank you for taking on another daughter and always making me feel at home in your presence. I am blessed to have you.

To Pamela Williams, my sister, you've proved you don't have to share blood to be family. Thank you for being in my life for the last twenty years, for believing early on my book was good enough to be published, for listening to me talk about my characters as if they were real people, and for always telling it like it is.

Donna Booker, our mothers met when you were a toddler and I was still in the womb. I believe they knew then we were destined to be tied at the heart. Thank you for your many cards and gifts of encouragement, which always arrived on the days I needed them most.

My godmother, Vanessa Liggett, you have the biggest heart and most loving spirit of anyone I know. Thank you for never tiring of praying for me. Thank you for the music.

Nancy Stevenson, the first time I told you I was writing a book, you took me seriously and have from then on. Without wavering, you walked with me through the good days and the rough ones, too. Thank you.

Linda Poole, before I owned a computer, you allowed me to sit at yours (for hours) and write the first chapter of my book. Not many people would have done that, which goes to show just how beautiful you are. Thank you for all the Web site help, too.

God has blessed me with a camp of spiritual mothers: Dorothy Howard, Janet Wilder, Celeste Walton, Velma Spain, and Jacqueline Williams. Your daughter loves you.

Dexter and Tiffany Godfrey, I am honored to have you in my life. Thank you for standing on God's promises with me, and for opening your home when I came that way.

Mayola James, Carolyn Boston, Cheryl Threadgill, Robin Williams, Brenda Chamberlain, Charity Jones, and "my sista" Casey Hayes, whenever I ran into you, you had something positive to say about my writing and that meant so much.

There were those who poured words of motivation into my life early on: Mrs. Baxter, my fourth grade teacher, who assigned me the job of writing the class Christmas play. Former youth minister, Rev. Edward Cross, Jr., who made a "big" deal out of all my "little" essays. And the late James Jefferson, the first writer I knew.

Mrs. Jean Love Robinson, I'm so thankful God sent such a wonderful writer and person my way. Watching you, I've learned how to hold my head up higher and to make the most of every day. What a light you are.

Mrs. Katherine Reed, I am grateful for your prayers

through every stage of my life. And thank you for calling me on the morning I left for my first overnight writers' conference. I will always remember.

Prayer warriors: Mother Evelyn Simpson, Mother Vernice Copeland, Dr. and Mrs. David Stevens, Pastor Roxanna Puriefoy, Ms. Doris Miller, and Minister Gail King. It's been a comfort knowing you are going before God on my behalf.

Denise Thompson, Marion Taylor, Carla Cardwell, and Yolonda Marshall, you've been my girlfriends since before I was ten. How blessed I am! Crystal Miller, Hilarey Johnson, and Adria Carter, how blessed I am to have new friends like you!

To my Walk Worthy Writer's Group: Leslie, Claudia, Olivia, MaRita, Aubrey, Kristin, Rodney, Colette, Pamela, and Gloria, meeting you face-to-face was one of the greatest events in my life. Thank you for reading my first one hundred pages and sharing your insight.

To my first church families, High Street Church of God and West Oak Lane Church of God. It is in these places I received a firm foundation. Thank you for all the love and prayers.

To my current shepherd, Pastor Alyn E. Waller. I continue to grow spiritually because of your love for the Word of God. Thank you for your commitment to Jesus Christ and your unconditional love for your flock.

Denise Gause of Denise's Delicacies, you patiently explained the ins and outs of running a bakery. You also make the best butter pound cake I have ever tasted!

Lisa Crayton, you are a gift to the writing/publishing industry. Thank you for pulling me aside and speaking those words of life into my life. They continue to resonate through my heart.

To Diana Urban, thank you for helping me navigate through the editor and agent appointments at the ACFW conferences. Although I was tired, you wouldn't let me cancel.

To the authors I met along the way who deposited a strong word of support: Carmen Leal, Dr. MaryAnn Diorio, Linda Windsor, Kimberley Brooks, Kendra Norman-Bellamy, Marilynn Griffith, Andrea Boeshaar, Louise Gouge, Kathleen Y'Barbo, Sharon Ewell Foster, Carrie Turansky, and Yolonda Tonette Sanders. I appreciate your willingness to help another writer make the journey.

To author and speaker Yolanda White Powell, you are a dynamic voice for God. I have learned so much from you.

To my publisher and mentor, Denise Stinson, under your guidance I've discovered what it means to be a writer for God and that nothing, not even writing for Him, is more important than Him. You are an inspiring woman of faith, and I thank you for the privilege of writing for Walk Worthy Press.

To my editor, Frances Jalet-Miller, thank you for the attention you dedicated to every aspect of my story. You made the editing process a pleasure. My sincere appreciation is extended to the entire Walk Worthy Press and Time Warner family for taking this novel to the next level.

Before I sign off, Anthony, wherever you are, thank you. You said this day would happen way back when we were in the sixth grade.

acknowledgments

And to anyone I may have forgotten to list, truly you are not forgotten, but I am simply imperfect.

Finally, to everyone who reads this book, I am humbled that you selected it. God bless you.

forgivin' ain't
forgettin'

prologue

She'd been taken.

He'd been left behind.

The man seated on the first pew gazed at the closest window. Strong, frequent gusts of fresh air blew into the room, yet he felt like a prisoner in the mouth of a skin-scorching oven. He dipped his fingers into the inner pocket of his suit jacket and retrieved a pack of antacids. With a slow fire rolling through his belly and the toast and orange juice he'd forced down this morning threatening to reappear, he placed a tablet on his tongue.

Perspiration dribbled from his sideburns and collected under the stiff collar of his shirt. He drew his hand along his throat, down to his tie, and pulled on the knot. It seemed like hours, but he'd only been in the stone church about thirty minutes, gathered with hundreds of others to say farewell. As sunshine illuminated the enormous stained-glass window at the front of the sanctuary and colorful rays of light crisscrossed above the pulpit, he closed his eyes and wrestled against the tears he refused to let drop, agonizing that nothing would ever be the same. It was the beginning of a whole new way. And like a man unjustly sentenced for a crime he did not commit, he could not believe life had dealt him this hand.

He recalled the hour his world toppled with the ease of a preschooler's blocks. The long hand had slipped to 12. The short hand hovered on 2. The clock on the hospital wall ticked death as a bedside monitor howled and a throng of scrubs-dressed people circled the bruised and broken body of his other half. The doctors and nurses did everything medically possible while he looked on from the other side of the door—hoping, praying, begging God for a miracle.

That was six long days ago. Restful sleep had eluded him since, the bags under his eyes as dark as his suit.

The heartburn that had caused such discomfort minutes prior began to ebb, his skin cooling now. Hopeful the music might numb the pain of a broken heart, he stared through the semidarkened lenses of the sunglasses he hadn't bothered to remove and settled his sight on the choir. The director raised her hands, and the robed singers stood. But as the musicians began to play the introductory notes of a known-to-please spiritual, the man's focus relocated to the place it had lingered so many moments already this morning. He studied the shiny pearl-tinted casket centered before the altar rails and surrounded by hundreds of bright full blooms.

It was difficult to tear his eyes away from the casket, but he brought his heavy gaze back to the choir. As the singers harmonized with the force and the grace of angels, a tiny hand slid along the inside of his wrist and up to the lines of his palm. He managed a slight smile at the four-year-old sitting beside him on the padded bench, then lifted her to his lap and hugged her to his chest. Two small legs dangled between the V of his large ones. Two forlorn eyes searched his before asking, "Daddy, why did Mommy leave us?"

He clasped her hands between his, the same gentle way one would shelter a fallen baby sparrow separated from the security of the nest. He whispered around the lump of tears in his throat, "Everything will be all right," although he was skeptical that it was the truth.

A perfume that had been with him in the limousine continued to cloud around his head. The scent belonged to the woman leaning against his shoulder—his children's godmother. Unrestrained sobs shook her shoulders, and he squeezed her hand. She pulled their joined hands into her lap, and the tears her handkerchief missed trickled between his fingers and over his wedding band. By now, the choir had reached the pinnacle of its song, rocking in the enraptured fashion expected. Many of the mourners were on their feet, clapping, bouncing. Those electing to remain seated displayed their joy with waving hands or handkerchiefs, toe tapping, and shouts of praise that coasted like wing-stretched doves to the high ceiling. But the musical gospel failed to console him. Close to weeping, he drew a breath for composure, dug his heels into the carpet, and blinked back all stinging tears before they could run rivers down his face.

He had to be strong for his girls.

He glanced at his older child, an arm's length away on the same pew, her small hands folded so tightly they must have ached. The paternal longing to hold her as he was holding his little one knocked at his heart, yet he left her as she was, nestled in the curve of her aunt's arm. The time when he had possessed the power to hug and kiss this daughter's problems away was only a murky memory. She had withdrawn from him since her mother's passing. Perhaps she wished it had been he who died. He had wished it. He would have gladly taken his sweetheart's place so his children could have her back.

But God had not allowed it to be. And so it seemed he had not only lost his wife. He'd also lost his firstborn.

*

Three twenty-something women sat together near the rear of the crowded church. The one in the middle extended her polished nail and swept a piece of lint from her dress, the hem of the red garment inching toward her thighs as she crossed one slim leg over the other. She unzipped a small handbag, withdrew a compact, and popped it open.

"Can't you go anywhere without that thing?" a disapproving voice said.

Ignoring the female sitting on her right, the woman in the red dress and red heels continued to idolize her reflection.

"Do you really think it's appropriate to do that now?" The whispered question shot from the left this time.

The woman rolled her eyes. Any sensible female knew a funeral was one of the top ten places for meeting a man, making it essential to look her best. She extracted a tube of lipstick from her handbag and applied an additional coat, sharpening the color. "I look so good," she cooed, bouncing her shoulders to a beat in her head.

"I know exactly what your butt is up to," the petite lady on the right snapped, and several people in the vicinity sent reprimanding glances. She quieted to a whisper. "Anyone who knows you can see straight through your brain."

"What are you talking about?"

"I'm *talking* about the reason you're here."

"I'm here for the same reason as everyone else." She tried to sound sad. "I'm in mourning." Batting her eyelashes, she returned the glamour accessories to her purse.

"You never even liked her," she hissed.

The slender female on the left eased her back away from the pew and turned her head. "Why don't you *both* save this drama for later? The pastor is speaking."

The female in the middle squinted at the woman who had just subtly told them to shut up. She was sick of her holiness ways and modest wardrobe. Today her girlfriend's black skirt was too long, the white collar of her blouse too high, and, as usual, the only makeup she had on was a tame shade of lipstick. "I'll be the first to admit that me and what's her name up there in the coffin were never close, but I do feel terrible about what happened to her," the woman in red said as she toyed with a lock of her long curls. "However, *she's* dead, not me. So why let the opportunity to delight in all these hard *chocolate* male bodies just slip by?" She stuck out her tongue and jiggled it. "*Taste* the chocolate."

In a voice tense with rebuke, the woman on the left whispered into her ear, "Show a little respect. This is a church, not a club."

Her chin jutted out. "I know where I am. And maybe I'll start coming more often." She nodded amen in response to the last statement the pastor had made, although she had no idea what it was.

"You don't fool me, girl." The woman on the right cooled herself with a straw fan. "Now that the man of your habitual delusions is single, you think you have a chance. You've always wanted him."

The woman in red snatched the fan and fluttered it near her exposed cleavage. "Yes, at one time I was *minimally* attracted to him."

"But you have no interest in him now?"

She stared ahead, waving the fan with increased momentum. "No interest at all."

$\mathscr{L}$

She was no stranger to visions, but certainly, a funeral was an odd time for a vision of a wedding. Startled by the arresting image, the gray-haired church mother jerked, sending the purple leather-bound Bible open on her lap to the floor. Bending to retrieve the divine book, she glanced across the aisle at the new widower. He was holding the hand of the beautiful woman next to him. They appeared to be dealing with their loss together. The church mother meditated some more on the vision, then leaned forward and helped herself to another look at the widower and the pretty-faced woman. A faint smile of enchantment and approval played on the church mother's lips as she pondered how God would bring the marriage in her vision to pass.

chapter one

Ear-piercing screams filled the air. Cassidy Beckett *tucked the towel around the baby and hugged him closer. She kissed his wrinkled forehead and rocked back and forth.*

"What's the matter with it?" Minister's voice crackled with hostility.

"I don't know." Cassidy gulped, and more of her tears fell onto the bundle in her arms. Earlier, she had cleaned him up the best she knew how, then rubbed lotion on his tender skin. Now Cassidy pressed her cheek against the baby and sniffed, holding his soft scent inside her nostrils until her lungs gave way. "I don't know how to calm him," she cried, her voice shaking with each word.

"Well, you better hurry up and figure something out." Contempt blazed in Minister's eyes as he stared at the baby.

Cassidy's cell phone hummed a series of notes, and she forced herself to stop thinking about Minister and the baby. Focusing on the present, she answered the phone. The caller had the wrong number, and after a polite exchange, Cassidy ended the call as the cab she occupied merged with the stream of traffic aiming for the next off-ramp. She was at least ten minutes from her destination, and so she had time to check her messages, and she logged in the code. One message waited in her voice mail box. Cassidy gritted her teeth and sighed from a place inside that was tired of dealing with Sister Maranda Whittle. She quickly scribbled Maranda's number on a small notepad, then called the number, ready to take on Maranda for the last time.

"Praise the Lord!" Maranda answered after the second ring.

"Hello, Sister Whittle. This is Cassidy Beck—"

"Oh, yes, Cassidy," Maranda cut in. Maranda smiled a full beam whenever she spoke to Cassidy at church, so Cassidy imagined Maranda was fully charged now. "I'm so glad you called. Have you given any more thought to our previous conversation?"

Cassidy's stomach burned. "No . . . not much."

"The Sparrow Ministry could use a young woman like you. Why don't you come to our next meeting?"

No can do. Cassidy could not make the next meeting, the reason enfolded in personal conflict, which she would never unfold with Maranda or anyone else. So why couldn't she just be blunt and answer Maranda with a no? Like the other times they'd spoken on this topic, her tongue hardened, and she could not lift it to speak one word that would let Maranda know without question she wasn't interested in joining the Sparrow Ministry. Maranda stated the time and place for the next Sparrow Ministry staff meeting, probably assuming Cassidy was writing the information down. As if she sensed Cassidy's desire to hang up, Maranda rushed through an oration on the ins and outs of the Sparrow Ministry that she had shared with Cassidy once before. "You be blessed," Maranda tooted at the end of the call.

"You, too," said Cassidy.

"Here we are," the cabdriver said. Cassidy suddenly realized the driver had parked in front of her house. He came around, opened her door, raised his cap, and scratched his bald, dark-colored scalp. He put his cap back on tight, and only the woolly gray sideburns were visible again. Cassidy stretched her legs through the doorway and vacated the burned-popcorn-smelling car she'd spent sixty minutes of her life in. As the hem of a denim skirt dropped below her calves, she smiled up at the three-story semidetached dwelling standing before her. The bulbs in the pine boxes that bordered the second-level windows had bloomed while she was away, and a breeze encouraged the tiny flowers to wave and bow at her as if they were welcoming home royalty.

After a sigh of optimism, Cassidy said, "It's good to be back." She harbored no doubts, questions, or regrets. Leaving San Diego, returning to her children, remained a wise decision.

The driver, who'd introduced himself as Benny at the airport, spoke with certainty. "I'm sure you missed your little girl."

Cassidy frowned, and Benny pointed toward the walkway leading to the brick house. A toy Corvette with an African American Barbie doll lounging in the passenger seat was parked in the dirt beneath a manicured shrub. Cassidy rubbed a hand over her microbraids from the start of her hairline to the bun at the back of her head. "One of the neighborhood girls must have left it there," she said. No children lived at this address, just she and her great-aunt, Odessa. Several years prior, upon completion of graduate school, Cassidy had planned on moving out of Odessa's house and renting an apartment. But Odessa had suggested that Cassidy continue living here and they would share the household bills.

Cassidy grinned as she thought of how surprised Odessa was going to be. Cassidy hadn't told her she was returning today.

Benny lifted a large suitcase from the trunk and started toward the house.

"No," Cassidy objected right away, "I can handle that." Benny shrugged and placed the luggage at the edge of the walkway, and she handed him the fare with a generous tip.

Rounding his vehicle to the driver's side, Benny shouted, "Enjoy the rest of the day . . . and the summer."

Cassidy planned to enjoy every remaining slice of summer vacation. Breathing in the delicate fragrance of her aunt's small garden, she flung aside the memory of Larenz Flemings, the man she'd dated at this time last year. Cassidy already vowed that *this* summer would be better, brighter, and by all means date-free, with the exception of Oliver Toby. Cassidy and Oliver Toby had a date every Wednesday afternoon.

A group of elementary-age girls drove by on bicycles, and Cassidy smiled, ACES stamped on her thoughts. The tutorial center, stationed in Charity Community Church, had been her idea. She had named it the Academic and Cultural Enrichment School. And while

ACES had been left in capable hands, Cassidy was eager to return. The students weren't just students. They were her children, those she loved and those who loved her.

The wind chimes hanging in the far corner of the porch tinkled as Cassidy looked over at her car, parked on the street. The previously owned Accord, hers for the last eight years, had been grounded, in need of significant repairs. Cassidy sauntered closer to the car and removed a brochure clamped beneath the windshield wiper. She skimmed the advertisement, an announcement detailing the grand opening of another neighborhood pizzeria. There was no room for pizza in Cassidy's diet, so she crumpled the paper into a ball and stuffed the wad into her pocket. She continued to study the car and decided it must have rained a lot while she'd been out of town, because except for the bird droppings splattered on the windshield, her car was immaculate, the front bumper "burnished to a luminous shine," she remarked to a squirrel scampering up a telephone pole.

Burnish.

It was Cassidy's word for the week. She collected words the way some people collected stamps or dolls or coins.

"Cassie gal, is that you?" Emma Purdue, Cassidy's longtime next-door neighbor, wobbled out onto her porch. Cassidy smiled in the direction of Emma's loud voice as Emma limped down the steps and along the walkway with the assistance of a cane.

"Yes, Ms. Emma, it's me." Cassidy advanced upon the only person in the world who called her Cassie. Emma Purdue, slightly deaf in both ears and adamant about not needing the support of hearing aids, had yet to discover that Cassidy's real name was Cassidy. With folks like Emma, once something got stuck in their head, it seemed to stay that way, and no matter how zealously the rest of the world poked, prodded, or protested, it didn't change a thing. Cassidy had long ago accepted that to Emma Purdue she would probably remain "Cassie" forever.

Cassidy embraced Emma, the odor of fried chicken and collards billowing from the stout senior's flowered housedress. The soul-food smell almost drowned out the thick and commonplace smell of the pomade Emma used on her short gray Afro.

"Whatcha doing back?" Emma asked, a hand on her hip, a hand resting on her cane. "Gal, ya not sick, is ya?"

Emma, with her Deep South upbringing and no more than eight years of school, often reverted to the way she spoke when she was a "gal" back home. Cassidy shook her head no to Emma's question, appreciating the motherly concern threading through Emma's voice.

"Did you eat enough while ya was at that teachas' convention?" With the back of her hand, Emma wiped the mid-June heat from her forehead. "I know the way ya can go without two, three meals straight sometimes." Her lips in a firm pucker, her eyelids close together, Emma bobbed her head down, up, down, up as she inspected Cassidy. "Gal, it don't look like ya put on a single pound."

"I ate three meals a day, Ms. Emma." Cassidy added what she knew the older woman would relish hearing: "Of course, none of the meals were as good as yours."

"I sho know that's right."

A mighty laugh burst from Emma, and Cassidy laughed, too, secretly, at Emma. The over-eighty-year-old didn't believe anyone could fry, bake, or even boil better than she could, and the truth was, up and down treelined Pomona Street, Emma was said to be one of the three best cooks on the block. The Vietnam veteran who resided in the corner house and Cassidy's aunt Odessa were said to be the other two.

"Well, I'm glad yer back," Emma said. "Shevelle and the baby is still here. Shevelle's been hoping she could get together with ya 'fore she goes home next week."

Cassidy was all for hanging out with Shevelle, but she prayed Shevelle left the baby at home. Last time Cassidy and Shevelle went out, Shevelle brought the baby along and insisted Cassidy hold her. It annoyed Cassidy when people with babies assumed everyone wanted to hold their little angels.

Cassidy reached for her suitcase, and the gold link bracelet she rarely took off slid to the end of her arm.

"Hold it." Emma's voice was uncompromising as she pounded her wooden stick on the sidewalk, the rubber tip stealing the strident sound she seemed to be after. "Robbie, come take this here suitcase," she hollered across the two-way urban street.

Their neighbor, a boy of nine, out for an excursion on his scooter, stopped the royal-blue contraption a few inches short of Cassidy's white canvas sneakers. "Hi, Cassidy," he said cheerily.

"That's Miss Cassie to you, boy." Emma nudged his ankle with her cane.

Cassidy put her arm around Robbie's shoulder and

sent a smile down to the child. An ache within Cassidy's soul intensified mercilessly, but she kept her jaw rigid, unwilling to let the agony show on her face. "Robbie," she said, "you keep right on calling me Cassidy."

"It ain't respectful." Emma aimed a sharp gaze at the youngster, further conveying that in her presence there would be no addressing adults without the preface of Mr. or Miss.

Cassidy gave Robbie a squeeze and patted his braided-to-the-scalp hair. "Your scooter looks new."

"It is. My dad gave it to me last weekend . . . when I stayed at his house."

"It's very nice. I like your knee and elbow guards, too. Where's your helmet?"

Robbie's stare widened. "I should go put it on."

"Good idea. I've got the luggage." Cassidy watched the boy ride home, her heart still aching. She turned back to Emma. Emma's expression was a sandwich of disbelief and disagreement.

"Ya should've let that chile help. It's never too soon for a boy to learn the ways of a man." She propped her cane on her hip and stacked her arms across a hefty bosom. "And like I've told ya time and time again, young lady, acceptin' a man's strength is not a sign of weakness."

Out of reverence, Cassidy kept her eyes from rolling, but she had to speak up. "I've got the Lord, and He's all the strength I'll ever need."

Emma laughed. "The Lord is the center of my world, too, baby. But the broad shoulders of an earthly man sho feels mighty good."

Not in the mood for one of her neighbor's love-and-marriage and how-good-a-man-can-make-you-feel talks, Cassidy hugged Emma good-bye, then grabbed her suitcase from the sidewalk and hurried to the house. Before she could drag her key from her purse, the Charity Community Church van pulled up to the curb and the driver blew the horn. Cassidy waved at Deacon Willie Linden and the three silver-haired female passengers on their way to the Knitting Circle, a club that met at the church on Friday evenings.

"Well, mercy," Odessa Vale exclaimed, pushing open the screen door. It squeaked and slammed behind her. "Baby girl, what are you doing here?"

Cassidy wrapped her aunt in a hug that pinned them close for several moments. She was forced to give the abridged version of why she'd come home early because Deacon Linden had blown the horn a second time, and now he was on his way up the walkway to escort Odessa to the van.

"We'll talk more when I get home." Odessa gave Deacon Linden, barely able to bend his arthritic knees, her bag of knitting supplies so she could hold on to his elbow and the rail as she eased down the steps. "I'll tell you all about Trevor," she said over her shoulder.

"Who's Trevor?" Cassidy called after Odessa, but she was engaged in a conversation with Deacon Linden and either didn't hear the question or elected not to answer.

℀

"Are there any questions or concerns?" No hands rose this time. Trevor Monroe clapped shut his binder and stood. "In that case, we're done for the day. You'll find refreshments in the lounge." He smiled at the newest teen employees seated around the conference table as they gathered complimentary pens and handbooks, preparing to exit. It was a first job for most of them, and their uncertainty was obvious. As was his custom, Trevor had tried to keep the tone of the meeting casual. Although he let it be known that he was boss and expected professionalism at all times, he wanted his employees to feel comfortable and free to approach him. At the door, he shook each teenager's hand. "My number is in the manual if you have concerns, job-related . . . or otherwise," he reminded them.

Without meeting his secretary's gaze, he knew she regarded him with dissatisfaction. Grace Armstrong had advised that his private number should remain private. The managers could handle concerns. But Trevor had disagreed. The concerns of employees, especially the teens, were paramount. Some of them couldn't, wouldn't, talk to their parents. He preferred they come to him rather than reach out to negative street influences.

Trevor looked Grace's way. Above the burgundy rims of reading glasses, set so close to the tip of her nose it seemed one quick move of her head and the frames would topple off, her eyes scrutinized him. After all of the teenagers had gone, Trevor strode over and glued a kiss to the cheek of the woman dear enough that he'd given her cards and gifts every Mother's Day since she started working for him. Trevor knew he had a special place in Grace's heart as well. Grace had miscarried a baby thirty-five years ago, and he was the same age that baby would have been.

Grace wriggled out of his embrace, fanning her hands as if shooing flies. "That lovey-dovey stuff will get you nowhere, Mr. Monroe."

At work, she insisted on addressing him formally, and that was one of the battles he'd let her win. "I know, but that lovey-dovey stuff sure is fun." He winked. "Just don't tell Houston. I'd hate to have him put a beat-down on me."

Grace's face softened. "It's been ages since I've had men fighting over me."

"Shattered many hearts in your day, huh, Grace?"

She chortled, not answering. Trevor could easily imagine she had broken hearts. Grace was attractive at fifty-nine. Her silver and black hair was cut in a modern style, and even with the makeup she often wore, her face appeared natural. Grace had a medium-size, well-defined figure, and her clothing, while befitting her maturity, stayed hip enough to gain oodles of compliments from younger workers. Grace was what Trevor imagined his wife might have resembled years down the line if—

Grace's voice interrupted Trevor's thoughts as she passed him on the way to the door. "I mailed you an invitation. Did you receive it?"

He frowned, not meaning to. "It came a few days ago."

"I'll be making that potato salad you eat by the ton."

At the least, Grace deserved a halfhearted grin, and he gave one. "The offer's tempting. I'll let you know." In all honesty, Trevor could have let her know right then. He would not attend the annual barbecue in honor of Grace and Houston's wedding anniversary. With his family one member short, such a gathering would be too painful. Trevor lifted his binder from the table remembering how difficult it had been to return to church without his wife. It was a full three months before he could sit through an entire service.

Trevor locked up his office for the day and exited through the rear of his Chelten Avenue bakery and café. Car keys hanging from his fingertips, he strolled across the parking lot blacktop to a hunter-green Expedition. The hot strikes the sun bombed the region with all week were held at bay by thickening, darkening clouds, but the air was still too clingy for Trevor's taste, and before boarding his truck, he pulled off his tie, undid his top shirt buttons, and rolled his sleeves to his elbows. After starting the ignition, he flipped on the air conditioner. A man pleased with the outcome of the workday, he drummed his fingers on the dashboard in time to the spry pulse of Bishop Colvin Culpepper and the Solid Ground Church Mass Choir. Trevor owned all four of Culpepper's urban praise CDs. The latest he'd purchased yesterday, and as he listened to a song he was hearing for the first time, he sorted through ideas of how to spend the evening. Like most things nowadays, his plans revolved around and often included the leading ladies in his life. Trevor removed his phone from the belt clip at his waist and punched the necessary buttons.

"Hello," a child's voice promptly said.

"Hey, baby."

"Daddy," Brandi Monroe sang. "When are you coming to pick us up?"

"I'll be there soon. And guess what?"

"What?" Brandi asked with breathless anticipation.

"I have a surprise for you and Brittney."

"A puppy," she squealed. "Are we getting a puppy?"

Trevor smiled, enjoying his baby daughter. "No, Poopie's enough." One ball of fur that tagged his toes before he could get his socks on in the mornings was all he could tolerate. "It's not a bunny, a lamb, or a raccoon," he said, satisfied he'd named all the critters on Brandi's most recent pet wish list.

"I have a surprise for you, too, Daddy," she said. "But you have to wait until Sunday."

Father's Day. Holidays drove the pain of loss in deeper, and whether it was Memorial Day, Thanksgiving, or Christmas, Trevor had become more of an onlooker than a participant. But God is good, he thought, determined to stay encouraged, and come Sunday, he'd wear a smile for the sake of his children. He requested gently, "Sweetheart, put Aunt Penny on, please."

After a brief silence, another familiar voice greeted him. "What's up, big brother?"

"Don't tell the girls, but I thought I'd treat you three to dinner and a movie." Penny Davies was worthy of more. She'd been a lifesaver, helping with the kids since the death of his wife. They were at Penny's place now because she'd taken on the weekly task of washing and braiding their hair. Trevor would never forget the way tender-headed Brandi screamed her misery the first and only time *he* attempted to comb through her coarse tresses. "So are we on for tonight?"

"I'll have to pass."

"Don't tell me you have a date with Kirk."

"And if I do?"

Trevor caught an earful of attitude. "Take it easy," he soothed, not intending to go one-on-one with Penny over this month's loser. Since her divorce, the quality of the men Penny chose to date balanced to zero. Yet Trevor had promised to keep out of her romantic affairs. He understood how vexing it could be when people angled their radar toward the love life of another. His wife had been gone only a little more than a year yet numbers had been slipped to him, names whispered, bouquets and baskets delivered. The bulk had been from fellow Charity Community Church parishioners ready to have their daughters or granddaughters, nieces or baby cousins, pursued, courted, and wed—and not necessarily in that order.

"I'd love to go out with you and the kids," Penny said, "but my throat's sore. I think I'm coming down with something. I plan to order Chinese food and call it a night."

"Just make sure you're all better by next Saturday, or else I'm dateless."

"I told you, I have several girlfriends who would *love* to escort my tall, so-fine brother."

"Not interested," he mumbled. Then in a lighter tone, he added, "I have an errand to run. Then I'll be over for the girls."

"Hey," she stopped him before he clicked off. "If it isn't too much trouble, bring a movie to go with my meal."

Asking what kind of film to rent was a waste of time. Penny appreciated a good love story as much as he did.

In fact, brother and sister, born eleven months apart, were very much like twins. They looked alike, had the same food favorites, and they could talk about anything together. But Trevor rarely talked to Penny, Grace, or anyone about losing his wife. And he had not spoken once about the cowardly decision he'd made the day she died.

chapter two

Trevor crossed the video store, passing the New Releases section. He halted behind a man his height and cleared his throat. Kregg Lattimore turned, and a smile appeared on his dark-skinned, clean-shaven face as the men performed their rendition of a handshake, a little something they put together during their Central High School days. A few minutes into the conversation, Trevor wanted to know, "Did you solve your scheduling problem?" Last week, Kregg had divulged he was having trouble juggling a full-time accounting career, two graduate courses, and his new high-maintenance girlfriend.

"I'm working it out." Kregg slid a pack of gum from the breast pocket of a knit shirt. He held the pack out to Trevor, who shook his head no. Kregg dislodged a stick, then returned the pack to his pocket. "So how's Penny? I haven't talked with her this week."

"She's coming down with a cold or something, but other than that, she's okay."

"Is she still going out with that jerk Kirkpatrick?"

Trevor grimaced. "Most likely. And for the record, the *jerk* prefers 'Kirk.'"

"I could care less what that cheating dog prefers." Kregg yanked a romantic comedy from the shelf. "I don't know why Penny can't see it. Anytime a man tells you not to call his house and won't give you a legitimate reason, it means another woman is the reason."

Trevor selected a movie he thought his sister might welcome. "Maybe if you'd shown more interest, Penny wouldn't have gotten involved with Kirk."

"Like I've always said, I can't date Penny. I've known her since she was in diapers. We're like family." Kregg looked down at the romantic comedy he was holding. Putting the film back on the shelf, he opined, "Romance is so overrated."

"Romance is a vital organ of the love relationship. Having a relationship without romance is like having candles and never lighting them. Where's the pleasure?"

Kregg grinned for a moment. "I remember how you and Brenda were always doing something romantic. Your love for each other was quality, and it showed, man. And speaking of love, guess who I ran into at the gym yesterday?"

A young male employee with short dreadlocks and two gold hoops in each ear ambled by with a stack of videos. Another employee straightened a nearby shelf.

"Sherron Markham," Kregg answered his own question.

Trevor stopped looking at DVDs and focused on Kregg. Sherron had played basketball with them at Penn State. Sherron's girlfriend Staci had also been a student, and when you saw one around campus, you saw the other. No one was surprised they married before graduating. Everyone was stunned when Staci died suddenly of an aneurysm two years ago.

"How's he been doing?" Trevor remembered Sherron had cried throughout Staci's funeral.

"Great. He showed me a picture of his fiancée."

"He's engaged?" There was total surprise in Trevor's tone.

"Engaged," Kregg echoed. "And he looks like a happy man. I gave him my best wishes and told him he better let us know when the big day is."

Trevor suppressed a frown. He was having a hard time bending his brain around this bit of news. It seemed like Staci had died only yesterday. And now Sherron was in love with some other woman. How could he disrespect Staci like that?

Kregg scrutinized Trevor intensely. "So what about you, man?" Kregg asked.

"What about me?" Trevor said uncomfortably.

"Do you think you'll ever marry again?"

"I seriously doubt it," Trevor responded from his heart, and walked away.

Wordlessly, the men trekked to the next aisle. Kregg pointed out an action film. "Rave might like this, huh?"

"I'm clueless."

"Help a brother out, will you?"

"Okay, two words"—Trevor made the peace sign for the number two—"*Fatal Attraction.*"

Kregg meandered a few feet down the aisle. "Look, I admit Rave's spoiled and self-centered, but she has a sweet side."

Trevor followed Kregg into lane four and dodged a

set of rambunctious boys about the size of his eight-year-old, hoping his boyhood crony was right about his girlfriend Rave. From what he'd heard of her, Rave Brown wasn't spoiled, she was rotten—a woman accustomed to having her wishes fulfilled, and more mercy on the man who refused to grant them.

"I'm bringing Rave next Saturday," Kregg said.

When Trevor learned that all the coaches were bringing dates to the City Champions awards banquet, he felt like he was in seventh grade again. It was one week before the spring dance, and he was the only boy without a date. Kregg, already possessing a charm that made all the girls blush and giggle, had asked Natalie Thomkins for him. Natalie was taller than all the boys and had beat all of them up at least once, but miraculously, Trevor got through the dance without a scratch.

"Is Penny still coming with you?" Kregg asked.

Trevor bobbed his head, signaling yes. The only other woman he would have felt no trepidation asking out was Kendall McBride. She had been his wife's best friend. She was also his children's godmother. Kendall lived on the West Coast, and flying her in so she could be his date seemed a little over-the-top. So it was either take Penny or attend the semiformal alone. Trevor coached an all-boys' basketball team, and Kregg a mixed-sex tennis team. In years past, at the season's close, the City Champions league rewarded the basketball, football, and tennis teams, comprised of kids from multiple Philadelphia neighborhoods, with an all-you-can-eat cookout in Fairmount Park. This year the board decided on an evening affair, something to inspire the kids to dress up and promote some manners.

"I hope we're at the same table. That way you can get to know Rave better. Just promise you'll leave off the ice."

Trevor thought if anyone left a chill in their path, it was Rave. He imagined the woman carried a pointed icicle in her purse and wouldn't think twice about impaling someone's heart with it. He shot a pitying look at Kregg.

"What's up with your face? You're the one who introduced me to her," Kregg reminded him.

It had been purely accidental. A couple of months ago, following Easter Sunday service, the two men were about to exit through the church doors when Rave intercepted Kregg. Trevor hurled Kregg a look of warning, but it was too late. The man was already salivating. Unable to quickly devise a purpose for pulling Kregg away, Trevor was left to do the polite thing and make introductions.

"Man, where are you?" Kregg questioned, two DVDs in his possession.

Trevor let the memory drift away and checked the time on his wristwatch. He needed to get going. The men joined a checkout line. "Look," he said, "if you're happy with Rave, that's all that matters. And I can see one good thing has come out of the relationship."

"What's that?"

"Rave has you coming to church more often."

"Yeah, well . . . I like being with her and doing the things she likes to do."

Trevor pulled out from the parking lot ruminating over what Kregg had said about him and Brenda. Kregg was right. Their love had been quality.

And Brenda Mosley had been his only love.

He was thirteen the first time he spotted her. She was dressed in a yellow blouse and a denim mini, a celestial sight, even finer than his Sunday school teacher, Sister Cornelius. He had a chronic crush on Sister Cornelius and planned to marry her—until Brenda.

Little Miss Mosley snubbed him at first, and understandably. He'd been a pubescent disaster—a mouth full of braces, a face stitched in acne, and too much corner-store cologne under his chin and armpits. Yet ugly and offensive as he had been, he had vowed then and there he would marry Brenda someday, giving Sister Cornelius to the second luckiest guy in the world. He, no doubt, would be the first.

Trevor turned on the windshield wipers, the thunderstorm forecast on the morning news coming in strong—building instant puddles, tugging down the temperature, and sending the unprepared scurrying for cover. For the length of the windy, rainy ride to Penny's, a hallowed collection of scenes shared with Brenda played on the stage of his mind, and it seemed almost sacrilegious, as well as ludicrous, to think he could marry again, love another as much as he loved Brenda.

♥

"Get moving. Your dad is here."

Trevor heard Penny's voice before she opened the door to her sixth-floor apartment. "Hi," he said seconds later, and pushed a DVD into her hand. The satisfied expression on her face reminded Trevor of his mother and grandmother. Penny wore her typical relaxation gear: sweat shorts and a tank shirt. Her hair was a group of short charcoal twists, untamed but vibrant.

"Daddy," Brandi screamed, and squeezed between the wall and her aunt so she could get to him.

Trevor caught the five-year-old under her arms, lifted her, and kissed her cheek.

"What's our surprise?" she said, giggling.

Keeping her in suspense, he answered, "Not yet."

"Aw," she whined, although her face was a circle of elation. She wrapped her arms around his neck and pressed her cheek against his. "I love you." The happy sound coasted into his ear.

"I love you, too."

A second little girl eased beside Penny.

"Hi, Brittney baby," he said, a lump fighting its way into his throat.

Brittney's hello was scarcely audible, and miles away from welcoming. She put her backpack on and progressed through the doorway without taking a glance at him. Trevor placed Brandi on her feet. When he straightened, Penny stroked his shoulder.

"Hang in there," she said supportively.

He nodded, masking inner chaos with a blank face. "Gotta go. I hope you feel better."

"Thanks. And thanks for the movie."

"Anytime," he said, and followed his children to the elevator, finally swallowing that lump.

chapter three

Cassidy relaxed beneath the water's warm flow. As the liquid soothed the tired muscles she hadn't realized she'd used while traveling, she listened to Minister's stern instructions.

"You're going to have to make it shut up."

"I'm trying," she cried, and put the baby to her breast again. "I can't get him to suck."

Minister stomped to her. "Give it to me."

She hesitated, then lifted the baby, secured in a bath towel. "Be careful with him."

Minister placed the bundle against his shoulder. He paced the length of the small living room, intermittently shooting her glances mixed with desperation and derision as he thumped the baby on the back.

"Please, Minister," she pleaded, "not so hard. He's so small. You'll hurt him." She began to quake with fear, and her sobs joined the baby's as she begged, "Please don't hurt him."

The recollection burdened Cassidy with sorrow.

Shoulders sagging, she tipped her face to the shower-head, and the steady spray washed the tears from her face. Turning off the water, she let the stinging memory trickle back to an ocean of others like it. At times like this, when depression approached with an engulfing wave, she sought safety within the arms of her Father. *"When my heart is overwhelmed: lead me to the rock that is higher than I. For thou hast been a shelter for me, and a strong tower from the enemy. I will abide in thy tabernacle for ever: I will trust in the covert of thy wings,"* she said aloud, encouraging herself with the passage from Psalms, a series of verses she had committed to memory so she could draw upon them at any moment.

Cassidy pushed aside the shower curtain, snatched the shower cap from her head, and stepped onto a terry bath mat. After drying herself and applying de-odorant and lotion, she dressed in panties and a T-shirt. The white top, beginning to fray in some spots, was small, barely reaching her thighs, but it was comfortable. She reached up and freed a shoulder-length mass of black braids that she often styled off-the-neck when the temperature and humidity were high. The braids were so thin it was difficult to tell that they were braids unless you were standing beside her. She let the silky strands remain on her shoulders, and following a quick comb-through with her fingers, she reached for the knob of her bedroom door, her hand stalling in the air. She tilted her head toward the door on the opposite end of the room—the door that linked the bathroom to the guest bedroom. The floorboards in that room were creaking, and what sounded like footsteps clomped closer. Someone was in the house.

Cassidy sensed it wasn't Odessa back so soon, and the skin on the back of her neck prickled as her heart suffered a twitch of anxiety. She spun around as the door flew open.

"You can't catch me!" a voice yelled, speeding by.

Cassidy jumped backward, bewildered by the sudden appearance of a little girl with light-colored skin and long dark brown beaded cornrows. Her small hand twisted the doorknob to Cassidy's bedroom, and the girl with the head full of clacking beads disappeared inside the room. It wasn't likely, but Cassidy was thinking the child might be an angel. What other logical explanation was there? Cassidy moved to follow the angel, but the sound of much bigger footsteps drew her attention. Not knowing what to think now, she swung around again and bumped into the wall.

Cassidy tottered, the jolt having disturbed her balance as much as the shock. There was no wall, at least not of brick and mortar. This one was flesh and blood, hard as any wall. Her hands flattened to the male chest in her face as she steadied herself. She swallowed tightly as she realized a pair of sturdy arms had slipped around her waist, and large hands, all ten strong fingers, had secured her back. Stranded between the urge to flee and the desire to remain, she wandered into the eyes that were searching her face. Cassidy lingered inside them, deeper than planned, and before she could gain control, a flurry of excitement throbbed through her, setting off trembling from limb to limb. Possibly, he had felt her shiver, because he lowered his arms, though he did not back away. Cassidy supposed it would be up to her to place distance between them. She gave a feeble push against his chest and began to retreat—one step, then another.

So this was the Trevor her aunt had referred to. Oh, Cassidy had recognized him mere seconds after impact. But though she'd seen him countless times at church, she had seldom looked at him for more than a quick beat and never from this intimate stance, where it was easy to inventory every detail of his face. The skin, baked brown like bread edges, was without crater, wrinkle, or pimple. A mustache colored the area above his lip ebony, while a goatee, trimmed short, embraced his chin. A complete head of hair was cropped close to his scalp, and his eyebrows, moderate slashes, held faintly noticeable arches.

But it was more than surface good looks that held Cassidy's interest. She'd immediately perceived something pure and good and gentle in this man. And she'd felt from the moment he touched her that he was trying his best to keep her from falling, and was not attempting to be forward. First impressions, however, could be misleading. And from her experience, men that looked like Trevor, the handsome, "I work out regularly" type, like Minister and Larenz, were shallow and conceited and endowed with the personality of a peanut, so she wasn't about to get caught up in him.

"What are you doing in my house?" she snapped. "And how did you get in?" She knew without a doubt she had locked the front door *and* gone back to check.

A fat bumblebee hovering outside the screened window made a persistent buzzing sound. After a stretch of long seconds, Trevor finally drowned out the humming bee with a low but firm answer. "Mother Vale gave me a key."

"Why would you need a key to this house?" Cassidy slung her arms across her middle as if she were placing a barricade between herself and the man, an undisputable three or more inches taller than her five feet nine, she was noticing now. Trevor stood as stiff-shouldered as she was, and she continued to thrash him with an unfriendly look, demonstrating that although she'd initially been jarred, she was no pushover. "Answer me," Cassidy insisted in a tone more suitable for addressing a child.

Trevor's face held more amusement than anything else as his gaze eased over her face and down her neck and straight past the neckline of her . . .

Cassidy's eyes ballooned with anguish as a gasp of humiliation escaped her half-open lips. She yanked her towel from the bar and quickly wrapped it around her body.

"I found it," the angel bellowed as she came skipping back into the room, cuddling a yellow jacket as carefully as a mother would her newborn.

"Good girl." Trevor hoisted her into his arms, kissed her cheek, and gave her back to the floor. "Now go tell Sis we'll be leaving for the movies in a minute. And no more running in the house," he gently admonished over his shoulder.

That's when Cassidy made her move. Holding the towel in place, she twisted on the soles of her feet and marched into her bedroom. The slam of the door reverberated in her ears, and the picture on the wall quivered from the force. She pulled off the towel and threw it to the floor, making it the victim of her frustration as she replayed how Trevor had surveyed her with a twinkle in his eyes as if the incident had a humorous side. Cassidy huffed, snatched open the door of her closet, and jerked an understated shirt from a hanger. There was nothing comical about what had just happened in that bathroom, and as soon as she could dress, she would give Trevor her opinion in spoken words.

♋

Cassidy laughed, putting the phone to her other ear. "That was a funny one," she said of the anecdote her friend had downloaded from the Web.

"I've got another one. Would you like to hear it?"

Cassidy looped a lock of hair around her finger. "No, save it for tomorrow's conversation."

"Okay," Dunbar Smith agreed. "So tell me why you're home. When I spoke with you a few days ago, you said"—Dunbar adjusted his tone to sound more like a female's—"my days are filled with conferences. There won't be much time for sightseeing, so I'm going to stay into next week and visit a couple of attractions, buy a few sci-fi books, and kick back in the lounge chair on the balcony outside my hotel room, order room service at least once, and watch Lifetime all day."

Cassidy giggled. Dunbar had repeated what she'd told him almost word for word. And count on Dunbar to put a smile on her face. She sipped water from a glass, and for the next few minutes, she unloaded the primary reason she'd come home. "I want to make sure the kids are ready for the spelling bee." The Interfaith

Spelling Bee was only weeks away. There was a trophy cabinet in the church's main hallway, the shelves lined with dozens of trophies and medals won by the gospel choir, the youth choir, and the men's basketball team. Cassidy had already picked out a space on the first-place shelf for the trophy ACES would win.

"It's all about the kids," Dunbar whined with exaggeration when Cassidy finished. "I thought maybe it had something to do with me."

"Oh, you know I missed you."

His voice was serious. "I missed you, too, C.C." Following a brief period of comfortable silence, he asked, "Are you going to buy new books?"

She sighed. "I hope to. It's essential the kids read every day." Before Cassidy called Dunbar, she had called Portia Washington. Portia had been in charge of ACES while Cassidy was away, and she was the one who gave Cassidy the disturbing news. Their small one-room library had been painted, and the painters, doing a good deed, removed the books from the shelves and packed them in boxes so they wouldn't be damaged. Unfortunately, the painters left the boxes next to another set of boxes destined for the trash, and the janitorial staff carried the boxes with the books away, too. "When will the pastor be home from vacation?"

"Next Friday . . . I think," said Dunbar.

"When he gets back, I'll ask him if ACES can use the money in the children's summer fund. There should be enough money in the account to replace at least half of the books." Cassidy looked up from her kitchen stool perch. She could see Odessa coming through the front door. "Aunt Odessa's home," she said, "and I want to get the scoop on Trevor. He was gone before I could get my clothes on and grill him myself."

"Sorry I couldn't be any help."

"That's okay."

"Hey," Dunbar inserted into the pause, "how's your boyfriend Oliver Toby doing?"

Cassidy smiled. "Great. I called him as soon as I got in."

"I think I hear wedding bells," Dunbar teased.

"You're so silly. I'll see you tomorrow night at the singles' fellowship."

"Can't wait," Dunbar said. "Bye, C.C."

Cassidy listened. Dunbar liked for her to hang up first. "Bye," she said, assured he was still there. She walked over to the wall and placed the phone in the cradle as Odessa strolled into the kitchen. A head and a neck taller than Odessa, Cassidy leaned over and kissed the top of her hot-combed silver hair, slicked back and molded into a bun same as every day, except Sundays, when it was curled under a stylish hat. "We need to talk."

Odessa planted her midsize hips in a chair and clasped her hands in the lap of a pleated skirt. "Yes, thank you, I *would* like something cold to drink."

Cassidy smiled, selected a glass from the dish drainer, and approached the refrigerator.

"Are you going to Caring Hands in the morning?" Odessa watched as Cassidy put the cap back on the water jug.

"Yes, I left a message on Arlene's machine letting her know I'll be in."

"That senior center is blessed to have volunteers like you."

Cassidy thumped a tall glass filled with ice and spring water on the table. "Subject change," she said, lowering herself to a chair. She folded her arms on the table and pinned Odessa's gaze. "Would you like to know what man walked in on me while I was in the bathroom wearing next to nothing?"

Odessa pressed a hand to her cheek. "Oh, no, Trevor walked in on you?" Her bottom lip vibrated as she struggled not to smile. "I'm sorry, honey."

"Oh, so you think it's hilarious, too. Well, I don't *think* so," she said with emphasis, and flopped against the ladder-back chair, arms laced across her chest. "What's he doing around here—helping with a few odd jobs?" It was the only sensible theory she'd been able to formulate. And it wouldn't be the first time her aunt had recruited a man from the church for small household repairs.

Odessa swallowed several gulps of water. "Trevor's living here," she stated as matter-of-factly as she would have said good morning or good night.

Cassidy straightened. "Why would he be living here?"

"There was a fire at his house. Not too bad—confined to the kitchen. A lot of smoke and water damage, though."

"Yes, Dunbar mentioned it," she said slowly, her brain processing the revelation at a deliberate pace. "But I don't see the connection to *our* house."

"At Bible study, when Pastor Audrey announced there'd been a fire at the Monroe home and that our prayers were needed, I decided there was more I could do than pray. I invited Trevor and his children to dinner."

"I thought people brought flowers or a dessert when they came to dinner, not their luggage."

Her aunt ignored her. "While the children were having a slice of my apple pie, Trevor stepped outside to take a call. It was then I began to feel the Lord nudging my heart. He reminded me that since we have three extra bedrooms, there was plenty of room for Trevor and his family. They'll be here until it's safe for them to return to their home."

"Why didn't you tell me they were here when I phoned from San Diego last night?"

"I was about to tell you when Emma rang the doorbell."

"Oh," Cassidy said, remembering Odessa had rushed her off the phone because the Purdues had locked themselves out of the house and needed the spare key.

"I was planning to call you back, but Brandi and I struck up a conversation. That child sure can talk—almost as much as you could when you were a little girl." There was a glow on Odessa's face, and Cassidy suspected Odessa was remembering the first time she and Cassidy met. Cassidy was two and had no recollection of the event, but she loved to hear Odessa tell the story of how she'd reluctantly taken Cassidy out of foster care twenty-six years before and brought her home to live with her. Never having had a child of her own, well into her fifties, recently widowed, and two months away from retirement, Odessa didn't think she was the best choice for the position of mothering. But God reminded her that He was her strength and that she could accomplish anything with Him in her life.

Cassidy smiled at the woman who'd raised her, the

only blood relative she had. But the smile departed Cassidy's face as quickly as it had arrived. "Doesn't Trevor have family?"

"Trevor's parents are deceased, and so are Brenda's. She had no siblings, and Trevor has one sister. She lives in a single-bedroom apartment, and that really isn't much space for growing girls."

"No," Cassidy said, not so much thinking about the issue of space, but that Trevor didn't have much more family than she did.

"Trevor said his secretary and her husband are as close as family, but they already had out-of-town guests, and he didn't want to infringe. Initially, Trevor didn't accept the invitation to live here, either. He went on about how his insurance company was going to put him and the children up in a hotel. But I reminded him that our house was close to the church, his job, and his house, and therefore, it would be convenient for him if he stayed here. I think the selling point was when I mentioned the children would probably be safer and happier in a loving home than some strange hotel." Odessa had a complete white smile, since she had yet to remove her partial plates for the night. "The girls call me Grammy."

Cassidy could easily believe Trevor's girls were fond of Odessa. She possessed a passionate love for God and life and people of all ages. Goodness seeped from her, sweetening the lives of all she touched.

Odessa suddenly raised her hands the way she did in church. "Thank God Trevor and the children managed to get out of the house safely. Jesus, thank You . . ."

As Odessa praised God for His mercy toward Trevor

and his brood, Cassidy recalled it was just the spring of last year when Brenda Monroe was killed. It was a sad time for Charity Community, as Brenda was well liked. Cassidy had never befriended her, but they had worked together a few times in the church bookstore. Cassidy thought Brenda had a sweet personality, and she especially admired the way Brenda had cared for her little girls—and husband.

"I'm sure Trevor will be paying you rent," Cassidy said, returning to the present.

"He most certainly will not. And don't you dare ask him for any. He tried to give me money this morning, and I wouldn't accept it. I did let him supply his own groceries, but that was only because I wasn't sure we had what the girls are used to eating." She finished her water and loosened the ice cubes lodged at the bottom of the glass with a shake. "Trevor offered to do the cooking while he was staying here. I told him we'd split it with him." She sucked on a piece of ice, then spit it back into the glass, and it clinked against the other cubes. "He seems to be somewhat of a handyman. I don't know if you've noticed, but the faucet no longer drips after you turn it off."

Cassidy glanced at the sink. She hadn't noticed.

"I just did catch the young man before he got his hands on my screen door," Odessa continued. "I told him that slam was as much a part of the house as the foundation." She smiled. "He did wash your car, though."

"So it wasn't the rain?" Cassidy mumbled, heavy on the sarcasm.

"Trevor took a look under the hood, too. He said he

doesn't know a whole lot about mechanics, but he has a friend who does that kind of work." Odessa stood and walked to the sink with her glass. She dunked it in a basin of soapy water and washed it with a red-and-white-checkered cloth. "I've given the girls the third-floor bedroom and bathroom, and of course, I gave Trevor our guest room," she said, placing the rinsed glass in the drainer. "If you're uncomfortable sharing a bathroom with him, feel free to use the master bath in my room."

Cassidy tapped her index finger on the table, trailing Odessa with a cool gaze as she left the kitchen. Like a turtle coming out of its shell, Odessa poked her head back into the room. "I told him he could have the bottom shelf of your medicine cabinet. I hope you don't mind."

Cassidy forced a smile of resignation as Odessa disappeared again. Her aunt had done what a Christian should, opening their home to those in need. But there was still a portion of Cassidy that was unhappy about it. She didn't wish misfortune on anyone, but why couldn't it have been Dunbar who needed a place to stay? He would have been a lot more fun to have around. She lifted her arm and admired the gold bracelet decorating her wrist. It was a present from Dunbar. At least twice a month, he'd leave a box on her desk at the church. The box was always wrapped in pretty paper and capped with a bow. Dunbar attached a card each time, the message the same: *I thank God for you.*

chapter four

Daddy, are you listening?"

It was a struggle. Trevor was absorbed, reflecting upon the woman who'd filled his arms this afternoon. They attended the same church, but he didn't know her. With a thousand members, there was no way you could know everyone. Mother Vale had spoken of her niece several times since he moved into the house, but Trevor couldn't remember what she'd said her name was. Catherine. Cassandra. He was almost positive it was the second.

Trevor decided Cassandra resembled Mother Vale. Both had the same coffee-bean coloring, rich brown eyes silhouetted by lashes short but full, and a face more oval than round. Cassandra's face and the rest of her, if he were honest, had become a tenant in his thoughts, difficult to evict. And that was an enigma, if ever there was one. Skinny women were not his type. Brenda had been full-figured, and full was how he liked his hands to be. But Cassandra's slim body was a perfect fit next to his.

And all these hours later, it seemed he could still smell her sweet-scented skin, still feel her ragged breaths tapping below his collarbone where his shirt was unbuttoned, still feel her soft palms lying against his chest. He had wanted to cover her hands with his larger ones and whisper against the flow of hair shading her ear that she shouldn't be alarmed. But what else would she be, considering the way he had barged in on her and held her longer than necessary, then gawked at her like a boy of twelve while she stood there in that little white shirt.

He hadn't meant to stare. Anyway, the material was thick enough that he couldn't see anything. Not that he was trying. And Trevor had every intention of apologizing for the way he and his daughter had intruded, but Cassandra had zoomed from the room before giving him the chance.

Brandi asked another question. "Do you want some of our food, Daddy?"

Trevor suspended his musings to concentrate on his girls, the two of them sharing a cheesesteak and a basket of fries. He'd only ordered a soft drink for himself. "No, baby, I'm not hungry." He wiped her mouth with one of the white restaurant napkins.

Brandi's naturally wide eyes stayed on him. "Do you got a tummy ache?"

"Do you *have* a tummy ache?" he corrected with a gentle voice, and noticed that his elder child had ceased chewing, a fry doused with ketchup dangling midair as she waited for his response to her sister's question. Brittney rarely had much to say to him anymore, but it did make him feel better to think she might harbor a pinch of interest. "No tummy ache, girls." He smiled at them, then playfully pulled one of Brandi's braids and rubbed a hand across the top of Brittney's thick cornrows. The children resumed eating, and Trevor contemplated how one might express to girls this young that what ached was his heart; it was lonely, and missing their mother. Additional pain screwed through it as he watched a couple in a neighboring booth share a kiss. He hoped they knew how blessed they were.

Trevor helped the girls discard their trash and accompanied them to the ladies' room door. He paced outside, leery over sending his little girls into a public restroom unattended—a single father's apprehension. Brandi exited the lavatory first, hands dripping with water. "Why didn't you dry your hands?" he asked, his voice on edge because he hadn't come completely down from worrying.

Brittney, having heard the question as she came out of the bathroom, answered for her sister, "No towels," and returned to the booth to collect the stickers the waitress gave all kids under eleven, drying her hands on the front of her shorts. Trevor grabbed a handful of napkins and gave them to Brandi before she also resorted to using her clothing. Outside, he whisked her into his arms.

"I want to see another movie," she whimpered, hugging his neck.

"No more movies tonight." He kissed Brandi's chin, sticky with ketchup. He reached for Brittney's hand. She immediately plunged it into her pocket.

Their seat belts fastened, Trevor cruised from the

parking lot. The rain seemed to be over, and a few stars brightened the sky. At the traffic signal, he peered around the headrest. Brandi's lids fluttered on the brink of sleep. Across from her, Brittney stared through the window. A week after Brenda's funeral, he'd sent both girls to professional grief counseling at the church, though he hadn't signed up for it himself. The sessions benefited Brandi, but Brittney would cry hysterically when it was time to attend, and he eventually gave in and stopped making her go. He just couldn't stand the crying anymore. And since Brittney continued to earn passing grades in school and was playing as energetically on the soccer field as normal, Trevor thought forcing her into counseling might do more damage than good and only make her hate him more.

The little girl who used to shoot hoops with him, help him make cookies, and confide in him about everything was angry with him. She had every right to be. His behavior on the day they lost Brenda was irresponsible, insensitive. But at this point, he didn't know what else to do or say to make things right. Not a day went by that he didn't hug his girls, kiss his girls, and tell them how much he loved them. What else could he say that would mean as much as "I love you"?

⁀

"I love you, too," Rave Brown whispered to the man in her daydream before concluding with a kiss to his lips.

She tossed her long hair over her shoulder. She rested a stem glass half-full of white wine on the nightstand and rose from the king-size canopy bed. The thick carpeting of the large bedroom snuggled the soles of her bare feet as she crossed the room and pulled open the door of a walk-in closet. She stepped inside and snapped on the light. Rave removed the pantsuit she'd worn to the firm, and for a long time, she stood motionless in front of a wide full-length mirror in a lace chemise and a matching thong. Finally, with her hands planted on her waist, she studied her curves from different angles and smiled applause. She had been blessed with her father's fair skin and straight hair and her mother's C-cup breasts and small shapely backside.

The satisfaction on Rave's face withered to disgruntlement. No matter how breathtaking she was, the man in her thoughts never appeared enamored. She stomped her foot like a contentious child and fussed at him, "You should be finished grieving by now."

Rave stared into the resolute eyes of her reflection. The woman staring back at her was an attorney. She didn't settle for no without a fight.

Rave jetted out of the closet. A hasty rifle through her bottom bureau drawer rewarded her with a pair of hip-hugging black shorts and a red top that was more bra than shirt, perfect for showing off her navel piercing. She slid into the clothes and a pair of red platform slides, then strutted to the kitchen to search for the ice pick.

Inside thirty minutes, Rave slammed her foot on the gas pedal of her Mercedes and whizzed out of the driveway of the Germantown Towers Luxury Apartments. A screech of tires turned heads as she swung a sharp and reckless right at the corner. "I'll get you,

Trevor," she swore, "by any means necessary." That's why she'd gone after his friend. Get close to the friend, and eventually, she'd get close to Trevor. Rave remembered the day she resurrected the age-old idea. Easter Sunday. She hadn't planned to attend service, but with several new outfits, she figured it would be a shame not to model at least one on such a holy day. The benediction spoken, she approached her targets. As always, Trevor's greeting was wintry. But Trevor's friend, like most men, fondled her with a lascivious gaze. Rave would have been flattered had it not been Trevor's lust she craved.

"Trevor," she murmured, anticipation building as she thought about tonight and how they would spend it together with candles and music and silk sheets. She disregarded a stop sign for a third time and sped along the route that would lead her to him, the road to happiness.

✑

Delight bubbled in Cassidy, her smile deepening as she rested in the arms of the unconditional love flowing from the piano. Over the years, the ivory and ebony keys had become her confidants. The music spoke to her, and she spoke to the music. The notes knew all about the despicable act she'd committed when she was a student at Tilden University, yet they could be trusted to keep her disgrace from the world.

Cassidy struck a final note with as much gusto as she had the first, and lowered the lid of the dark upright, a gift from Odessa for her eighth birthday. The older woman joined her in the living room, carrying a purple leather-covered Bible and a mug of coffee that perfumed the air with mint chocolate. Odessa put her mug on a side table and settled into her antique rocker. The chair had been upholstered twice in fifty years, but the sepia-stained wood remained sturdy and smooth.

"Since you're home, will you be attending the baby shower?" Odessa asked, flipping the pages of her Bible.

One of the sisters from the church was due next month, and her mother was throwing a shower at the church on Sunday afternoon. Cassidy wouldn't get into a long discussion with Odessa about it, but the last baby shower Cassidy took part in left her battling a three-week attack of the doldrums. "No, I'll probably hang out with Dunbar Sunday afternoon." Cassidy shot a look at the crystal clock on the mahogany mantel, the color of the woodwork throughout the room. It was close to nine o'clock. "I'm going up for the night," she said. "I need to go over my Bible lesson." The Bible lessons were the chief reason she attended Charity Community's twice-a-month Saturday night singles' fellowship, unlike many of her female counterparts, who admitted they were there for the solitary purpose of finding a husband. Cassidy used to be one of those women who checked out every half-good-looking male who walked through the door while entertaining the thought that he might be *the one*. But these days Cassidy didn't care one iota about who showed up. "Good night," Cassidy said, and pasted a kiss on Odessa's cheek. She got as far as plank one of the stairs when the doorbell chimed. Cassidy left the steps and followed Odessa to the door. She listened over the older woman's shoulder, pleased she was using the intercom. She had cautioned Odessa against opening the door without checking first.

"Who is it?" Odessa repeated. The first reply had been too fuzzy to decipher.

This time the blissful voice sailed through plainly. "Special delivery."

Aunt and niece looked at each other and chorused, "Lena."

"Hello, ladies," the charismatic five-foot-one body sang with enough vibrancy to light a Christmas tree. Lena Stroud strutted in, dressed in pale orange nursing scrubs and swinging a large shopping bag from Strawbridge's. The department store was Lena's home away from home and only a few blocks away from the hospital where Lena worked.

"I got the message you left saying you were back in town. I didn't have to work a second shift, so I decided to stop by and show you what I bought." Lena hugged Cassidy. She gave Odessa a tight squeeze, too, and they all moved deeper into the living room. Odessa lifted the mug she'd taken a few sips from and retreated to the kitchen. Cassidy knew Odessa would soon return with something for Lena to eat and drink. It didn't matter whether you called ahead or not, Odessa made sure everyone was served a heaping dose of hospitality.

Lena collapsed into a wing chair and stored the shopping bag on the floor by her sneaker-clad feet. "Today's the day. Did you remember?"

"Yes. Did you?"

"The twins are fine."

"Mine, too," Cassidy told her partner. They became

partners last year when the church sponsored their first Family Health Conference. At the women's wellness seminar, Cassidy learned that twenty-something was not too young to begin breast self-exams and that it was a good idea to team up with someone who would remind you to perform the exam once a month.

"So did you meet any cute and *eligible* guys while you were away?"

"I had better things to do with my time." Cassidy stretched her bare feet beneath a wood coffee table that matched smaller tables at both ends of the sofa.

"You know, you need to stop being so cold. There are some *good* men out there. I know I'm going to get me one."

"I thought you already *had* a good man."

"The only thing Floyd was good at was spending my money. I'm still paying for the laptop he bought with my Visa." She waved her finger in the air. "Don't say it. I know. I was stupid for letting that clown use my credit card." Lena reached into the shopping bag. "And since we're on the topic of credit cards"—she tossed a piece of black fabric across the room—"American Express just had to get this for you."

Cassidy caught the airborne item and held it up.

Lena grinned. "Isn't it hot?"

Cassidy stuffed the teddy that would leave very little to a man's imagination between her hip and a sofa pillow.

"Put it with the others." Lena winked, folding her petite legs and fingering a tress of the dark brown hair that bordered a round face and underscored the bronze hue of her skin.

"I should return it to the store."

"Trust me, one day all our lingerie will be put to good use."

Cassidy rolled her eyes and pursed her lips. Every month for about a year now, Lena bought the two of them a sexy piece of lingerie that they were supposed to tuck away to wear when they were married. An act of faith, Lena maintained. Cassidy only kept the skimpy garments to humor Lena. Cassidy was content as a single woman. She intended to live life to the fullest without a man by her side. She knew lots of single women who were doing just that. They weren't sitting around waiting for a mate who would make life grow wings and take off. They were flying high, working toward goals, serving God by serving others, being the best individuals they could be. In fact, they had more zing in their steps and larger smiles in their eyes than some of the married women she knew.

"I bought you one more thing," Lena said, uncrossing her legs. Her eyes were bright with excitement. "It had your name written all over it." A second later, she was on her feet singing, "Ta-da," as she exhibited a dress that was longer than she was.

A big smile found a home on Cassidy's face. "It's the dress I wanted." The store had every size except her size, and the sales associate had said they wouldn't be getting any more in.

"It's a return, but a couple of the tags are still on it, so likely it wasn't worn," said Lena.

Cassidy appraised the denim dress. Denim was her fabric of choice, and she liked the style of the dress so much she would have accepted it without the tags. "I'm

going to try it on," she said, her feet already in progress.
She wiggled out of a pair of knit leggings and an over-
size T-shirt and came from behind the dining room wall
attired in the straight, sleeveless, button-down white
outfit. She walked the length of the room with all the
spice and flair of a professional model.

"Work it now, girl," Lena rooted. Holding an invisible microphone, Lena rendered a specific account of
Cassidy's new clothing as Cassidy spun and struck a
pose.

"I hope I didn't miss much of the show," a smooth
tenor rumbled.

A current of alarm sent a shock wave through Cassidy, and she bounced in place, jerking her hand from
her hip. Not believing she could be this humiliated for
the second time in one day, she looked everywhere but
at Trevor.

Lena jacked a brow. "Well, isn't this a treat!"

Cassidy mustered the nerve and faced Trevor. He
was greeting Lena. While the duo exchanged pleas-
antries, Cassidy forgot her humiliation and secretly admired the Father's-Day-card image of a dad with a
sleeping child in each arm.

"I saw you on TV a few weeks ago," Lena said. Cassidy had also viewed the local news that day. Trevor had
been the guest chef for the cooking segment. "I love
how you label yourself a dessert artist instead of a baker.
It's so millennial." Lena stepped closer to Trevor. "I
tried making that triple-berry pie, but I made a mess instead."

"You'll do better next time," he encouraged.

Cassidy drew her mouth into a smirk. If Lena

stretched the grin on her face any wider, it would take surgery to correct it.

"So how long have the two of you been friends?" Trevor's pensive stare was on Cassidy, an obvious invitation for her to join the conversation. She prayed he wasn't planning to small-talk her to death. The only thing he should be saying to her was, *I'm sorry*, for the way he sabotaged her privacy this afternoon. Cassidy met his eyes, then steered her gaze away from his, unnerved when their eyes connected, her emotions as sheer as the lace curtains adorning the length of the living room window.

"I've known Cassidy since day one of kindergarten," Lena answered for her. "She was picking her nose"— Cassidy felt the heat of embarrassment kindling under her chin and snaking toward her ears, and she began faking a chain of coughs, but Lena ignored the sound— "and I rescued her with a tissue."

Cassidy hoped her eyes said, *You're a dead woman*, because she was going to kill her best girlfriend.

"Cassidy," Trevor voiced thoughtfully, "not Cassandra," and both women plastered him with searching looks. He smiled. It was semicrooked and sexy, and Cassidy wanted to kick her own behind for noticing. "I thought your name was Cassandra," he said.

Lena's eyes grew into question marks. Cassidy could certainly understand why Lena would be wondering why a man who'd just let himself into the house was still a stranger. "You two haven't met before now?" Lena asked.

"Not formally," Trevor responded. There was an awkward stillness in the room as he looked at Cassidy and she looked at the painting on the wall to the left of him.

Lena, a natural at keeping the fires of conversation burning, merely said, "Oh."

Trevor's smaller child yawned, slightly opening her eyes as she squirmed. "Well," he said, casting a fleeting but friendly look at Cassidy, "I'd better get my girls up to bed."

More questions piled into Lena's eyes as she glanced at Cassidy. "Would you like some help?" she asked Trevor.

He turned and started up the stairs. "No, thank you. I'm fine."

"That's for sure," Lena flirted in a husky singsong, and Cassidy glared at her.

chapter five

I can't believe you kept this from me," Lena exclaimed less than a full second after Trevor had disappeared. "I bet you told Dunbar that Trevor was here. You tell him everything."

"I do not. And for your information, I wasn't keeping anything from you. I just hadn't gotten around to telling you. And for precisely this reason"—she fluttered her hands in the air—"I knew you'd go all loco." Cassidy plopped down on the couch. "By the way, I don't appreciate you escorting Trevor along the memory lane of my life. Would you like me to tell him how you peed the bed until you were twelve?"

Lena upturned both hands above her shoulders. "Sorry," she said. "So why is he putting his kids to bed here? And what was up with *you*? You didn't say one word to him." Lena joined Cassidy on the couch as Odessa reentered and put down a tray of refreshments before excusing herself for the night. When Odessa was out of hearing range, Lena spoke up, fanning herself with her hand. "Trevor sure was checking one of us out, girl, and I'm sorry to say it was *not* me."

Cassidy shook her head. At times, she wondered if Lena was mentally stable.

"*Please,*" Lena went on, "he was trying to be all 'I'm not looking at her,' but he was on you, and you know it."

Cassidy twiddled her thumbs. Yes, she'd been completely cognizant of Trevor's intense gazes, but not talking about them made them less real and, consequently, less overwhelming.

Lena filled a glass with lemonade. "So are you going to tell me why he's here?"

Quickly, quietly, and with a face devoid of expression, Cassidy imparted the story. "I'm surprised you hadn't heard Trevor moved in."

"You know how crazy my shifts can get. I haven't had time to gossip with anyone from church this week."

Cassidy fired a peeved look up the stairs. "I'm just glad Brother Monroe's stay is going to be delimited." "Delimited" was one of her words from last month.

"What's *delimited* mean?" Lena took one of the shortbread cookies from the plate beside the pitcher.

"It means no need to get comfortable because you won't be staying long."

"Girl, do you know how many women would love to be living under the same roof as Trevor Monroe?"

It was pathetic. Dozens of women at the church were planning their weddings around Trevor. Cassidy hardly thought him worthy of all the attention he drew. "I guess we should add your name to the list of Trevor-chasers."

Lena swallowed a swig of lemonade. "I'm not ashamed. I'd be all up on him if I wasn't talking to Dondre. I told you about him, remember?"

"Um-hmm"—Cassidy crossed her arms—"I remember."

Lena sampled a chocolate cookie this time, and dark brown crumbs rained onto the napkin perched on her palm just south of her chin. "We had dinner at his apartment last night."

"Is that all?"

"Yes, Mother dearest, that's all." Lena's smile became impish. "Though I ain't saying I wasn't tempted to move things from the dining room to the bedroom. The man knows how to push all the right buttons."

"Did he get saved yet?"

Lena sucked her teeth. "No, and before you start reminding me of the merits of dating *saved* men, remind yourself that some of them so-called saved brothers who have their hands raised in the air praising the Lord on Sunday are using the same hands that attempted to roam all up under your skirt the night before."

Cassidy's memory tumbled in reverse to the first saved guy she'd had a serious relationship with. During her freshman year at the small, rural, upstate Tilden University, she started seeing a popular upperclassman nicknamed Minister. He could quote entire chapters from the Bible, and one day he was going to be the pastor of the church where his daddy served as pastor, and his daddy's daddy had, too. Looking back now, Cassidy could clearly see how self-absorbed and confused Minister was. But at that time, all she could see was his alluring smile and chiseled body. All the women from freshmen to seniors wanted to be with Minister. But he only wanted to be with her—at least that's what he told her—and she had fallen for it and kept falling until she crashed into a reality still too distressing to deal with.

"Don't look so concerned," Lena said, and Cassidy realized Lena was responding to the intense frown weaved into her forehead. "I'm staying before the Lord in prayer. But this saving-sex-for-marriage business is hard on the nerves. Maybe it would be easier if I'd stayed a virgin like you."

Cassidy dropped her gaze to the spread of magazines on the coffee table and turned her features to neutral.

"Hey," Lena said, finishing another of Odessa's homemade cookies, "remember how we used to create stories about our husbands?"

"Our husbands" filled many teen journal pages. And back then, Cassidy believed those penciled dreams would come true.

"Mine's going to be at least six feet tall, dark-chocolate-coated, built to perfection." Lena rattled off the updated qualifications she expected her man to meet. "*And* he's going to have a college degree, a job in corporate America, and a—"

"Relationship with the Lord," Cassidy interjected.

Lena smiled. "I was going to say that." She propped a pillow on her lap and hugged it. "Now let's talk about what *you* want in a husband."

"You know not to even go there." Cassidy employed the impassive tone she used whenever the subject was broached. Her relationship with Larenz had sealed her decision to remain single, to completely turn her back on dating. The three guys she'd dated before Larenz—

Joseph, Zair, and Bertram—all Charity Community members like Larenz had once been, hounded her for sex, but each of them had simply taken her home and never called again after she'd denied their propositions. Larenz, however, had chosen a different plan of action when Cassidy turned down his advances, and it turned out to be one of the scariest nights of Cassidy's life.

$\mathscr{L}$❤

Soon after Lena had gone home, Cassidy sprinted down the stairs into the living room, a fierce dash to seize the teddy she'd left on the sofa. With the way her day had been going, Trevor would find it, and even if she tried to pin it on Odessa, there was no way he'd believe a mother of the church owned something so racy. Surprised to find the front door ajar, Cassidy edged to it, eased it slightly wider, and peeked outside. The streetlights provided sufficient gleam for her to see Trevor as he stood on the sidewalk with a woman pressed against him.

chapter six

Trevor pried Rave's twiglike arms from around his neck. She had run to him, embraced him, rambled on about having a flat and how scared she'd been at the prospect of being stranded for hours on a dark city street.

"How fortunate for me you're living here now." Her red lips became a smile. "This must be heavenly intervention."

"Heavenly" wasn't the word that surfaced in Trevor's mind as he massaged the constricted muscle at the back of his neck. "What are you doing out? Kregg said the two of you were spending the evening together."

"I canceled," she said. She fluttered her eyelashes, and Trevor got the impression it was a rehearsed action. Rave directed a thumb over her shoulder. "My convertible is just around the corner. Can you help me?"

Rave's gray eyes beckoned like jewels. Cheap ones, Trevor mused. "Wait here," he said, and walked four cars back to his Expedition, parked in what was the closest available space to the house. In case Rave didn't have the necessaries, he grabbed the black duffel bag that held his roadside emergency equipment. He thought about going back to lock the front door of the house but figured the task of changing a flat wouldn't take long. He would have Rave well on her way within the half hour. "Lead the way," he said when he returned, neither smiling nor frowning at the woman who'd blocked him before he could get to his vehicle to retrieve the Bible he'd left under the front seat.

Caroling crickets filled the night with music as Trevor assessed the situation. Rave's Mercedes did indeed have a flat. "Keys," he said.

Rave coiled her fingers around his wrist, lifted his arm, and dropped the ring of keys in his open palm. She stared at him with wide-eyed innocence, but as she flapped her lashes again, her expression seemed more sinister than sincere when she whined, "I must have run over some glass or something."

Trevor removed the spare, the jack, and the tire iron from the trunk of the white car and went to work while Rave disappeared around the other side of the vehicle. Suddenly, as if he'd been slapped across the back of the head, he jerked his shoulders, censure crossing his features. Rave had turned on the car's sound system, and a blast of hip-hop drowned out the peaceful serenade of the crickets. She was beside him now, snapping fingers, flailing arms, swiveling hips, and chanting lyrics. From his squatting position, he looked up at her. "Here, hold this."

Rave accepted the flashlight, continuing to bop.

"I need you to hold it still," he ordered.

"I'll hold it any way you want."

Her purr had been close enough to warm his ear.

Trevor continued working, ignoring the long bare legs she rubbed against his slacks. He soon put the damaged tire in the spot from which he'd taken the spare, Rave on his heels. He wasn't sure if he bumped into her or the other way around as he slammed shut the trunk. "Watch out," he grumbled.

The pink tones creeping into Rave's cheeks told Trevor she'd been wounded by the brusque command. But what did he care? Rave's bruised feelings could heal on their own. After all, she'd been far more offensive to him . . . and to Kregg, carrying on like this behind Kregg's back with Kregg's friend. "I'm sorry," Trevor apologized anyhow. "I didn't want you to get hurt." He perceived any hurt feelings to have been soothed when she trailed a fingernail along his arm from elbow to wrist and smiled up at him. Trevor hastened to the front of the car and opened the door, an invitation for Rave to take her seat.

Rave advanced, her chunky heels loudly hitting the asphalt. She stopped toe-to-toe with him, threw her arms around his middle, and leaned into him from the waist down. "How might I compensate you for your services?"

Trevor tightened his grip on the door while his other hand found that muscle cramping again at the base of his neck. "No payment necessary," he said, and deliberated when he would tell Kregg about this.

"Oh, come on. Let's go get a soft pretzel"—she smiled—"share a soda. Or if you want, we could go to my place and have *Bible* study." Rave giggled.

"No, thank you, Rave." His voice was unyielding. "I have to get back to my girls."

"I'm sure the old hag will keep an eye on them."

Patience waning as swiftly as the time, Trevor replied austerely, "Rave, let's say good night. Like I said, I need to get back. I didn't tell Mother Vale or Cassidy I left the house."

Rave's eyes narrowed to slits as she loosened but didn't unfasten the cinch on his waist. "I thought Cassidy was away."

"She came home," Trevor said, thinking about the other young woman who was this close to him today and how much he wanted to return to the house and offer the apology he had intended from the beginning.

"Another time, then," Rave relented, pouting as she gradually released him.

He watched her drive away before hurrying back to his truck and returning the duffel bag. He snatched his Bible from beneath the passenger seat and jogged to the house. He tried to twist the doorknob, but the door was locked, the first floor dark. It seemed Cassidy had retired for the night, the opportunity to apologize postponed until morning. Disappointed, and pondering why he was, Trevor lingered beneath the brightness of the porch light. As moths tagged the overhead bulb, he pushed his key into the lock. It was much harder to push away the memory of Cassidy walking across the living room floor—poised, graceful, and with enough sass to incite a man to want to see her sway like that some more.

✿

It was a pity Lena left when she had. She could have seen for herself whom Trevor was checking out. Cassidy had no idea those two had hooked up. The last time she talked with Rave, she was seeing some guy named Kregg.

Cassidy smeared a glob of toothpaste onto her toothbrush. She knew Rave had been attracted to Trevor
long before Brenda died. A month after joining Charity
Community, Cassidy had invited Lena and Rave to
come with her to church. Rave gabbed during most of
the Sunday worship service and slept through the entire sermon. Well rested by the benediction, Rave was
ready to indulge in her favorite sport—flirting with
men of all ages, shapes, and shoe sizes. But there was
one man Rave was particularly enthralled with.

"Married," Cassidy informed her.

*And Rave asked in the curt soprano everyone was ac-
customed to, "What's marriage have to do with anything?"*

Well, it seemed that after years of wishing, dreaming,
and drooling, Rave had snagged her man.

Cassidy spit and returned her toothbrush to the
holder. For the first time, she noticed the other toothbrush hanging there. Trevor's toothbrush.

Slowly, as if performing something forbidden, she
curled her fingers around the knob of the medicine cabinet, pulled open the door, and fixed her gaze on the
row Odessa had assigned their houseguest. Aligned
from left to right were a can of shaving cream, a bottle
of aftershave, and a brand of deodorant designed for the
most rugged of men, according to the commercial. A
small bottle of cologne ended the parade of items. Fas-
cination teased Cassidy as she removed the blue container, unscrewed the tiny top, and lightly inhaled. The
smell of the man she'd been body-on-body with in the
bathroom this afternoon rushed up her nose and down
her throat, and Cassidy sniffed a second dose.

chapter seven

It's time to get up," Brandi sang the wake-up call. She straddled her father's lower back, clapped her hands against his skin, bounced her body, and sang the song again.

Trevor growled, and Brandi giggled as she plopped onto her back, landing beside him. Giving a longwinded yawn, Trevor rolled over, meeting morning and his daughter. He wasn't sure which was brighter: the broad strips of sunlight reaching in from under the window shade or the smile on his kid's face. He grabbed the miniature clump of happiness. She was dressed in pink shorts, a pink shirt, and one pink sock, the items he'd laid out the night before. Without effort, he lifted Brandi above him, as high as his arms would extend, then dunked her onto the mattress and tickled her tummy. All giggles, she scrambled beneath the sheet to escape, and Trevor granted her a recess, reaching toward the nightstand for the wristwatch Brenda had given him for his thirtieth birthday. He read the time, and Brandi finally stopped giggling. "Grammy told me"—she pressed her finger to her chest—"to tell you"—she pointed to him—"that Derek called *three* times this morning." The child raised three fingers.

Entombed in sleep, Trevor had heard neither the house phones nor his cell phone. He backed his upper frame against the headboard and tossed the sheet aside, uncovering the lower portion of his body. He had on the lightweight sweatpants he'd done sit-ups and push-ups in before climbing into bed last night.

"Are you going to call Derek back?"

Traces of concern for Derek were vivid in his little girl's eyes. As he well knew, Brandi had become very fond of Derek, adopting him as a big brother. Trevor leaned forward and kissed her forehead. "Yes, I'm going to call him back." He grabbed the foot without the sock and kissed the big toe. "Where's your other sock?"

"I can't find it." She laughed, pulling her foot out of his hand.

"Well, go find it, and I'll call Derek."

Brandi began to crawl away, then stopped and saddled him with a look that indicated she had a life-and-death matter on her mind. "Who was that lady in the bathroom with us yesterday?"

"That lady," Trevor said slowly, "was Cassidy. She lives here." He sat up straighter. "And that was her bedroom you entered without permission. From now on, if you would like to speak with Cassidy or Mother Vale, you're to stand outside the door and knock, then wait for them to invite you in, even if the door is already open." Trevor's eyebrows went up, a customary signal that he meant business.

"Okay," Brandi said, and rolled over twice before reaching the brink of the mattress.

Trevor had not interrogated Brandi yesterday and asked now, "Why was your jacket in Cassidy's room?"

"I left it under the bed when I was hiding from Sis."

"Stay out of there," he reinforced, taking his cell phone from the nightstand.

Brandi climbed off the bed. "I love you, Daddy."

"I love you, too."

"I love you more than banilla ice cream," she said, initiating the game she loved to play with him as she jumped-hopped-skipped to the door.

Trevor was about to press the button to speed-dial Derek but could not neglect the opportunity to provide his daughter the joy of playing in this simple way. "I love you more than vanilla ice cream with chocolate syrup."

"I love you more than banilla ice cream with chocolate syrup and sprinkles."

Trevor added another topping, and it was Brandi's turn.

"I love you more than banilla ice cream with chocolate syrup, sprinkles"—she rolled her eyes to the top of her head, making sure she remembered in sequence—"coconut, and cherries," she yelled, finalizing the building of the sundae as she scurried out of sight.

Trevor listened as the phone rang for the fifth time, also concerned about Derek Hines. Derek was the only person other than his secretary and his sister whom Trevor had given Mother Vale's phone number to. He'd told the boy to use it only in case of an emergency, so as the phone continued to go unanswered, Trevor's worry over the fourteen-year-old doubled. Like Brandi, he had become quite fond of Derek, despite a shaky beginning.

Six months ago, Derek had been caught stealing from Seconds. Trevor had planned to come down hard on him, teach him a lesson while he was impressionable. But after learning the youngster wanted the food for two small brothers, Trevor decided against notifying the police. Instead, he set Derek up with part-time employment and homework help, and when he discovered Derek's passion for basketball, he gave him a spot on the City Champions team. Derek excelled on the court, and his grades and attitude improved as well.

"Who dis?" Derek's mother answered the phone.

Trevor grimaced at the ragged salutation. "Hello, Miss Hines. This is Coach Monroe. Is Derek there?"

"Oh, Coach, how you *doin'*?"

"I'm fine, Miss Hines, and you?"

"Oh, I'm doin' real good, now."

Trudy Hines's routine flirtation dance had begun and would swing into full gear if Trevor didn't end it pronto. "Have Derek call me when he gets in, please. And you have a good day."

"Wait," Trudy said before he could disconnect.

When Trudy didn't say anything more, Trevor asked, his voice even, "Is there something I can do for you, Miss Hines?" He wrinkled his face as soon as the words were released. That had definitely been the wrong way to put it.

"Oh, there's a lot you can do for me," Trudy said like she was auditioning for a phone-sex job.

Trevor was sure he heard Derek's voice in the background, amid the cries of a younger child and the brouhaha of the television. "Is Derek home?" he asked again.

"Yeah, he home!"

The phone had been slammed against something hard, and Trevor had to pull the receiver away from his ear. He brought the phone back to hear Trudy discharging a string of obscenities while informing Derek she wasn't his secretary.

It amazed Trevor how well Derek dealt with Trudy, a reckless mother if ever there was one. If it had not been for Derek's pleas, Trevor would have turned Trudy over to Social Services months ago. But Derek vowed he would help his mom raise his brothers to keep them from being separated. At times, Trevor questioned whether he was doing the right thing, keeping his mouth shut. At times, he was downright uncomfortable with the decision. So he kept in close contact with Derek and donated groceries or clothing for Derek and his brothers as needed. Of course, Derek's mother thought her son purchased these items with the money he earned at the bakery, but Trevor had opened up a savings account for Derek, and that's where most of the boy's paycheck resided.

"Yo, yo, yo." A voice not quite a man's ripped through the wires.

"Hello, Derek. What's going on?"

"Aw, Coach, you ain't gonna believe it. All my stuff for the awards thingy next Saturday is missin'. The suit, shoes . . . even the socks." He lowered his voice. "I think Trudy might have sold everything . . . for more forties."

Trevor was accustomed to Derek using his mother's first name. It was Trudy's idea. Only thirteen years older than her son, she'd been heard to say, "I'm too young for you to be calling me Mama." Derek's voice shot up a few decibels. "What I'm gonna do? I ain't got nuffin' else nice to wear."

"Are you sure the clothes aren't in the house?"

"I done looked everywhere. Trudy must've got my stuff when I was at my cousin's girlfriend's sista's house last night, gettin' my hair braided. I gotta keep that Iverson look, ya know."

If Derek was near a mirror, Trevor imagined the teenager was looking in it—patting his head and grinning at himself.

"So can you take me shoppin' today, Coach?"

Trevor looked at the time again. Following breakfast, Brandi was to be dropped off at a play date in the park, and Brittney had to be taken to a 10:30 dental appointment. Trevor prayed the dentist was running on time because he was scheduled to teach a twelve o'clock baking class at Seconds. At the end of the class, he would go back and pick up Brandi and drive both girls to Grace's. She'd agreed to babysit after Penny phoned late last night and said she was feeling worse and didn't want the kids to catch anything.

Neither did Trevor. Two kids sick at the same time— he'd been down that harrowing road twice last winter. All the hot soup in the world couldn't replace what his children really wanted. Their mommy.

Trevor swung his feet off the bed. Sitting on the edge of the mattress, he pinched the bridge of his nose, rushing his thoughts through the rest of today's schedule, trying to find a spot for Derek. There didn't seem to be one. This afternoon Trevor had a meeting with a potential client that he couldn't cancel on again. And then he had to do laundry, or they'd all be staying home from church tomorrow. "We've got all week, plenty of time to figure something out. So don't worry, okay?"

Derek didn't answer right away. "Yeah, okay."

Trevor disconnected, sorry he'd disappointed Derek, but he had almost more than he could carry on his back for one day. This single-parenting thing—well, he'd developed a new respect for it.

Trevor exhaled a gust that seemed to come all the way from his toes, then reached for his Bible and slid from the bed to his knees. He quickly searched for the familiar scripture that reminded him where his help for today's challenges resided. *Our help is in the name of the Lord, Who made heaven and earth.*

ℒ❤

Cassidy cringed and covered her mouth, smothering a scream as she walked into the kitchen and a ball of fur the size of a subway rat, wearing a red collar with a silver bell, skittered across her undressed feet.

"Don't be alarmed, that's just Poopie." Odessa watered the small potted plants on the windowsill above the sink. "She's with the Monroes. Poor thing was accidentally locked in the basement. Guess that's why you didn't meet her yesterday."

Cassidy tightened her lips with a grimace. She was *not* a cat person. "That thing was in my room," she complained. Cassidy had wanted to catch an extra hour of sleep, since Arlene, the senior center administrator, called last night and said a replacement volunteer had been scheduled, and Cassidy wouldn't be needed at Caring Hands today. But the customary quiet of Cassidy's morning had been shattered by a chain of meows coming from under the bed, as well as the brutal sound of Trevor singing in the shower. Right now the wannabe Fred Hammond was at the counter tapping an egg against a mixing bowl. He was dressed in slacks and a V-neck shirt that hung over his waist. Cassidy flipped him an antagonistic sideways glance before pinning a similar one on the short-haired feline washing its pink nose by the back door.

"You're just in time, baby girl," Odessa said to Cassidy, taking plates from an overhead cabinet. "Trevor's making breakfast for everyone."

Cassidy watched Trevor's daughter follow Odessa to the table. The child was carrying a pink Barbie-doll car, most likely the one Cassidy had seen outside yesterday. Odessa put down the plates, smoothed her housedress as she lowered herself to a chair, and pulled the child onto her thighs.

"You're the lady from the bathroom," the child said to Cassidy.

The girl's smile was contagious, and Cassidy smiled, too. "You must be Brandi." She extended her hand. "I'm Cassidy, Mother Vale's niece."

"I'm a niece, too."

Odessa interjected, "One who's supposed to be helping me set the table."

The old and young went to collect the silverware, and

Cassidy strolled to the refrigerator. She opened the door and removed a plastic bag stuffed with ready-to-eat carrot and celery sticks when someone came up behind her. Every inch of Cassidy's body stiffened with awareness as Trevor reached around, returned the eggs, seized the milk, and stepped away without once uttering, *Excuse me.* For a homeless man, he was terribly presumptuous, and Cassidy couldn't stand him! She shut the Kenmore with so much force the jars on the door jangled.

The way Trevor kept sneaking up on her—it had to stop. Cassidy fed the raw vegetables to a juicer, deciding she would surely speak to Trevor about his ghostlike behavior. Then she would present the topic of when Poopie would be relocating to a shelter. Cassidy consumed her breakfast beverage while Trevor helped Brandi stir the pancake batter. It suddenly dawned on Cassidy that he hadn't offered her a word of greeting this morning, and for a reason she couldn't label, it irked her. She smacked her glass on the counter. "I have yet to taste pancakes that are better than yours, Aunt Odessa," she said, intent on insulting the source of her irritation, albeit indirectly. She stole a peek at him, but it was difficult to tell if he was offended, with his back to her as he tended the griddle.

"Well, the man can bake a cake better than I ever could," Odessa said. "Don't you remember me telling you about the dessert I ordered for the last senior citizens' fellowship? That caramel cake was the talk of all the desserts served."

Cassidy shrugged. She had a vague recollection of the conversation. "Since when did you start using *bakery* cakes?"

Odessa glared at Cassidy with shock followed by disapproval. Cassidy pretended not to notice as she strutted over to the small portable radio/cassette player sitting on the counter. Much to Cassidy's displeasure, someone had altered the dial, and a local R&B station was about to play number three of the morning's Top Ten. Cassidy's gaze flitted around the room from person to person. Odessa didn't listen to this type of music, so Cassidy figured the dial-changing culprit was Trevor. She grasped the button and returned the dial to the station of her choice. She liked R&B and smooth jazz and pop, too, but her mornings were reserved for classical radio, and she was not modifying her daily routine for Trevor. Assured he'd received that message, she took a victory walk back to the opposite counter, slapping her soles against the linoleum. She disassembled the juicer and at the sink washed the sections that could be submerged in water.

Odessa snaked up beside her and whispered, "Something ugly woke up with you this morning."

The juicer cleaned and reassembled into a whole appliance again, Cassidy dried her hands with a paper towel. She tapped a short manicured nail on the countertop as she eyed the pancakes Trevor had piled on a plate. She'd only seen pancakes so perfectly round in television commercials. Cassidy shook her head, condemning the amount of butter Trevor was topping his pancake stacks with. After a few seconds, her vision settled on his hands. He had long fingers with rugged knuckles, and she could see that whether it was making a cake or fixing things around the house, Trevor was a hard worker.

He whistled an unidentifiable chord of notes, and she instantly looked up at his face and discovered him watching her, something soft and perhaps playful in his eyes. Entirely conscious of him yet in the same breath entirely self-conscious, Cassidy spun and trotted from the room, the house, with the hope that a few gulps of fresh air might calm her nerves.

Still gripping the screen door so it wouldn't slam, Cassidy bounced to a stop to keep from stepping on a girl, larger than the one inside. She was sitting cross-legged on the porch floor, several neat rows of cards spread out on the welcome mat. Cassidy gently released the door, and it closed with a dull thud. "Hello," Cassidy said as the child below placed a card on what was obviously the beginning of a new row. She did not return Cassidy's greeting. Not ready to close the book on this girl yet, Cassidy crouched beside her. This one had Trevor's square jaw, flat forehead, full lips; Brenda's eggnog complexion, brownish black hair, and ginger-brown eyes. "Umm . . . WNBA trading cards. I have some myself."

Uncertain eyes studied Cassidy. "*You* collect WNBA cards?" The voice was much raspier than Brandi's flute-like pitch.

"Only September through June."

"Huh?"

Cassidy laughed aloud at the quizzical expression on the child's face. "From my students," she hinted, letting the riddle dangle in the air.

"You're a teacher," the girl concluded, scrunching her face as if she'd bitten into a detested vegetable.

"That's right . . . third grade. Sometimes I have to

take cards from students when they have them out at the wrong time. Do you know what I mean?"

"Yeah, I lost some of my cards to my teacher because I took them out during a spelling test." She looked back to the cards in her grasp before refocusing on Cassidy. "My name's Brittney."

Cassidy smiled. "I'm Cassidy."

The budding of a smile appeared at the corners of Brittney's lips, but she herded it back before it could bloom. "You signed once for Kidpraise."

"Yes, when Brother Simpson was out of town." Lately, Cassidy had been thinking about becoming a regular children's church staff member. The congregation was swelling with parents of young children, and the Kidpraise Ministry was in need of workers. Cassidy had talked it over with Dunbar, and he thought it would be a good place for her, too.

The child's voice pulled Cassidy away from her rumination. "Where'd you learn how to do sign language?"

"Right here in Germantown . . . at the Pennsylvania School for the Deaf."

"Oh." Brittney's voice became close to a whisper. "I don't like Kidpraise anymore."

Cassidy knew children well. They usually didn't unearth things they didn't want to talk about. "Why?" she asked.

Brittney pumped her shoulders, a shadow too old for someone so young clouding her eyes.

Cassidy understood. There were dark things from her own past she couldn't bring into the light. She lifted one of Brittney's cards. "I played basketball in ninth grade."

The child stuck her fingertips between two rows of her cornrows and scratched her scalp. "How come you stopped?"

Cassidy gave Brittney her card back. "My grades were slipping, and my aunt told me I needed to devote more time to studying. I couldn't imagine giving up my piano lessons, so I came off the team."

"My dad played in high school, too. He's good. We used to play together all the time."

Brittney suddenly seemed depressed, as before, and something unexpected and maternal arose in Cassidy. She wanted to take the child into her arms and rock as much of the sadness away as she could. Another moment, and she would have, but Trevor appeared at the door.

"It's time for breakfast, Brittney." Trevor cleared his throat. "Cassidy?"

"Oh . . . no, thank you," she answered, speaking to him politely for the first time as she glanced up at him through the screen. It was hard to see his eyes, but she could tell that his face was stiff, like something was heavy on his brain. She might be wrong, but she sensed that his dour mood had something to do with Brittney. She faced the girl, but out of the corner of her eye, Cassidy watched Trevor's leather loafers turn and move away. "We'll talk some more another time . . . if you want to, Brittney."

Brittney was slow to consent. "Okay," she finally muttered, and this time she let her smile grow wider.

chapter eight

The smile beaming from her date's face was all it took to encourage Cassidy to quicken her steps so she could get to him faster. She leaned over and covered him with a hug. "Oliver Toby," she said in greeting, happiness highlighting both words.

"How's my sweetheart?"

"Perfect." She smiled down at him, then dabbed his baggy cheek with a kiss. They talked for a long while, then Cassidy helped him stand. She kept her hand locked on his elbow until he was steady and had firm control of his walker.

"I'm sorry about your library," he said. "If I had the money, you know I'd give it to you."

"And you know I wouldn't accept it." Confidence pumped through her. "Everything's going to work out. My pastor will surely understand how critical the situation is and give ACES permission to use the children's summer fund."

The path leading to the rear of the Serenity Home for the Aged was smooth and direct, and they stayed on the paved trail until they came to a garden that looked and smelled as if it had been sent from heaven. Oliver Toby, still a gentleman at the age of ninety-two, waited for Cassidy to take a seat on the wrought-iron bench before he bent and began the slow descent to the place beside her. Oliver Toby had once been a client at Caring Hands. But when his son and daughter-in-law divorced, and his son moved into a small apartment, Oliver Toby was placed in a nursing home. Adored by the staff of Caring Hands, he was given a big party his last day there, and Cassidy promised she would visit him at least once a week here at his new home. They settled on Wednesday afternoons.

Whenever Oliver Toby spoke, his voice was low and casual—his standard tone and tempo. Occasionally, a tremor passed through his words, a sign that his vocal cords were not as strong as his mind. There was nothing wrong with the former college professor's brain. "What's our word for the week?" he asked.

"Pietistic."

He stalled for only a moment, then his head swayed from side to side. "Too many people like that in the world."

"I give up." Cassidy breathed deeply. She thought for sure she finally had a word he wouldn't know the meaning of.

The old man chuckled, and Cassidy offered her friend a grin. He was about her height and more bone than meat. His coarse hair was white, and his wrinkled skin was a tad darker than brown sugar. An avid wearer of sweater vests, he had on a blue one with a gray stripe across the chest.

"Have you considered what we talked about the last time?" His fond gaze was that of a father who without question wanted the best for his child.

Rather than answer, Cassidy pretended to be interested in the birdbath and the sparrow fluttering around it. When she looked back at Oliver Toby, he was staring forward. During Cassidy's last date with him, they'd sat in this same area, and he shared that he'd been blessed with a sense that showed him when a heart was obstructed with adversity. She remembered his words.

"You have a heavy burden," he said. "I don't know what it is, but it hurts you, child."

She sat as rigidly as the larger-than-life stone figures, replicas of squirrels and bunnies, positioned throughout the flowered garden. As much as Cassidy loved and revered Oliver Toby, she couldn't find the courage to tell him about her pain or even acknowledge that his assessment had been accurate.

She couldn't find the courage today, either. Oliver Toby seemed to know this and said softly, *"Cast thy burden upon the Lord, and He shall sustain thee."* Cassidy read and studied her Bible regularly and knew that scripture well; but completely relinquishing the burden of her past to God was a step she didn't feel worthy of taking.

Romans 8:1 immediately penetrated her thoughts. *There is therefore now no condemnation to them which are in Christ Jesus.* Another scripture whispered, *As far as the east is from the west, so far hath He removed our transgressions from us.*

Yes, Lord. Cassidy silently acknowledged God's Word as truth, yet couldn't fully accept that the verses were for her.

She remained quiet for the rest of the visit, and Oliver Toby did not push her to speak. Close to the dinner hour, they walked back to the two-story L-shaped building. Cassidy escorted Oliver Toby to the dining room, and when he was comfortably seated, she kissed his forehead.

He folded his hand around hers, and the inside of his age-roughened palm gently scratched her skin. "I'm not trying to hurt you. I simply want to see you walking in the freedom God has called you to." He set a kiss on the back of her hand.

Cassidy swept her blue feelings away behind a big smile. "I'll see you next week."

⚘

The following evening Cassidy dialed and waited for a member of the Purdue house to answer the phone.

"Hello."

"Hi, Shevelle."

Shevelle Tapp was Emma's granddaughter, and every summer since Shevelle was ten, she came from her home state of Delaware to visit with the Purdues. Naturally, Cassidy and Shevelle had played together, and their bond of friendship had endured into adulthood. "What's going on?" Shevelle asked, and the women conversed for several minutes.

"So would you like to go to Little Curly's tonight?" Cassidy asked. Shevelle loved seafood. "My treat," Cassidy offered.

"I'm going to the movies with my cousins tonight, but tomorrow night would work."

"Sure, but we'll have to make it late. I have a ministry meeting at six." Their talk drifted to the subject of Nigel, Shevelle's husband. He was a marine stationed overseas and would remain there for at least four more months. Nigel and Shevelle had been through a lot of tough times during their young marriage, yet they seemed to still love each other as much as they had on the day they said their vows. It was refreshing to know a couple who loved God and each other. Cassidy often prayed that one day Lena would find a strong-in-the-Lord man like Nigel.

"Hey, Cassidy," Shevelle said as the conversation began to wane, "the Word says we have not because we ask not, so I'm going to put this out there. It's last-minute and all, but do you think you could watch Nile tonight?"

Cassidy's heart quickened. "Watch Nile?" she repeated with a tremble in her voice.

"I would ask Nana and Papa, but they're going to that revival over at Full Joy Fellowship. It's going to be a packed house, and Nana and Papa don't need the stress of taking care of Nile if she starts crying or something."

Cassidy paced her bedroom floor. She loved Nile. Nile was a blessing. All babies were blessings. But Cassidy didn't know how to be with babies. They revived her insecurities, represented her failures.

"I haven't been to a movie since Nile was born." Shevelle didn't sound disturbed by that fact, she was simply stating it. "I can take her with me and take her out of the theater if she gets antsy . . ." As Shevelle continued to talk, Cassidy shifted her thoughts all around, trying to figure out how she was going to get out of this one. She couldn't say she had plans after just inviting Shevelle to do something tonight. And she couldn't pass Nile off on Odessa because Odessa was going to the revival with the Purdues.

"I'll take her with me," Shevelle said.

"No." Shevelle was her friend. True friends were there for each other. Cassidy sat on the bed. "I'll watch Nile."

"Are you sure?"

"I'm sure. You go and have a good time."

Cassidy pressed the phone's off button and curled on the bed as her stomach cramped and the memory came crashing forward.

"Don't do it," Colvin begged, torment visible in his expression.

Cassidy stared at him and then at Minister and finally at the baby in her arms.

$\mathcal{L}$♥

Trevor sauntered toward the five-month-old. "Hey, sweet as peaches, what's the matter?" he asked. Cassidy lifted her finger from the piano, ending the one-handed lullaby meant to soothe Nile. She gazed at Trevor as he squatted close to the cranky baby.

"I just changed her, and before that she had a bottle," Cassidy said, letting him know she wasn't ignorant about baby basics.

"Maybe she just wants to get out of this thing." He unfastened the safety straps, then scooped Nile from her car seat that doubled as a rocker. The baby's cries quieted to coos as Trevor cradled her close to his chest. "That's better, isn't it?" He wiggled his fingertip against Nile's chin. The baby kicked one chubby foot and pumped her hands as a smile filled her entire face.

Trevor brought the baby to Cassidy. Before he could hand her off, she stood and lowered the piano cover. She moved to the coffee table and one by one packed Nile's toys in the baby bag. Shevelle would be back soon.

And Trevor would be leaving soon. He had dropped in to pick up something, and then he was going back to his office. The first of the week, she'd overheard him telling Odessa that June was a whirlwind month, filled with graduations, weddings, and family reunions. He and the children wouldn't get in before eleven some nights.

He tickled Nile some more, and the baby giggled, dribbles of spit wetting her chin and his finger. Trevor smiled at the baby. "You're a real cutie," he said, lowering himself to Odessa's rocking chair. He wiped Nile's face with her bib as Cassidy strolled toward the window, away from them.

☙

At exactly 5:30 the next evening, the chime of the doorbell was followed by a knock that shook the screen door. "Hey, girl," Yaneesha Polk called, cupping her hands above her eyes and peering through the screen at Cassidy.

Cassidy hung the straps of her tote bag on her shoulder and joined Yaneesha outside. A sister from church, Yaneesha was one of those who might engage you in casual chitchat one Sunday and walk by you without half a glance the next. Cassidy smiled. "Thanks for the ride, Yaneesha."

"Ain't nuttin' but a thang." The ends of Yaneesha's black shoulder-length perm were dyed raspberry. She was wearing purple jeans and a shirt with the word "Yummy" written across the chest. "So where's Trevor?" Yaneesha appeared as excited as a fan on the verge of coming face-to-face with her favorite pop star. It was clear why Yaneesha had insisted she pick up Cassidy.

"He's not here," Cassidy stated, and headed for Yaneesha's Jeep. Yaneesha pranced beside her, her super-size hoop earrings rocking every time she moved her head. She straightened her gold cat-shaped eyeglasses and glanced back at the house as if Cassidy had lied and Trevor would suddenly appear.

During the thirty-minute ride, Cassidy thought of Sister Maranda Whittle several times. The Sparrow Ministry staff meeting Maranda had invited Cassidy to attend was also scheduled for this evening.

Yaneesha swung into a spot in the underground garage of the Diamond Retirement Condominiums, and the women waited for the elevator. After a ride that consisted of four stops, they reached Mother Almondetta Hartwell's floor. Yaneesha, having been here before, led the way to 22G.

Cassidy's pastor encouraged members not only to pray before joining a ministry but also to attend a few of the staff meetings to get the feel of things. Truthfully, Cassidy hadn't prayed about whether or not she should join Special Day. The ministry responsible for making sure each senior citizen member received a birthday card, present, and visit on their birthday seemed a logical place for her to serve, since her time spent at the senior center and the nursing home had proven how much she liked interacting with the elderly. But Cassidy would do as the pastor requested and sit in on a couple of the meetings first. Then she would decide if she would join Special Day or Kidpraise.

Their hostess for the evening, the facilitator and founder of Special Day, opened her door.

"Hello, Mother." Yaneesha smiled, and light from the living room chandelier hit Yaneesha's gold tooth, making the upper incisor gleam.

"Say hello to Delightful," was the first thing out of Almondetta's mouth.

"Hello, Delightful," Yaneesha cooed at the white Chihuahua and gave it several pats on the head. Cassidy smiled at the dog, solely to appease Almondetta. She found Delightful altogether too creepy for her taste. On the way over, Yaneesha had given Cassidy the story about Delightful. The little dog had passed away two years ago, but Almondetta, unable to part with her canine companion of thirteen years, had her freeze-dried.

Within moments, Cassidy and Yaneesha were standing barefoot on Mother Almondetta's white wall-to-wall carpeting.

"Can't have folks tracking in dirt and germs," she said in a tight voice, pointing to a basket. Cassidy placed her shoes in the basket next to Yaneesha's. Her appraising gaze sweeping the length of Cassidy, Almondetta's lips formed a pink frown. Cassidy decided not to take offense at the greeting that thus far felt icy. "Hello, Mother Hartwell. I'm Cassidy Beckett." She gave a genuine smile and offered her hand. "I'm glad to be here. I believe Special Day is a fundamental ministry." A segment of the senior population had lost their spouses and many of their peers to death and their children to relocation. Surely, a special hello on a birthday was a welcome occurrence.

The widow and church mother barely touched Cassidy's fingers before dropping her hand. "Yes, I know who you are," she muttered, and turned. Once again, Cassidy chose to dismiss Almondetta's snobbish behavior. Focus on the more important matter of learning about Special Day. She and Yaneesha followed Almondetta out of the living room, painted and furnished in blue tones, onto a terrace with a table set for three.

"Isn't anyone else coming?" Cassidy asked. Special Day had been active for several months. Of course, there were more workers.

"People usually come to one or two of the meetings, but they don't join," said Yaneesha, plopping down at the table.

"Goes to show how people are all talk and no action," Almondetta sniped, setting Delightful on her doggie chaise. Almondetta lowered herself to one of the chairs, smoothing her crocheted dress over her thin bones. She adjusted her wig as if it were a hat and stared at Cassidy. "Church ministry is serious business. It's not for the lazy."

Cassidy folded her hands in her lap. "I love the Lord. I love serving on His behalf, and I aspire to give my all."

"We're still in the planning stages. Yaneesha was

supposed to collect the names of our seniors, but she hasn't given me a list yet."

Yaneesha didn't seem bothered by Almondetta's report. The young woman sipped from her glass and reached for one of the brownies on a tray in the center of the table.

"Perhaps I can help Yaneesha get things started," Cassidy volunteered, seeing a need. She decided another meeting wasn't necessary. She was ready to join the Special Day team now, although an internal siren beeped that she'd taken a wrong turn and was facing a dead end.

chapter nine

Ms. Emma and her husband, Harold, babysat Nile while Cassidy and Shevelle went to dinner. The two women talked and laughed nonstop through the meal and all the way home. Shevelle parked her car in front of her grandparents' house, and Cassidy and Shevelle hugged good-bye. Shevelle was going back to Delaware in the morning.

Back at Odessa's, Cassidy prepared for bed, turned up the radio, pulled the top sheet up to her chest, and propped her back against two pillows. On Fridays, the host of her favorite Christian talk program asked a series of trivia questions. The first listener to call in with all of the correct answers won a CD or an inspirational book. Cassidy had her Bible open and was searching for the answer to question number four when she heard Trevor ushering the kids up to the third floor. They were just getting in.

The bare stairs creaked as he came back down. Cassidy peered at the digital bedside clock. It was midnight, and Solid Ground Church Ministries was opening its daily radio program with its popular gospel theme song. The Chicago church was one of the largest black congregations in the nation, and its leader was the young, gifted, and energetic Bishop Colvin Culpepper. Cassidy and Colvin had been friends once. Good friends. And when she stood at the crossroads of a heart-wrenching decision, Colvin had offered wise advice. But she hadn't followed it, and now his voice simply reminded her of the decision she longed to travel back in time and change.

Cassidy turned to her beloved classical station, lowered the volume, and snapped off the lamp. She could hear Trevor moving about in the guest bedroom, and soon the bathroom. Her lids hung heavy and her limbs began to loosen as she identified the splash of water hitting the sink and the scrub of toothbrush bristles grazing Trevor's teeth. She listened as he juggled what was probably mouthwash at the top of his throat, and she eventually heard a steady trickle as he relieved himself. Three more sounds followed that one: the flush of the toilet, more water hissing from the spigot, and finally, the click of the light.

Cassidy heard these same sounds, in the same order, around the same time every night now. And she'd discovered them to be a melody as gentle as the one streaming from the radio.

❧

Trevor changed into a pair of sweats and grabbed his Bible. Once downstairs, he opened the front door and stood for a couple of minutes, allowing his shirtless chest to drink from the refreshing breeze while he studied the slice of moon and sprinkle of stars hovering over the houses across the street. "Thank you, God," he whispered. It had been a good day. It was always a good day when his family was safe in bed. Life was fragile. Here one moment, gone the next. That being the case, Trevor always remembered to thank the Lord for getting them all home in one piece.

He walked into the kitchen, flipped the light switch at the top of the basement stairs, and carefully navigated the narrow steps leading to the bottom level. The basement had become the late-night hangout Trevor retreated to—a quiet, kid-free zone he needed now and then. Brandi didn't venture down here because she found it spooky. And he supposed a child would. The length and depth of the room gave it a cave effect, and the only dependable sounds boomed from the water heater. Peeling paint scarred the walls, and the cemented floor was a carpet of cracks. Brown boxes of all proportions cluttered the walking space, and cobwebs and spiderwebs mingled and dangled from the rafters above. Brittney, tomboy though she was, wouldn't tread anywhere near a spider. That alone kept her from opening the door leading to the basement.

Trevor laid his Bible on the old, rickety desk Odessa said he could use. He pressed his bottom into a cushioned chair that had lost its plush feel, and opened the book before him to the twelfth chapter of Romans. It had been Brenda's favorite passage. He read the entire chapter, the last verse a second time. *Be not overcome of evil, but overcome evil with good.* It was a challenge for him to make something good stem from Brenda's death. He'd made sizable monetary donations to anti-drinking-and-driving organizations, but he felt there was something more that he should do, in Brenda's honor. What it would be, he had no idea.

"Brenda," he mused, closing his eyes, leaning deep into the cradle of the tattered leather chair. He remembered Brenda's eyes, skin, voice, her smile. She had the most beautiful smile on her face the morning of the day she died as they shared a kiss and a hug and a few quiet moments before he left the house.

Trevor drew a hand over his face and let out a lengthy sigh. The events of that last day with Brenda were charted with indelible memories, and each time he viewed them they seemed to unfold in slow motion.

He was in the middle of an interview with a potential driver for one of the Seconds delivery vans when Grace uncharacteristically burst into his office.

"Excuse me, Trevor," she quaked, rushing to his desk.

Right away he knew something was wrong, Grace calling him Trevor, instead of the formal Mr. Monroe. Struggling to remain calm in the face of calamity, Trevor prayed and quoted every scripture of faith, healing, and deliverance he knew as he drove too fast to the hospital.

"It could go either way," the doctor told him.

Thirty minutes later, Brenda was dead, and Trevor had to figure out how he was going to tell his children.

Trevor let the memory dissolve and sat up straight. He closed the Bible, but his ring finger caught his eye, and the past immediately took over his thoughts again. About two months after the funeral, he had removed his wedding band, and it rested with Brenda's in a small box in his top bureau drawer. Putting the rings side by side had been his way of paying tribute to the bond he and Brenda shared and always would share; it was not a signal to the world that he was ready to start dating again, as Kregg had mistakenly assessed.

Trevor resumed a reclining pose, his long legs extended beneath the desk as a conversation he had with Kregg a few weeks before sprang to mind. On the way home from a City Champions meeting, they'd stopped at the market to pick up beverages and snacks to go with the boxing matches they were planning to watch on television. Two young ladies walked by, one whispered something to the other, and both burst into giggles. The women smiled over their shoulders at them, and Kregg nodded and smiled back.

"I hope they don't think we're a couple," Kregg said.

"What does it matter? I thought you only had eyes for Rave," said Trevor.

"Maybe I'm looking out for you." Kregg grinned. "Helping you get back in the game."

Trevor passed on a wisecrack and resumed the task of deciding between sour cream-and-onion or plain potato chips.

"Do you think you might want to hook up with us sometime?"

Trevor frowned. "You mean double-date?"

"Maybe even get a good-night kiss out of the deal," Kregg said, and patted him on the back.

Trevor had to admit he missed kissing and all the good feelings it entailed. But he only wanted to kiss Brenda, and she was gone.

Slightly swiveling the chair, he thought more about dating. The opportunity had presented itself if he'd been interested. His church sisters began pushing up on him a week after his wife's burial.

Lynette Graham, her grandmother leading the way, stopped by his house without calling. Said they wanted to make sure he was okay. Lynette barely offered more than a complete sentence of conversation, whereas her grandmother prattled incessantly, and by the time they left, Trevor had a throbbing headache and more information about Lynette than he was comfortable knowing.

Then there was Judith Long, who believed candor paved the way to love. She came right out and admitted she was alone and lonely; while her twin sister, Edith, seemed to think the way to a man's heart was through food poisoning. She showed up at his job with two covered casseroles and a roast. He hadn't had a bout of diarrhea that deadly since he was seven and accepted Kregg's challenge to a worm-eating contest.

Priscilla Barnes, missing a front tooth and armed with a body odor that lingered well after she'd left the room, also made his diet a priority.

"Have you eaten?" she asked one evening, pushing her way into his foyer.

"No," he croaked. Depressed over Brenda's absence, he hadn't eaten since breakfast that day. And he didn't want to eat dinner or anything else with Priscilla, who'd flounced into the kitchen, planted a brown bag on the table, and withdrawn two TV dinners.

"I got you a Hungry-Man," she announced in a husky alto.

Trevor stared, voiceless and numb, as she rummaged through drawers and shelves in search of tableware, running

*her uninvited hands over Brenda's things. It seemed unholy
and it made him angry. While he was in the process of de-
vising a tactful way of asking her to leave, she accidentally
shattered the cup Brenda had sipped coffee from each
morning. A rock of pain weighting his chest, he overlooked
politeness.*

"*You need to go,*" *he said.*

*The glower Priscilla flashed him could have sharpened all
the knives in the knife block, and Trevor wondered if she
was entertaining throwing the hot dinner she'd pulled from
the microwave in his face.*

Honestly, Trevor didn't understand all the hoopla
women made over him. He considered himself as ordi-
nary as the next guy and as flawed. His eyes were too
dark, his nose larger than average, and at certain angles,
it seemed his ears stuck out.

Trevor closed his eyes, but not the subject. If he were
to date, whom would he ask? And what could he offer
a woman when he still craved Brenda? He pondered
how Brenda might feel about him dating. They had
never discussed what one would do if the other died.
He'd just taken for granted, as she probably had, that
they would be together forever.

chapter ten

Cassidy popped straight up and grabbed at her throat in a plea for air as her speeding heart geared to drive through her chest. After so many years, she thought she'd be immune to the nightmare that commonly bruised her nights. But she was as rattled as she'd been the first night she bolted out of sleep like this, back when she was a student at Tilden.

Cassidy refused to crumple in despair. *"When my heart is overwhelmed: lead me to the rock,"* she whispered. She shoved aside the covers and switched on the bedside lamp, erasing the darkness. Sticky with cold perspiration, an extra-large T-shirt clung to her skin. She went to the bureau and pulled out a clean shirt. This one had the name "La Salle" across the front. After walking out on a four-year scholarship to Tilden, she completed her undergrad and grad courses at the locally based La Salle University, funding tuition and books with loans, part-time jobs, and ultimately a chunk of Odessa's life savings because Odessa wouldn't have it any other way.

Cassidy sat on the bed and plowed her shaky fingers through her hair. The scarf she'd used to contain her hair had come off during her fitful sleep. She tied the scarf back on her head and stared at the bold red clock numbers. It was after one o'clock. Concerned she might slip back into the lair of the nightmare, Cassidy wouldn't attempt to sleep again, not right away. Sometimes a warm drink helped her mellow, and she eased into her all-season robe and trod downstairs.

No chamomile available, Cassidy chose a peppermint tea bag and dunked it into a mug of hot, bubbling water. As the unsweetened liquid cooled, she switched on the radio, finding shelter under an umbrella of classical music. She lifted the mug and settled at the table. She and Odessa had shared many good times in this room, at this table, especially when Cassidy was of elementary school age. On any given afternoon, while waiting for a pie to bake, a pan of bread to rise, or a bowl of beans to soak, they sat and had tea parties or clipped coupons or did cross-stitch patterns. Cassidy looked up at the wall above the table. A large wood-framed stitching, sewn by Odessa when her eyesight had been sharper, read, "As for me and my house, we will eat a home-cooked meal."

Cassidy swallowed a first sip of tea, and the warm flavored water kissed the length of her throat. She peered around the room, finding additions to the quaint kitchen setting tonight—vestiges of Trevor Monroe. Several boxes of cereal, sugar-sweetened brands she'd never consider buying, lined the top of the refrigerator. And on the counter, a jar filled with jelly beans set her face in a grimace.

Stroking one bare foot with the other, Cassidy gazed through the vapor and into her tea. Her mind returned to the nightmare.

She jumped in the river, joining the little boy. They laughed as they smacked the water with their hands, splashing each other. Suddenly, the boy's laughter turned to cries as the river pulled him away. "Help, help," he wailed, his small arms thrashing like the wings of a bird that couldn't get off the ground.

Cassidy began swimming toward him, but the faster she swam, the larger the distance between them grew. "I'm coming," she cried. "Hold on, hold on."

"Help me, please, help me." The child's pitiful calls sounded more like echoes now.

"Hold on," Cassidy screamed, although the child had disappeared.

✐

Trevor and Brenda were barefoot, the beach sand filtering between their toes. A light wind whistled under the hem of Brenda's long white dress, and the fabric billowed like a sail. The same friendly wind wafted through Trevor's open white shirt. Laughing, hands locked, they cantered to where shore met sea, and the waves lapped at their ankles.

Trevor pulled Brenda into his arms. As their bodies molded, he became oblivious to the sand, waves, and wind. He was conscious only of Brenda, an angel, warm against him. He closed his eyes as his lips caressed hers. The tender trail stretched to her jaw, her neck, her shoulder. Trevor couldn't keep his lids shut any longer. He had to see her.

Had to behold the beauty he was about to cuddle with on the sand. He opened his eyes . . .

Trevor came awake, shooting from the chair with enough force to send it rolling into the wall behind with a powerful punch. Decayed paint loosened from the wall and rained to the floor, sounding like the patter of a million tiny feet. Trevor gripped the edge of the desk, his fingertips stinging from the pressure while he reluctantly rewound to the final frame of his dream.

He had been kissing Brenda, but when he opened his eyes to see her lovely face, it wasn't Brenda he held. It wasn't Brenda he desired.

"Cassidy," he whispered.

⌇❤

Someone had turned the light off. Forced to feel his way up the darkened basement stairwell, Trevor groped through the blackness, stumbling along the way, smacking his knee on the wooden stair, then scratching his hand on something unidentifiable. "Ouch," he hissed. Displeasure tightening his face, he rounded the doorway to the kitchen and found Cassidy. Her eyes flashed aggression as she stood holding an aluminum bat, poised to take a swing at his head.

A perceptible sigh rushed through her lips, and she relaxed her arms, lowering her weapon. "Oh, it's just you," she stated, leaving him to speculate on whether she was relieved he wasn't an intruder or disappointed it was him. "I would have left the light on if I'd known you were down there." Her expression showed complete disregard, yet her tone had softened, and he decided she was telling the truth. She returned the bat to its place between the baker's rack and the microwave cart and tied another knot in the belt of her robe before approaching the table.

Trevor filled a bowl with milk and cereal, then moseyed in Cassidy's direction. Her gaze was fixed on her cup, and he presumed she would prefer he take his bowl upstairs or at least sit at the island on one of the two stools. "I'll take this seat," he said, then pulled out a chair and placed his bowl on the vinyl tablecloth. Cassidy slid her mug closer to herself and straightened her back, and Trevor lowered himself to the chair thinking he'd seen mannequins less tense than this woman.

He dipped his spoon and brought up a hill of cereal. He chewed with his mouth closed, but the room was so quiet he was sure Cassidy could hear him crunching. Poopie brushed against his ankle, and Trevor scratched her between the ears, keeping his scrutiny within the boundaries of Cassidy's face. Some of her features Trevor had noticed before, like the slightly pronounced cheekbones many models would date the devil for. Other features, like the pencil-point mole on the bridge of her nose, he was discovering for the first time. "Are you all right? Your eyes are red." There were several crinkled napkins on the table, and Trevor believed she had been crying.

"I'm fine," she said to her unfinished tea.

"Well, if you want to talk," he said smoothly, "I'm a good listener. And if you want to pray, I've been successful in getting a few through." He bounced his eyebrows and noted that his ploy to lighten her load had elicited from her only a sealed-lips smile.

Cassidy spoke to the tea again. "No. But thanks."

Trevor put down the spoon, reached the short distance, and slipped his fingertips between her hand and
the cup. He felt a tremor pulse through her palm as she
watched him through large, baffled eyes. Considering
the dream he'd just awakened from, he thought he
would want to stay as far away from Cassidy as possible.
But here he was, holding her hand. It had been a bold
move, but one he could honestly say felt right as he said
a short, silent prayer for her.

In a voice that lowered with each word, she said, "I
think I'll go upstairs now."

"Before you go, there's something I need to say."

"Daddy," Brandi called out, bringing the moment to
an abrupt standstill. Cassidy ripped her hand from his as
his little girl trudged toward the table, accompanied by a
stuffed sandy-brown bear, half her size, led by its ear.

Trevor backed his chair away from the table and hurried to meet his daughter before she tripped over the
hem of the nightgown that once belonged to Brittney
and was still a bit big for Brandi. He lifted her into his
arms. Brandi rested her head on his shoulder, retaining
a grip on her bear. Trevor caressed Brandi's back, cognizant of the smile in Cassidy's expression as she
watched them.

"Can I get in *your* bed, Daddy?" Brandi whined. "I'll
tell you a sleepy-time story."

"Okay." He smiled and kissed her nose.

Cassidy transported her cup to the sink as he offered
Brandi warm milk. "I want you to wait upstairs," he
said, putting Brandi on the floor. He filled her Snoopy
mug with milk and placed it in the microwave.

"I'm going that way." Cassidy smiled at Brandi. "We can walk together."

Brandi looked as if she were about to pop with approval. "Do you want to hold my bear? His name is Sammy."

Cassidy's posture was perfect as she passed Trevor without a glance. "I'd love to hold Sam . . ."

Her voice dwindled to silence as Trevor reached and circled her wrist, slowing her hurried exit. She sent a derisive gaze to the hand on her arm, then threw the same to his face. Trevor uncurled his fingers and mulled over why a woman who only a few minutes prior had accepted his touch suddenly found it repulsive. "Sweetheart," he called to Brandi, "take Sammy on up and tuck him in. Daddy needs to speak with Cassidy."

"Will you come and say good night to Sammy and me?"

Cassidy cradled Brandi's chin. "I'll be up soon."

His baby out of the kitchen, Trevor gave Cassidy his full gaze and said what he had been on the brink of saying at the table. "It's a week late, but I owe you an apology. Brandi and I had no idea you were in the bathroom. We didn't mean to frighten you."

"I wasn't frightened," Cassidy asserted a bit too frantically for it to be believable. She put calm in her next sentence. "I was surprised."

"Then . . . I'm sorry we surprised you."

"Well, I am accustomed to the privacy of *my* bathroom."

"You don't have a problem with me using the same bathroom as you, do you?"

She raised her face to him. "Actually, I do."

He felt a strong impulse to laugh at Cassidy's frown. But he kept a straight face and pulled a container of cocoa from the cupboard. It would make a nice treat, since Brandi loved anything chocolate. "Then I have good news," he said. He took the mug from the microwave and stirred in the cocoa.

Cassidy uncrossed her arms and appeared relieved. "Thank you for deciding to use the third-floor bathroom instead of mine."

"When did I decide that?" He stood in front of her, the mug of hot chocolate between them. Lowering his head and voice, Trevor leaned in close and said near Cassidy's ear, "My good news is that I'll always knock first. That way you'll have plenty of time to grab a towel if you don't have that T-shirt handy."

Shock turned to fury on Cassidy's face. "Move," she ordered. When he didn't budge, she seemed to deliberate pushing past him, but realized this might jar the cup, risking burns for one or both of them. She squared her shoulders and retaliated with words. "Anyone with a third of a brain knows not to give a child who can't sleep chocolate milk. The sugar and the caffeine in the cocoa will simply make her fidgety."

Trevor lowered his eyes to the hot chocolate before returning to Cassidy's faultfinding gaze. He thought she looked sexy in her scarf, and for a moment, he thought about pulling it from her head just to see what she would do. Cassidy's neck-cradling, ankle-shading robe also appealed to Trevor in a way he hadn't expected. The cottony-looking garment, colored in the blue family, gave her the appearance of being wrapped in a piece of twilight-time sky. But right now the stare "Sky" was giving him was anything but heavenly. The woman's pupils were pitchforks. Not wanting things to get out of hand, he stepped aside, careful not to step on Sky's pretty polished toes.

"There's one more thing," Cassidy said, her tone still tetchy. "In the future, I'd appreciate it if you'd refrain from walking around like that."

He squinted in confusion. "Like what?"

"Naked," she said sharply, and hurled a glare of disapproval toward his bare chest.

He taunted her with a grin. "This isn't naked for a man. In order to be naked"—he tugged on the waistband of his sweatpants—"I'd have to take off—"

"That's enough, Trevor," she scolded, and turned away.

He chuckled and followed her to the top of the stairs. "Don't forget you promised to tuck my daughter in, Sky." He rumbled the nickname much deeper than the other words.

Her voice snapped through the air with the spunk of a whip. "What did you call me?"

Finished teasing Cassidy for now, he gave her a dense stare and strolled away. He found Brandi nestled between the sheets, Sammy tucked in on one side. "You were almost asleep. Maybe we should save this for morning," he suggested, setting the cocoa on the stand beside the bed. He didn't know if it was myth or fact that sugar made kids hyper, but if Brandi were to drink something now, she'd be peeing the rest of the night.

"I was not almost asleep," his daughter whimpered, rubbing droopy eyes with small fists.

"You looked just like a sleeping doll to me." Cassidy

positioned herself on the edge of the bed. "I have an idea. Why don't I tell *you* a sleepy-time story?"

Tired from a demanding workday and from being up so late, Trevor was thankful Brandi acquiesced without tears, pouting, or additional whining. He eased the cup of untouched cocoa off the table and returned to the kitchen. He washed Brandi's mug along with the things he and Cassidy had dirtied, confounded by the magnitude of his attraction to Cassidy. Only one other woman had ever stirred him like this. "Brenda," he whispered, hoping that when he fell asleep, his darling wife would meet him again in his dreams.

chapter eleven

Cassidy!" A quartet of girls from the neighborhood squealed and ran toward her.

Cassidy smiled at the seven- through eleven-year-olds. Their skin tones ranged from the darkest of chocolate to French vanilla.

"Look at my necklace," one said after hugging Cassidy. She pointed to the rope of bright beads around her neck. "I made it myself, and I'm making one just like it for my mom."

"It's beautiful," Cassidy exclaimed. The smallest of the girls continued to hang on to Cassidy. Crumbs circled her mouth, and some of them were sticking to Cassidy's coordinating cotton shirt and pants. Accustomed to having crumbs and marker stains and snot from runny noses rubbed into her clothing, Cassidy continued to grin.

The girl smiled up at Cassidy. "I'm going to make you a bracelet."

"You should put lots of pink in it," her friend recommended, "so it'll match her outfit."

The girl beamed in agreement. "I'll have it ready for you when you get home."

The girls dashed back to the steps of the house where they'd been sitting, and Cassidy walked to the corner, increasing her pace until she reached the speed she wanted to maintain. A swift walk three times a week was her prime method of exercise, and although Germantown had its share of unkempt properties and streets, a walk through the area was especially rewarding on sunny afternoons like this one. The predominantly black, predominantly working-class neighborhood was a city within a city, and there was much to appreciate if you took the time. Within a ten-block radius sat several elite private schools and a host of historic house museums. One of her favorites, located on the same street as Charity Community Church, had once been a stop on the Underground Railroad. A lively shopping district comprised of numerous thrift and antique shops stretched up and down Germantown Avenue. Cassidy often frequented the thrift stores, on the lookout for scarves and hats and mittens she would give out during the winter to students who were without.

Today Cassidy stopped at the bank, the post office, and the produce market. She weaved through the heavy volume of Saturday shoppers, past the farm-fresh eggs and around a huge ring of fruit and vegetables. She ended up in front of a display of jarred preserves, boxed baked goods, and see-through canisters packed with nuts.

"Ah, Cas-si-dy, how are you?"

Cassidy always smiled at the way Gabriel divided her name into syllables. "I'm fine, Gabriel. And you?"

He laughed, his baritone thundering over the countertop. "As long as the Father above affords me breath, I have no grievances. What will you have today?"

"The usual," she requested of the sturdy black-bearded Amish gentleman in the straw hat. He opened a plastic bag and scooped from a well of almonds. Remembering that Brittney and Brandi were staying at the house, Cassidy quickly changed the order to a half pound, more than enough to share, and better for them than the sweets their father provided.

"Anything else?" Gabriel twisted a tie on the almond-fattened bag.

"A quarter of walnuts and quarter of pistachios . . . unsalted." She would have a broader offering in case the sisters didn't like one or the other. "I don't see Beatrice today," Cassidy mentioned while waiting.

"There's a good reason for that." He boomed, "My wife is going to make me a father this winter. She had morning sickness today and couldn't make it."

Cassidy was sure she'd never seen Gabriel smile so. She congratulated the proud father-to-be, elated for anyone who found joy in the prospects of parenting.

"How awful," Lena was saying as Cassidy entered the kitchen, returning from her walk. There was an open container of strawberry yogurt on the table, and the spoon in Lena's hand was poised to dip.

"What's so awful?" Cassidy dropped her bag of nuts on the kitchen counter.

"Mother Vale was telling me how she isn't feeling

the best. She's unsure if she'll be able to go out this evening."

Cassidy sat at the table with Odessa and Lena. She checked Odessa's forehead for warmth. Cassidy couldn't recall the last time Odessa had something as mundane as a cold. "Is there something I can do for you?"

"Well . . . yes . . . there is something you may be able to help with."

Cassidy expected to be asked to run an errand or heat some soup. Waiting for instructions, she began removing the pink and purple bracelet her young neighbor had tied on her wrist. The beaded jewelry was cutting off her circulation.

"I was scheduled to sit for Trevor's girls this evening," Odessa said.

A smile filled Cassidy, and she flaunted it on her face. "I'd be happy to take care of the girls. Brandi and Brittney are extremely nice." Cassidy remembered their father and could think of nothing pleasant to say about him, or his overactive cat, in the corner right now, chasing her tail.

"That's not what I need you to do," Odessa clarified. "You see, originally, Trevor's sister, Penny, was supposed to go with him to a banquet tonight. But just after you left, she called and said she was still sick. So Trevor invited me to go with him." Odessa yawned, and the wrinkles in her face bunched. "Certainly, I suggested he go with someone closer to his age. I even told him I could fix him up with one of the sisters from our church. But he insisted I was his choice, that I deserved a night out on the town. I think that was very sweet of him." She looked at Cassidy, as if waiting for her to agree.

Lena gave her vote. "That *was* sweet of him, Mother Vale."

Odessa smiled. "Yes, I do think—"

Cassidy's voice cut in, "Can we stick to the main street, please?"

Odessa shrugged. "Like Penny, I won't be able to attend this evening. I simply don't feel up to it. So I thought you could accompany Trevor in my place. It would be so sad for him to go alone," she said with graveside soberness.

"Amen," Lena punctuated, and bit back a smile.

Cassidy tossed her tablemates a glare as potent as the lingering aroma of the breakfast bacon Odessa had oven-fried.

"Trevor most likely would have had Brenda by his side, but . . . well . . ." Odessa's voice disappeared.

Lena guided a spoon of pink to her mouth. "It must be difficult to do things solo, after you've adapted to doing them as a couple."

Cassidy considered herself as humanitarian as the next person, but why should she be the one to pay the bill for Trevor's singleness? Gathering her jumbled wits at the same time that she cooled a rising temper, she succeeded in speaking without a trace of the hysteria roaring within. "I'm sure Trevor could get one of his girlfriends to go with him."

"Trevor doesn't have girlfriends," Odessa piped, seemingly without doubt.

"That's not the way it looked last Friday night. I saw Trevor holding Rave, right outside this house."

Cassidy had told Lena the following day. Odessa looked as skeptical as Lena had. "I know what I saw," Cassidy argued. "Rave was stuck to Trevor like an adhesive strip."

Lena licked her spoon clean. "Maybe the woman just looked like Rave. Anyway, Rave doesn't seem to be all that interested in Trevor anymore. Remember, she admitted as much at Brenda's funeral. I didn't believe her then, but she really does seem to have her sights set elsewhere."

"Lena's right," Odessa said. "Trevor hasn't dated Rave or anyone."

Cassidy held her mouth open. She finally formed the words. "You mean you've been all up in the man's love life?"

"I told him you weren't seeing anyone, either, and it wouldn't be a problem for you to go with him tonight."

Lena howled with amusement as Cassidy blurted, "My personal affairs are none of Trevor's business." She pushed away from the table but remained in her seat, her arms crossed in rebellion as she drummed her fingers just above her elbows. "What makes you think he would want to go with *me?*"

Odessa's response was matter-of-fact. "He said it was fine with him."

Anxiety stewed in the pit of Cassidy's stomach, and she bit on her thumbnail as the memory of last night burned on her brain. The pores in her skin had tingled with responsiveness the moment Trevor pried his hand between hers and the cup. Cassidy had wanted to be furious with him for taking such a liberty, but anger had not come, and she had pondered why until falling asleep.

"What about you?" she addressed Lena. "An evening out with Trevor would be a dream come true for you."

"Girl, you ain't wrong. I would love to take this tour of duty. But I have a date with Dondre tonight." Lena winked.

"I would make a much better babysitter than a . . ." Cassidy didn't know what to call it. An escort . . . a date . . . a companion. These terms all left a bitter taste in her mouth.

"Pastor Audrey's Natasha will be doing the babysitting," Odessa said.

"There you go." Cassidy clapped once. "Natasha could go with Trevor, and I'll watch the kids."

Lena frowned. "Natasha's only fourteen."

"A big one," Odessa incorporated, "but only fourteen."

Cassidy knew that, but she was grabbing at every straw. She sighed, in dire need of some sensible excuse, because she was going down fast. "I don't have anything to wear."

Lena popped to her feet. "If we get started now, we'll have time to hunt for something at the mall."

Cassidy stayed defiantly put. She gazed steadily across the table at Odessa. Her aunt's features were overcast and distant, and Cassidy began to wonder if Odessa was feeling worse than she'd admitted. Maybe Odessa really did need her. It was only right for her to be there when her aunt was in a crisis. Odessa had made so many sacrifices for her over the years, never with complaint. Not once had Odessa scolded her for giving up her Tilden scholarship and returning to the city with no explanation other than she missed home.

Cassidy gave the matter more thought. Time alone with Trevor could prove advantageous. She still wanted to tell him how much she hated the way he was always sneaking up on her and how much of an irritant his early morning shower singing was and that she'd appreciate it if he'd leave the toilet seat down, in addition to a list of other complaints she'd cataloged in her head.

"Okay," she decided. Determination held Cassidy's face firm as she strutted from the room. "I'll go with him."

chapter twelve

Lena hugged Cassidy. "Don't worry. It's going to be a perfect night."

Cassidy thought about it. On a perfect night, she would be spending this tranquil, dusk-colored evening sprawled on her bed, absorbed in a good sci-fi read, dressed in sweats and a T-shirt. On a perfect night, she would be barefoot as a newborn instead of jammed into black high-heeled footwear. She had to settle for size 8½ shoes because the store was out of 9s and they had run out of time.

Before leaving the bedroom, Cassidy took one last glimpse in the mirror, checking the hair she'd upswept to capture a look of elegance. The makeup Lena helped her apply looked great, and she approved of the tips Lena put on her nails.

Despite sore feet, Cassidy rushed down the steps, less than exuberant about going out with Trevor. She merely wanted to get the whole evening over with. She was already sorry she'd agreed to go. As soon as she walked into

the living room, those dark eyes of Trevor's began appraising with quiet intensity. The man was at least six
feet away, yet she felt as if he'd put his hands on her in a
warm, gentle way. How he did it, she couldn't imagine.

"Cassidy," he breathed more than spoke. Pleasure
and praise gathered in his eyes.

Cassidy smiled lightly. Although she knew she
looked good, it was nice he thought so, too.

Odessa, watching with all the interest she invested
in her favorite Court TV show, folded her hands at her
chest as if the moment were sacred. "Oh, sweetheart,
you look like a princess."

"Thank you." Cassidy spoke softly, placed a light
kiss on Odessa's cheek, and turned toward Trevor. Now
that he was up on her, she detected his cologne. It had
become as familiar as the scent of the body wash that
engulfed the bathroom after he showered. She looked
him over. He was faultlessly dressed in black leather
shoes and a blacker suit. Beneath it he wore a light gray
shirt and a gray tie, a color that made his eyes appear
more attractively darker, and Cassidy almost forgot she
didn't like him.

✍

Trevor escorted Cassidy to the car, checking her out
as much as he could without being obvious. She was ar-
rayed in a short-sleeved straight black dress that
squared at her collarbone and circled above her ankles
and lightly cuddled her curves. There was a string of
silver looping her neck, and a teardrop pearl dangled
from the chain. He thought the jewel looked like a tiny

ship on a sea of chocolate silk. Before clicking the car lock with the handheld opener, he attempted to catch Cassidy's attention, but she refused him, her eyes darting somewhere beyond his shoulder. It suddenly struck him that perhaps she was more naturally shy than purposely aloof, and an ache to know more about her dawned deep in his inner man.

He opened the car door, taking pride in his last-minute decision to go to his house and get the Maxima that once belonged to Brenda. As beautifully as Cassidy was dressed this evening, he would have hated to ask her to climb up into his SUV. When she was seated, he leaned in and guided the seat belt around her, moving so deftly there was no time for protest.

"Comfortable?" he asked.

"Yes," was her answer, yet she sat twisting the cord of her black beaded purse, revealing she was not at all comfortable with the proximity of their heads.

Trevor stepped back, then came forward, bringing their heads even closer this time as he welcomed the fragrance of her perfume. "I disagree with your aunt." Their gazes locked. "You don't look like a princess." He retreated and pushed the door, letting it shut with a resounding thud.

Cassidy's mouth was still open like a doughnut hole as Trevor filled the driver's seat. Her eyes shot missiles of extreme dislike, and although he didn't know Cassidy well, he knew that she would have unleashed a storm of remarks if he had not hurried and said, "You look more beautiful than any princess I've ever seen." He retrieved a package from beneath his seat and piloted it toward his passenger.

Her unsteady hand paused in the air before grasping the edge of the gift. She peeled away two layers of pink wrapping, and her gaze met his. "Music," she said.

"I've noticed you keep classical on the radio, and I thought you might like to listen to it during the drive. It's a peace offering, too. I really am sorry about walking in on you in the bathroom."

She had a smile in her tone. "You do have a way of suddenly appearing."

"Maybe I should get a bell like Poopie's."

She chuckled, and he smiled with her. As they departed Pomona Street, a blend of wind and string instruments permeated the car's interior. Cassidy exhaled. "I like this song."

Trevor liked the long lovely leg smiling up at him through the knee-to-ankle split in Cassidy's dress. He fought to keep his eyes on the street and off of Cassidy's sheer nylons.

Moments later, Trevor avoided a pothole, a swift dagger of guilt piercing him where it hurt most—his heart. *What is wrong with me?* he wanted to shout. He shouldn't be admiring Cassidy's legs. Brenda's legs were the only legs he should be thinking of.

❦

"Yo! Coach Monroe!" LaKell Biltmore called. He and several members of Trevor's team, including Derek, dressed in the new suit, shirt, tie, and shoes Trevor had bought him, rushed toward him as he walked through a sparkling glass door into the hotel lobby. Trevor grinned, feeling especially proud of how mature Derek looked. He introduced the youngsters to Cassidy, and she politely said hello, then excused herself and headed for the ladies' lounge.

"We ain't know you had a girlfriend, Coach." Thirteen-year-old LaKell, slightly taller than Derek's six-foot figure, elbowed Trevor.

"Yeah," Derek said, "I thought I knew everything about you."

Trevor set them straight. "Well, you don't. And I don't have a girlfriend, not that it's any of your business."

"Then who is she?" The question rang from Keon Carmichael, also thirteen, and cleaner tonight than Trevor had ever seen him.

"She goes to my church," was all he supplied.

"She looks good, Coach," LaKell stated, as if his stamp of approval were required.

Derek asked the circle, "Why can't I meet fine sistas like that?"

" 'Cause you ain't nuttin' but a lit'l boy."

"I'm older than your ugly-mugly rump." Derek and LaKell exchanged jabs not intended to do any harm.

"Chill, fellas," Trevor urged. "Remember we agreed you'd try civilized behavior for one evening."

The boys obeyed, and Trevor excused himself so he could go and say hello to one of the sponsors of tonight's affair. Once he gave the boys his back and began walking away, LaKell called out, "Make sure we get an invitation to the wedding, Coach."

"Make sure I'm the best man," Derek yelled through their snickers.

Trevor never turned to look at them. He did not want them to see the blush on his face.

The ceremony began promptly at seven with the singing of the national anthem, followed by the black national anthem. After an applause-drawing welcome address by one of the youngest players in the league, a comedian kept the audience in hysterics until dinner was served. At the conclusion of the main course, they came to the crux of the ceremony: the presenting of the awards. Cassidy clapped and cheered with the others as the youngsters proudly strutted forward to claim their trophies and medals. She even applauded heartily when Trevor's name was read as one of the contenders for Coach of the Year, and the boys on his team jumped up, whooping and clapping.

"I didn't know you were a nominee," Cassidy whispered. He smiled, a shy kind of smile that had her pulse beating between rapid and life-threatening, and she quickly turned back to the podium. Trevor did not win, and Cassidy did not know how she was going to survive the night if he kept smiling at her.

"You look as if you're having a nice time," he said as the last of the awards were presented.

If Cassidy were responsible for grading the event up to this point, she'd give it a big red A. "Yes, I am having a nice time," she replied. She smiled, and decided she would wait until morning to voice the list of complaints she had written on a piece of paper and stuck in her purse. Surprisingly, Trevor had been the perfect gentleman, and he *had* taken her musical flavor into account. She was actually looking forward to the drive home when she would be able to listen to the remainder of her new CD. Cassidy reached for her water glass and shared a pleasant glance with Trevor. Tonight she would be an ideal escort, but first thing tomorrow, she would have a talk with Mr. Monroe. There were some things he needed to do differently if he was going to remain under her roof.

✐

"This has really been nice." Lydia Rodriguez popped the morsel of white-chocolate cheesecake that had fallen next to her empty dessert plate between her lips.

Everyone at the round dining table nodded and grinned in agreement with Lydia, except for Rave. Her evening had been dismal. She was at the right table, but with the wrong man. Rave cast her gaze beyond the floating-candle centerpiece and observed the pair across from her. She didn't know what to make of something she'd witnessed earlier. After Trevor was announced as a candidate for Coach of the Year, Cassidy whispered in his ear, and though a smile curved his lips, it was his eyes that leaked the story. They sparkled with the stardust of a man in the early stages of falling in love.

Kregg murmured close to her head, "Everything all right, babe?"

Rave laid her hand atop Kregg's and smiled into his eyes. "Everything's wonderful as long as you're by my side." They shared a light kiss.

"Break it up, you two," Shelby McNeil advised. "We have minors in here."

"And they're doing a lot more," Eduardo Rodriguez pointed out. Several tables away, two teenagers were kissing as if they were the only ones in the room. "I better go cool 'em off." Eduardo lifted the water pitcher, earning laughs from the others at the table.

"Give me that, Eddie." Lydia took the pitcher from her husband, and he strode toward the kissing teens.

A section of the large ballroom had been reserved for dancing. The whoop of a DJ and the commanding sound of hip-hop sent teens flying from their chairs to the dance floor. Dimmed lights gave the room a club effect as the music screamed.

"Whose idea was this?" Lydia rested her forearms on the tablecloth and leaned forward to be heard.

Kregg thumped his fingers on the table to the beat of the music. He spoke extra loud like Lydia. "The planning committee thought the kids would enjoy it."

"I'm enjoying it, too." Rave wiggled to standing. The maroon silk clinging to her skin revealed shoulders and back to the waist. A slit running from ankle to center thigh exposed leg exactly the way she liked it. Licking her lipstick-layered lips and smoothing her hands over her figure, she fantasized about how it would feel to kiss Trevor while his hands became acquainted with her body.

Rave's heart turned cold. If her ice pick stunt had played out the way it should have, she wouldn't have to imagine. Maybe she should have stabbed two tires. At least she would have gotten to spend a little more time with the man she desired more than life.

She looked into the stare of her date. She made sure everyone at the table could hear her. "How about dancing with the sexiest female in attendance?"

Kregg kissed her palm. "Lead the way."

chapter thirteen

Rave and Kregg disappeared inside the crowd of dancers, and Derek approached the table. As Cassidy peered at the young man's face, an arctic tongue licked her spine, and she hugged herself, chasing the icy sensation away.

"You senior citizens havin' a good time?" A glowing smile followed Derek's question.

"I'm having a great time." Chantalle Williams, the coach of a girls' basketball team, straightened her dress as she stood. "Let's go dance."

Derek's eyes bulged as if to say that he couldn't believe a grown woman wanted to dance with him. He swaggered as he escorted Chantalle across the room, nodding at the other boys who looked equally perplexed by Derek's good fortune.

Lydia smiled. "This takes me back. Remember how we used to party, Eddie?"

Leaning back in his seat, Eduardo grinned.

"Would you care to relive old times?" she asked.

"Lydia, I think my gyratin' days are over."

"That's not the way it seemed last night."

"All right, now!" Shelby slapped Lydia with a high five, and Lydia led her blushing husband to the dance floor.

"Come on, Byron"—Shelby grabbed her escort's hand—"let's show these kids how it's done."

"You didn't eat your dessert," Trevor thundered over the music.

Cassidy glanced at the wedge of untouched cheesecake on her plate. "I don't eat junk food." The music softened some as she enveloped Trevor with a direct stare. "Do you know which disease kills more American women than any other disease?"

He grew pensive. "Breast cancer?"

"No. Heart disease. Many women believe cancer is their ultimate enemy, but heart disease poses the greater threat. A healthy diet will help lower the risk of developing heart disease *and* type 2 diabetes, which has surfaced in our community at an alarming rate." Trevor seemed dazed by her words, and she supposed such facts were a lot for him to digest, considering he marketed sugar for a living. "The program really was lovely," she said, changing the subject to something she knew he felt more at ease discussing. "I love anything that encourages children to do their best, then honors their accomplishments."

Trevor nodded and shared the history of City Champions, but since the loud music made it difficult to converse in normal tones, they ultimately sat quietly, enjoying the dance moves of the young and not so young. A sappy love song came on, enticing the dancers to sway closer to their partners.

"Do you like to dance, Cassidy?" Trevor gripped the slim stalk of his glass and drained the last drop of sparkling cider.

Nerves nibbled at Cassidy's insides. She prayed this wasn't Trevor's roundabout way of asking if she wanted to dance. There was no way she was dancing with him to something this slow, which required that partners touch. "It's been a while since I've danced," she answered, likewise choosing evasiveness. She glanced at him. He was staring ahead, seemingly a trillion miles away.

Trevor was actually a year and some months in the past, reliving the night he danced with his wife under the moon and the stars in their backyard. Brenda had loved to dance, to Natalie Cole mostly, before they made love.

A waiter came to clear the table. Affording the young gentleman more room, Trevor slid his chair closer to Cassidy. She gave him an uneasy smile, but her personality stayed open.

"A few moments ago you seemed to be deep in thought," she said. "What was on your brain, if you don't mind me asking?"

He answered without looking at her. "How fortunate I am to be sitting next to the most stunning woman here."

"Rave looks pretty," she said, and he thought he heard a crimp in her tone. "Have you been friends long?"

Trevor followed Cassidy's stare and focused on Kregg and the woman mashed against him. "Kregg and I have been friends since the day our tricycles collided on the playground."

"I meant you and Rave."

A dry chuckle left Trevor's throat. "Isn't Rave one of *your* friends?" He didn't wait for an answer. "I believe I've seen the two of you rather buddy-buddy at church."

"We attended the same high school. She's more acquaintance than friend. But last week I got the impression that you two were"—she parroted his words—"buddy-buddy."

The fingers of his hand folded into a fist. Had Cassidy seen Rave hanging all over him? What that must have looked like! "Rave had a flat, and she asked for my help." Trevor felt he didn't need to explain himself, but he wanted no misinformation about Rave and him simmering in anyone's hearsay pot. He faced Cassidy, secured her gaze for as long as she would allow, and made it clear: "There's nothing going on between me and Rave."

✺

Rave stopped pumping her pelvis. "I want to go," she blurted to Kregg. Trevor and Cassidy were sitting like two doves in a nest, and it was giving her stomach pains. Rave spun on her spiked heels and stomped toward an exit sign. She tossed her long hair over her shoulder, an insecure gesture much more than vanity, although she knew most assumed it was only the latter.

"Leaving so soon?" Lydia asked as Rave passed.

"Yes," Rave snapped. She had to leave. As volatile as she was feeling, she dared not stay.

☙

"Take me home now," Cassidy insisted.

"I don't think so," he growled, and stopped the car in a woodland section of Fairmount Park. "Not until you give me some." He leaned over to the passenger side. Clutching the back of her neck, he aimed his lips at her mouth.

His husky whisper had the odor of the breath mint he'd eaten. "I told you no, Larenz, and I'm not changing my mind. When I have sex, it will be with my husband." She kept her voice strong, although her insides felt weak and queasy.

"That's unfortunate." A thick layer of ice covered his voice. "Get out of my car."

Cassidy peered around. The headlights were the only glow. Even the moon and the stars had forsaken her. "Just take me home, please," she said in as conciliatory a tone as she could manage, recognizing she was at Larenz's mercy.

"If you don't get out, I will take what I want," he barked.

He pulled at a button on her blouse, and she knocked his hand away. Fear gouged her heart, but she wouldn't give Larenz the satisfaction of tears. She opened the door. The inside light came on, giving her a clearer view of the evil, stark and hungry, in Larenz's eyes.

"I can't believe you call yourself a man of God," she chided, giving him some of her anger now. She stepped onto the grass and slammed the door. He sped away, and she began walking in the same direction, hoping it would lead

her to civilization. Her imagination became her worst enemy, and she came to numerous breath-holding stops, listening over her shoulder to make sure her footsteps were the only ones there. Despite being dizzy with fright, Cassidy was determined to maintain her assurance in God, and as she staggered through the darkness, searching for the way out of the park, she called on Him. He would get her home safely.

Cassidy shut down the memory and leaned out of the car window. "Can you fix it?" she hollered.

"No," Trevor hollered back over the rumble of a passing truck. He popped from under the hood of the car, whacking his head. "Ow."

"Are you all right?"

"I'm fine," he grumbled. He rubbed the sore spot on his head as he came up to the passenger-side window. "Maybe if I knew what was wrong with the car, I could fix it. I've never been too good with mechanics. I was scheduled to take a couple of auto clinics but never got around to actually going."

Cassidy didn't think his not being able to fix the car was anything for him to look so embarrassed over. "One person can't know how to do everything," she said, touched by the little-boy-who's-lost-his-puppy tint in Trevor's eyes.

Don't fall for it, her good sense advised.

Not even, she promised.

Trevor had turned his back to her. He was on the phone, plugging his left ear with a fingertip to drown out the steady groan of the City Avenue traffic. Cassidy pinned him with a studious squint. He'd taken off his jacket, and she had no trouble seeing the effects of weight lifting in his broad back. Trevor clicked off the phone and did an about-face, and Cassidy jerked forward so fast she thought she might have sprained a muscle in her neck.

"A friend of mine, Hulk, will be out in an hour or so to take a look at the car. If Hulk can't get the car running, it'll have to be towed. I'll call a cab so you can go home. I apologize for the inconvenience and for not being able to take you myself." He rapped his knuckles on the roof and looked somewhere off into the distance. "This was Brenda's car," he continued. "It hasn't been driven in months, and I should have had it checked out before putting it back on the road."

Trevor lowered his gaze to Cassidy. She lifted hers to his.

"I'll make that call," he said.

Cassidy pulled her phone out of her purse. "I can do it."

He nodded and stepped away from the door. "Then I'll call Natasha and let her know I won't be back until late."

"Dunbar should be here in fifteen minutes," she called out to him a few minutes later.

Trevor frowned and sauntered closer. "Dunbar?"

☙

A black Saturn parked in front of them, and Trevor assisted Cassidy with a hand as she climbed out of the Maxima. Trevor wore a smile he didn't feel. Cassidy had a right to call whomever she pleased to come and take her home, but the fact she'd called Dunbar annoyed him. It was probably because of the way Cassidy was with Dunbar. Trevor had been at the house one evening when Dunbar stopped by. Cassidy seemed happy and relaxed in Dunbar's presence. Cassidy was at the opposite end of the spectrum around Trevor most times, so uptight and guarded.

Dunbar greeted him first. "Trevor."

"Dunbar," Trevor responded. He reached and pounded hands with Dunbar, a wiry, average-height, clean-cut, dark brown man with small brown eyes that looked as if they were pressed too close to the lenses of his eyeglasses. The assistant funeral director of Smith Funeral Home was rarely without a tie or the gold stud in his left ear that Trevor thought didn't quite blend with the other parts of Dunbar's stiff personality. Trevor had never talked one-on-one with Dunbar for any length of time, but he had heard the young minister preach over the years and had never been disappointed. Dunbar Smith always had something to say that left Trevor feeling inspired to live a better life.

"Thanks for coming," Cassidy said to Dunbar. "As you can see, we're stranded."

"I'm always here for you, C.C., day or night."

Trevor's gut tightened. They were not stranded. And what was up with the nickname? It was as if he'd asked the question out loud because in the next breath Dunbar said, "I don't know if you know it, but Cassidy's middle name is Christine. I call her C.C. for short. I think I'm the only one who calls you that, right?"

Cassidy nodded and smiled at her rescuer. She had a wide, white smile, balanced with the perfect alliance of sweetness, charisma, and sensual energy. Every time she flashed it, it sent a rush of excitement through Trevor's heart, and he wondered what it would take to get her to smile at him the way she did at Dunbar.

"Well," Dunbar said, "we'd better get going. That movie you wanted to see is still playing. Why don't we catch the eleven o'clock?"

"Sure," she said. "But I want to go home and change first."

"By the way"—Dunbar's voice deepened—"you look wonderful as always, C.C."

Trevor smirked. The nickname "Sky" was a thousand times prettier than "C.C."

Cassidy peeled her gaze from Dunbar and pressed it on Trevor. Her smile, Trevor noted, had weakened. "I'll see you in the morning," she said.

"Good luck with the car," Dunbar wished.

Trevor forced out the word "Thanks." His posture was like granite and his arms rigidly crossed his rib cage as the others turned away and he watched Dunbar clasp Cassidy's hand with the confidence of a man who had done so many times before.

chapter fourteen

Cassidy climbed out of Lena's Neon and glanced indifferently at the SUV parked in front of the house. The Monroes had gone to the earlier worship service and apparently had already returned.

"I'll call you later." Lena hung a huge grin. "You can finish telling me about your date with Trevor." She hit the gas pedal and waved.

Singing the praise song the choir had ministered during the offertory, Cassidy bounced up the steps to the porch and poised her key to go into the lock when the front door jerked open.

"Hi." A jolly Brandi hugged Cassidy's thigh. She stayed this way as she chattered, "I saw you when you got out of the car. My daddy said it would be okay for me to open the door for you."

Cassidy hugged the child in the red sundress for several breathless seconds, overwhelmed by the warm welcome. Was this the pleasure a mother experienced when arriving home to her child, eager to receive her?

"Hi," the other Monroe child said softly. Her hands were hidden in the pockets of her denim shorts. Her eyes were more tentative than Brandi's and her cheeks less cheerful, yet her spirit seemed to whisper, *I am friend.*

"Hello, Brittney," Cassidy said.

"Are you going to eat with us? We're having peach cobwer for dessert." Brandi grabbed Cassidy's hand. "Come on, me and Sis set a place for you."

As Cassidy was led into the dining room, she chuckled at Brandi's attempt to say "cobbler" and at being invited to dine in her own house.

"Hello," Trevor said from the doorway dividing the dining area and the kitchen. He leaned against the door frame. A mitten pot holder covered one hand. The thumb of the other was hooked in the pocket of his sand-colored slacks. A white dish towel, a huge contrast to his black T-shirt, was carelessly draped over his shoulder.

Cassidy drew a breath, met and challenged his gaze. There was no reason for her to wilt beneath his keen perusal. To her surprise, Trevor was the first to look away—somewhat shyly, she was sure she perceived. Cassidy was shocked that Trevor's attitude toward her was so pleasant. This morning she had lambasted him for leaving little hairs on the bathroom sink, and then she had gone through the items on her complaint list one by one.

"Do you like baked chicken?" he asked, his attention back on her.

So that was the good smell flirting with her nose and convincing her mouth to water. "Yes, I do," she said. It was much healthier than fried.

Volcanic glee spilled from Brandi. "So you're going to eat with us?"

"Yes." She smiled at the girls. Trevor turned and went into the kitchen, and Cassidy followed. She watched him ladle green beans from pot to bowl. "I noticed there are only four places. Aunt Odessa's not feeling any better?"

"She said she would have something later."

"I should check on her." Cassidy went straight to the stairs, not another glance at Trevor and the green beans, as she tried not to let minimal concern deepen into mammoth worry. But Odessa had stayed home from church today, the first Sunday service she had missed since Cassidy was in middle school.

When Cassidy returned to the kitchen, she'd changed from the skirt and blouse she'd worn to church into a pair of pants and a sleeveless sweater. The hair she'd worn on her shoulders had been twisted and pinned up.

Trevor's smooth tone eased across the room. "How's Mother Vale?"

"She's sleeping, and I didn't want to wake her." For the second time, Trevor was the first to avert his gaze, and Cassidy was unsure which she liked least. The way he could stare at her as if he had nothing better to do, or the way he could tear his eyes from her as if it pained him. Both turned her knees to foam.

Trevor placed an oval plate of parsley-garnished chicken in the center of the linen tablecloth between crystal candleholders. A tiny flame stood on its toes at the top of each white candle. The dimmed lights of the chandelier partnered with the rays of sun coming through the side window, bathing the dining room in subdued radiance. The table looked holiday lovely, and Cassidy, impressed with the way Trevor had made a simple meal elegant, praised him, saying, "Everything looks wonderful."

Trevor said the blessing, including a special prayer for Odessa, and he and Cassidy helped the children fix their plates, then served themselves. Cassidy helped herself to the chicken and string beans.

"No, thank you," she said when Trevor held up the plate of biscuits. She also refused the lemonade she had watched Trevor dump two cups of sugar into, and politely nodded no to the macaroni and cheese. The casserole's golden top was hot and bubbly with thick yellow cheese, and Cassidy cringed at the thought of how much butter Trevor had probably stirred into it.

"I helped snap the beans," Brandi announced.

"I helped Aunt Odessa cook when I was a little girl." Cassidy carved off a small piece of meat. "Often we'd have enough to feed an army, and Aunt Odessa would invite a family to eat with us."

"Like she invited my family." Brandi grinned and wiped her mouth with the back of her hand.

Trevor buttered one half of a biscuit. "It sounds as if you had a nice childhood."

"Yes, thanks to Aunt Odessa."

A lump of macaroni and cheese flew back to Brandi's plate as she jerked her fork away from her mouth and ogled Cassidy with curiosity. "Didn't you have a mommy and daddy?"

"My father wasn't a part of my life, and my mother died when I was very young."

"Oh." She blinked. "My mommy died, too."

Brittney dropped her fork against the stoneware plate. The pinging sound joined her hiss of exasperation. "Can I be excused?"

"It's 'may I.'" Trevor reached for the salt shaker. "And no, you may not."

The child slouched even lower in the chair and wheeled her green beans around with the fork tines.

"Don't play with your food," Brandi pestered.

Brittney raised her fork like a torch, both fists knotted. She slammed them to the table. "Don't tell me what to do!"

Trevor tamed his daughters with scolding stares. Cassidy cleared her throat and then tried to clear the air, too. "Someone tell me how Poopie came to be a part of the family."

"We found her," Brandi said.

"Truthfully, she found us." Done with the salt, Trevor sprinkled pepper across his food. "She appeared in our backyard one afternoon. The girls latched onto her right away, and I was outnumbered three to one. We took her to the vet, where she was inoculated and flea-dipped, and she's been with us since." He shrugged his eyebrows and his shoulders, a gesture of penitence. "I'm sorry about her being in your room. If it's any consolation, I can't seem to keep her out of mine, either."

Cassidy accepted Trevor's apology . . . and accepted the cat, which she understood was as much a member of the family as a person and one the girls wouldn't easily part with. Nor could she ask them to so soon after losing their mother. "How did Poopie get her name?"

Brandi giggled, and Cassidy saw even Brittney smile some.

"We had a difficult time housebreaking her," Trevor recalled. "The litter pan was as foreign to her as sleeping on the floor. She kept leaving piles of—"

"Don't, Daddy," Brandi blasted, covering her ears with her hands.

He winked at Brandi and finished, "I gave her the name on her calling card."

Brandi smiled at Cassidy. "I wanted to name her Powder."

"She didn't smell anything like powder to me," her father said.

Cassidy let out a buoyant laugh, delighting in the company of this man and his children more than she'd ever imagined she could. She reached to the center of the table and forked up a chicken leg this time. She sipped from her glass of water as Brandi said in a small voice, "Mommy would've loved Poopie."

Trevor dabbed the corners of his mouth and returned the napkin to his lap. His voice matched the softness pouring from his gaze. "Do you remember what I told you?"

Brandi bobbed her head up and down. "Whenever I feel sad about Mommy not being here is when she's looking down blowing kisses to me."

Cassidy's heart swelled. The longer she sat with the man at the opposite end of the table, the more she considered him to be a warm and caring and patient father. It was clear Brittney was not through testing that patience this afternoon.

"I can't eat any more," the child said, using her

forearm to nudge aside a plate of barely touched food. She fired on Brandi, "You're so stupid." Her voice rose. "Mommy's dead. She can't see you." She jumped from her chair and ran from the room, Poopie dashing after her.

Abandoning her own meal, Cassidy put down her fork. To a degree, she agreed with Brittney. Cassidy didn't believe the dead looked back, either. But Cassidy also recognized a mutinous child when she saw one. However, defiance wasn't the only emotion affecting Brittney. The little girl was . . .

Trevor said what Cassidy had been thinking. "She's so angry." He sighed from deep within. "I really don't know what I'm going to do. Nothing I've tried has worked." Brandi, sobbing openly, climbed into her father's lap. She looped her small arms around his neck. He looped his big arms around her waist.

Leaning back in her chair, Cassidy assessed Trevor. He looked as helpless as she felt. It seemed she should say something that might support this father. Though she was still unable to label him as one of her favorite people, she would gladly tell anyone how strong was his love for his little girls.

ℒ❦

"Girl, don't you ask me again. I told you I'm fine. I stayed home today because I was tired, not because I was sick."

Cassidy marched behind Odessa from the counter to the table. The older woman hooked a hand over a chair, pulled it back, and sat with their young housemates. The children were gobbling up apples candied with chocolate, Trevor's idea of fresh fruit, Cassidy supposed.

"Take note I said *was* tired. There's not a tired bone in my body as of now." She smiled. "The girls and I are going to do a jigsaw puzzle once they've finished their snack."

"I'm ready," Trevor stated, his footsteps clobbering the floor, sounding his return as he jogged downstairs, toting car keys.

The nursing home had called and said Oliver Toby was demonstrating abnormal behavior. When the staff couldn't reach his family, they called Cassidy. Since she couldn't use her car, Trevor had offered to take her to check on her friend so she wouldn't have to take the bus.

Cassidy showered Odessa with a gaze of uncertainty.

"I'm fine. Now, get going," Odessa ordered.

❧

"What's with everyone calling him Oliver Toby? Why not Dr. Toby or just plain Oliver?" Trevor turned onto Chew Avenue. There was little traffic, and he drove at a moderate speed.

"His mother called him Oliver Toby from birth, and it stuck. Even when he was a practicing professor, his students called him Oliver Toby."

"What do you think he's so upset about?"

"I don't know. But it must be something terrible to make him break down and cry."

Trevor scowled. "He was crying?"

"That's what the nurse said."

"In front of people?"

"I guess." Cassidy shrugged. "What's the big deal?"

"From the description you painted of this Oliver Toby, I imagined he was an emotionally strong man."

"Are you suggesting that men who cry are weak?"

"It depends on what they're crying over. Whatever it's about, I don't think crying should be done all out in the open, with everyone watching."

"Wait here," Cassidy told Trevor once they arrived, and she went to find her friend.

Oliver Toby occupied his favorite spot in the garden, and Cassidy glanced up at the green leaves swaddling the arms of the kingly-looking tree behind him. She eased down beside her friend, joining him on the iron bench. She curled her hand around his.

"I'm leaving," he whispered.

She dived into the solemn pools of Oliver Toby's eyes as her fingers clamped tighter over the stony protrusions of his knuckles. She kept her voice calm, although a sliver of misgiving crawled through her. "Leaving?"

"My son told me this morning. He's taken a job in Denver, and he's getting a bigger apartment. He wants me to go with him, and we'll live together again." He sighed. "How can I say no? He's my boy. I love him. And I don't want to stay here, so many miles from him."

The totality of what Oliver Toby said began to sink in, and Cassidy blinked hard. A sense of abandonment washed over her, and she felt tears in her eyes. It was selfish of her to pull the spotlight onto herself, but she asked, "What about our date day?"

"You'll have to fly to Denver every week?" he jested.

There was no playfulness in Cassidy's heart. She stared directly at the man who'd become a father figure, so he could see her wound.

Oliver Toby rubbed the back of her hand. "I'm feeling equally bad. After all, I've lived in this city all my life. My church family is here." He gazed at the clear blueness above them. "Moving to a strange place and starting over is a scary step for someone my age."

She pushed the emotion from her throat with a forceful swallow. "I promise to come and visit." She found a smile she didn't think she had. "And I'll write you every week."

He smiled, too. "You better." After a long pause, he said, "As frightening as moving is, I know I'm not going anywhere God isn't. And I know He has a plan for me. The way I see it, there's something God wants me to do in Denver."

Cassidy looped arms with Oliver Toby, willing herself to look on the positive side of things with him. They talked a few minutes more before she rested her head on his shoulder.

"Who's the young man who gave you the ride?"

She raised her head. "I never said it was a young man." She remembered. She said she came with a friend.

"I suppose it was the sparkle that highlighted your cheeks when you mentioned this friend."

"A sparkle of irritation," she said. "He's such a pain."

Oliver Toby chuckled. "Are you going to introduce me to him?"

She shrugged. "I guess I have to. But that can wait.

This is our time now." Again she leaned her head on Oliver Toby's shoulder, but suddenly, it was the man waiting inside the building who filled her thoughts.

☙

Trevor opened the bathroom door and peered into Cassidy's bedroom after trying to wake her with several knocks. The light from the bulbs above the bathroom mirror glowed over his shoulder, through the darkness, and he could see her blanket-covered profile.

"Cassidy," he whispered, and she shifted slightly. He called her name again.

"What's the matter?" she murmured. She leaned on one elbow and shielded her face from the light with her other arm.

His voice remained a whisper. "I need to talk to you. Can you come closer?"

"Just a minute," she said, and he pulled the door shut while she climbed out of bed. "What is it?" she whispered a few moments later as she opened the door and peeked around it far enough for him to see her face and one shoulder.

"Derek's in a bit of a jam," he said. "I need to go check on him." Cassidy opened the door an inch more. She was wearing her blue robe. "Would you—"

"I've got the girls covered," she cut in. The kindness in her eyes assured him she didn't mind looking after his children.

"I won't be long." He smiled and walked to the other end of the bathroom.

"Trevor," she called, and he turned. "I'll be praying."

"Thank you," he said, and they both stepped backward but not before exchanging looks that wandered deep into the other's consciousness.

☙

"I hate her," Derek growled, pulling on the sweatpants Trevor had loaned him. Trudy had put him out of the house wearing nothing but his boxers. This was not the first time Trudy had put her son out half-naked and not the first time the owner of the deli on the corner of Derek's block had let the youngster come inside and telephone for help.

"Does it make you feel better to hate her?" Trevor asked as they stood near the back of the small eat-in or take-out restaurant.

"No," Derek rumbled. "But *she* hates *me*. Always telling me how much I remind her of my father and how he ain't nuttin' but no good and I'm gonna end up in jail just like him." His bottom lip slid forward. "Why can't I hate her back?" There were two patrons inside the deli tonight, and they glanced back at Derek as he slipped into one of Trevor's old workout T-shirts. Trevor also brought along flip-flops. They were too large for Derek but would protect his feet from sharp debris along the pavement.

Derek's face was hard with contempt, his lips twisted into a frown. There was no point sending Derek home when he was this close to imploding and when Trudy most likely was as explosive as always. Trevor purchased two hot chocolates and chose a booth for them. They sipped their drinks as steam spiraled from their cups.

"You ain't answer me," Derek said, his voice less of a grumble. "Why is it wrong for me to hate Trudy when she hates me so much?"

"Were you serious when you asked God into your heart?"

"Yeah, I was serious." Derek swiped the back of his hand across his lips.

"So you're a young man of God now, which doesn't mean you're not going to make mistakes. But it does mean you made a commitment to live your life in accordance with God's Word to the best of your ability. And His Word commands us to—"

Derek intercepted him with a moan of "Love everyone."

He that loveth not knoweth not God; for God is love. Trevor silently recalled the verse and was instantly drawn inside himself, forced to examine his own heart. He didn't hate the man who had killed Brenda, but he couldn't say he loved him, either.

Derek's eyes were calmer by the time their cups were empty. "Come on," Trevor instructed, and they stepped outside, the neon lights from the deli lighting the first segment of their trail up the street. They reached a house near the corner and climbed the six steps to the porch. The Hineses' screen door had been removed, and Trevor knocked on the steel front door. Trudy opened the door and held on to the knob and the jamb, dressed in a red teddy and a brazen smile with Trevor's name on it.

"Hey, baby, where you been?" The alcohol in her system slurred her words. "I've been waitin' for you." Trudy had not glanced at Derek once.

"Miss Hines, Derek would like to come home."

Derek shifted in place, head bowed, apparently embarrassed by the whole scene.

"Well . . . it depends." Trudy stared at Trevor. "Are you comin' in, too?"

Derek sucked his teeth in disgust. "You need to go get some clothes on."

"You need"—she poked a finger at him—"to keep your mouth shut."

"Look," Trevor butted in, blowing away Trudy's smoke before it became a flame, "Derek just wants to come in and go to bed. He works in the morning and needs his rest."

"I got needs, too." Suggestion sizzled in her eyes as she teetered toward Trevor. Derek reached and caught his mother's arm, lending support.

"Get off uh me," she snapped, jerking away.

"Please, Trudy." Derek's tone was respectful. "Coach ain't here for you. Now, let me come in."

Trudy slowly stepped aside, her stare a weapon rather than a welcome.

"Good night, Coach," Derek mumbled, and the house received its missing occupant.

"I don't know what gets into that boy." Trudy patted her hair into place as Trevor turned to leave. Her raspy yell grated against the quiet night. "Oh, you don't want me now. But day is gon' come when you gon' need me to do you a favor. Day is gon' come."

chapter fifteen

A tall, lean woman clothed in suit and pumps, conservative in style and shade, greeted Cassidy as she entered the waiting room outside of the pastor's office.

"Good morning, Francine," Cassidy replied. Francine Philmont, recently into her winter forties, listened to Cassidy's request to see the pastor with her usual all-work-and-no-play air. Some of the parishioners had complained about Francine's austere nature, maintaining that a pastor's personal secretary should be more outgoing. But Cassidy had often overheard Pastor Audrey defend Francine as a blessing. During a sermon, he'd praised Francine by saying she was privy to many of the problems that came in and out of his office, yet he could depend on her to keep those problems confidential. He went on to say that in his opinion, this alone far outweighed how unsociable she was.

Francine marched into the pastor's office with a manila-bound collection of documents. She came back empty-handed and with a message for Cassidy. "Pastor Audrey has a few minutes. You can go in."

Cassidy rose from the cushioned chair. "Thank you, Francine."

Francine gave a curt nod, and Cassidy entered the office. The pastor closed the magazine lying on his desk.

"Cassidy, how are you?" The tall and wide middle-aged preacher, muscular in some areas, flabby in others, left his seat, strode across the room, and presented a hand that swallowed Cassidy's as she remembered the first time she met Clement Audrey.

She was a student at La Salle and taking a walk between classes. They were both waiting for the light at a busy inter-section when an elderly woman, crossing the other way, dropped one of her grocery bags, sprinkling the street with canned goods. Cassidy and the stranger next to her rushed to rescue the frail woman's cans and usher her safely to the sidewalk. The stranger introduced himself as the pastor of Charity Community Church and invited the woman to service. He turned and asked, "How about you, young lady? Do you have a church home?"

She shook her head no. "Sometimes I attend All Saints' Baptist with my aunt." She paused. "A lot's happened in my life, and I've strayed way off track."

He smiled. "You can never stray too far away for God to hear you."

As the rumble of an incoming subway erupted from the mouth leading underground, and passengers scuttled up the stairs to the streets and hurried around Clement and Cassidy, he continued to minister. On the corner of Broad and Olney, Cassidy rededicated her life to Jesus Christ.

Clement left the door to his office ajar and went to his desk. Cassidy sat on one of the chairs facing him. She glanced behind him to a few of the books filling the shelves of a unit extending from ceiling to floor and wall to wall.

"Thank you for seeing me," she said, looking straight at him now.

"Let's pray so we can get started." The pastor bowed his head. At the end of the short prayer, he leaned back in the plush chair customized to accommodate a man of his proportions. He rested his folded hands on a belly that hid his belt buckle. "It's interesting you should stop by this morning." Clement exposed his thoughts. "The Lord laid you on my heart yesterday. I believe our Sparrow Ministry would be a good place for you to utilize your gifts."

Cassidy's insides turned liquid. She clenched her hands. How could someone with a past like her own inspire courage in unwed pregnant women?

But, Cassidy, there is no condemnation to them which are in Christ . . .

Cassidy resisted. She was the last person God would designate for the Sparrow Ministry. The pastor's signals were crossed, just like Sister Maranda Whittle's.

Cassidy found her means of escape. Clement often advised members to commit to one or two ministries, do them well, and avoid becoming involved in too many things. "I've already joined the Special Day team," she said.

The pastor's face was compassionate, but his silence pressured Cassidy to glance away. "If that's where the Lord has led you to serve, then that's where you should be. But why don't you give the matter a little more prayer time?" Clement smiled. "Now, what's on your mind?"

Cassidy relaxed her hands, although her guts still felt like they were sliding around. "I would like to use the remainder of the children's summer fund on ACES."

"Problem," Clement murmured.

☙

"Some lady is here for you," one of a group of twenty-one boys announced.

"That's no lady, that's Sister Cassidy," another corrected him with a grin.

A smile danced around Trevor's mouth, too. He pushed his pen behind his ear, his clipboard under his armpit, and turned to face the reason that his heart cartwheeled.

"How could you?" she attacked.

Even with the layer of sweat clinging to the room's atmosphere after the rigorous workout he'd just put his boys through, Cassidy's familiar fragrance reached his nose. "How may I help you?" he queried, struggling to keep comedy out of his voice. When angry, Cassidy was as appealing as whipped cream. He licked his lips, stepping forward, gently invading her space, the tips of his black sneakers nearly kissing the soles of her sandals.

Cassidy held her position. "I would like to speak with you." The acerbic request drew everyone's attention. They both glanced at the boys, who were all eyes, all ears. "In private," she said less astringently.

"We can talk in the hall."

"Fine," she agreed, and swirled to exit, the hem of her dress whipping about the calves of her legs.

"Three laps," Trevor ordered. He lifted the whistle dangling around his neck and blew, signaling for the boys to start.

Outside the gymnasium doors, Cassidy fumed, "I don't appreciate you going behind my back."

Leaning against the cinder-block wall, he crossed his arms, clasping the clipboard against the big number 5 on his jersey. "What are we talking about?"

"The money you drained out of the reserves. I went to Pastor Audrey to discuss the possibility of using the funds for ACES. I was informed that the director of SAFE, whatever *that* stands for, had squandered the money on gym mats and basketballs."

Trevor cleared his throat. "'SAFE' doesn't stand for anything. It simply means we provide a wholesome and danger-limited environment for kids to play." He talked much slower than she had. "And your facts are inaccurate. I did not deplete the funds."

She threw her hip to the side and put a hand on it. "You barely left enough to purchase an adequate supply of pencils. Just how many basketballs does one team need? And what was wrong with the old mats? They had a few good years left."

Trevor curbed his resentment and suppressed his urge to give Cassidy a few choice words. "As I understand it, your tutoring program, this sports camp, and the vacation Bible school are allotted the same amount of money. Funds banked afterward are up for grabs. It may not be the best way to do business, but that's how it's been done, at least up to now." He paused for a second. "As for your questions about the manner in which I elected to expend the funds . . . well, that's really none of your concern, now, is it?" Her lips parted to answer, and he realized she was raring to give him a good verbal beating, but he wasn't ready to pass the microphone. "I don't come snooping around your classrooms to see how much chalk is being wasted each day. Why do you need all those different colors? My grade school teachers seemed to do fine with basic white and yellow."

Anger narrowed her eyes. "Under my supervision, not one *inch* of chalk or anything else is wasted. I run a very serious program, and I planned to use the money in the reserves to replace the library books we lost." She hurled a glance through the square window at the top of the gym door. "My children come to work, not play. As you know, we're preparing for the Interfaith Spelling Bee."

Trevor peered through the same small glass at the top of the door. The boys had completed the laps, and most were playing with the basketballs he'd told them not to touch until later. The others were running about like jungle cats. He glanced at his watch. One of his assistants had car trouble and wouldn't be in until this afternoon, the other called in sick with a stomach virus, and his teen counselors were not due in until midweek. He didn't have another second of free time to donate to Cassidy's grumbling. "It's our first day of camp, and I have a long list of dos and do nots to cover, so if there's nothing else?"

"Why are you here?"

"Excuse me?"

"Pastor Audrey had an appointment, so there wasn't time for me to ask him, so I'm asking you: why aren't you utilizing the recreation center down the street like last year? Coach Snyder said the boys loved being there."

"I guess you haven't heard. Mold was discovered in the building, so it's off-limits."

Her expression became suspicious, as if to suggest he had somehow planted the mold himself. "What about that church over on Greene? Coach Snyder and the boys used their facility one summer."

"I know, but why pay to use someone else's space when there's ample space here?"

She answered with a question. "When was all this decided?"

"While you were away, I guess. Your assistant . . . uh . . . what's her name . . ."

"Portia," Cassidy answered.

"Yes, Portia agreed with me and the pastor that having the camp here shouldn't be a problem."

"Well, I disagree. Having the camp here *is* likely to be a problem. Listen to them." She tapped her ear. "Your boys are absolutely *obstreperous*."

The walking, talking dictionary had a know-it-all look in her eyes. Well, he hadn't had as much college as she had, but he did graduate. And he knew the meaning of plenty of big words, though he had no idea what the twenty-syllable word she'd just flung at him meant.

A smile slinked across Cassidy's lips. "It means—"

"I don't care what it means." Impatience roughened his voice. He was ready to return to the gym and restore order before someone got hurt. "We can talk later," he said. "Give me a time, and we'll meet in our office."

Cassidy drew back. "Our office?"

"Yes, the one down the hall."

"That's *my* office."

"*Our* office," he corrected. "Portia gave me her desk."

⌁

Give up? No way. Cassidy lifted the nearest pencil and tapped it on the desktop as she brainstormed. ACES needed books, and right now that was synonymous with money, so she needed to come up with a way to raise money. Cassidy smacked the pencil on the desk. "It will take months to raise enough money to buy books." She sprang from the chair. "I need some help here, Lord." She crossed her arms and strolled back and forth across the room, the rubber bottoms of her sandals squeaking a steady cadence. With each step, her thoughts grew more intense, and she could feel the skin on her forehead tightening as she frowned. Suddenly, as if someone had lassoed her shoulders, Cassidy halted, spun, and marched to her desk. She grabbed the pencil she had been so hard on, and reached for a pad of paper to record notes. She had an idea. "Thank you, Lord," she said, chuckling.

chapter sixteen

According to the radio announcer, the time was 4:10. Trevor backed from the driveway of his stone house. He had just left a meeting with the contractor in charge of remodeling the kitchen Trevor had set on fire as a result of leaving potatoes frying unattended.

During the short commute to Seconds, he thanked his Heavenly Father for helping him to find a day camp for Brittney and Brandi that came with van service. This meant he wouldn't have to pick them up in the evenings, and until they moved back home, the girls would be dropped off at Mother Vale's. After a long debate, she'd finally convinced him she was strong enough to assist and would care for them until he arrived home from work.

Trevor had showered earlier this afternoon in the men's locker room at the church, directly after dismissing the SAFE boys. Now, instead of shorts and sneakers, he was clothed in slacks, a button-down shirt, and a pair of semicasual oxfords. He greeted Grace and strode to his desk. He landed in his chair, sifted through the mail, and held up the last envelope in the pile. It reeked of perfume, and he twisted his face, holding back a sneeze. He grabbed the gold-tone letter opener from the holder, sliced the flap of the envelope, and pulled out a photocopy of what appeared to be a newspaper article. Trevor muttered the headline, "Tilden U. Student Saves Lives." He read on silently. *Cassidy Beckett shared the dangers of drinking and driving at a local youth meeting. Beckett, driving under the influence . . .* Trevor stopped. He felt his world tilt. Collapsing against the back of the chair as if he'd been punched in the chest and the breath knocked out of him, he let the information sink in.

Cassidy had been a drunken driver.

The statement became a deafening echo in his head, drowning out every other thought. Finally able to silence the offensive sound, Trevor flicked the newspaper clipping to the desk. His mind flared with images of the man serving time in a Pennsylvania prison for running down Brenda as she attempted to cross the street. Several scriptures on love and forgiveness came to Trevor, yet he stared sorrowfully at the desktop photograph of Brenda and turned his thoughts over to the article again. Perhaps the black print he'd just read wasn't about the Cassidy Beckett he knew. Maybe, by some bizarre coincidence, there had been another Tilden student with the same name. With a slight sense of relief, he lifted the article and focused on the date of publication. To his dismay, it matched the year Cassidy was a student.

Trevor unclasped the paper and tightly folded his

hands on the desk. Questions raced through his mind. Would Cassidy drink and drive again? Were his children safe in her presence? How could Cassidy have done something as unthinking and unfeeling as driving inebriated? But, then, drunk drivers didn't think, didn't feel. They simply went on their merry, oblivious, selfish way, endangering lives or ending lives and devastating loved ones left behind.

✐

Brandi dashed to Trevor before he could set his briefcase down. "Can we go, Daddy?"

He placed the leather briefcase on the floor and scooped up Brandi. "Can you go where, sweetheart?"

Cassidy and Brittney came all the way into the living room. "There's a double-Dutch contest this evening at the recreation center around the corner," Cassidy informed him. "I was about to call you and ask if the girls could go and watch. They ate dinner with me and Aunt Odessa, so they're all set."

Trevor's eyes bored into her as if he were trying to see through to her bones, and not meaning to, Cassidy squeezed the hand Brittney had linked with hers. After what felt to Cassidy like an eternity, Trevor's gaze lowered to his older daughter but soon returned to Cassidy.

"You're only going around the corner?" Trevor's tone was unusual. Even when they argued as they had this morning outside the gymnasium, his voice had not been as hard.

"Yes," Cassidy answered. "I'll bring them directly home after the competition."

Once again Trevor regarded Cassidy with prolonged contemplation. "All right," he said. "Just be careful with my daughters."

Cassidy blinked. Because the girls were listening and observing, she managed a gentle reply. "I'm always careful when it comes to children."

Cassidy and the little Monroes walked to the inter-section and crossed the street. The children raced to the next corner and waited for Cassidy to catch up with them. Cassidy walked slowly and wondered what was up with Trevor. Perhaps he was more annoyed with her than he had let on at the church. She had confronted him again this afternoon about the noise the SAFE boys had been making. And at that time, she also told him, in not the kindest of tones, how she caught two of the SAFE boys teasing some of the smaller ACES kids. But as Cassidy latched onto Brittney's and Brandi's hands and they moved across the street, she felt there was something else that had made Trevor study her with so much concern. The children darted ahead, and Cassidy's hands and neck and back pumped out cold sweat as she immediately thought the worst.

Trevor knew.

Somehow Trevor had found out about the baby.

He knew what she had done to her baby.

chapter seventeen

I've written several suggestions," Cassidy said, attempting to redirect the conversation and keep the reason for the meeting in clear view.

Mother Almondetta continued with her own agenda. "In my day, women knew the importance of getting married and starting a family. Nowadays young ladies want to work and make money. They wait until forty to settle down, then rush and try to have some babies." She grunted. "It's a shame how mothers are sticking their kids in day care all day. Then when they come home from work, they're too tired to play with them. They put the kids in front of the television for hours and expect them to have some sense. Modern women, what's wrong with them?" Almondetta looked at Cassidy.

Cassidy decided it was best to reply so they could move on with the meeting. "There's nothing wrong with modern women. We simply have a different perspective. Today's woman understands she can have both a career and a family. There are many women at our church who have both."

"What about you two?" she asked Cassidy and Yaneesha. Her tone had the prick of a thorn. "Why aren't you married?"

"Marriage isn't for everyone," Cassidy stated.

"It's for me. That's why I don't wear *no* ring on this finger. I don't want nobody thinkin' I'm unavailable." Yaneesha raised both hands but only wiggled the finger where a wedding band traditionally went, the only one of her fingers without a ring on it. "When I do get married, I want to stay home. Let my man work and take care of me and his babies."

Cassidy expected Almondetta to be smiling after that statement, but the church mother wore a look identical to the one Cassidy often gave students when they were wasting time during class. Cassidy lifted her pen and pointed toward her notes. "I created a list of gifts we could buy our seniors. As you'll see, each item is practical as well as economical, so we shouldn't have any problem staying within our budget." She studied Almondetta and Yaneesha. "I'd like to have your input."

"I have to use the bathroom," Yaneesha said, and pushed away from the table.

Mother Almondetta didn't have her wig on, and the few strands of hair on her apple-shaped head lay straight against her scalp. Cassidy's gaze slipped away from Almondetta's head and down to her eyes. Almondetta's stare was blank. "Would you like to see the list?" Cassidy tried again.

Almondetta clasped her throat. "What I'd like is some water. Would you mind?"

"Of course not," Cassidy said before laying down her pen and leaving the terrace.

"Bring the cake that's on the table. The two of you got here early, and I didn't have time to set out the refreshments." Cassidy opened and closed two drawers before finding a knife large enough for the cake. "And look there in the fridge," Almondetta continued. "Since you don't eat cake, I bought you grapes. You eat grapes, don't you?"

Cassidy smiled and called out, "Yes." She placed a pitcher of ice water, three glasses, the cake, and a bowl of grapes on a tray and exited the kitchen. "The woman in the picture in the hall looks so much like you. Is she your daughter?"

Almondetta pressed a cloth napkin over her lap. "She's my daughter. That picture was taken the day she graduated from medical school," Almondetta said as Cassidy filled a glass and passed it to her. "She's a surgeon now, too busy and big-time to stop by and say hello."

In an attempt to lessen the gloom surrounding Almondetta, Cassidy smiled. "I appreciate the grapes, but you didn't need to go to the trouble of buying them for me."

"As grown as I am, I don't think I need no young girl like you telling me how to spend my money."

"That's not what I was trying to do." Cassidy sliced cake for Almondetta. "What I was trying to say was—"

"Where's Yaneesha?" Almondetta interrupted.

Cassidy glanced at the terrace door. It *was* taking Yaneesha a long time. "I'll make sure she's all right." Cassidy moved to stand, but Yaneesha rushed back in.

"Umm, cake," she exclaimed, and reached for the knife.

By the end of the meeting, nothing of substance had been determined. A stress headache activated, Cassidy arrived home and went straight to the piano. One hour of playing effortlessly became two.

Cassidy slid her fingers from the keys, dropped her foot from the pedal, and the music left the room as Trevor entered, wearing a serious expression on his face and balancing a pizza box on a flattened palm. The children scampered in behind him.

"This is for you," Brittney said to Cassidy, and she handed over a drawing. "I did it while we were waiting for the pizza."

Cassidy held up the picture and smiled. "It's gorgeous, Brittney."

Brandi jumped in place. She used both hands to hold her own drawing by the top edge. "Look at mine. I made it for Grammy. Do you like it?"

"I love it, and I'm sure Grammy will, too." Silently, Cassidy gave God praise. Her aunt hadn't had any more tired spells and was back to a full routine of attending worship services, visiting the sick and shut-in, and nurturing her garden. Odessa had promised she would go to the doctor if she felt the slightest bit ill, and this put Cassidy's nerves at ease.

"Go wash your hands," Trevor instructed the children as Cassidy lowered the lid of the piano. The artwork in hand, Cassidy offered Trevor a half-there smile and hastened to leave the room and the tense air between them, which remained as thick as the unrelenting humidity they'd been dealt today.

"Truce," he said, stopping her.

"What?"

"I want to call a truce. I'm tired of the tension."

"You're the one that's been moody lately."

"You're right," he acknowledged. "I received a piece of disturbing mail earlier this week . . . and it's been on my mind."

Conflict rolled across Trevor's face, and Cassidy was tempted to ask questions. She opted against it and glanced at the pizza box, remembering a time when she could eat six slices of pepperoni pizza in one sitting.

"You're welcome to eat with us." His expression softened some. "Half of this pizza is topped with healthy mushrooms," he added as incentive.

Cassidy replied politely, "No, thank you." Refusing to break bread with the Monroes had much less to do with her practice of healthful eating and much more to do with the noxious fumes escaping the box. She resisted making an ugly face at Trevor's dinner so she would not offend him, but the urge to throw up grew stronger with each intake of breath. Eager to leave the room before she puked all over Trevor's shoes, she gasped, "Really, I'm not hungry. Maybe some other night, okay?" Trevor nodded, and Cassidy refused to breathe, an attempt to thwart nausea as she rushed away from the pizza smell.

ℒ♥

The scent of the bath oil the girls gave him for Father's Day lingered on his skin, and Trevor swatted at the bee that insisted on coming close as he waited on the front porch for his mechanic. Several years ago, Brenda had locked her keys in the car and was stranded in a deserted shopping mall parking lot. Horace "Hulk" Hudson happened along, and with the assistance of professional door-opening tools, he had Brenda safely behind the wheel of the car in less than sixty seconds. Brenda took one of Hulk's cards, and later that evening Trevor called him to extend thanks and inquire about payment.

"Bring me your business" had been Hulk's only demand.

Hulk pulled up to the curb. He jumped from his GMC pickup, Trevor darted from the steps, and the friends pounded fists. As Hulk checked things out under the hood, Trevor glanced in the direction Cassidy would probably be returning, then checked his watch. If Cassidy stayed married to her schedule, she wouldn't be back for at least three more hours, plenty of time for Hulk to deliver an official diagnosis and perhaps do the necessary repairs. Lucky for Trevor, he'd learned through Odessa that Cassidy kept a spare set of car keys in the kitchen drawer. In addition, Odessa had shared that Cassidy was reluctant about Hulk working on her car. But Trevor knew Hulk would do a first-rate job without overcharging. Cassidy shouldn't have any complaints.

Lena rolled up and parked across the street. She strolled over and exchanged hellos with Trevor. Hulk was on the ground, under the car, only visible from the waist down, so Trevor decided introductions weren't necessary.

"How did you talk Cassidy into letting you help with the car?" Lena peered at Trevor.

"I didn't."

"She doesn't know?"

"Not yet."

"Oh, baby, you like livin' dangerously, now, don't you?" Lena chuckled. "Well, tell Cassidy I stopped by, okay?"

"Sure thing," he said as she stepped off the curb and into the street at the same instant Hulk pushed from under the Accord. Hulk bumped his boots into Lena's sneakers.

"Sorry about that," he said. "Let me get your feet."

Lena's eyes became enchanted as Hulk raised himself up off the ground just enough to pull a handkerchief from the back pocket of his jumpsuit and dust all over the red Reeboks that went with the red stripe in her white running suit. She flashed a smile at him as he stood, put the handkerchief away, and removed the disposable gloves from his hands. He smiled in return, a marble-size dimple in his left cheek. Trevor introduced them.

"It's nice to meet you," Hulk said.

"Same here," she said, keeping her head tilted so she could remain eye-to-eye with Hulk, who was much taller than she was while much shorter than Trevor. His round head was bald, and a hint of a mustache bordered his lips. Lena slid her hand inside the hand Hulk extended. As her hand slipped slowly from his, a gaze passed between them that suggested it hadn't been nearly slow enough.

chapter eighteen

Y ou gave Hulk Lena's number?"

Trevor backed against the counter and crossed his arms over his midriff. "I did."

"Why would you do that?" Cassidy snapped.

"Because he's a nice guy, and he asked for it."

Blowing a puff of air, Cassidy snatched her dangling keys from the tips of Trevor's fingers. "I didn't need you to get Hulk to fix my car. I already had three estimates, and I was going to make a choice next week." She glared at him. "I'm not a weakling woman who can't take care of business. Not anymore."

Her gaze wavered away, and Trevor thought she seemed embarrassed that she'd exposed a small measure of herself to him.

Cassidy slammed the keys into the drawer, then slammed the drawer shut. "You might run things at your butter and sugar factory, but not here. In case you've forgotten, this is not *your* house."

"How could I forget?" His voice was grouchy. "You

certainly haven't gone out of your way to make me feel at home. But I guess you wouldn't have time to complain about *everything* if you took time and did that."

Cassidy did what Trevor called the ghetto-girl pop: neck roll, eye roll, and the sucking of teeth, all in the same beat. "I haven't complained all *that* much," she protested.

He calmly refreshed her memory. "You don't want me to sing in the shower. You don't want me to wash your car. You don't want me to help you bring the groceries into the house. I put too much salt and butter in the food." He moved away from the counter. "I can't even give my kids a *cookie* without you gawking at me as if I'm forcing an illegal substance down their throats."

Cassidy rolled her eyes again.

"Why can't you just say thank you and admit that I saved you a couple hundred dollars today?"

Cassidy nudged a chair with her hip and dropped to the seat. For the third time, she studied the invoice Hulk had left. "It is a good price," she conceded, although she continued to scowl.

A leisurely stride brought Trevor to the table, and he clutched the top crosspiece of the chair. "It never crossed my mind that you were weak and couldn't handle the situation on your own. I can see you're an intelligent and self-sufficient woman. And those are qualities I admire and respect." She glanced up at him. "Helping out around here is simply my way of thanking you and Mother Vale for opening your door to my family. It's my pleasure to do what I can to demonstrate how appreciative I am."

Trevor stared as Cassidy laid the invoice on the table near the fruit-bowl centerpiece. A bunch of bananas, too green to enjoy yesterday, appeared ripe enough to eat today. He lifted and turned the chair, straddled it, and stacked his arms across the top. He lowered his chin until it rested on his arm. From this angle, it was easy to see through the window above the sink. Birds dotted the sky in the distance and white clouds crossed the sky in slow motion, and Trevor wondered what was happening to him. Only weeks ago, if someone had told him a woman other than Brenda could make him feel this crazy, he would have labeled *that* person crazy. "You know what I think, Sky?" Cassidy was observing him as he spoke. "I think you like me a lot more than you're willing to show," he said.

Cassidy pursed her mouth. "I think you're dreaming."

It was corny, but he responded, "Only about you."

A child's giggle turned Trevor's head, and he discovered a little girl in the kitchen entrance. Brittney slid in and stood next to her sister. "Well," he said, pushing out of the chair. "I'm glad you small folk are here. I have good news. Grandmom Grace called and invited us to her cookout again. I told her we'd be there."

"Yes," Brandi shouted, punching the air with a fist.

A good feeling took root through Trevor. Not totally, but to a large extent, he'd been living in limbo, permitting grief to keep him from engaging in the activities he and the kids loved. But it was a new day, time to walk ahead. He didn't know how far he would get. But going to Grace and Houston's barbecue today would be a step in the right direction, not only for him but also for his children. And he wasn't taking these steps alone. As a child of God, he was never alone. "We're going to leave soon, so get on your swimwear."

A soft question drifted up to him. "Can Cassidy come with us, Daddy?"

Shock left Trevor speechless. This was the most Brittney had spoken to him all day. And her brown eyes, wide with waiting, were staring pointedly at him. He unclamped his tongue from the roof of his mouth. "That's up to Cassidy, pumpkin."

All gazes settled on Cassidy, and Trevor felt bad that she'd been put on the spot this way. The look she gave Brittney was soft and apologetic. "It's sweet of you to think of me, but there's a singles' meeting at the church tonight I'm planning to attend."

"What time is the meeting?" Trevor asked.

"Seven."

"I'll get you back in time."

They studied each other before turning to the girls. The optimism on their small faces pulled on Trevor's heartstrings. He knew Cassidy's heart was being tugged as well, and after a long pause, she gave her decision.

chapter nineteen

The smooth sound of R&B played in the background, and the hickory-smoked scent of an outdoor grill in progress wafted through the air. The Armstrong lawn was a green stage littered with chairs and tables and people of all ages. Most of the guests were already eating the hamburgers, baked beans, coleslaw, seafood salad, corn on the cob, and the many other appetizing items Grace had prepared. Grace waved and hurried across her property to welcome the Monroes. "We have on our suits," Brandi blurted as soon as Grace was in hearing range. She hiked up the hem of her T-shirt so Grace could see.

"You look so cute," Grace cooed as good as any grandmother. She bent at the waist, giving Brandi and Brittney one kiss and one hug each. She straightened and embraced Trevor. "I'm glad you came." Trevor squeezed Grace hard, sending her the private message that he appreciated her going the extra step, giving him that call this afternoon and reminding him that she loved him.

As if standing on hot coals, Brandi bounced from foot to foot. "Can we go swimming?"

"I don't see why not," Grace replied.

The girls ran toward the in-ground pool. Trevor lifted his voice. "Be careful," he called after them.

"Don't worry," Grace said. "I have two of the neighborhood girls who lifeguard at the Y helping out."

Trevor slowly withdrew his attention from the children and focused on Grace. "I have someone I would like you to meet," he said, and cupped Cassidy's elbow while Grace's eyes sparkled like a mother who was happy her son had finally brought a nice girl home.

&

"How was the potato salad?" Grace asked later, joining Trevor and Houston at the grill. She stood between the men and looped her arm around Trevor's middle.

He placed his arm around Grace's shoulder and kissed her temple. "Awesome as always."

"I set some back for you to take with you."

"Thanks," he said.

"I talked with Cassidy. She seems like a good down-to-earth soul." Grace looked at Houston. "She teaches at that school where Blanche's grandboys attend." Houston nodded as he sipped punch from a tumbler and Grace stared up at Trevor. "You and the girls bring Cassidy over for dinner one evening, you hear?"

"Uh-oh, son, you better watch out." A chuckle ended Houston's warning. "You see that look on her face. It says matchmaker."

Grace snatched up the flyswatter and whacked her husband's behind. "My face says no such thing."

"Yeah, that's why them three are ready to eat this boy alive."

Trevor glanced over at "them three," a cluster of three females who'd been staring at Trevor as if he really were their next meal. He shook his head at Grace, a light smile of *No hard feelings* on his lips. "Should've known you were behind that."

"I only hinted that you were a good catch." She rubbed Trevor's back. "Just looking out for you, baby."

Houston snorted as he brushed his secret sauce on a batch of ribs. "You call karate-killer Debbie looking out for him? The woman's looking more like a man every day."

"Oh, she is not," Grace responded. "She looks terrific. She's worked very hard to get her body like that."

Trevor glanced at the ladies. He knew exactly which one Debbie was because her biker shorts and spandex vest fit like a glazed topping over a physique that supported Grace's argument. As a man who appreciated the gym, Trevor admired Debbie's exercise ethics.

Grace poked Houston in the shoulder with her finger. "Her sport's not karate, it's wrestling. She's competing next Saturday, so make sure you find time today to wish her well." Grace rolled her eyes to the corners. "That is, if you're not afraid of her."

Houston flexed his arm as if to say, *Not a chance*, as a smile grew beneath his gray mustache. Grace's aunt Alcie hobbled toward them. "Those ribs ready yet, Houston?" Her voice sounded like a scratched record.

"Not yet, Auntie," Grace answered.

"You'll be the first to get a plate when they are," Houston promised. "I heard you forgot your teeth, but not to worry, these babies are tender 'nough for you to eat without 'em."

"I'm countin' on it." Alcie's grin was all gums as she turned around with her cane and shuffled back to her chair in the shade.

"Oh, look." Grace lit up with delight. "Dolly and Pete made it. Let me go say hello."

Houston put down his utensils, wiped his hands on his apron, and grabbed her arm before she could go. "Not so fast, young lady." He tilted his head, his white chef hat leaning, too, as he pecked Grace on the mouth. "I love you," he growled.

Grace blushed like a new bride and walked off to meet the latest arrivals while Houston grinned like he'd just won a million dollars. Trevor took it all in with a sigh as the voice flowing from the stereo system sang, "Love is a beautiful thing."

$\mathcal{L}\text{♥}$

Cassidy stepped behind the podium and gazed across the crowded auditorium. The weather was sunny and warm, and on Sundays like this, many of the parishioners who ordinarily attended the second service came to the first so they could spend a large fraction of the day enjoying outdoor activities.

Cassidy cleared her throat and held her head higher. Standing in front of a class of children was easy. Standing in front of hundreds of people was another story. But all the jitters in the world could not discourage her from making this announcement. "I'm before you on behalf of ACES. If you haven't heard, we lost all of the books in our library." A murmur rippled through the congregation. "The good news is, we're starting a readathon tomorrow, and the ACES children need your help." Cassidy explained that the ACES students had been asked to read ten public library books in three weeks. A sponsor would give one dollar for one book read. "If any of you would like to sponsor a child, there's a . . ."

Cassidy swallowed what was left of the sentence as she stared at Trevor. He was seated on the left side, about twelve rows back, middle of the row. She had warned herself not to look at him, but somehow her brain lost control of her eyes. Cassidy clutched the sides of the wood podium, a scatter of tingly pimples springing up on her arms. Being aware of a man was a terrible thing, especially when you didn't want to be aware of him. But no matter how many people were in the room, she always knew exactly where Trevor was.

Cassidy glanced at Clement Audrey. He smiled and nodded that she should continue. She smiled at the congregation, focusing on no one person, as she regrouped. "As I was saying, there's a sign-up sheet on the announcement board for anyone who would like to be a sponsor. You can sponsor a child for one book or as many books as your pocketbook or wallet can support."

"Amen," someone shouted.

Cassidy presented another smile, this one more cheerful. She said a few more details, offered a word of thanks, and hurried out of the pulpit to her seat between Lena and Dunbar. She found it difficult to con-

centrate on the rest of the service. Mental flashes of the
Armstrong barbecue merged with Pastor Audrey's
sermon, and Cassidy admonished herself for not being
fully focused on the message. Trying to do a better job
of paying attention, she sat up straighter and flipped
through her Bible to the scripture Pastor Audrey asked
the congregation to find. As he read the selected passage, Cassidy tuned out his voice and once again began
entertaining memories of the barbecue and the peaceful
scene that played out much later as she apologized to
Trevor for the way she responded to him upon learning
he'd had her car fixed. The razor tongue she slashed
into Trevor from time to time was not a reflection of
her heart. The truth of Cassidy's heart was that she
liked Trevor. More than she was comfortable admitting
with words or deeds.

Days later, Cassidy was still thinking about all this as
she snacked on grapes while the other two women updated their gossip files. "Have you heard about Deacon
Stanley?" Almondetta asked, dabbing at her lips with a
snow-colored napkin.

"No." Yaneesha released the word with a combina-
tion of dread and too much drama as she cleaned the
lenses of her eyeglasses with the edge of her shirt.

Almondetta began her oral report, and Yaneesha put
on her glasses. The young woman's eyes grew big, indicating there was still space in her life for more of Deacon
Stanley's business. But before Almondetta could broad-
cast additional details, Cassidy excused her way over the
church mother's voice, then said, "Four of our seniors
have birthdays next week. I'll visit two and, Yaneesha,
you can take two." Making sure she included Al-

mondetta, Cassidy suggested, "Since you don't get out much, I thought it would be nice if we wrapped the presents here and you wrote a special message on each card."

"Yes, that's fine," Almondetta answered in the soft but severe manner Cassidy disliked but accepted as the way Almondetta spoke. Yaneesha helped herself to a second cinnamon bun. "They're from Seconds," Almondetta said. "Delicious, aren't they?"

"Ummm-hmmm," Yaneesha hummed, then spoke without shame, "And so is Trevor. I'm going to marry him one day." Yaneesha went on for several minutes about the home she and Trevor were going to build, the cars they were going to drive, the cruises they were destined to sail.

"Trevor is a wise choice," Almondetta said at the end of Yaneesha's plans. "Stay away from those deacons and preachers. Most of them are like doctors—too busy taking care of others. You want a man who's going to be at home in bed with you instead of sitting at the bedside of every terminally ill parishioner." Almondetta smoothed a wrinkle out of the tablecloth. "Can you cook? As big as you are, you ought to know how to cook a husband a decent meal."

"I cook in the bedroom, and that's where it matters the most," Yaneesha said with confident twinkles in her eyes as she raised her palm for Cassidy to slap with *Amen*.

Cassidy passed on the invitation while Almondetta voiced her opinion. "That may be so, young lady. But you just make sure you aren't slinging your meals all over the church. A God-fearing man like Trevor ain't about to eat out the same pot as another."

chapter twenty

Pork chops smothered in gravy. Creamy mashed potatoes seasoned with bits of bacon. Green peas and mushrooms glazed with garlic and butter sauce. "And a beautiful woman, too," Trevor gloried, placing a bouquet of lilies on the table. He rushed Brenda away from the stove and into his arms, close to his heart.

"Happy anniversary," she said, and tied her arms around his neck as she reared slightly, resting her back against the support of his locked hands. The joy in her eyes was a reflection of what he felt, but unable to adequately express the enormity of his emotions with words, he spoke with a kiss that put the anniversary meal Brenda had prepared on hold until much later.

" . . . not speaking tonight," Cassidy said.

Trevor immediately gazed at the woman across the room as he came back to live in the present. He'd been dwelling on the past so deeply he didn't remember parking his vehicle or unlocking the front door or walking through the house to the kitchen. He stared at

Cassidy as she wiped the countertop with a dishcloth. Trevor wondered how many times she had said hello and received nothing in return. "Hi," he responded, doing his part yet leaving his heart out of it. He dropped a bouquet of flowers on the table and strode to the refrigerator. He pulled out a bottle of grape soda, untwisted the cap, and guzzled a third of the beverage with high hopes Cassidy wasn't going to say anything about the drink's sugar content. He could certainly do without her rebuke tonight, considering the way his day had shaped up. The craziness started this afternoon when a teen employee, packing a nine millimeter handgun and a grudge against the world, threatened to blow out the brains of another teen employee. After the police arrived and things returned to normal, Trevor received a call from one of his delivery van drivers. The largest van in the fleet of four, stocked with the monthly order of breakfast pastry he supplied for a band of local schools, had been a player in a fender bender on I-95. Trevor was thankful the driver was fine, the van would only be out of commission for a week, and the packaged baked goods had survived without a scratch.

Cassidy folded the dishcloth and hung it over the front of the sink. She carried a bowl of fresh strawberries to the refrigerator. "The girls and I had strawberry-banana smoothies for dessert. Aunt Odessa taught them one of her favorite hymns while they put on their pajamas, and we made sure they were tucked in. There are plenty of leftovers if you would like dinner." She smiled slightly at him and then at the flowers. "Well . . . good night," she said, walking toward the back stairs.

"Cassidy," he called.

She stopped and turned and offered him her face, a softness to it that sidetracked his thoughts. More than a couple of moments filled the silence around them before he moved his tongue. "Thanks for helping Mother Vale with my children. I'm sorry I'm so late getting home."

"No problem. Aunt Odessa told me you phoned and said you would be late."

Cassidy left the room, and Trevor plunked down in a chair and finished off the soda. He reached for the pocket dictionary and small spiral notebook Cassidy had left on the table. He'd seen her writing in the notebook once and had asked her about it.

"It's where I record my word for the week," she had said.

Tonight the notebook lay open, and an unfamiliar word stood on the first line of the page. As he read the second word, one he recognized, he heard a soft shuffling sound coming from the back stairwell. At first, he thought it was the cat, but cats didn't have polished toenails or long jean-covered legs or soft brown eyes that made him want to curl up inside them and tell her all about his bad day. But Cassidy wouldn't want to hear about his bad day, would she? She probably came back to the kitchen for her books and wanted to hurry and collect them so she could get away from him. So if that was the case, why was she still standing there?

"You . . . you look bad," she stammered.

"Thanks," he said dryly, and wiped his soda-wet lips with his palm.

"I mean . . ." She inched closer. "I mean, you don't look like yourself. Is something wrong?"

The question *Why would you care?* slid to the tip of his tongue. But the fact that she'd asked about him pleased him, and he wasn't about to do or say anything to chase her away.

"Come sit down," he said, making sure the sentence sounded like an offer and not an order. Cassidy selected the chair across from him and placed her hands in her lap. "How's the readathon going?" he asked. His grandmother used to say asking about others is just as important as telling about yourself.

"The sponsor sheet I hung up on Sunday is filled." Radiance showed in Cassidy's cheeks. "God's Word is true. He supplies all of our needs."

"Yes, He does." Trevor's smile was fleeting. He tapped the plastic soda bottle against the table. "Today would have been my wedding anniversary."

In a gentle tone, Cassidy responded, "So close to Houston and Grace's anniversary. No wonder you didn't change your mind about going to their barbecue until the last minute."

"I had planned to take these flowers to Brenda's grave today . . . after work." They both glanced at the blossoms. "But the cemetery had closed by the time I arrived."

"I bet you gave Brenda more than enough flowers to fill a garden when she was alive."

Trevor folded his hands on the table and met Cassidy's gaze. "Yes," he answered softly.

"That means Brenda had her flowers when she could appreciate them, and that's what counted."

The statement carried comfort, and more tears than anticipated stung Trevor's eyes. He dropped his gaze to an old stain on the tablecloth. A small smile tugged at his mouth. "I can see why my girls are so Cassidy-crazy."

"They're Daddy-crazy, too. You're all Brittney talks about."

Trevor measured Cassidy, disbelief in his heart.

"My daddy makes the best chocolate muffins in the world," Cassidy repeated his daughter's words. "My daddy taught me how to ride a bike . . . my daddy taught me how to skate . . . my daddy taught me how to spit."

The fond memory inspired Trevor to chuckle. "She told you I taught her how to spit?"

Cassidy grinned. "The whole disgusting truth."

Trevor chuckled again, but moments later, he placed his elbows on the table and his face in his palms. All of sudden, he didn't care if Cassidy saw this tormented side of him. He sighed in his hands before dragging them over his face. "I hurt my children. On the day Brenda died, instead of coming straight home, I stayed away until sometime after midnight, knowing they'd be asleep by then. I knew they would have questions, but I was afraid I wouldn't know how to answer them." He leaned back in the chair, an ache in one shoulder growing strong enough to menace. He massaged the muscle. "I remember feeling like such a failure that night because I couldn't bring my little girls their mother."

"You had no control over whether Brenda lived or died."

"Logically, I knew that. But at the time, my emotions were in the driver's seat." Regret weighted his voice. "I should have been the one to tell them about their mother. I can only imagine how scared and confused they must have been—their mother dead and their father missing. Brit and Bran are probably always going to remember their dad wasn't there for them that day."

"I disagree," Cassidy said. "I'm sure your daughters are going to grow up remembering all the times their dad *was* there for them, all the times you *did* dry their tears." She eased her hand forward, then pulled it back, and Trevor sensed she was fearful of extending that much of herself. "You're a good father, Trevor. There are many little girls who would give every doll they own to have a father as kind and as loving as you. I should know. I never knew my father or much about him. Aunt Odessa said my mom only spoke of him once. He was some guy she had an overnight fling with. She didn't even know his name."

"How did your mother die?" he questioned, hoping he wasn't asking too much.

"She overdosed on pills." Cassidy shrugged her shoulders as if to say, *No big deal*. Or maybe the shrug meant, *Let's not go there*, because she asked him a question now. "Did you have a good relationship with your parents?"

"Yes. In fact, I spent a lot of time in the kitchen with my mother. She believed girls *and* boys needed to know their way around a stove. I wasn't even eye level with the rim of the kitchen sink when she taught me how to roll the dough for the sweet potato pies." He would have stopped there, but Cassidy stared at him with strong interest. "By the time I was ten, I could make the whole pie on my own. And before I graduated from high school, I knew I just had to share all of my mother's delicious creations with the city of Philadelphia. Sooooo after graduating with a business degree, I took some culinary courses and Seconds was born."

"Tell me about your dad," Cassidy invited.

Following a string of reflective moments, Trevor responded, "He was kind, genuine . . . hardworking"—he paused—"and eternally optimistic. I don't think he ever had a bad day in his life. If he did, he never showed it. He died when I was fourteen. I remember I was sitting in a chair by his bed as he struggled with his final breaths. I began to cry, and he reached out and with the last of his strength, he took hold of my arm and said, 'No tears, son. You're the man of this house now, so you're going to have to be strong for your mother and grandmother and sister.'" Trevor breathed deeply, understanding what a life-molding moment that final conversation with his father had been. It was the sum of why he had never let his children see him cry and had never shared with them how he felt about losing Brenda.

Time on top of time, he'd had the chance.

He recalled the morning he found Brittney in his bedroom holding the cap to a bottle of Brenda's perfume as the bottle, an apparent victim of a fall, oozed its liquid contents into the carpet. Both he and Brittney stood like statues, only moving their eyes, first to stare at each other and then back to the scene on the floor while Trevor's heart hammered in his ears as he wondered what was going through his little girl's mind. What had she been doing with her mother's perfume? Had she been trying it on because that's what little girls did, or had she simply wanted to smell it, an effort to smell her mother again? It was the reason he had not gotten rid of the fragrance. He had kept it so he could smell Brenda whenever he wanted and pretend she was standing next to him.

Trevor raised his gaze and stared at Cassidy, unsure of how much time had passed. "Did your mom and dad attend Charity Community?" she asked.

He sniffed to clear his airways and projected a stable voice. "No. And Brenda and I didn't become members until she became pregnant with Brittney. We weren't married and hadn't planned to marry for a couple of years. But we loved each other, and with a baby on the way, we decided not to wait. Neither of us had a personal relationship with the Lord," Trevor continued, "but Brenda wanted to be married by a minister. So a friend pointed us to Charity Community. We met with Pastor Audrey, and during one of our counseling sessions, we both gave our hearts to God. The following Sunday we joined the congregation, and two weeks later we had a small wedding."

"Brenda was blessed to have a man who loved her and the baby they created." Cassidy's eyes darkened for a long moment, as if she was revisiting a bad memory. She blinked and came back to him, then offered a simple yet genuine smile. "Do you mind if I make a couple of suggestions that might help you with your daughters?"

"Go ahead," he said.

"For one . . . you should take them out once in a while."

Offense taken, Trevor struggled to push it from his tone. "I take my children out all the time."

"I know, but this would be different," she explained. "I saw it on a talk show. This guy had three daughters, and one day out of the month he took each one on a well-thought-out date. It makes each girl feel special, it's a chance for you to get to know them better and vice versa, *and* at the same time, you're modeling how they should be treated when a boyfriend eventually takes them out."

The stubborn set of his jaw slackened and he humbled. "Keep going."

"Well," she began as if doubtful she should proceed, "have you ever told Brittney and Brandi you were sorry you didn't come home the day their mother died?"

Trevor drifted into a state of intense meditation. "No," he finally admitted.

"An apology might be the key that will open the door to Brittney's heart."

Trevor slowly digested the words. Cassidy bowed her head, and he did the same as she began to pray for him and his children. At the end of the prayer, Trevor opened his eyes, any doubts about Cassidy erased. Since receiving that anonymous envelope and article, he'd been wrestling with the notion of Cassidy having been a drunken driver. But it was getting easier to let it go. The woman sharing the room with him cared deeply for his daughters, and she would not do anything to endanger their lives. He was sure about that now.

Trevor would have taken Cassidy's hand, maybe held both of them, but she had put them under the table, out of sight, out of reach. "I plan to take your advice and talk with Brittney and Brandi as soon as they get back from California," he said. Penny and the girls were flying out early tomorrow morning to visit Kendall McBride, and there wouldn't be time to sit and talk the way he wanted and the way the girls deserved.

"Your children have been going on and on about this trip to see their godmother. They told me she and their mother were very close."

"Brenda and Kendall were like sisters." Breaking into a slight grin, Trevor stroked his goatee. "Kendall McBride . . . ," he mused softly, but kept the rest of his thoughts about Kendall private.

chapter twenty-one

A wave of pandemonium penetrated the classroom in spite of the closed door, and Cassidy disguised her frustration with a smile. "Good try," she encouraged the eleven-year-old standing in front of the chalkboard. He had spelled the word "indivisible" incorrectly. She gave him a sticker, and he swaggered back to his seat with a pleased expression on his face. Cassidy stared from desk to desk. None of the children were concentrating this afternoon. And why would they want to prepare for a spelling bee when down the hall, Trevor's boys were whooping it up in the gym? Portia Washington, in her last year of college, sauntered in and set up things for a science project. Cassidy dismissed the students to the water fountain three at a time, then turned the reins of responsibility over to the younger woman.

Annoyance prompting Cassidy to walk with pep, she hurried through the hall, scarcely able to refrain from going inside the gymnasium and lecturing Trevor about the high level of noise. The spelling bee was tomorrow, and he knew she needed every available second to get the kids ready. "Men can be so inconsiderate," she muttered, crossing the threshold of her office. She snapped to an immediate halt upon noticing Derek on the telephone at Trevor's desk.

"What's up, Miss Beckett?" Derek swung his feet off of the desk and launched from the chair. His eyes brightened the way they did whenever he said hello to her.

"Hello, Derek." Cassidy fought to keep the chill out of her voice. "What are you doing in here?"

The young man flattened a palm over the mouthpiece of the receiver. "Coach Monroe . . . is treating . . . the boys to pizza. He . . . asked me . . . to order." Cassidy was aware of the way Derek took his time and formed each word, attempting to impress her with good grammar, she gathered. His voice fell manly deeper as he spoke through the receiver. "Yes, sir . . . that's what I said . . . five plain . . . five pepperoni"—he smiled tooth and gums at Cassidy—"and five hot sausage."

The inside of Cassidy's mouth thickened with a slimy cardboard-tasting film. It seemed Trevor loved pizza as much as she detested it. Ignoring Derek's voice as he completed his call, she went to the file cabinet and began searching through the J to L folders.

"Can I help you find something?"

Cassidy jumped at the voice that came out of the young man standing only inches behind her now. She braved a look at his face, and suddenly, the years rolled backward. Cassidy was a student at Tilden, and Minister was yelling at her.

"We talked about this." Bubbles of sweat formed on

Minister's forehead, *and his hands were tight balls at his sides. "We had it all planned out, and we're sticking to those plans." He frowned at the baby. "We're getting rid of it."*

"No help needed." Cassidy's tone was firm as she pressed a guarded stare on Derek. Everything about the youngster's face strongly resembled Minister's. The tea-colored skin, the broad smile, the long, thick eye-lashes—all Minister. Cassidy pulled out Twyla Keary's folder. Twyla had been out ill, and Cassidy wanted to check on the child's condition and let the family know Twyla was in her prayers. She closed the metal drawer and asked the camp counselor, "Shouldn't you be getting back to the gym?"

"Yeah." Derek winced. "I mean, yes . . . I should be on my way." His smile faded into a serious expression. "I . . . I've been meaning to ask . . ." He momentarily averted his gaze. "Well, I had a hard time . . . with some of my subjects last year . . . and I was wondering . . . if you could tutor me when school starts up?"

Derek's eyes were loaded with hope. But how could Cassidy help someone who gave her flashbacks to a time when her life was in shreds? "I'm sorry, Derek. I'm busy with my own students in the fall. I won't have the time."

The light in Derek's eyes clicked off. "I . . . I understand. Thanks, anyway." He turned, his shoulders curved with rejection. "I'll see you."

"Bye," Cassidy said softly, and slumped to the chair behind her desk, pondering what God was up to. Why would He bring Derek into her life at this time? Why had He used Sister Whittle and Pastor Audrey to drop seeds into her heart about the Sparrow Ministry?

Cassidy closed her eyes and tried to make sense of her thoughts.

∠❤

A spunky fifth grader with dimples you could hide your fingertips in was the first to jog down the stairs of the yellow school bus parked in front of Charity Community Church. "We came in second," she shouted, mesmerizing the day-care center children playing in the tot lot.

Cassidy chuckled and strolled up and down the bus aisle, making sure all the kids were off the bus before thanking the driver.

"Congratulations," Trevor cheered, and high-fived some of the youngsters. The kids, staff, and parent volunteers walked into the building, all talking about the spelling bee victory. One of the bigger children carried a silver-plated trophy.

"You must be proud," Trevor said as Cassidy approached.

She smiled. "Of course, I am." The thrill on the children's faces when their second-place standing had been announced was a prize she would forever cherish. And the second-place trophy, though only half as tall as the first-place statue, would look beautiful in the trophy cabinet.

Cassidy looked down on the boy at Trevor's side. Herbie, the smallest and the youngest boy in the sports camp, wore a baseball cap that came down over the tips of his ears. Cassidy raised the flap of the cap so she could get a peek at Herbie's eyes. Big brown circles pinned Cassidy with worry.

"I'm waiting for Mommy Jean," he said, and looked in the direction she ordinarily walked.

Cassidy attempted to comfort him. "I'm sure she'll be here soon."

The child had come a long way. When Herbie first began attending SAFE, he cried whenever his foster mother was late picking him up. And who could blame him? Last year, two days before Christmas, his biolog-ical mother put him on a city bus with instructions to get off at the last stop, and she would meet him there. Herbie stood at that stop all alone for three hours waiting for a mother who later admitted to authorities she never planned to come for him.

Trevor clamped Herbie's head with one of his big hands. "I told Herbie not to worry. Mommy Jean is on her way."

Cassidy squatted and pulled Herbie into her arms. "Everything's going to be fine." His chin wobbled against her shoulder as he nodded. Cassidy released him and moved along the walkway and into the building, the strong desire to go back and hold Herbie beating in her heart.

The ACES students were dismissed for the day, and Cassidy entered her office. "Looks like Dunbar's been here," Portia said. An enormous silver box sat on Cas-sidy's desk. Hit with a surge of excitement, Cassidy smiled and crossed the room to see what Dunbar had left. Without delay, she raised the rectangular top, decked with one large blossom of curly white ribbon, and pulled out a children's picture book. There were at least fifty others and a heavy plastic container full of . . .

"Chalk," Portia said with awe, peeping into the box

as if she were standing on the edge of a mountain and looking down into a faraway valley. "Check out all the cool colors. I don't think I've ever seen red chalk be-fore."

"Neither have I." Cassidy opened and read the card that had been attached to the chalk bucket.

"Dunbar really knows how to make a girl blush. Check out your face."

Conscious of the warm lines stretching up her neck and into her cheeks, Cassidy slid the card into her pants pocket, then touched her heated jaw.

"God is just too good," Portia praised. "First the spelling bee win and now this." She picked up her tote bag and said good-bye with a giggle.

Cassidy groped a colorful paperback about trains, meditating on the man who'd blessed ACES today, while jubilation and fear, equal in portion, did battle within her. The room was still, and the tiny tick of the clock on the wall seemed to elevate to the sound of thunder as she reached inside her pocket, removed the card, and reread the penned message.

> All the colors of the rainbow are here
> But none color the world as pretty as your smile.
>   Love,
>   Trevor

chapter twenty-two

Trevor joined a long line of congregants entering the sanctuary. He chose a partially filled pew in the middle of the vast room, approximately where he sat most Sunday mornings. While a steady flow of people streamed through the rear and side entrances, and the musicians, already positioned up front, began playing soft music, Trevor opened a large black Bible to the chapter he'd started reading last night. This was the time Pastor Audrey had suggested his members use for meditative reflection, but some used these pre-service minutes for talking and laughing and strolling up and down the red carpet like it was Oscar night. Trevor looked up from the Bible in his lap. It was apparent Yaneesha was feeling like a celebrity this morning. She was standing at the end of the aisle, talking on a cell phone. Trevor returned to the scriptures, only to suspend reading as he gazed out of the corner of his eye at the woman in the tight orange sleeveless dress as she slid into the space next to him.

"Good morning," she said, crossing her big sheer-covered legs, sending her hemline racing up her thighs.

"Good morning, Yaneesha." Trevor eased an inch over, putting a thin line of space between their arms.

"You look nice," she said.

The smile she blazed was as lascivious as the shimmer inside the gaze that climbed up the legs of his black pants and up each button of his black shirt. Trevor considered moving to another pew, but remembering that Yaneesha was bold enough and crazy enough to follow him—she'd done it once before—he decided to stay put, avoiding a scene sure to amuse any onlookers.

"What were you reading?" She slid over, and their elbows were touching again.

"The second chapter of Daniel."

Yaneesha adjusted her glasses on her nose. "Daniel the one that killed that giant, right?"

"No," he clarified, "you're thinking of David. Daniel is better known for surviving the lion's den."

"Oh, well." She giggled, digging in her purse. "I knew he was one of dem disciples." She generated another wanton smile. "Do you want some?"

Trevor glanced at the roll of candy she was sticking at him. "No, thank you," he said. A pain at the base of his head spread to his shoulders, and he closed the Bible, stared ahead, and prayed, *Lord, let the service be a short one.*

✍❥

"Go, share the good news of Jesus Christ with someone today," Clement said as parting words to the congregation. He and a ministerial staff of five walked down the center of the aisle, and the choir exited the choir stand through a side door that led to the room where they would shuck out of their robes. Once the pulpit was vacant, the ushers stepped away from the doors so the crowd could depart.

"That's a good color on you," Lena said of Cassidy's full-length lilac dress and matching slides as they waded through the human ocean gathered outside.

"Thanks," Cassidy replied, and they stopped at a people-free spot near a row of white flowers bordering the lawn. She brushed aside the lock of hair curving along the side of her face. The rest of her microbraids were pulled back into a high ponytail.

Lena smiled. "Hulk loved the fruit basket."

Cassidy had sent the basket as an additional thank-you for the work Hulk did on her car.

"I think I'm falling for him," Lena said, and passed Cassidy a picture she'd taken of Hulk. Cassidy studied the not-quite-average-in-height, bulky-structured, light-skinned man.

"What happened to your 'what my man has to be' requirements? I believe some of it went a little something like 'tall, dark, and slim.'"

"What can I say?" Lena shrugged. "I've evolved. None of that stuff is important. Hulk has an honest and loving heart, he's a hard worker, and he likes to have fun, too. We have quite a few of the same interests." Her smile grew brighter with every word. "He's coming to service here next Sunday, and I'll be going to Bible study at his church the following Wednesday. Can you believe I've actually met a guy who sincerely loves the Lord? Hulk's even inspired me to reevaluate my relationship with God." Lena unbuttoned the jacket of a white pantsuit, and now you could see the black tank she was wearing underneath the jacket. "I've been playing church, girl. I was just coming because that's how I was raised. Hulk and I . . . well, we prayed last night, and I recommitted my life to Christ." Her face was radiant. "I want the kind of relationship with the Lord that Hulk has. I want to serve God with my whole heart, not a piece of it—and not just when it's convenient." Lena and Cassidy nodded hello to a middle-aged couple as they passed. A moment later, Yaneesha shot by, a large black Bible clutched against her chest.

Lena arched an eyebrow. "Yaneesha with a Bible. I've never seen that before."

"Maybe she's getting serious with the Lord, too."

Lena didn't look convinced. "So do you want to go tonight or not?"

"Sure," Cassidy said. There was a gospel stage play at the Merriam Theater. Hulk's sister and brother in-law were supposed to attend, but one of their kids was sick, so Lena had offered their tickets to her.

"Who are you going to bring?" Lena asked.

Dunbar, Cassidy's first choice, had a speaking engagement this afternoon. "Portia's an avid listener of gospel music. Maybe I'll see if she wants to join us."

Lena heaved a sigh. "I was thinking more on the lines of Trevor."

Cassidy could see Trevor clearly from where she stood. He was talking to a man she didn't know. "No, that would be too much like a date."

"Girl, I'm about two days away from my period. Please don't get on my last good nerve."

"And don't get on mine." She glanced at Trevor again. "Anyway, his children are flying home, and he has to pick them up from his sister's later on."

"What time?"

"I don't know."

"Well, let's ask."

"No," Cassidy said, but Lena was already in motion, jetting across the church lawn toward Trevor.

"Is everything okay?" Rave stopped beside Cassidy.

Cassidy peered into Rave's perpetual stony, narrow eyes and wondered if Rave's clients ever trusted a thing she said. "Everything is fine, Rave." She complimented the choir member. "Your solo today was beautiful."

Rave tossed her hair over her shoulder along with a nasty glance at the church pianist. "I would have sounded better if it weren't for him. I told him verse, chorus, verse, chorus, chorus, chorus, but the simpleton got it all mixed up and threw us both off."

"I'm sure no one noticed."

"Or *cared*," Lena interjected, joining them.

Rave perched her hands on the waistband of a short black skirt. "I wasn't talking to you."

"But you were talking loud enough for everyone in the immediate area to hear you. That makes us all a part of your conversation."

Rave moved in on Lena. "Do you know what you can do for me?"

"I know what I'd like to do." Lena took a step forward, and now she was eye level with Rave's plunging neckline.

Cassidy kept a smile prisoner. She knew that Lena would kick Rave's butt if they were to get into it. She squeezed Lena's elbow. "That's more than enough, you two."

Rave huffed and stomped off. The cord of Lena's purse had slipped to the bend in her arm, and she returned it to her shoulder. "That girl has some major issues."

Cassidy stared after Rave. "Don't we all?"

Lena didn't dwell on it. "I have good news," she announced. "Trevor said his daughters won't be in until late, well *after* the play."

In the parking lot, Portia leaned against Rave's Mercedes. "What should I do?"

Rave tugged her car keys out of her purse. She scrutinized Portia. Her bones were too big, eyes too small, hips too wide, and lips too thin to be considered pretty.

"Let him know how you feel." Rave fingered the small crucifix dangling between her breasts. "Trevor is shy. You have to come on strong. Be obvious. And by all means, be persistent." Such tactics had gotten Rave nowhere with Trevor, and she knew Portia was in for the same.

"Are you sure?" Portia wrinkled her face. "I've never thought of Trevor as shy. And he certainly doesn't seem the type who appreciates aggression."

"You asked me what I thought, and now I'm telling you." Rave's words speared the air as she deactivated the car alarm, and it blurted a distinct *bleep-bleep*. "If you want Trevor, go after him. Send him a gift or write a cute little letter. That will grab his attention, and you'll soon be the next Mrs. Monroe."

☙

Rays of sun rubbed Trevor's back as he bent over and tied the laces of his right shoe. But the heat from the sun failed to dilute the chill he felt when he removed his foot from the running board of his vehicle and straightened to his full height to discover Rave glaring at him from the other side of the parking lot.

Merging with the parade of cars exiting the lot, Trevor questioned what was going on in Rave's mind. That was the third time today he'd found her eyes pinned on him, and each time the stare had burned hostile. Surely, she wasn't upset with him for refusing to have that soda and soft pretzel with her the night he fixed her tire.

Trevor had discussed Rave's behavior on that evening with Kregg. Kregg insisted Rave was just naturally flirty, and it was no big deal. Trevor had decided not to make a big deal out of it, since Kregg wasn't. Still, he didn't trust Rave. He had the strong and disconcerting feeling that Rave was the one who'd sent him the newspaper clipping about Cassidy. Rave had known Cassidy for a long time and would know things about Cassidy others might not.

Trevor inched the Expedition forward, passing Rave. She stood alone and had donned a pair of sunglasses. He pulled out of the lot with the impression that behind those black lenses her gaze was still linked to him, and it was no less vicious than earlier.

He left the parking lot and started home, all Rave-thoughts behind him as he realized he did not have his Bible. Believing he'd left it on the pew, he drove back to the church and returned to the area where he'd worshipped. The Bible wasn't there, so he made a visit to the Lost and Found. No one had turned in his Bible.

chapter twenty-three

Stop talking and finish your breakfast," Trevor scolded.
"We need to leave soon."

Brandi stared as Trevor peered over the newspaper at
her before looking at the watch on his arm. She pushed
a spoonful of cereal into her mouth, watching as he
touched his thumb to the tip of his tongue before
turning the page of the newspaper.

Cassidy, sitting at the center island, sipped warm tea
and took small bites out of a wheat cracker. She glanced
at Brittney, who had finished eating and was in the
corner playing with Poopie.

Brandi decided to speak before her bowl was bare and
buttered toast eaten. "I covered Grammy with another
blanket so she wouldn't be so cold," she said.

Trevor folded the newspaper and frowned. "Mother
Vale complained of being cold this morning?"

Brandi poked out her chin. "No. She *felt* cold. So I
got a blanket from the hall closet and put it over her. I

didn't even wake her up," she added, and made an "I'm a big girl" smile.

Apprehension suddenly fanned Cassidy's heart, and she pushed from the stool, its four feet scratching the floor, and the floor screeching as if it were upset with the stool. "Aunt Odessa!" Cassidy yelled as she ran upstairs.

✿

Casseroles came all afternoon. The latest was a zucchini in a disposable pan.

"Let me take care of that for you, honey babe." Emma waddled over and emptied Cassidy's hands. She made space for the tray in the refrigerator while Harold Purdue and a few of Odessa's closest Knitting Circle girlfriends sat around the table sprinkling their stories about Odessa with laughter and tears. Cassidy watched from the sidelines, wishing the childlike wish that somehow she could bring Odessa back. A heart attack had taken her away. When Cassidy and Trevor found her, she had been dead for hours, the blanket Brandi had supplied pulled up to her chin and a smile on her face that gave her the presence of being in the arms of a very pleasant dream.

"Don't ya want somethin' to eat, Cassie baby?" Emma said. "I'll be glad to dip ya up a bowl of my gumbo."

Emma thought her shrimp gumbo was the balm for every sorrow. "No, Ms. Emma, I'm not hungry," Cassidy answered. Cassidy had never been able to eat much when she was hurting. Tears hemmed the rims of her eyes, and she walked out of the kitchen before Emma noticed and locked her in a hug and started singing "It Is Well with My Soul" again. Grief seemed to be sucking the energy out of Cassidy, and she climbed the stairs, the lift and land of every footstep lethargic. "Jesus," she whispered, powerless to say more, thankful for the comfort that this one word delivered. Earlier, she had locked herself in Odessa's bathroom and wept. Lena came over, and the two of them had sat in the middle of the bathroom floor and talked and prayed until Cassidy felt like coming out and greeting the first wave of visitors.

Cassidy continued her climb up the steps, tiptoeing to the third floor, to check on the children. She recalled the devastation on their faces when given the bad news about Odessa. Both girls had cried to exhaustion, Brandi in Trevor's arms, Brittney in Cassidy's. Then Trevor put them down for a nap.

Cassidy cracked the door and peeked in on them. Sound asleep, they appeared to be fine. Cassidy eased down the steps. Trevor and Dunbar were in the living room, a man dotting each end of the sofa. As if choreographed, they stood in unison as she entered the room. "You look tired," Dunbar said, stepping around the coffee table and rushing forward. "Maybe you should lie down."

"Maybe later," she said.

Dunbar held her hand in his. "I have a service to attend to tonight, so I have to get back to the parlor. But I should be done by ten. I can come back." Trevor had planted his body in front of the fireplace, and Dunbar looked at him.

"No, that won't be necessary"—Cassidy squeezed Dunbar's hand—"but thank you."

Dunbar and his sister, Irenia Smith, were handling the arrangements for Odessa, and he said, "I'll be by tomorrow so we can finalize everything."

She nodded, and Dunbar pecked her cheek. She walked him out onto the porch. When she returned, Trevor was in the same spot. He'd picked up a framed picture of Odessa, taken when she was twenty-five. Cassidy stood beside Trevor, and they admired the young face behind the glass.

"I feel responsible," she confided. Her throat was taut with emotion, and it hurt as she swallowed. "I should have insisted Aunt Odessa see a doctor. There were signs she wasn't herself."

Trevor returned the picture to its home on the mantel. His words were gentle. "Don't even go there, Cassidy. Mother Vale was her own person. There was no making her do anything. She died peacefully, and I believe she wanted that."

Cassidy nodded yes. "Aunt Odessa always said she would prefer to go home to be with the Lord a few years early than suffer a few years longer. I wish we could have said good-bye, though." It was as if her aunt had just walked off. "Did you get to say good-bye to Brenda?"

"No," he replied, and neither of them seemed to know what to say next, so they stood in the silence, scanning the assortment of mantel pictures.

"Have you spoken with Portia?" she asked.

"Yes, she'll take care of everything until you return. I've also made arrangements for SAFE and Seconds so that I can be with you for the next day or so."

Trevor's face, voice, exuded a strength that Cassidy lacked, yet she protested, "No, I don't want to take you away from your work." She nodded in the direction of the kitchen, and a benign smile worked its way onto her face. "Don't forget, I have the whole gang in there."

"But I want to be here." He extended a slow but confident hand and cupped the side of her face. His thumb slid back and forth across her cheekbone.

Cassidy's lids grew listless, drooped, and shut as she leaned her face into the core of Trevor's hand, without explanation as to why his touch seemed to console more than any other today. When her lids eased apart, Cassidy's unsettled gaze lifted to Trevor's stare, and he gingerly urged her forward until the gap between them was filled. She followed his lead, curving her arms around him. With her head against him, she could hear his heart pounding. Cassidy closed her eyes, a fresh wave of grief spanning her heart, and she silently longed for Odessa . . . and for the beautiful baby she'd lost years before.

✑❤

Trevor entered the bedroom as Brandi said, "That was a good story." He smiled, humbled by the sight of Cassidy on the bed, shoulder blades against the headboard, one of his daughters on each side of her. She had been reading them a bedtime story, comforting them despite her own torn heart. She was so much braver than he had been when Brenda died.

Seated on the side of the bed, Trevor massaged one of Brandi's bare feet and met Brittney's eyes. "Girls, I need to talk with you." Over the weekend, while they were out of town, he'd been praying diligently, asking God to give him the right words to say to them and the courage to say it. His intentions were to take them to the park this afternoon, spread a blanket, and have this talk. But once the children had been told about Odessa, Trevor changed his mind and let them grieve. Yet he didn't want another night to pass without saying, "Daddy needs to let you know how sorry he is." Cassidy started to move from the bed. "No, stay . . . please," he said.

"Are you sorry because Grammy died?" Brandi crawled onto his thighs.

"I'm very sad we've lost Aunt Odessa." He joined gazes with Cassidy. "I feel as if I've lost a member of my family. But there's something else I'm sorry about." He checked to ensure he had both daughters' attention. "On the day Mommy died, I did something that wasn't very smart . . . or brave." He paused, Brittney receiving the larger portion of his focus. Her head was against Cassidy's shoulder and her eyes turned down. "I didn't come home to be with you that day because I was afraid to face your pain, and I felt really bad that I couldn't bring Mommy home. I'm sorry I wasn't there when you needed me. I'm sorry I chose to cry alone instead of with you."

Brittney raised her eyes to his. "You cried when Mommy died?"

"Yes, baby, I cried. I cried at the hospital and in my office and sometimes in my bedroom." How well he remembered rolling to Brenda's side of the bed one night, clutching the last nightshirt she'd worn and sobbing until he was empty of tears, but remarkably still so full of pain. During that sleepless, solitary night, angry at God for taking Brenda, he'd been tempted to shut God out of his life. But somehow he found the strength to pray and to reflect on all the blessings God had poured into his life over the years, Brenda one of them. Not much later, he fell asleep, and he slept through the night. When he awoke in the morning, although he yearned for Brenda, the road ahead of him didn't look as dark.

He cradled Brittney's chin. "I made a big mistake. I should have let you know how much I missed Mommy." Ready to start handling things differently, he said, "Sometimes it still hurts when I think about her and how I can't reach out to her, but do you know what I do?"

Both girls, wide and misty-eyed, shook no.

"I talk to God about it. And that's when I feel His presence and His love, and I know I'm going to be all right." Tears trickled from Brittney. She covered her face and let out sobs that wobbled her small frame. Trevor signaled to Cassidy to take Brandi, and he pulled Brittney to his chest. He let her cry, rubbing her back, rocking her until she was done. "I'm truly sorry I hurt you."

"We forgive you, Daddy. Don't we, Sis?"

"Yes," Brittney panted through her anguish.

The quick forgiveness from his children pushed tears from Trevor's eyes, and he let the drops fall, open and free. Brandi crawled to him and wiped his face. As Trevor held her baby-soft palm in place against his cheek, he decided a tissue could not have been more delicate. He positioned the children so they could share his lap and kissed their foreheads. "I love you both," he whispered, "so much." Trevor carried his gaze to Cassidy. "Thank you . . . for everything."

Cassidy nodded and brushed away the tears that were standing on her face.

Suddenly, Trevor felt the truth of God rising on the inside of his conscience. *You must forgive, too. Give the anger you have for Brenda's killer to Me.*

Brandi's eyes sparkled like Brenda's had when she was happy. "Can I say a scripture, Daddy?"

"Sure you can, sweetheart."

Brandi began reciting a familiar Psalm. At the start of the second verse, Brittney spoke with her sister and another tear slipped from Trevor.

chapter twenty-four

Cassidy opened the back door and stepped onto the wooden porch. The sconce high up on the wall produced rays of white light that showcased Trevor from head to naked feet. "Are you sure that's something you want to start?" she asked.

He smiled, ogling her shoeless feet. "You make it look so comfortable." He sat up straighter, and the lawn chair shifted backward as it accepted his new angle.

Cassidy set a decanter of insect repellent on the railing. The small flame inside the decanter's belly shimmered. "I thought the service was beautiful," she said of the funeral that had taken place earlier that day. She stared through the window behind Trevor's head. With the screen in place, it was difficult to see clearly into the kitchen Odessa had loved, but Cassidy could see the curtains Odessa had hand-sewn. A breeze, handling them as gently as Odessa had, sucked the curtains against the screen, then blew them away.

Cassidy lounged against the railing, both hands gripping the paint-chipped wood. "Thank . . ."—she paused, sought and held Trevor's eyes—"thank you for being so supportive through everything." At one point following the burial, when she had been surrounded by church members offering their condolences, he had even reached through the crowd and pressed a note into her palm that reminded her he was close by if she needed him.

Cassidy turned suddenly and faced the skinny crooked tree standing barely three feet tall in the corner of the yard. She arched her neck and observed the full moon as the same breeze that had moved the curtains made the empty clothesline sway.

"Sky," Trevor said.

Sky. He was calling her that more and more. Secretly, Cassidy had come to like it. She had no clue why he called her Sky, though. Whenever she asked him why, he'd smile and change the subject. "Yes," she answered.

"Come sit next to me."

A plane roared through a sky freckled with stars as Cassidy turned and found Trevor's hand, palm side up, in the space between them. Their surroundings grew quiet as she stared into a pair of eyes that whispered, *Come to me . . . I won't hurt you . . . trust me.*

She took a step forward and reached and laid her hand against his warm palm. His steady grip tightened over her fingers, and he led her to the chair beside him.

"Tell me something about you I don't know," he said.

A memory of the night she lost the baby formed in Cassidy's mind. But that memory was too complicated to put into words, though sometimes she wished she could find the courage to talk it through with someone. She studied their joined hands, deciding to disclose accounts from her childhood and high school days. "I was in the twelfth grade when I decided I wanted to teach," she said. "One of my friends had to babysit her brother after school each day. He was failing math, and my friend didn't have the patience to help him, so she asked me. Soon I was tutoring him and four of his friends."

The sky had turned several shades darker by the time Cassidy and Trevor strolled inside.

The following night, the children in bed, Trevor did most of the talking after Cassidy accepted his invitation and sat again, her hand in his, on the back porch. He told her how he'd met Brenda and how Brenda had rejected his first six offers to take her out and what had happened when they finally did have their first date on Brenda's fifteenth birthday. Trevor recounted some of the stupid things he and Kregg did as teenagers, and he talked briefly about how scared he'd been when he became a first-time father. He shared his future plans for a second Seconds, and finally, Trevor exposed his most embarrassing moment in life. She and Trevor laughed about it, their buoyant tones like musical notes meshing and shaping one happy sound under a post-midnight sky.

✐♥

"Cassidy?" someone called from the sidewalk behind Cassidy.

She spun around. Grace stood a few feet away,

dressed in a moccasin-brown pantsuit, sandals the same color as her clothing, and a smile that surpassed the temperature in warmth. Cassidy flashed a similar smile, and the two hugged like they'd been friends for years.

"Are you here to meet Trevor?" Grace asked. "He had business to take care of, and he's not back yet."

"That's fine. I didn't tell him I was coming by. I was out for a walk and decided to stop."

"Well," Grace offered, "come on in and have a cold drink on the house."

Cassidy observed the large modern edifice. The tinted windows and revolving middle door gave it the face of a polished office building rather than a bakery, and Cassidy instantly recalled that this facility was once home to an insurance company. "I've never been inside Seconds," Cassidy said.

Grace's mouth fell open for a moment. "You're kidding."

"I'm not much of a sweet-eater."

Grace held the glass side door open, her eyes shining. "Welcome to Seconds."

Outside, the aroma had been pleasurable. Inside the building, the aroma was simply divine, and Cassidy snatched quick puffs from the air, determined to give a name to the scent.

"Corn bread," Grace revealed. "People come from all over the city for it. We make blueberry, raspberry, cinnamon raisin, maple pecan, and, of course"—she grinned—"plain ole corn bread."

Cassidy strolled behind Grace, taking note of everything. The front half of the room housed little round tables and chairs. A pinball machine stood on the left, a jukebox to the right, and potted trees were decoratively placed. Paintings of families from various ethnic backgrounds lined the walls, as well as numerous culinary awards and photographs of many famous Philadelphians who had been patrons. A giant square of display cases filled with every type of baked good one could imagine sat in the middle of the bakery. An espresso-cappuccino machine and soft drink machine were near the registers. Workers, teenaged to seniors, uniformed in denim jeans, white shirts, and navy-blue baseball caps with the Seconds logo above the bill, hustled behind the counters. "How many people does Seconds employ?"

"Forty. We have bakers, decorators, dishwashers, porters, cashiers, and delivery personnel." She opened and held the door of the kitchen so Cassidy could view the room of wall ovens, ten-burner ranges, mixers with bowls large enough to bathe a small child in, and walk-in refrigerators.

"Why is it called Seconds?" Cassidy questioned, pondering why she had never thought to ask Trevor.

"Take a guess," Grace suggested.

"Your order is ready in . . . *seconds?*"

"No"—Grace chuckled—"you always come back for more."

"Apparently," Cassidy said, observing the long lines. At a display case, a little white-haired woman pointed to a round cake lathered with creamy yellow icing and crowned with a wreath of mint-green petals and vines. Cassidy gave the floral decorations a harder look. "Are those real?"

"They sure do look it, don't they?" Grace waved a

hand. "This way." She led Cassidy to a room in the rear. Cassidy continued thinking about the cake. Trevor was right. Dessert artist *was* a fitting title for anyone who could decorate a cake with such precision and creativity. "This is our lounge," Grace said. "Mr. Monroe wanted employees who were also students to have a quiet place to study before or after school. Some Saturday afternoons we rent this space for small birthday parties, and we supply a complimentary cake."

The women climbed a narrow flight of stairs leading to the second floor. "Occasionally, Mr. Monroe ventures into the kitchen or jumps behind a register," Grace chatted on the way, "but he mostly works behind the scenes now." At the top of the steps, she pointed. "Our offices are on this level. She opened the second cherrywood door in a line of three. "Make yourself comfortable. I'll be right back."

Counterclockwise, Cassidy examined Grace's office, typical of many: one desk, several chairs, twin plants, and scattered pictures of family from desk to bookshelf to wall. The room had an air of kindliness. Much like the soul it belonged to, Cassidy mused.

While awaiting Grace's return, Cassidy noticed two doors. The closest was ajar, so she peeked in, discovering it was a closet. She assumed the other door led to Trevor's office. Since she knew he wasn't in, the temptation to open the door and catch a glance of his room was getting the best of her. Another minute and she would have peeped in, but Grace emerged, clutching a tray that held two tall plastic cups and a small white paper bag.

"I brought sugar packets so you can sweeten your

iced tea to your preference. There's a corn muffin in the bag"—she jiggled her eyebrows—"in case you want to be adventurous."

With a smile, Cassidy thanked Grace and sat in the armchair at the side of the desk.

Grace settled in the padded chair on wheels behind her desk. She crossed her legs and folded her hands atop her knee. "Trevor tells me you're back to work."

Cassidy pulled the cup of iced tea away from her lips. "Yes, I didn't want to stay away from the children too long."

"Getting back into routine after losing a loved one can be good, but make sure you do what you need to do to heal."

"Yes, I am. I've already been to my first grief support meeting at the church."

The phone beeped once, interrupting their conversation. "Excuse me," Grace said, and pushed a button.

The beats of Cassidy's heart ran closer together as she listened to Trevor's smooth, low-key voice over the speakerphone. "I'm back in the office," he said, and she found it too hard not to smile.

ᴄ~

"I'd like you to call Rothwell Enterprises, please," Trevor requested as Grace neared his desk. "Find out if they're still interested in using us for Sam Rothwell's birthday party." He handed a disk across the desk. "Here's that list of potential clients. Send advertisements out as soon as possible, please." Trevor grinned, recollecting how intimidated Grace had been by the computer when she started. During the secretarial search, he'd received résumés from more qualified applicants, but Grace, a homemaker much of her adult life, had expressed the desire to do something different, and Trevor had wanted to give her the chance. "Also"—he stuck a fingertip in his ear and scratched—"I ran into Suzanne Holloway today. She was quite satisfied with the dessert bar we set up for that black-tie affair last month, and she wants to use us for her daughter's wedding next Saturday."

"Not much notice."

"They want her married before she starts showing."

Grace puckered her modestly shaded lips. "I see."

Trevor leveled full concentration on the stack of baking catalogs that had come in yesterday. Flipping through one, he noticed that Grace was still lodged in place. "Is something the matter?"

"No," she said, and smiled at him. "There's someone here to see you."

Trevor put down the magazine and picked up another. "I wasn't aware of any appointments this afternoon."

"It's Cassidy, Mr. Monroe."

Trevor faked interest in the cookie cutters on page 17 of *Better Baking.* Grace seemed to be waiting for him to say something. He didn't, so she asked above the tangible hush, "Should I send her in?"

His head stayed bowed, and his voice held no emotion. "No, I'll be over in a few minutes." Grace remained unmoving and quiet, and he sensed her desire to ask questions. She finally turned and left him, closing the door behind her. Trevor unleashed the breath he'd been holding, put down the magazine, and swiveled around to stare through the large square window behind him. He drew his fingertips across his forehead as if he were trying to smooth out the lines, thinking he might be losing his mind. Cassidy had been consistently entwined in his thoughts since the funeral last week. He and Cassidy hadn't known each other long, yet he felt as if he'd known her all along. And the more time they spent together, the more he wanted to spend with her.

He swung around and lifted the photo of Brenda from his desk. His head was congested with questions, and he began throwing some of them out to God. *Are the feelings I have for Cassidy the real deal?* Maybe he was just looking for a quick replacement. *Shouldn't I wait a few years before getting involved with someone?* A three- to five-year interim following the death of a beloved spouse seemed honorable.

He placed Brenda's picture alongside the one of his daughters. Minutes later, outwardly composed, Trevor penetrated the adjoining office. Cassidy was wearing the white denim dress he'd become familiar with, and he thought she looked as beautiful as the white carnations in the vase on Grace's desk.

"Hi, Trevor," she greeted warmly, and set aside her drink. "I hope I haven't disturbed you."

✎❧

Cassidy smiled at Trevor. Her smile was not returned, and she was sure she *had* disturbed him. "Your establishment is quite impressive," she said, giving friendliness another try. Trevor's expression remained closed, as did his mouth. Uncomfortable with the gaping silence, she felt obliged to fill it. "That's a compliment coming from someone who'd rather have vegetables than cake, Trevor."

Grace chuckled nervously. Trevor shoved his hands in his pockets and rocked on his heels. "Thank you," he said flatly.

Grace shot him with a look of chastisement before turning to Cassidy and softening the emotion in her eyes. "Well, now, you didn't get to see everything." Grace talked rapidly, as if she were trying to rescue Cassidy. "How about an inside look at how we get the cream in the puffs?"

The stern creases streaking Trevor's forehead encouraged Cassidy to refuse. She smiled at Grace and said, "Perhaps another day." Cassidy grabbed her purse and hurried to the door.

"Well, you're always welcome to come by for a visit," Grace said, her heels clicking behind Cassidy. "Don't forget your muffin, love." The bag passed hands as the phone rang. "That might be the call I've been waiting for." She looked at Trevor as sternly as before, yet her tone held respect. "Why don't you see Cassidy out?" she said.

"That won't be necessary, Grace." Cassidy marched out of the room and down the hall, her glare stamped upon the steel door in front of her.

"Don't open that," Trevor warned gently as she was about to push the handle. "It's a fire exit. You'll set off the alarms."

Alarms were going off in Cassidy's head. What an idiot she'd been. She hadn't opened the door to her heart, but she had cracked a few of the windows by sitting with Trevor, holding his hand for a pair of nights, dishing out pieces of her life. And every night since, they'd stayed up late, talking at the kitchen table or on the front steps.

Cassidy had felt safe with him.

She was sure it had much to do with the type of person he was. Trevor was a quiet man. The way he handled his daughters, spoke his words, moved his body—all unassuming confidence and strength she admired. She remembered how initially she hated the unnerving way he could enter a room so inconspicuously. Now it was something she found utterly appealing.

And she had not ended up at his workplace today by chance. Wanting to see him and his business, she had come on purpose. During one of their late-evening conversations, Trevor had told her how hard he had worked to start Seconds and how it had flourished. She woke up this morning with the giddy urge to see it firsthand.

"Which way is out?" she bit into the air.

He turned into a narrow corridor and led the way. Stepping aside, he held the door. "These steps will take you down to the main floor. Make a left and go straight."

Her hand on the banister, Cassidy stomped down the first three stairs before stopping, turning, and lifting her gaze. Her fire-and-vinegar stare tangled with eyes too dark to read. Angry words steamed inside her, but the will to vent them disappeared under a cloud of disappointment. She had thought Trevor was different, but she returned to her original assumption: Trevor was a jerk, no better than Larenz and Minister . . . and nothing at all like Dunbar.

chapter twenty-five

Houston sauntered through the entrance of Time Out, and Trevor waved him over to the booth.

"I'll have what he's having," Houston instructed the waiter of the bar-and-grill restaurant. He slid onto the seat, looking to Trevor. "What are you having?"

Trevor lifted his glass. "Strawberry lemonade."

"Strawberry lemonade it is, then." Houston smiled at the young waiter.

Trevor passed Houston the small plate on the end of their rectangular table. "Help yourself to the appetizers."

Houston's grin looked hungry. "Grace would have a conniption if she saw me eating this stuff. Every meal I've had since our barbecue has been green, leafy, and taste-free. It's been fourteen years since my heart attack, and I'm still under surveillance."

Trevor hadn't given Houston's diet restrictions a thought when he ordered the appetizers. "When the waiter brings your drink, I'll order you a salad."

Houston laughed. "You'll be the one eating it." He forked two cheese-stuffed potato skins and several spicy chicken fingers onto his plate. "So to what do I owe the pleasure of this invitation?"

Trevor paused as the waiter served Houston's drink. When they were alone, he said, "I'm having strong feelings for someone."

Houston wiped his greasy fingers on a napkin and said, "Cassidy Beckett."

Trevor frowned. "How did you know I was talking about Cassidy?"

"I saw the way you were grinning like you'd taken a drug for it when you brought her to the barbecue." Houston chewed and swallowed. "Your children seemed to like her, too."

"It's remarkable how well the girls respond to her."

"So what's the problem?"

Trevor dunked a chicken finger into a miniature cup of honey mustard sauce and bit off a large chunk of the tender meat. He picked up his napkin and wiped his mouth. "I didn't expect to feel like this toward someone so quickly behind Brenda. I'm thinking that maybe the timing's all wrong."

"When would the timing be right?"

"I didn't just ask you here to stuff your mouth with food. You're supposed to help me figure that out."

"I see." Houston grinned. "Well, have you ever read Proverbs 3, verses 5 and 6?"

"Yes."

"Then there's the answer." Houston quoted a portion of the passage. "*In all thy ways acknowledge Him, and He shall direct thy paths.*"

Trevor smirked and leaned all the way back in the seat.

The waiter came and took their orders, then Houston counseled further. "Look, I'm not trying to be callous about what you're going through. But it would be easy for me to give my opinion, which, by the way, I will. However, my opinion pales in comparison to the Word of God. And the Word is where every problem and concern we have is addressed. All the answers are there. If you approach God with a sincere heart, He'll steer you down the right road, and you'll have peace about the situation."

"Proverbs 3, 5 and 6," Trevor repeated.

"That's where it's at. And remember, son, God's time is never early or late. And it's His pleasure to bless you. Now, I'm not saying Cassidy is, or isn't, that blessing. But wouldn't it be better to find out than live with the regret of never knowing what could have been?" Houston held Trevor's gaze. "We both know Brenda would want you to share all that love you have inside you with the woman of God's choosing. So"—he raised his glass—"here's to finding out who she is and to new beginnings."

✦

"These are for you." Trevor's tone was sensitive as he presented a dozen red roses. Cassidy was seated at the table and refused to glance at him as she ingested a thick greenish orange substance he suspected was something she had created with her juicer.

Cassidy stood and traveled toward the sink, gripping the glass. She had changed out of the dress she'd had on earlier and into faded jeans and a sweatshirt. Still, he thought she looked perfect. Wringing water out of the dishcloth, she finally spoke, a tart response Trevor felt he deserved. "You can put them with the others."

From where he stood, he searched the room. A vase of roses, twice as many as he was holding, decorated a corner of the counter. He marched over and removed the card lodged between two of the red blooms. It was none of his business who sent the flowers, but he wanted to know just the same. He opened the small envelope and read the card.

> C. C., *I'm always here for you.*
> *Dunbar*

Trevor tightened his hands, putting an unintentional dog-ear in the card from Dunbar as he contemplated pulling Dunbar's flowers out of the vase and putting his bouquet in their place. Resisting the childish urge, Trevor hunted for another vase. He filled it with water, stuffed his roses inside, and pulled each one up high so it looked as if there were almost as many in his presentation as there were in Dunbar's.

"There," he said, and whipped around to find he was alone.

Cassidy had gone to the basement, and he joined her by the washing machine, where she measured detergent. No tolerance for guessing games tonight, he asked, "What is the extent of your relationship with Dunbar?"

Cassidy replied with the iciness of an East Coast winter, "I'm not discussing that with you."

Trevor calmed himself with a deep breath. "Listen, I know I behaved poorly this afternoon." Creating emotional distance until he'd sorted through his feelings for Cassidy had seemed the best thing to do. Now he saw it for what it was. Stupid. One by one, Cassidy pulled towels from a laundry bag and pitched them into the rising water. He grasped her elbow with his fingertips, halting her work. "Today, when you showed up, I was shocked, and I wasn't ready for you or Grace or anyone to see how happy I was that you were there." She gunned a glance at him, then wriggled out of his clasp. "I realize I hurt you, and I'm sorry."

She threw in the last towel and slammed down the top of the machine. "Yes, you are sorry. As sorry and insensitive as most of the men I've gotten too close to." Moisture dampened the fire in her eyes. The washing machine grunted as it began washing the towels, and she looked at it instead of him.

Bothered by the hurt he saw, he longed to embrace her, but he settled for the next best thing and caressed her with a warm voice. "You still have open wounds, courtesy of Larenz."

Curtly but softly, she said, "My issue with Larenz is none of your business."

His tone lingered soft, too. "Mother Vale told me what happened with him—how he wanted sex, but that ever since you were a teenager, you wanted your husband to be the first man you gave yourself to." He cupped her chin and lifted her head, sinking his eyes into her watery gaze. "She told me how he deserted you in the park when you wouldn't submit to his demands." A pulse in Trevor's clenched jaw started jumping. He had never respected Larenz. Larenz was quick to gossip about the women of Charity Community whom he'd dated. Once, Trevor led him aside and told him it was inappropriate to spread details about his church sisters throughout the congregation. Larenz became defensive and stepped up in his face, but when Trevor didn't back down, Larenz stormed away.

"Aunt Odessa had no business telling you what happened between me and Larenz."

"She told me because she understood how much I care for you." He waited for her to respond. "Sky," he whispered deeply, his fingers still caressing her chin. "Look at me."

Cassidy hesitated, complied, then lowered her eyes again.

"I'm just as scared as you are," he confessed. "But I'm not going to let fear keep me from loving you." Her wide eyes, vulnerable and truth-seeking, rose and examined him. "That's right," he reassured her, "I love you." His gaze and voice never faltered as he said it again, then did what he could no longer resist. Clasping her upper arms, he leaned forward and pressed his lips to the gold stud in her ear. He slid his mouth along her warm cheek and kissed once . . . twice . . . a third time, drawing an invisible line to the corner of her lips as her breathing touched his face with the softness of a butterfly and her palm came to rest on the flat of his chest. He slowly pulled back so he could not merely feel but also read her reaction. She studied him, too, her eyes dreamy with wonder and welcome. It was the permission he needed to continue, and Trevor's heart soared as he drifted down and hovered over her mouth as if saying a prayer of thanks before relaxing his lips against hers.

As their lips parted, she whispered, "He's only my friend."

"What?" Trevor eased up his head, but kept her close.

"Dunbar. We're just good friends."

Trevor hugged Cassidy and smiled. He'd forgotten about Dunbar. And right now Trevor didn't want to think about him. His mind was on the woman in his arms, and he thanked God for bringing her into his life at the perfect time.

chapter twenty-six

Picnic tables draped with checkered cloths stretched across a large area of thriving green grass. There was enough food spread from table to table to feed all of Charity Community's families and then some.

Vivaca Audrey kissed Cassidy's cheek. "I wasn't sure you'd be here today."

"The last thing Aunt Odessa would sanction is me sitting at home moping in her honor," Cassidy said as Clement enveloped her in a giant bear hug. The pastor and his wife turned to Trevor and the children.

"Now, who do we have here?" Vivaca asked.

Brittney put her hand on Herbie's shoulder. "This is Herbie."

Brandi smiled and took hold of Herbie's hand. He was only a couple of inches taller than Brandi, although he was closer in age to Brittney. "He's our special guest," Brandi exploded.

"He's one of my SAFE boys," Trevor added.

Vivaca and Herbie had a similar medium brown skin

tone, and Cassidy had always thought Vivaca's brown eyes seemed to sing when she smiled. Vivaca clutched Herbie's face and gave him a kiss on the forehead. "It's nice to meet you, Herbie."

Cassidy smiled, a happy dance taking place in her heart as Herbie nodded.

Clement snaked his arm around Vivaca's shoulder, and the couple walked away to say hello to others attending the annual Charity Community Church picnic.

One of the youth workers announced it was time for games and all participants were to convene at the bottom of the hill in fifteen minutes. Sheila, a little girl the same age as Brittney, skipped up to her and said, "My dad's going to race with me in the father-daughter relay." Sheila skipped away.

Like watercolors on paper, shades of emotion washed together in Trevor's expression. There was hope that Brittney would ask him to be her partner, and fear that she wouldn't, and happiness when she looked up at him, her countenance timid, as if she thought that after so many months of pushing him away, he might now do the same to her. She asked no louder than the wind, scarcely blowing today, "Will you be my partner, Daddy?"

Cassidy continued to stare as Trevor heaved a sizable breath of hallelujah. "I'd love to be your partner," he said.

Brandi poked out her bottom lip, tugging at the hem of Trevor's long shorts. "What about me?"

Trevor scooped Brandi from the grass, and he and Brittney and Herbie walked out of sight. Cassidy looked sideways. She was under intense scrutiny.

"You seem different today," Lena remarked.

"Do I?" Cassidy let a mischievous smile form.

"Oh my goodness, something's going on," Lena squealed, and bounced up and down. "Tell me, girl. You better tell me."

Cassidy saw that her friend was a bounce away from combustion, and she decided to do the humane thing and put her out of her misery. "Trevor kissed me."

Lena grew bug-eyed. "He what?" she whispered, then screamed, "Get . . . out!"

Two church mothers and the president of the usher board stopped talking long enough to glare with suspicion.

"Will you shush?" Cassidy commanded. "You're drawing attention."

"Let's walk over here." Lena hurried to lead the way up and down a small embankment. "So when did all this happen?" Her smile was excited.

Cassidy slipped her hands in the pockets of her Bermuda shorts. "Last night."

"I can't believe you didn't call me." Lena frowned, but the lines quickly lifted. "Does this mean the two of you are a couple?"

Cassidy wasn't ready to divulge what Trevor had confided. She was struggling to process it herself. "We haven't talked about it," she said. This morning, while the girls were upstairs and Trevor and Cassidy found themselves alone in the kitchen for a few minutes, they talked about today's picnic-perfect weather and that time about five years ago when the picnic was turned into an indoor potluck because of heavy rain. But neither of them had mentioned last night.

~~~

"We would have won first place if Sheila's legs weren't so long." Brittney collapsed on the blanket. She lay on her back, arms and legs sprawled, a second-place ribbon in one hand. Trevor sat on the blanket next to Cassidy and leaned back on his elbows. "Next year," Brittney said, "I'll be a lot taller, and Sheila and her dad had better watch out."

Brandi's eyes were sincere. "What if Sheila grows more, too?"

Brittney smacked her hands to the sides of her head. "I didn't think of that."

Everyone laughed but Brittney. "I hope Sheila's not going to brag tomorrow during Kidpraise." She whined, "Daddy, do I have to go?"

Trevor sized up Brittney. It was time to talk. Cassidy had shared that Brittney was uncomfortable attending children's church but felt that Brittney should be the one to tell him why. "Britt, I'll listen to whatever it is you want to say. So can you trust me enough to tell me what it is about Kidpraise that upsets you?"

The little girl pushed up and sat on her bottom. "Yeah, I guess so."

Cassidy stood. "I'm going to fix our plates." She asked Brandi and Herbie, "Would you two like to help?"

"Yes," Brandi said, shooting to her feet, and Herbie jumped up, too.

"I'm here for you, Britt," Trevor said, and twisted one of her braids around his finger.

She seemed to be weighing his words or her thoughts

or both. "It's not the same since Mom's not there," she finally said.

The simple statement belted Trevor in the throat. What was wrong with him? How could he not have considered Brittney and Brandi's predicament? It had to be difficult for them to go to Kidpraise, the ministry their mother had served on. He slid closer to Brittney.

"Mommy used to let me help pass out the crayons and the glue sticks. Sister Peterson only lets the eleven-year-olds help. I wish I could still help."

"Brittney," was all Trevor could say, and he encouraged her to rest her head on his rib cage as he thought of a suggestion. "Sister Peterson's here today. Why don't we ask her if you can help some Sundays?"

"What if she says no?"

"What if she says yes?"

❧

Cassidy stood among a light crowd watching the annual Ping-Pong tournament play out between the trustees and the deacons. Trevor came up behind her, close enough to catch the gentle scent of her skin. His voice was a whisper. "Will you walk with me?"

She turned and took a step backward, adding inches to the space between them. "Where are the girls and Herbie?"

"Having their faces painted." As Cassidy bit her lip and hesitated further, Trevor did not show his disappointment.

"Okay," she ultimately said, and his heart felt light

again. She asked, "What did Sister Peterson say about Brittney helping in Kidpraise?"

Trevor smiled. "She said yes."

"Good," Cassidy said, and smiled her happiness, too.

Now that they could no longer be seen by Charity Community members, Trevor took Cassidy's hand. The two walked along a stony trail balanced with trees and wildflowers. A stream running parallel to the path gurgled, and above, birds whistled and cawed. Not ready to bring up last night, for fear of pushing, Trevor decided to let Cassidy start the conversation. As they approached the banks of the stream, she spoke. "I love walking."

"Brenda and I used to . . ." He let the words fade, supposing it might not be appropriate to go on and on about Brenda now that he'd declared his love for Cassidy. "I don't mean to talk about her so much."

"I don't mind. At the grief support meeting, the counselors advised us to talk about our loved ones." She kicked a pebble, and it scooted ahead. "Have you ever gone to any of the meetings?"

Trevor crouched low to the ground and tugged up a few blades of grass. "No."

"You should," she said. She watched as he twirled the blades between his thumb and index finger. "What were you going to say about Brenda?"

Trevor appreciated that Cassidy was okay with him talking about Brenda. He stood, releasing the grass. The strands floated to the earth and blended into a carpet of green. "I was going to say that Brenda and I used to take long walks." He reached for Cassidy and united their hands again. They watched the moving water. "I meant what I said last night," he said, turning and tipping his head to stare down at the beauty by his side. "I love you." The hope she would say the same bubbled over in his heart. "I'd like to get to know you a whole lot better. Spend more time with you. How do you feel about that?"

There was no stalling. "I've been through a lot, Trevor." She ducked her eyes, then raised them. "I don't want to get hurt again."

"I don't want you to get hurt." He stepped in front of Cassidy and captured her arms near the shoulders, his thumbs rubbing there, bunching the sleeves of her cotton shirt. "I'm not into games, Sky. I didn't say I love you because I didn't have anything else to say." He stroked her with a thoughtful gaze. "Before you decide a committed relationship can't work between us, go home and pray about it. That's all I ask. Will you pray about it . . . about us?"

A slow, bashful smile made an appearance on her lips while her eyes reflected the sincerity of her verbal vow. "Yes," she said, "I'll pray."

⁀♥

Putting her ears close to other people's business, Rave listened as Lena told Hulk that Trevor had kissed Cassidy. So incensed she couldn't swallow, Rave pitched her half-full plate of fried chicken, deviled eggs, and pasta salad into a nearby receptacle. She hung her thumbs in the back pockets of her low-rise jeans, her mind reeling with mischief. It was time to put an end to this Trevor-Cassidy crap, and she knew exactly how to do it.

Walking as if fire nipped at her heels, she stomped through a group of children nearing completion of a sand castle in the sandlot, obliterating their handiwork with one swift kick. She ignored their sad wails and the furious exclamations of one of the mothers. However, Rave paid close attention to the whistles of a group of volleyball-playing young men and slowed her steps to bask in the attention, assuming a hip-swinging stride that inspired old Brother Henshaw, reclining in a lawn chair, cataracts in both eyes, to sit up straighter.

Rave located the root of her anger. Shielded behind the body of a large tree, she opened her purse and wrapped her hand around the medium that would deliver the punishment she sought. She caressed the body of the black instrument, thrill shooting through her heart as she lifted the device. She steadied and aimed at the couple. Her finger on the spot that would ignite the blow, she whispered, "Bang."

chapter twenty-seven

Cassidy," Yaneesha screamed repeatedly as she entered the ladies' room, drowning out the voices of the after-church crowd. She banged on several stall doors before reaching the door Cassidy stood behind. Cassidy flushed the toilet and straightened her skirt. Still on fire from the sermon Pastor Audrey had just preached on over-coming the enemy, Cassidy unlocked the door and, without fear, stepped out to face Yaneesha to find out why she was behaving like a lunatic.

Yaneesha puffed her cheeks and huffed, "You knew I had feelings for him."

Cassidy observed Yaneesha. A band of sweat had turned the edges of her head glossy. "I don't know what or who you're talking about."

"Trevor," she snapped. "I told you I was going to be his wife." She threw her words. "You said you didn't want to be with anyone. You said you were satisfied not having a man. So why did you kiss him?"

"What?"

"Why did you kiss him?" she screamed, and held up a flyer-size sheet. Some of the sisters who had backed away eased forward to get a better view of the large color print of Trevor and Cassidy doing exactly what Yaneesha had alleged. The kiss had taken place during the church picnic by the stream. One brief kiss that was more Trevor kissing her than she kissing him. It must have lasted all of five seconds.

"Oh, my dang," one young woman drawled over Cassidy's shoulder, while another told Cassidy, "You go, girl."

Cassidy snatched the paper from Yaneesha. "Where did you get this?"

"Someone put them on all the cars in the parking lot." Yaneesha removed her glasses. The rage in her eyes turned to sadness, and tears marred her makeup. Cassidy felt the urge to apologize but wasn't sure of what exactly she would be apologizing for. She hadn't purposefully tried to hurt Yaneesha.

"Oh, come on, now," a deaconess said, putting her arm around Yaneehsa and leading her from the bathroom. "There are plenty of young men at this church who'd be interested in getting to know you . . ."

The ladies' room slowly returned to normal as a new set of women came in, unaware of the events that had just taken place. Cassidy threw the picture in the trash and washed her hands.

"It's not even funny," Cassidy said to Lena that night.

"Yeah, it is a little funny but only because you're taking it too seriously. Who cares that someone took a picture of you and Trevor and passed it out? Somebody's just jealous is all."

"It's creepy," Cassidy said, continuing the phone call that had started fifteen minutes ago.

"Only if you make it creepy. Now, if it happens again, I'd start to get concerned. Otherwise, just forget about it and go on with life." There was a pause. "So are you seriously considering coming off the Special Day team?"

"I'm serious. Mother Almondetta and Yaneesha aren't taking it to heart. When they aren't gossiping or eating cake, Yaneesha's in the bathroom doing who knows what. I'm doing all the work. Yaneesha has yet to visit one senior, whereas I've visited everyone on my list *and* hers. And now with Yaneesha acting all crazy because of this picture mess, I'm not sure I feel like dealing with her right now."

"I think we need to close this call with some prayer, girl."

"Sounds good. I need direction about this and . . . and what to do about Trevor," she admitted softly. It was difficult to believe she was actually open to praying about exploring a serious relationship with someone. But Trevor had altered her thinking. She knew his heart really wasn't anything like Larenz's or Minister's. Trevor had a pure heart. One that strived to please God. One that genuinely cared about others.

Lena prayed with confidence and authority, differently than Cassidy had ever heard her pray, evidence Lena was spending more time with the Lord. After Cassidy hung up with Lena, Cassidy reached for the Bible

Odessa had cherished, Cassidy's Bible now. Over the years, Odessa had highlighted many verses in yellow or pink, and Cassidy read a few of them now. She ended with *It is good for me to draw near to God* as she eased from her bed to her knees.

✑❧

Rave listened to the jingle of keys and the click of metal that foretold the opening of the front door. She smiled impishly, enjoying the shocked look on Dunbar's face as he walked in and found her sitting on his glass dining room table with her legs curled to one side as if she were in the palms of a photo shoot.

"How did you get in here?" he demanded. He tossed his briefcase onto the sofa and put his hands on his hips, pulling the front of his suit coat back on both sides.

"Your neighbor let me in," she said. "He found me waiting in the hall and asked if he could help. I told him I was your cousin, here for the weekend, and had forgotten the key you gave me." She slid a slim finger up her naked leg to the hem of her micromini. Dunbar's gaze followed the path. "That's when he said you and he had exchanged keys in case of an emergency and, well, you can guess the rest." The wicked smile continued. "I missed you at the church picnic yesterday. Where were you?"

"I had to do a funeral."

"That's too bad," Rave said, "because your girlfriend had a good time without you."

"I don't have a girlfriend," he snapped, removing his jacket. "Now, what do you want?"

"I want your help."

"Rave, it's almost midnight. I've been in Baltimore all day, where I preached two youth services. I'm really tired, so I need you to get to the point. And then get out," he said as politely as those words could be delivered.

"I want you to help me break up Trevor and Cassidy," Rave said.

Dunbar flashed her a tense glance, then marched to the kitchen and pulled a can of ginger ale from the refrigerator, popped open the top, and drank. He lowered the can. "There's nothing to break up."

"I believe the picture hanging inside your freezer says differently."

Dunbar opened the top half of the refrigerator and pulled out one of the sheets she had paid some kid in the neighborhood to attach to all the cars in the church lot.

"Now, now, Dunbie," she cooed, "I know you've seen the way Cassidy watches Trevor when she thinks no one is paying attention." She scooted from the table. "And the way she stands still and stops breathing whenever Trevor comes close to her." She walked slowly toward Dunbar. "And the way her eyes sparkle whenever Trevor laughs."

Watching Dunbar turn grim with jealousy pushed Rave close to giggles, but she pulled on her "let's get down to business" face and came to stand in front of him. She took the can from his hand, filled her mouth with soda, and swallowed. "I know you want to do Cassidy as much as I want to do Trevor," she said after the soda bubbles cleared her throat. "That's why we'd make the perfect relationship-sabotage team." She softened her voice. "Now, why don't we go into your bedroom and discuss things further?" she suggested, sliding her hands to his belt buckle and unfastening it.

☙

"Is Pastor Audrey in?" Rave never intended to wait for an answer. Dressed in a conservative gray suit and low heels with her hair spun into a back-of-the-head bun, she flounced past Francine's desk, creating a breeze that carried a small sheet of paper to the floor.

Francine halted her work at the PC. "You cannot barge in here, Sister Brown. Pastor has a jammed schedule today." She rose and thumped to the side of her desk.

Rave panned Francine from the top of her outdated hairdo to the toe of her old-lady pumps. "I'm sure Pastor Audrey can squeeze me in."

Clement opened the door of his office. "Francine, here's that document for review."

"I'll see to it right away," she said, her glare tacked on Rave.

Clement's scrutiny rested on Rave as well. "Good morning, Sister Brown."

"Pastor," Rave greeted, rolling her eyes at, then away from, Francine. "I've been informed that I *don't* have an appointment. However, there's a matter that requires *prompt* attention."

Clement took a moment and assessed Rave. He smiled at the other woman. "I have a few minutes, Francine. It's okay."

Rave perched on the edge of a desk-front chair, crossed her nylon-covered legs, and began speaking without affording Clement the luxury of taking his seat. "As you know, I'm a dedicated member of your flock." She folded her hands on her knee, observing her fingernails, palely polished, solely for this encounter. "I pay tithes, I attend our weekly Bible study, I—"

Clement silenced her with a wave of his hand as he sat behind his desk. "Let's open with prayer, Sister Brown."

Rave projected a smile, simply to appease Clement. "Of course, Reverend. Communication with the Lord should never be neglected. Will you be doing the honors?" Her pastor's face was a picture of no nonsense as he planted his elbows near the edge of the desk and merged the tips of his fingers and thumbs, forming a replica of a steeple. He shut his eyes.

Rave's remained wide open, the prayer falling on uninterested ears as she tinkered with the idea of kissing her shepherd. Not on the cheek like the church mothers and little girls did after Sunday morning service, but on the lips, like his wife would. Clement Audrey wasn't Rave's type, so broad and bald. Yet he did have his finer points. Smooth skin. Full lips. Generous hands. She fantasized about the pleasure those hands could bring.

"Rave!" Clement chopped the air with a heavy voice.

Rave jerked as if someone had whacked her with a paddle.

"That was the third time I said your name."

She covered the embarrassing moment with a synthetic grin.

"You were about to tell me why you needed to see me," he said.

"Yes, and I'm sure you don't mind me speaking to you frankly." Rave batted her lids. "The children and youth of this church and community are of the utmost importance to me," she began.

"Oh, I was unaware you served on any of our children or youth ministries."

Rave, remembering to exhibit her best behavior, caught a nasty retort before it escaped through her lips. She made a short succession of phony, high-pitched chuckles. "Pastor Audrey, you're so the comedian."

"I'm also very busy today, so if you could fast-forward to the crux of your concern, it would be a blessing."

Rave's tone quickly changed from melodic to slicing. "I question, as I'm sure you will, too, the appropriateness of two of your members' living arrangements."

Hands clasped and propped on his belly, Clement leaned back in his chair. "Of whom are we speaking?"

"Trevor Monroe and Cassidy Beckett." Rave said the names as if she were turning in two of America's most wanted. "They have heated feelings for each other, or did you not see the picture someone posted all over the church grounds yesterday?"

The room became quiet, and Rave felt like she'd opened a window and Pastor Audrey could see she was the culprit behind the production and distribution of the photo. She reached into her vault of smiles and found something sweet that would give her spirit the shine of virtue and continued in a demure tone, "I think it's unwise for Trevor and Cassidy to be sharing a house. Why, I've heard you preach many times how a man and a woman who are attracted to each other should not place themselves in a situation where it's difficult to say no." She leaned forward as if she were divulging top-secret information. "Trevor is a young man, Pastor, and it can't be easy for him to be without the luxuries of married life." She straightened, pulled a lace hankie from her purse, and pressed it to her lips as she whispered, "Well, I need not say more." Yet she did. "Satan will use a woman like Cassidy to lead Trevor straight into the snare of sin and shame. I'm sure you've heard of how she tried to seduce Larenz Flemings."

"As difficult as it may be to believe, Sister Brown, I try not to hear about everything that goes on around here."

"Well, I just hope it's not too late."

Clement resumed an upright posture and placed his folded hands on the desk. "Just what are you trying to say?"

Although the room was comfortably cool, Rave dabbed the perimeters of her face with her handkerchief, feigning fluster at being asked for specifics. "Trevor and Cassidy may already be indulging in"—she fell to a whisper—"*the works of the flesh.*"

"Okay," Clement said abruptly, and stood. "It's time to adjourn this meeting."

Fine! She'd said what she'd come to say. With an upward thrust, she stood, ironed the wrinkles out of her skirt with an open palm, covered Clement with one last disapproving look, and strutted the short distance to the door.

Trevor jumped into his truck and drove back to the church from Seconds. He needed to remind the custodial staff that the SAFE kids would be staying late tomorrow for a volleyball tournament, and they would not be able to clean the gymnasium until after four. The church parking lot was empty except for three cars, and Trevor grabbed a spot near the gym door and entered through the rear of the building. After speaking with Charlie Young, a member of the custodial crew who was the man to see when you needed information transmitted efficiently, he was hailed by Portia in the stairwell.

"I didn't know you were still here," she said.

"I had to come back. Are you finished for the day?"

"Yes," she said in a soft voice.

. "Then I'll see you tomorrow. Have a good evening." He held the door so she could exit first, but Portia remained where she was. Trevor let the door close. "Is something wrong?"

She brought her hand from the pocket of her skirt, transporting a small box. "I want you to have this."

He grinned. "Did I forget my own birthday?" he joked, but Portia's expression was no less somber. He applied more sincerity to the moment. "Would you like me to open it now?"

She nodded, and he opened the box and pulled out a whistle—a miniature basketball. "Hey, this is cool. Thank you."

"You're probably used to getting gifts from women all the time. Believe it or not, mine is from the heart."

"That's what makes it special . . . like you."

She gazed at him, and he hung her gift around his

neck. "God has a man for you, Portia. He's preparing him, right now, just as He's preparing you for him." Her eyes were broad with the shock that he was speaking with such frankness. "If you wait for *God's* man, you'll never be sorry you did." He kissed Portia's cheek as Clement rounded the stairs from the upper level.

She blushed and smiled. "Thanks, Trevor. You're a true brother in the Lord. A girl can't have too many of them in her corner." She pushed open the door and looked back at Trevor. "I'm going to wait for him," she promised, and walked away.

Loosening his tie, Clement slowly strode down the steps toward Trevor. "That Portia's a sweetheart."

Trevor glanced at the door she'd exited. "She is. Like my new whistle?" Trevor jiggled the device.

"Nice," Clement said, aiming his rear end at the steps. He designated his lap as a table for his briefcase and folded his hands. "Why don't you join me, Trevor?" Clement's gaze was resolute. "There's something we should discuss."

ℒ♥

"Are you telling me that Trevor's moving out of the house?" The man's deep voice barreled through the room.

Rave paraded around the office executing dance moves and watching as torches of desire burned within her companion's eyes. "That's right. You know as well as I do he's going to want to do the"—she made quotation marks in the air—"*righteous* thing."

As if there were an invisible leash between them,

the general practitioner swiveled his head and followed Rave's path. She leapt onto his desk and jiggled her hips with the finesse of an experienced stripper. "So you're getting your way this time," he said from the chair below.

"No thanks to you." Rave jumped to the floor, climbed onto his legs, and straddled him. She removed the stethoscope curled on his shoulders like a snake, hooked it on her neck, and listened to his heart.

"I told you, I'm not getting involved in your games," he said as she played doctor. "I was recently made a deacon over at Living Right Temple. I need to stay out of trouble"—he swallowed—"for now."

Rave gave him a powerful kiss on the mouth. She broke the kiss as harshly as she'd started it. "It took an eternity, but I convinced Dunbar that he should tell Cassidy how he feels about her." She giggled. "Dunbar and Cassidy—those two will be so cute together. They'll probably be engaged by the end of the month. Then Trevor will belong to me." The urge to rejoice in dance hit Rave. She returned the stethoscope to the place from where she'd taken it and scampered back to her desktop stage. She smiled down on Larenz Flemings. He groaned deeply and grinned widely with every twist and turn of her figure as she rejoiced out of her clothes.

chapter twenty-eight

Trevor paused at the front door. The sound of music had come to be one he looked forward to at the end of the day. A composition he didn't know by name but associated with Cassidy because she played it so often flowed from the front room, and he wanted to stand there longer and listen to the concert she made with her hands. But it was imperative that he talk with her.

He eased next to her on the piano bench, and the sleeve of his shirt caressed her bare arm. "I talked to the pastor today. He voiced concern about me living here given the fact that I have such strong feelings for you." Trevor hung his folded hands between his legs. He wasn't perturbed by Clement's counsel. It was confirmation of the message God had spoken into Trevor's spirit. "Honestly," he continued, "there's no reason for me to still be living here. I can't use my kitchen yet, but the rest of the house is fine, and we could've returned before now." Cassidy surveyed Trevor with startled eyes for a few notes of music, then looked straight ahead. "When

Mother Vale died so suddenly, I wanted to stay and make sure you would be all right. And"—he halted to get the words right—"I wanted to stay with you because I feel good when I'm around you. Anyhow"—he sighed—"the girls and I will be leaving tomorrow." Cassidy's fingers raced across the keys, and he thought her playing sounded harsh. "The children can visit whenever you like. I know they'll miss you."

The music softened some.

"I'll miss you, too."

The music slowed.

"As I've expressed before, I'd like to see you regularly, without the children." He cleared his throat, and the masculine rumble mixed with the flutter of piano notes. "I have to pick up the girls, so I'll see you later." He stood and kissed the top of Cassidy's head, giving her shoulders a kind squeeze while his heart beat with the faith that Cassidy would give him a chance. *I love her, Lord,* he prayed as he stepped outside and the sun greeted him again. *But I love You more, and I want to do Your will in every area of my life. Show me Your will. If it's not Cassidy, somehow I'll survive, but if she's the one for me . . .*

L❧

"Do you love him?"

Instead of answering the question, Cassidy asked one of her own. "What if he breaks my heart?"

Oliver Toby responded with warm feeling. "There's always the possibility of broken hearts when it comes to love. Love is as fragile as it is fierce." He cast a chuckle into the air. "Young lady, you are taking me back in time today."

"Are you thinking about Louise?"

He answered with a nod. "My sweet Louise. It was love at first sight."

"There's no such thing as love at first sight."

"I beg your pardon." Indignation wrestled with amusement on Oliver Toby's face, and Cassidy knew she was about to be *told*. "I'm not talking about strong desire energized by physical attraction. Although the first time I saw Louise, I thought she was hot stuff." He chuckled again. "But when I say I loved Louise the first moment I laid my eyes on her, I'm saying that I only wanted good for Louise. She immediately became a part of my prayers. Every day I asked God to bless everything she touched, to draw her closer to Him and give her the desires of her heart, whether that was me or not. That's what true love is: wanting the best for the other person."

They talked about Louise and love and Oliver Toby's approaching moving day until it was time for Cassidy to leave. She and Oliver Toby would have only one more Wednesday date, and she was taking him out for a special lunch. "I'll be here an hour earlier than usual," she promised, and kissed his cheek.

"I'll be in my best suit."

She was about to walk away, but he let go of his walker and tightly clutched her hand. "Not so fast."

This was one of the few times she'd witnessed his eyes cloud over with such a serious expression, and Cassidy paid close attention to what he was about to say.

"I want an answer." He repeated firmly, "Do you love him?"

"Don't you love me, baby?" Kregg parted Rave's hair at the base and nuzzled the skin of her neck while his fingers took a ride along her spine.

With a knuckle, she covertly bumped a tear from the corner of her eye. "You know I do," she whispered, sitting up and tugging the sheet around her body. She stepped over their clothes, a disheveled pile on the floor, and hurried into the cozy refuge of her bathroom.

Still wearing the sheet, she filled the tub with water as hot as she could stand it. She pushed the sheet from her shoulders, and it glided to the floor, while her burdens remained chained to her back. She stepped into the tub and submerged everything but her head beneath a layer of white bubbles. The water slid over her skin, fondling her in a way that felt decent and pure, so unlike the countless male hands that knew her as well as the water. But submitting her body to the hands was her drug, a hit that made her feel wanted, and sometimes loved, if only for a moment.

With her head against the tub, Rave shut her eyes and listened to the voices that bled from the past, staining her life with bitterness. She had been schooled early about the opposite sex.

"All men are dogs, Rave," her mother cursed.

"All men have needs, Rave," her father cooed.

An hour later, her skin scrubbed until it was bruised and sore in places, Rave wrapped herself in a towel and returned to the bedroom. A pile of pillows supported Kregg's head, and a blanket shielded him from his waist to his feet. His adoring stare clung to her as if she walked on water as she made her way to the nightstand, and she had to fight hard against the prickling urge to scurry back to the tub and wash some more. She picked up her earrings and put them on. "Why do you always rush to bathe after we're together?" he asked.

Perfect timing, Rave thought. Her cellular phone was ringing, so she didn't have to answer Kregg. She answered the phone instead.

Kregg grabbed the latest issue of *Shades of Women* magazine from the shelf built under the canopy bed while Rave took the call. When she was done, he snatched her towel and asked, "Who was that?"

She snatched back the fluffy cotton and groaned, "Brandonberg. He wants to see me right away."

ℒ♥

Silas Brandonberg monopolized the balcony doorway of his riverfront penthouse. Rave slipped under the arm he was leaning against the frame and stepped outside. The bright lights of the boats below twinkled as the stars above called back with a resplendent sparkle of their own. Rave viewed Silas with a long face. "Why can't you send someone else?"

"It's settled." He sipped brandy from a glass. "You're going to Phoenix. This is a groundbreaking case, and I want you there as an observer. I'm sure we'll be handling something similar in the future, and you can't be too prepared."

She sighed. "How long?"

"Three weeks . . . but plan for four."

Silas was the reason Rave had this job, and she

wouldn't do anything to jeopardize her position at Dougherty Wells, a prestigious city firm. Rave nodded okay and forced a smile at the tall, lean, tanned man. She'd met him in a South Street club. He was thirty years older than she, and she had been attracted and intrigued from the start. Silas wasn't the first over-fifty male, the first Caucasian, or the first senior partner to ask her back to his place. But Silas was all three of these things in one, and that won him a yes to his invitation.

Rave scooped Silas's glass from his hand and poured a swallow from it into her mouth, batting the idea of Phoenix back and forth in her mind. Maybe a change of scenery would be good. And a month wasn't that long. Actually, it was the perfect amount of time for Trevor to get Cassidy out of his system once she dumped him for Dunbar. Rave could start dating Trevor as soon as she returned. That thought pumped Rave's spirits, and she raced into the bedroom and belly flopped onto the king-size bed. She turned over, stretched her legs, and kicked the bedside photo of Lucretia Brandonberg, Silas's wife of thirty-odd years, face over, as the bird popped from the clock on the wall. It cuckooed that there was plenty of time for Rave to run home, pack her bags, and get to the airport for her morning flight. But first, Rave would show Silas how much she was going to miss him.

chapter twenty-nine

The meteorologists had been wrong about the Sunday before Labor Day. There wasn't an overcast spot in the sky. Cassidy strolled from the church, down the steps, and along the walkway, weaving through the crowd outside of the church.

"Cassidy," the voices of children rang above the chatter in the air. Cassidy swept a quick glance through the crowd and saw the whole-face smiles of Brandi and Brittney. She hurried toward them as they darted in her direction. Both ACES and SAFE terminated with the advent of the new school season, and with Trevor and the children typically attending the earlier service, Cassidy hadn't seen or spoken to Trevor or his children for two weeks. Cassidy realized it wasn't altogether what Trevor wanted, but she appreciated his giving her space to pray and meditate about the course of their friendship.

Casting aside any worry of getting her pants dirty, she dropped to one knee and received the girls as they thrust their bodies against her in an embrace. A burst of love that she could only describe as overwhelming exploded inside her as she drowned her senses in the dainty scent of powder and fruity-fragranced perfume.

"I miss you," Brittney said.

"Me, too," Brandi said.

"Your hair is nice." Brittney stroked a lock of Cassidy's hair. Cassidy had taken out her braids, and her shoulder-tapping natural strands had been pressed and curled into soft, wavy layers. Through unshed tears, Cassidy focused on the long navy legs standing in front of her. She stood, straightening her suit jacket.

"Hi, Trevor," she said. A familiar softness illuminated his dark eyes.

"Hi," he said with huskiness in his throat. He kissed her cheek, and she grew warm with approval.

Cassidy clutched the handles of her purse, holding the medium-size item in front of her thighs while eyeing the sisters, attired in white cotton with lace hems. Their white ankle socks were also frilled with lace. "Where'd you get the pretty dresses?"

"Grandmom Grace," they chanted in the same breath.

Like a sponge, Cassidy soaked up their smiles. "How are Grace and Houston?"

"They're fine," Trevor said. "I'll tell them you said hello."

Cassidy nodded and stretched her gaze toward the parking lot as awkwardness continued to stand between them.

"We didn't mean to keep you," Trevor said. "Were you on your way to your car?"

"Oh, no," Cassidy blurted, and felt a blaze of embarrassment. "I . . . I mean yes." She took a breath to avoid stammering into the next sentence. "I was on my way to my car, but you all aren't keeping me. It's really good to see you." She pinched her lips together, although she wanted to say more. So much more.

"Can we walk you to your car?"

Cassidy sighed into a smile. "Sure," she said, and they all moved ahead, Brittney and Brandi telling her about the recent back-to-school shopping trip with their daddy and Aunt Penny. Cassidy reached inside her bag and retrieved her car keys. As she aimed the key at the car door, Trevor gently pulled the keys from her fingers. He unlocked and opened the door, and she slid into the seat. The keys slipped from his grasp to hers, and he grabbed both daughters' hands and they all stepped back as she started the ignition.

"Bye, Cassidy," Brittney said, and Brandi's echo followed.

With a tight two-handed grip on the steering wheel, Cassidy elevated her chin and accepted Trevor's tender gaze by returning one made of the same feelings. She asked, "Will you and the girls come to dinner on Friday?"

✑❥

Neighbors swayed, glided, or rocked in porch furniture. Others sat on cemented steps. All chatted about much the same thing they had the evening before. The streetlamps clicked on, bouncing a shine off the parked cars as fireflies decorated the stagnant air with specks of

light. Trevor opened the door he'd been standing behind and walked onto the porch. He stood by the rail
separating the properties and small-talked with Harold
Purdue until Ms. Emma asked if anyone cared for a slice
of pecan pie. Trevor and Cassidy politely thanked her
but refused. Harold followed Emma into the house,
saying, "Put a scoop of vanilla ice cream on mine,
honey bun."

Trevor studied Cassidy. Her smooth hair was pulled
into a ponytail, and small gold hearts dangled from her
ears. He walked over and sat next to her as she rested
on the wicker sofa with her legs crossed at the ankles
and her arms crossed at her stomach. He had insisted
she come outside and relax while he and the girls
washed, dried, and put away the dishes. His daughters
were still inside, Brittney with the broom and Brandi
with the dustpan, tackling the kitchen floor.

"Dinner was excellent," Trevor praised.

Cassidy glanced at him, and a smile quivered
through her eyes. "Thank you."

Trevor watched a spider bungee jumping from the
roof. "I'll cook for you next time." He wondered, would
there be a next time? He wanted to ask, but he let the
quiet spill and puddle around them.

As the sky grew darker, Cassidy unfolded her arms
and placed her hand on the sofa close to his. She whispered, "I'm glad you came tonight."

No mention of the kids. Just him. She was glad *he*
came tonight. Trevor jumped with joy inside himself,
and somehow he kept the barbed wire around his cool
and refrained from cradling Cassidy close and kissing
her. Trevor had decided he wouldn't share anything

that intimate with Cassidy again without knowing how she felt about him. As much as Trevor relished kissing and holding Cassidy, he wanted more. He wanted a relationship. He wanted Cassidy's heart.

"Wait here," he instructed, and hurried down the steps.

"Where are you going?" she called.

"Watch the girls for me. I'll be back soon."

⟋⟍

Talk and laughter fluttered through the kitchen as Cassidy served Brandi and Brittney fresh strawberries. Trevor returned with Natasha Audrey, and the jeans- and T-shirt-covered teen threw down her knapsack and joined the children at the table as comfortably as she would have in her own home. "I'm going to be hanging out with you for a while."

"Can you do my nails like last time?" Brandi asked.

Natasha pointed at her denim knapsack. "I've got my gear."

Preparing a dish of fruit for Natasha, Cassidy questioned Trevor, "What's going on?"

"Meet me outside in five," was all he revealed, swiping a strawberry from Brandi's plate.

"Hey!" Brandi objected.

"You can have one of mine," Brittney offered him instead, an arm spiked and her head back so she could find his mouth.

Trevor plucked the berry from Brittney's fingers with his front teeth. "Five," he reminded Cassidy, gesturing the number with his hand while backing from the room.

Cassidy probed Natasha's face for answers as she handed her a filled plate. The teenager shrugged. "Don't ask me. He just showed up at my house and asked my parents if I could babysit tonight."

*

"Where are we going?" Cassidy demanded as Trevor took Germantown Avenue into the Chestnut Hill section of the city.

"We're almost there."

"Where's there?" she wanted to know.

He responded by cranking up the volume of the radio.

"This is it," he said three minutes later, and parked the Expedition.

"This is a basketball court." Wariness entered her voice. "A deserted one."

His voice was easy. "Get out of the car, woman."

Frowning but obeying, she inquired, "Why did you bring me out here?"

"To play ball," he said as they sauntered toward the court. He tossed her the basketball he'd removed from the rear of the truck. She made no effort to catch it, and it rolled between her feet to center court. "I thought you said you knew how to play," he bantered, running after the ball.

"You really expect me to play?"

He dribbled in place. "I really do."

"In this skirt?"

"The skirt won't matter"—he rotated the ball on the tip of his finger—"if you're good."

"I'm good. Perhaps a little rusty because it's been a long time, but good."

"Show me." He passed her the ball. Her reflexes sharp, she seized the pumpkin-colored ball with open palms.

"Impressive. Show me more," he challenged.

She began bouncing the ball, never taking her eyes off her opponent. Beneath the glow of the moon and court lights, they played, she in white canvas sneakers, a blouse, and a long loose skirt, and he in black leather Nikes, a baseball shirt, and blue jeans. He won the first game by so many points they stopped counting, and she the second, because he went easy on her. Trevor returned to his vehicle, snatched two bottles of water from a small cooler, and they retired to the bleachers.

"This is crazy," she commented.

"What is?"

"Playing ball at this time of night." She twisted the white cap off the bottle.

"It's only nine-thirty." He drank from his bottle.

"It seems later."

He rested his elbows on the tiered bench behind. "It's fun, though, isn't it? Doing something you usually don't. Experiencing it with someone you love." He hit her with a sideways glance, then set aside the bottle and clamped the basketball between his hands. He stood and bounced the ball, then galloped to the net and made a layup. Cassidy squeezed her bottle, and it made a popping sound as Trevor charged to the basket with the ball again. It circled the rim and paused, as if deciding whether to fall through the hoop or not. The ball eventually rolled out, and Trevor caught it and jogged back to the bleachers. He placed the ball on the ground and knelt on the bench below her, flattening his hands on the metal to the left and right of her skirt. "Do you know when I started loving you?"

She shook her head no.

"The moment you crashed into my chest in that bathroom. All I wanted to do was protect you, keep you from falling and hurting yourself. I didn't know how to express it then, but it bothered me when I saw how upset you were about that whole thing."

"That's why you were laughing at me."

"I wasn't laughing at you." He grinned. "Well, maybe a little, but only because you were trying to be so tough." Cassidy had folded her hands in her lap, and Trevor placed his hand over the clasp. "I've been praying about you and me," he said. "What about you? Have you been praying?"

"Yes," she answered gently. "I told you I would." She stared into Trevor's eyes. "I saw your heart that day we met in the bathroom. I saw how sincere you were about keeping me safe."

"And what do you see now?"

She slipped her hand from beneath his and laid it along his face. "A man in love with God . . . a man in love with me." She spoke softly. "I love you, too."

"Then marry me," he whispered.

$\mathscr{L}$♥

"Married?" Rave snorted. Kregg's facts had to be wrong. "Where did you hear such an absurdity?"

Rave envisioned Kregg smiling as he said, "Straight

from the mouth of the future groom. I'm going to be the best man."

"Are you telling me Trevor asked Cassidy to marry him?"

"Yeah, babe, he proposed last week. Isn't that great?"

Rave's brain could barely keep up. "Cassidy's not dating Dunbar?"

"What are you talking about?"

"Never mind," Rave said impatiently as vivid streaks of red marred her vision. She felt as if she'd been slapped in the face by the cold hand of betrayal, and standing there holding the phone to her ear, she was suddenly more sad than irate. "Why didn't you tell me this before now?" Not that she could have done much here in Phoenix.

"I've been trying to reach you." Kregg's words were edgy. "Why haven't you returned my calls?"

"I've been busy."

"Too busy for our relationship?"

The question went unanswered. Rave was thinking about Trevor and wondering where she'd gone wrong. Why hadn't Trevor wanted her? Every man she'd ever come on to had wanted her. Even dull Dunbar, although he had not taken her, had wanted her. The heat in his eyes had testified to that. Rave plopped on the edge of the king-size hotel bed. Kregg was talking, but she wasn't listening, her mind a swirl of voices and memories that seemed only as far away as yesterday.

"Don't be afraid, Rave baby," her father mumbled as he slipped into bed with her. It was the first of his middle-of-the-night visits. She was nine.

"Don't you tell nobody about this, Rave," her father's

best friend whispered, holding her down on his lap. She was twelve then.

Following her parents' divorce, her mother's boyfriend came to her right before the start of her sweet-sixteen birthday party. "I want you, Rave," he whispered, the stench of alcohol and tobacco on his breath. "I want to make you feel good." Nothing he did to her that afternoon made her feel good.

"Hey, babe, you there?" Kregg's deep voice rumbled.

Rave rolled her teary eyes. "I'm here."

"How much longer will you be in Phoenix?"

"I don't know." Four weeks had already turned into more. "Nothing about this case has been predictable."

"I want to see you. How about I fly out this week, stay a few days?"

"Sorry, Kregg, this week's no good." She switched the phone to the other ear. "I have to go. I'll call you soon."

Housekeeping had not been to her room, and Rave slid between the tousled bedding. She pulled the sheet above her head, banishing the light that reminded her it was a beautiful day outside. Her face down, she pumped her sorrow into a pillow. Wave upon wave of agony coursed through Rave, and she cried louder, longer moans in a desperate attempt to survive the pain, although she was unsure whether she wanted to live.

chapter thirty

The next months passed quickly, bringing autumn and winter. Spring arrived, and the following weeks were met with many dreary, rainy days, but Cassidy was too excited about her upcoming wedding to be bothered by the weather. As night nestled in and today's showers ended, cool dampness lingered in the April air. Cassidy hugged herself tighter, sponging warmth from the over-size sweatshirt she wore. She'd stepped outside while Trevor took Kendall McBride's phone call. Cassidy had yet to meet Brittney and Brandi's godmother. Since Kendall had been so close to Brenda and still had a bond with the children, Cassidy hoped that she and Kendall would become friends.

Trevor came out onto the deck and stood behind her. He looped his arms around her center, and Cassidy immediately leaned into him. "How's Kendall?" she asked.

"She's in the hospital."

Cassidy frowned with concern. "What's wrong?"

"She has pneumonia. She'll be okay, but she won't be coming to our wedding."

"Oh, no," she said in earnest. "I'm sorry. We'll have to send her a DVD, then, all right?"

"Sounds like a good idea."

"I wish Aunt Odessa was here to see our wedding." At times, it was difficult not to feel sad when she thought of her aunt. But she found comfort in remembering all the wonderful times she and Odessa had shared.

"She'll be there . . . in our hearts," Trevor said.

"I can't wait to see Oliver Toby." Cassidy smiled. The professor was flying in from Denver to walk her down the aisle next Saturday.

"Maybe we'll be going to his wedding next."

Cassidy giggled. Oliver Toby was doing fine in his new home and had become good friends with his elderly neighbor, a widow named Ramona.

Cassidy rubbed Trevor's arm. "You know what I was thinking before you came out here?"

"What's that?"

She pointed to a space some thirty feet away, adjacent to a wall of trees that separated Trevor's property from his neighbor's. "I'm going to put an herb garden there." She'd observed enough of Odessa's greenthumbing over the years to feel confident she would be successful at managing something small.

"I think you'd look sexy in a straw hat and overalls, out there tilling the land."

Cassidy nudged him in the rib cage, and Trevor tightened the embrace.

"I love you so much, Sky," he said, the husky whisper gently buffeting her neck.

She smiled. "You still haven't told me what that nickname is all about."

He placed his lips against her cheek, and she felt him smile. "Your blue bathrobe reminds me of the sky at dusk. And like the sky, you're beautiful . . . and expansive . . . and limitless."

"Expansive and limitless," she repeated with an air of question.

"You're expansive," he explained, "because you have a lot of love in your heart. And you're always showing it to your students"—he pecked her cheek—"and to the seniors at the center"—another peck—"and to me and the girls."

Consciously floating on his cloud of flattery, she grinned wider. "And limitless?"

"I see you as a limitless woman. One that can reach any dream she climbs toward."

"Tell me more," she purposely cooed.

"Whenever I see you in your robe, it just makes me want to . . ." He whispered the remainder of the sentiment in her ear. Cassidy's mouth fell open, and she turned and gave him a featherweight punch in the chest. Trevor drew her closer, their bodies becoming a solid line, and she shut her eyes, reveling in some of the fun memories they'd made since Trevor proposed to her last summer.

They'd attended twelve premarital counseling sessions and planned a church wedding. They had their first Thanksgiving and Christmas and Easter dinners together. And they'd refashioned the master bedroom from corner to corner. Early on, Cassidy had reservations about moving into the home Trevor and Brenda had shared for the second half of their marriage. Cassidy thought it would be best if they started out fresh, bought a new house, a place of their own. Trevor had no objections. He was the one who initially broached the subject by asking if she wanted to purchase something new. He was even willing to move into her house, if that's what she wanted. They had spent several weeks looking at real estate options, but they hadn't found anything as elegant as Trevor's titanic vintage home. And when it all came down to it, neither she nor Trevor wanted to relocate too far away from the girls' school, his place of business, or the church they loved. So Cassidy decided she'd be okay moving in with Trevor and the children. Trevor had made it easy for her to come to that decision by giving her the clearance to redecorate the house as she pleased.

She leaned back and looked up at him, glimpsing the starless sky. He placed a mild kiss on her mouth. Ready for more, she molded a hand to the back of his neck, rose up on her toes, and reached for another kiss as he pulled back and whispered, "I want you to go home."

Her heart echoing her wish to remain close, she leaned forward and nibbled at his throat. He clutched her shoulders and with the lightest touch, pushed her away. The warmth of passion became replaced with the chill of confusion until Cassidy looked into the amorous depths of Trevor's eyes. Instantly, she realized he wanted to kiss as much as she did, and he wasn't refusing her because he didn't desire her . . . but because of how much he did. He dusted his hand along the length of her face. "Just eight more days, and we won't have to say good night."

With the same flirtatiousness she'd been feeling all evening, she tilted her chin up and rasped, "Then I can have all the kisses I want."

"Wherever you want," he added, and she blushed, but inside her heart, like every bride-to-be, she looked forward to the unbridled intimacy she would share with her new husband. They would be honeymooning in Jamaica, but their flight wasn't until Sunday morning, so they decided to spend their first night at home. Trevor had been sweet enough to sleep in one of the extra bedrooms so that they could christen their new room—and bed—together. Cassidy knew exactly what she was going to wear on her wedding night. At her bridal shower, Lena had given her a lacy-at-the-top, sheer-at-the-bottom nightgown. It was delicate yet sexy, and Cassidy was sure Trevor would think the same.

She lifted her eyes to his. She was the center of Trevor's attention, and she blushed as if he could see what she'd been thinking. "I should get going." She scooped her purse from a celery-green patio table, a match to four chairs and a recliner. Trevor reached for her hand and laced their fingers, and they walked to her car, sitting in a driveway that curved around the back of the house to a one-car garage.

"Call me when you get to Lena's so I know you're in safely," he said.

Cassidy had sold the house she'd inherited from Odessa and moved in with Lena two months ago. "Don't forget—have Brittney and Brandi ready by ten." The sisters would be their flower girls, and they had a final fitting with the seamstress in the morning along with bridesmaids Portia, Shevelle, and Penny and maid of honor Lena.

"They'll be ready."

"What time are you picking up Herbie?" she asked. Trevor was taking their ring bearer shopping for shoes tomorrow. Her question seeping into the silence, about to go unanswered, Cassidy gently called, "Trevor," her hand balled as she tapped him on the forehead. "Where'd you go?"

He blinked abruptly, as if he'd landed back on earth from a fantasy. "I was thinking about Kendall. I wish she could make the wedding." He smiled. "When you and Kendall do finally meet, I'm sure you're going to like each other."

Cassidy couldn't determine why, but a crumb of uneasiness suddenly fell into her prewedding happiness. She fished the unwelcome tidbit out before it could settle, and smiled up at Trevor.

❧

A tower of empty pizza boxes, twenty deep, sat against the wall in the recreation room of Kregg's town house. The trash can was full of soda cans and dirty paper plates. The speakers pumped out a steady thump of urban praise while an intense pool match progressed between Clement and a twenty-five-year-old named Linwood. All the other men were standing around, quiet as a surveillance team, eager to see if the unbeatable Linwood would finally be brought down by the pastor.

A few minutes later, Linwood emerged undefeated,

and the pastor asked the men to join him upstairs in the living room. Some of the thirty-five men in attendance seated themselves in the burgundy-wine leather sectional and matching chairs. Others sat on folding chairs that had been borrowed from the church, on stools carried in from the kitchen, or on the carpeted floor. Kregg came over and gave Trevor, seated on a leather chair, a white envelope. He gripped Trevor's shoulder. "Congratulations from all of us, man," was all he said, and stepped away.

Trevor pulled out a brochure and read the bold writing on the front flap aloud. "Welcome to the Pocono Mountains."

"We all chipped in," Houston said, "and got you and the soon-to-be missus an all-expense-paid week at one of them all-inclusive resorts. It's good for three years."

"Thanks." Trevor smiled and took another glance at the brochure. "I appreciate it. I appreciate this entire afternoon." Trevor thought he was coming over to help Kregg and Hulk install new flooring in the kitchen. Instead, he found this bunch. Nearly all of them were members of Charity Community's Men Movement— Men of Purpose. They usually met two days a month, one for biblical exploration and fellowship, the other for community service. Last month the men put their time, talent, and money together and painted fifteen units of a homeless shelter. Later this month they would sponsor an indoor fair for the children's wing of a hospital. A back-to-work clinic for former prison inmates would be hosted by Men of Purpose next month. With gratefulness in his eyes, Trevor regarded his bachelor party participants. "Thanks," he verbalized again.

"Well, we're not done yet," Clement said.

"Time for the stripper," Durante Jackson called out, and everyone laughed.

"Here's something from me and Vivaca." Clement gave Trevor a large box wrapped with gold paper and tied with white string that met at the top, forming an artistic puff that resembled a flower. "Vivaca insisted on all the frills," he said, backing away and shaking his head.

Trevor removed the decoration and found three books on marriage. "Thanks, Pastor," he said, and passed them around so everyone could get a closer look.

Sam Myricks read the blurbs on the back cover of one. "Maybe a book like this could help me figure out Leandra. She's been whining about how I don't understand her needs." He added sheepishly, "Especially in the bedroom."

Clement scooted forward in his seat and said, "Listen, fellows, I had planned to keep this afternoon light, but since it's just us men, there's something I'd like to say, if it's okay."

Everyone nodded or murmured for him to continue.

"Well, I want to talk to my married brothers first." His gaze fell on Sam. "Perhaps what I'm about to share will help."

Sam nodded that he was paying attention.

"Last week," Clement said, "I had a young lady come to see me. She told me she loves her husband but she hates having sex with him."

One of the men let out a long whistle.

"As the young lady and I spoke further, she confided, 'He doesn't know how to touch me, and when I tell him

how I'd like him to touch me, he gets angry.'" The room
was still. "This is not the first woman to come to me or
Vivaca or one of our counselors with the same heavy-
hearted burden. So if I may, I'm going to give you gen-
tlemen a scripture that will help you." Every eye was
alert. "Ephesians 5:28," Clement said.

"So ought men to love their wives as their own bodies,"
Hulk said.

"It's really as plain as the nose on your face. My friends
and my brothers," Clement said with calm authority,
"you don't rush into bed, grope the most sensitive areas
of your wife's body, and expect her to be turned on.
Listen," he told them, "hold your hands up for a moment." All the men held up their hands. "These hands
have power . . . the power to encourage a woman to
please you, if you know how to use them the right way."

"Power," Sam boasted. "I like the sound of that." He
pounded hands with the man next to him.

"Now, hear what I'm saying, guys. I'm not talking
about possession or dictatorship or manipulation. I'm
talking about preparation and presentation." Clement
leaned forward. "Let me break it down into language
you all can understand."

"Break it down, Preacher," Houston supported.

"Football," Clement said. "We all love the game. I
know because Sunday morning male attendance drops
drastically the closer it gets to the Super Bowl." A few
couldn't look Clement in the eye. "Now, when that
Sunday game is on, it has your total focus. Amen?"

"Amen," deep voices responded.

"Well, you guys need to love your wives with the
same devotion and passion. There are four quarters to a

game. Tell me why you can't dedicate the same amount of time or more to making love to your wife." The eyes of some grew large, suggesting they couldn't believe the pastor was going there. Others chuckled because the pastor did go there. "Most of you all in here are younger than me, and you mean to tell me you can't hang for four quarters? And how about a little pregame activity?" Clement picked on one of the chucklers. "Joel, how do you approach your wife?"

"I usually grab her butt and tell her it's time to get busy."

"Crude, man," someone said.

Clement's focus remained on Joel. "Is your wife receptive to that type of invitation?"

"Sometimes. But she usually gets an attitude," he admitted.

"So why don't you change your game plan?" His gaze shifted from man to man. "Start with a light touch to her face or a gentle squeeze of her hand. Hug her without mauling her. Kiss her without shoving your tongue down her throat. And by all means, massage her back or rub her feet." Clement taught on, "Love your woman *softly*, brothers. Would you like it if your wife grabbed you the same way she might grab that last pair of shoes in her size from the sale table?"

"Ouch," Durante said, bringing his legs together.

"Your wife's body is just as sensitive. She needs you to handle her the same way you want to be handled."

"What do you do when she doesn't want to be handled?" Bryce Stanford pretended to be his wife and stood up with his hands on his hips. "I've been taking care of these kids *all day* and I'm too tired."

There was laughter, but Clement was serious. "What have you done to ease her load?"

Bryce shrugged and took his seat.

"Did you do the dishes for her? Did you run her a bath?" Giving none of the married men the benefit of the doubt, he aimed the rhetorical questions, like football passes, around the room. "Did you let her sit and read while you put the kids to bed? When's the last time you opened your mouth and told her how much you appreciate her? Said I love you? I guarantee if you did a couple of those things consistently, she'd respond differently."

"What do you do when she says she's bored?" a young man named Marcelle asked.

"You've only been married a year," Bryce pointed out.

Marcelle looked to his pastor.

"If you approach the same team with the same strategies every time you play them, you're going to have difficulty. You've got to change the game plans. Women love variation, so throw a new play in from time to time." All the men were quiet and attentive. "Look, brothers, I surely don't claim to know all the answers. But there are dozens of books on the market, many of them Christian-authored books, on sex and romance and intimacy. The three go together, you know. You can't have one without the others and expect your wife to be satisfied."

The men signaled acceptance of Clement's message with nods.

"So do you have some words of wisdom for us single men?" someone asked.

Someone else moaned, "Don't get him started, man."

"Well, I'm going to get started," Clement said, his voice beginning to rise like it did when he was in the pulpit. "I've got a homework assignment for you single brothers who label yourselves men of God."

"Take your time, now, Preacher," Houston said.

"I want you to go home, get on your knees for more than three minutes a day, and ask the Lord who you're supposed to be dating"—Clement looked at no one in particular—"because I'm sick of some of you running around the congregation from woman to woman like you don't know no better."

"Some of the women in the church are chasing *us*," Durante was quick to say.

And Clement was quick to jump into Durante's gaze. "The chase will stop if you plant your feet firm in God's Word, look that fast sister in the face, and tell her and the *devil* in her to get away from you."

Amens echoed from several directions.

"Let me tell you how God operates," Clement said. He was in sermon mode now, voice charging up and down in all the right spots and eyes focused on the congregation. "God doesn't need to have you experimenting with a bunch of different females to see which one is right for you." Joel handed Clement a paper towel so he could wipe his brow. Clement said, "Thank you," and surged on. "Our God already knows who you need, and He's just waiting for you to get serious and consult with Him about who she is. And until the Lord reveals her to you, you should be fervently asking God to get you ready to be the kind of husband she's going to need." Clement creased the towel and used it. "While you're waiting, you should be fasting and praying for her, although you don't know who she is yet. Now, I'm not saying that once you marry her, everything is going to be perfect. But if you've prayed and got the right one, at least you'll have the peace of knowing that no matter what the problem, this is the one God gave you, and He doesn't make mistakes." The volume of his tone decreased but not the sobriety. "And, my good brothers, please stop getting *caught up* in the packaging. Some of you are so focused on looks only, you gonna live out hell on earth because of it. Just because a gift is wrapped in what you think is perfect paper doesn't mean that what's inside the box is good for you. So you better take time and get to know the character of that woman before you run with her to the altar. Proverbs 31 says what?"

Trevor answered, *"A woman that feareth the Lord . . . shall be praised."*

"We're not to base a woman's value on the size of her body." Some of the men started laughing. "I'm serious, fellows," Clement said, ending the laughter. "Not too long ago, I asked a brother who came to me for advice to name some of the qualities he was looking for in a wife. The dummy started out by telling me he wanted her to be at least a D-cup. I said, 'Young man, you better hope she can get a *prayer through* in the time of trial and tribulation.'" Clement met as many eyes as he could with one sweep of the room. "I'm the man I am today because Vivaca intercedes in prayer for me."

"But for real, Pastor," Durante voiced, "the woman you marry needs to have physical attributes that turn you on."

Clement responded with a smile. "Yes, she does. And that's how good God is, son. God will give you a woman who you will see as the most beautiful woman in the world, while the rest of us would rather scratch our eyes out than look at her." All the men laughed now, including Clement, as he motioned for them to stand and for Trevor to take a seat on a folding chair. Moments later, Trevor was in the center of a huddle, and he felt the firm pressure of Clement's hand resting on his head. Some of the others stacked their hands on Trevor's back and shoulders, then Clement asked God's blessings on Trevor and Cassidy and the family they would form next weekend.

Later, as Trevor drove away from the party, his new books on the seat beside him and the brochure tucked inside the glove compartment, he continued to pray. He believed he had been a good husband to Brenda. He wanted to be all that and more to Cassidy. He pulled his SUV into the Willow Grove Mall parking lot. An hour later, Trevor came out of the complex with shopping bags full of candles, bath and body items, and classical music, some of the ingredients he would use to fill next Saturday night with memories that would make Cassidy smile for the rest of their marriage.

ℒ❧

Strain lined Cassidy's face. After months of reprieve, the nightmare had returned. Cold sweat on her chest and back glued her nightshirt to her skin. Cassidy left the damp short-sleeved shirt on, though, too weary to get up and change.

Tears pushed against her closed eyes, demanding freedom.

Not tonight. There would be no tears tonight. Tears would make her eyes puffy and red. She could not have puffy and red eyes tomorrow on her wedding day.

The wet nightshirt gave her a chill that reached her bones, and Cassidy pulled the covers tighter around her. Although her eyes were wide open, she could hear the piercing pleas of the little boy fighting to keep his head above the water. Gripping the bedding, Cassidy wondered if the dream was in any way related to the terrible thing she had done to her baby. A few times, she had come close to telling Trevor about her child. Once, during a premarital session, the minister encouraged them to speak about anything that might have the potential to register as a problem somewhere down the road. Cassidy's mouth had stayed tightly closed. After all, didn't the Bible say to forget those things which are behind and press toward the new?

Cassidy turned onto her stomach, keeping the covers close to her frame as she pondered what good could come out of taking old baggage into her life with Trevor. It would be best for their future if she remained silent about the baby.

"*Forgetting those things which are behind,*" she muttered several times as sleep drifted near and lulled her into a cradle of calm.

chapter thirty-one

Trevor sat in the church parking lot and listened as Luther Vandross sang one of the songs that had been performed at Trevor and Cassidy's wedding. The last note rang from Luther, and Trevor turned off the radio, got out of the truck, and walked inside the church. He signed in with Clement Audrey's secretary, Francine, and took a seat in the small waiting area outside of the pastor's office. Two months ago, when Clement married him and Cassidy, Trevor never imagined that he would be in need of a session with his pastor.

"Are we still on for lunch?" Francine loaded a new bundle of paper into the copy machine as she talked with Barbara, the secretary from across the hall who handled the Sunday bulletins, all incoming announcements, and general church business. Francine and Barbara finalized their lunch plans before Barbara dashed from the room to answer her phone. Midway through the return trip to her desk, Francine glanced at Trevor. "Are you sure I can't get you a cup of coffee?"

"I'm sure, Francine. Thank you." Trevor patted his shoe against the carpet, every nerve in his body unraveling while he sat and waited for his appointment with Clement Audrey. He closed his eyes and willed himself to think of something pleasant. Something . . . anything other than the reason he'd scheduled this meeting. Every time he gave himself permission to meditate on the reason behind this meeting, his stomach grew fists and swung punches.

Clement opened the door of his office, and a young man and woman Trevor didn't remember seeing before walked out. The man had quiet but stern eyes. The woman's eyes were filled with tears. "Come on in, Trevor." Clement stepped aside.

Trevor glanced at the pastor and entered the office.

"Have a seat." Clement gestured to the chairs in front of his desk.

Trevor eased onto the nearest chair, keeping a firm grip on the leather arms. "I'm not sure where to start."

Clement smiled lightly. "Prayer is always a good place." The pastor prayed as the Spirit of God led him to pray, and some of Trevor's nervousness receded.

Clement leaned back. "How can I help?"

"Cassidy and I are having a . . ."—he cleared his throat, yet spoke lower—"a marital ministry problem." Trevor briefly rubbed his left ear as if that might silence his pulse, a steady drumbeat playing deep in his head. Otherwise, the office was quiet, and he continued to look down at the creases in his slacks. Sometimes the pastor referred to sex as marital ministry when speaking about it over the pulpit. Trevor was finding a marital ministry problem a humiliating thing to own up to, especially to another man, and especially since he and Cassidy had only been married for two months.

"Can you be more specific?" the pastor asked.

Lifting the barbells of bravery, Trevor looked at Clement. "Our marriage has never been consummated." With a swipe of his palm, Trevor wiped the sweat from his hairline and told the whole story.

Clement was silent for a few seconds. "Vaginismus," he concluded.

Trevor stared deep into Clement's face. "What?"

"What you described sounds like vaginismus. It can be quite traumatic for those involved."

"Yeah, tell me about it," Trevor said before asking, "What is it?"

Clement answered, "It's classified as a dysfunction." Trevor perched on the edge of the chair, his eyes rarely leaving Clement as he explained in detail. A few minutes later, the pastor concluded, "Any attempt at physical union is enormously painful for the woman, if not impossible."

"Do you know what causes the condition?"

"There are a variety of factors, physical or psychological, that may cause it, and it's important that a woman who suspects she has it see her gynecologist so that physical reasons such as infection can be either established or ruled out."

"You said it could be psychologically induced?"

Clement bobbed his head. "A psychological condition can cause the physical symptoms. Sometimes females who've gone through the traumatic experience of rape or molestation suffer from the dysfunction. Or sometimes the condition develops after a woman has had an unpleasant sexual experience and she fears the experience will repeat itself."

Trevor lapsed into intense thought, then said, "Cassidy was a virgin. She didn't have a prior experience. And she would have told me if she had been raped."

"Not necessarily. Some sexual assault victims are so ashamed about what's happened to them they won't speak about it. And some of them can't speak about it without help because they've blocked bits and pieces, if not all of it, out. But we shouldn't jump to conclusions. Like I said, there are many factors that can bring on this particular disorder."

A sudden sense of insecurity crept through Trevor. Maybe *he* was the cause of Cassidy's dysfunction. Maybe she was repulsed by something he was or wasn't doing. He'd never known Brenda to be dissatisfied, but now he wondered if maybe she had been, but had failed to mention it. Now, with Cassidy tense and in pain every time they attempted marital ministry, Trevor had to consider that he could be the problem. His skills might not be as tight as he thought they were.

Clement clutched the bottle of orange juice sitting on the desk and took a drink from it. "I met a couple some years back that were in the same situation as you and Cassidy. The wife was raised in a home where intimate relations, even in marriage, were viewed as perverted. Although she was married to a man she loved dearly, the negative messages she heard as a youngster continued to play in her head, affecting her ability to lead a normal intimate life. But with much prayer and some therapy, she was able to overcome. She's been married for eight years, and she and her husband have two children."

Trevor felt slightly better knowing that someone else in the world had gone through the same thing as he now was. Not that he wished the problem on anyone, but if this other couple had been cured, then there was hope for him and Cassidy.

Clement swiveled back and forth once, and the hinge underneath the seat sang a tune. "What does Cassidy say about all this?"

The question reminded Trevor of how isolated he'd been feeling lately. "The subject's not discussed if I don't bring it up. When I do bring it up, Cassidy simply apologizes for not being an adequate partner. I told her I don't see her as inadequate, I just want to find out what's going on."

Trevor continued, "I would have come to see you sooner, but Cassidy doesn't want anyone to know about her . . ." The problem belonged to them both. He hurt because she hurt. "*Our* problem," he corrected. Trevor propped his elbow on the arm of the chair and squeezed his forehead. "Cassidy is going to be furious when she finds out I came to you."

"From what I've read, many vaginismus sufferers initially find the condition embarrassing to talk about. And unfortunately, many go for years suffering in silence. I'm glad you took the first step and came to me."

"I needed to talk to someone." He wasn't going to shut the world out and try to cope on his own as he had when Brenda died. "There's something else worrying me," he confessed, connecting with Clement's attentive eyes. "I've always known Cassidy to eat nutritiously, but for the last two weeks, I haven't seen her eat much of anything."

Clement looked at his watch. "Cassidy should be downstairs with the ACES kids right about now, correct?"

Trevor glanced at his watch. It was 9:15. "Yes, she should be here."

"If it's okay with you, I'm going to have her come up. I'll have Vivaca come over, too. Considering the nature of the discussion, Cassidy might feel more at ease with her present."

Cassidy respected Vivaca. Trevor nodded consent as the grip of tension on his shoulders pinched to the point of pain, and the only way he could combat it was to leave the chair and walk across the room. He stopped at a wall lined with divinity degrees and prayed that Cassidy would forgive him for talking to their pastor without her approval.

Cassidy pulled two folders from the file cabinet and hurried upstairs to Clement's office, certain the reason she'd been asked to come up was Marvin and Karvin Frank. The twin ten-year-olds had serious behavior issues, and their parents had not responded to any of Cassidy's phone calls or letters. Yesterday Cassidy had recommended they be dismissed from ACES. However, no child could be expelled from the program without the pastor's authorization.

Cassidy knew the meeting wasn't about the Frank boys the moment she entered the pastor's office and found Vivaca and Trevor there. Alarm stampeded her heart. Surely, Trevor had not shared the delicate details of their personal life with Clement and Vivaca. They could have worked through their problem on their own. Cassidy plodded to the center of the floor and stood like an iron pole as Clement nodded welcome and offered her the empty seat between Trevor and Vivaca. Cassidy did not want to sit there. She did not want to be here. The walls were closing in on her, and she licked her dry lips as if that would eliminate the sudden need for a glass of water.

"It's okay, honey," Vivaca interrupted the silence. "There's plenty of love in this room."

Her emotions shattering, Cassidy gave Trevor a wary stare. His face was firm with tension, yet his eyes were soft with sensitivity, and she understood he didn't want to be here any more than she did. Like the pastor, Trevor was standing, waiting for her to sit. She slowly lowered herself to the chair, and Clement began. "Cassidy, first of all, Trevor did the right thing by coming to see me. You can't fix a problem if you don't seek out the necessary tools. Second"—Clement smiled gently—"I want to remind you that everything that's said here is confidential."

Cassidy placed the Frank boys' folders on the edge of the desk, cleared her throat, and found her voice. "What did he tell you?"

Clement reviewed the information Trevor had given. Humiliation burned Cassidy's cheeks, and she lacked the courage to lift her head.

"Cassidy"—Clement's voice sounded tender—"do you believe your husband came to me because he wanted to embarrass you?"

"No," she ultimately whispered.

"Do you believe he loves you?"

She raised her heavy gaze and faced Clement. "I know he loves me."

"And how do you feel about him?"

"I love him."

"Then are you willing to let Vivaca and me help you through this difficult period?"

Cassidy angled her gaze toward the pastor's wife. There was a consistent quality to Vivaca's character that reached out and made you feel special. "Yes," Cassidy answered.

"Good . . . because that's why we're here. Jesus had twelve disciples. We need people in our lives, too. You and Trevor don't have to walk alone." Clement's gaze drifted between Trevor and Cassidy. "I believe you're suffering from a condition called vaginismus. Of course, I'm not a physician, and therefore, you should see one as soon as possible and get an official diagnosis."

Cassidy swallowed with difficulty. "I've already been to the doctor."

Trevor fastened his hand on the arm of Cassidy's chair. "You've seen a doctor?"

It was much easier to look at Clement than at Trevor. "Yes. I do have vaginismus."

"Why didn't you tell me you saw someone about this?" Disappointment lay at the foundation of her husband's words.

Cassidy clenched her hands in the lap of her skirt. Tell him? How could she tell him without him asking a million questions that she didn't want to answer?

Trevor laid a hand over her hands. "Well, do you know what's causing the condition?"

This was one of the questions Cassidy feared, yet she answered, "I'm afraid I'll get pregnant."

Trevor stared, confusion heightening the intensity of his startled expression. "But you're on the pill," he said as if he couldn't believe he needed to remind her of this fact.

She shrugged. "There's still a possibility I could become pregnant."

"So what would be so terrible about that?" He gave her hand a squeeze of encouragement. "You're a good mom to the girls."

Pain filled Cassidy, nearly extinguishing her breath.

"Cassidy," Vivaca said, "did your doctor tell you that vaginismus is curable?"

She struggled, but whispered, "Yes."

"This means professional therapy was recommended?"

Cassidy shook her head yes and dropped her gaze, her heart hardening. No way! She was not going to see a therapist!

chapter thirty-two

"May I have the last piece?"

A smile curled Dunbar's lips. "It's all yours."

Cassidy dug her plastic fork into the remaining chunk of cantaloupe. Fruit was the only thing she had an appetite for these days. "You shouldn't spoil me like this." Dunbar had started bringing fresh fruit to their one-morning-a-week power walks. Last week it was red grapes and the week before sliced peaches.

Dunbar stared across the picnic table at Cassidy. "I like spoiling you. It makes my day brighter."

"Your wife is going to be one lucky woman."

"If I ever find a wife." A sharp blade cut through his voice.

"Of course, there's someone for you, Dunbar."

He shrugged and put the empty storage container in a small cooler. "Lean forward," he said. Cassidy frowned and he smiled. "Just do it." She leaned toward him, and he raised a napkin to her chin. "A tiny piece of melon missed your mouth."

She smiled. "Thanks."

Dunbar threw their forks and napkins in the trash, and they walked to the curb where their cars were parked. "I'm glad we still have this, C.C. I thought that after you became a married woman, you wouldn't have time for me."

"You're my friend. You always will be, and I'll always have time for you."

Dunbar stepped closer and kissed her cheek, the ritual send-off he gave her after their walks. "I'll see you on Sunday."

The smell of cologne eased under Cassidy's nose, and she compared it to the brand Trevor used. Trevor's smell was richer, more compelling.

Dunbar shut her door after she was behind the wheel of the Honda. "When are you going to talk to your husband about Herbie?"

"Later today," she said, and all the way home she prayed Trevor would be as enthusiastic as she was about the idea of adopting.

☙

"No," Trevor said, "it's almost time for dinner."

Brandi placed the candy bar in her father's hand and stomped toward the bedroom door.

"You better walk like you know, little girl," he warned.

"Okay," Brandi moaned, and exited with a normal stride.

"And close the door," Trevor said. A moment later, the door was shut. He sat on the bed, pulled off his tie, and removed his shoes. "How was your day?"

Cassidy guided a pen across the blue line of the notebook page, recording her word for the week. "I had a good day. We're practicing for the spelling bee."

"I have a feeling you guys are going to take the gold this year."

Cassidy grinned and brought her pen to a halt, giving Trevor her undivided attention. "How was *your* day?"

"Hectic. Business at the Main Street location is doing as well as I thought it would."

Trevor had recently opened a bakery in the city's Manayunk section and in the fall would expand the franchise to the Gallery at Eighth and Market. Cassidy moved the notebook from her lap to the bed and slid close to her husband. He slipped an arm around her middle and tickled her tummy, wrinkling the sleeveless zipper vest that coordinated with knit sweatpants.

"Stop!" She giggled, struggling to subdue his wiggling fingers.

"I don't want to," he whined, and gently pushed her by the shoulder to their sleigh-shaped bed. He ceased tickling, stretching his broad hand against her flat belly. A series of warm kisses ended with the words "I love you," first from him and then from her. As Trevor's mouth lingered above her lips, he asked the same question he'd asked every day since meeting in the pastor's office last week. "Did you schedule an appointment with the therapist?"

Her reply bordered on a whisper. "Not yet."

"Why haven't you?" he asked patiently.

Cassidy leaned her head to the side and stared at the framed art above the bed, denying him entrance to her soul. The inside of Trevor's hand surrounded her chin, and he turned her face so her gaze was back on him. His eyes were penetrating and loving and waiting for an answer.

Cassidy opened her mouth to give one, but could not translate her thoughts into words. Trevor sat up straight and clapped his hands to his knees. "This is ridiculous." There was less patience in his tone. "I don't understand what you're so afraid of."

The truth. If she were to talk to someone, the truth would come out. And Trevor would know what she had done. And he would be as disgusted with her as she was with herself. And most likely, he would walk away like the other man she had loved.

"I saw Herbie today," she said. Changing the subject might drain some of the tension from the room.

Trevor sighed with resignation and took part in the new topic. "How is he?"

"He misses you." Cassidy rose to a sitting position as Trevor unbuttoned his shirt. "He said he wants you to come back and be the SAFE coach like last summer."

"I wish I could. But with another bakery to operate, it's not going to happen." Trevor stood and crossed the leaves patterned in the hand-hooked rug covering much of a hardwood floor. "I'll try to come by and say hello to Herbie and the other boys one day next week."

"Did you know Herbie is eligible for adoption?" Cassidy asked as Trevor disappeared inside the closet they shared.

"No, I didn't know."

"I've talked to his new foster mother a few times."

Cassidy exhaled, forcing relaxation. "She's not inter-ested in adopting him."

Trevor emerged from the closet dressed in long draw-string shorts and a tank shirt. "Well, we'll have to keep Herbie in our prayers and ask God to send him a loving family."

"I know the perfect loving family." It was easy to smile. "*We* could adopt Herbie." They'd already decided she would adopt Brittney and Brandi.

Trevor sat on the edge of the dresser and folded his arms. He shook his head. "No."

"But we'd be ideal. I mean, think about it . . . Herbie would have two responsible parents, two sweet sisters . . . and it's not like we don't have the space or the finances."

"No," he repeated softly.

She spoke with disappointment. "But why not?"

"In case you haven't noticed, our relationship has some major holes in it. Just because you refuse to deal with our problem doesn't make it go away. Maybe if things were different, if you were in counseling—"

"Oh, so this is your way of punishing me for not going to counseling." She popped from the bed as if the mattress had bitten her backside.

"If that's what you want to believe, go for it. All I know is that before we even consider something as se-rious as adopting Herbie, we need to get things straight-ened out between us."

Cassidy turned from him and approached the French doors that led to a small balcony.

"I'm not getting it, Cassidy." His voice was much closer, indicating he was only steps behind her. "Why are you okay with bringing a child into our lives through adoption, but opposed to having a child the natural way?"

Tears with the sting of broken glass lined Cassidy's eyes as she wrapped herself in her arms and remembered her pregnancy. It had been a lonely time, especially the final trimester. In an effort to keep the pregnancy a secret, she terminated all social activities and only went to classes when absolutely necessary. Minister wasn't around much, so she talked to the baby in her womb. She prayed for him every night before she went to sleep. She marveled each time she felt him moving inside of her. She loved him, and she believed she was going to be a good mother. But a month before the baby was due, Minister came up with a plan. Cassidy took the anger she felt for Minister out on Trevor and snapped as she turned to face him, "Dunbar said you would probably say no."

Cassidy became the immediate recipient of an unfavorable squint. "You can tell Dunbar to mind his business. And while you're at it, tell him to find his own wife."

"What's that supposed to mean?"

"It means I don't like the way he looks at you. It's like he wants to lick you or something."

"You're being disgusting," she said.

"I'm being real, which is more than I can say for you. Think about it, Cassidy, you're a married woman, yet the man still leaves gifts on your desk."

"That's simply Dunbar's way of showing how much he values what we share."

"And what exactly *do* you share?"

She put her hand on her hip. "Are you implying that my friendship with Dunbar is something other than platonic?"

"All I'm saying is that the man is attracted to you, and has been since before you and I were serious, and it's hard to believe you haven't seen it."

"Well, I haven't 'seen it,'" she said, and turned from him again. Even if Trevor knew what he was talking about and Dunbar *had* ever been attracted to her, Lena would have surely noticed and made a big deal out of it the same way she had when Trevor came into the picture. She turned and faced her husband. "Why haven't you said anything about the way you think Dunbar looks at me before now?"

Trevor's eyes grew colder. "Because you haven't brought his name into our marriage before now."

She crossed her arms as she vibrated with acrimony. "I guess you don't want me to be friends with him anymore."

One of the children knocked on the door, and they both looked toward the white wood.

"We're hungry," Brittney called from the other side. "When are we going to eat?"

"Soon. Go wash your hands," Cassidy answered, exchanging the combative tone she'd used on Trevor for something gentler.

His tone remained militant. "Are you going to eat with us or just *watch* us eat?"

"Some people overeat when they're stressed and others undereat. I'm in the second category." She marched to the door.

He marched behind her. "Maybe you wouldn't be so

stressed if you'd open up and talk about *what it is* that's got you so stressed."

Her stare was as uncompromising as his. "Maybe I wouldn't be so stressed if you'd stop pressuring me to talk about what it is that's got me so stressed."

chapter thirty-three

Lena and Hulk's engagement had been announced during the first service. Cassidy watched from the parking lot as a group of well-wishers surrounded the happy couple and Lena showed off her ring. Cassidy glanced at the engagement ring and wedding band adorning her own finger. She tilted her hand beneath the sun, wishing her marriage had the glow the pear-shaped diamond registered.

She had not been naive enough to believe she and Trevor would never argue, but she had imagined any disagreements would be quickly settled, since they loved each other. But now she could see it wasn't that simple. Small disagreements could become big, ugly arguments, and it was easy to say things you didn't mean and do things to make the situation more explosive. And just because you loved the person didn't mean you were always instantly apologetic or forgiving.

Cassidy climbed in the passenger seat of the Expedition to wait for Trevor and the children. She pulled her cell phone out of her purse and dialed. Her call was answered in the middle of the fourth ring.

"Hello, celebrity," Cassidy said.

"Cassidy?"

"Yes, it's me. Can we talk?"

"Where are you?"

"In the parking lot."

Lena peeped around the burly body of a man in the crowd circling her and Hulk. She waved when she spotted Cassidy. "I'll be right over," she said into the phone.

After five minutes of waiting, Cassidy pulled out the latest letter from Oliver Toby. They wrote to each other twice a week and spoke by phone at least once—on Wednesdays. As Cassidy absorbed the nice feelings that came from reading Oliver Toby's thoughts, she imagined they were at the nursing home, on the bench, under the tree, looped arm in arm. "All my love to you, too," she said, responding to Oliver Toby's closing sentiment as she refolded the letter and placed it back in her purse. She glanced at Lena, who was still in conversation, then opened her Bible to 2 Corinthians 5:17, the text Pastor Audrey based the morning's sermon on. *Therefore if any man be in Christ, he is a new creature: old things are passed away; behold, all things are become new.*

Cassidy lifted her eyes from the page and remembered the sermon.

"*As Christians, we have a new character and should not continue to engage in any activity that opposes the Word of God,*" Reverend Audrey's strong voice taught the congregation. A little later, he inserted, "*We have been redeemed by*

Christ and are not to look back on our old life with guilty hearts. God's grace has removed our guilt . . ."

Cassidy halted her reflection as Lena limped across the parking lot. When Lena was close enough for Cassidy to speak without yelling, she offered, "Do you want to sit on the other side?" staring at Lena's feet, glamorous with new high heels.

Lena hobbled around to the driver's side and climbed up. "Thanks," she said, kicking off the footwear. "I only wore these shoes because they go so well with this dress, *and* because I wanted to look my best today with our engagement being announced." She asked through a brilliant grin, "So are you excited?"

"Of course, I'm happy for you and Hulk."

"I know that. I was referring to the news about Bishop Culpepper. I can't believe he's coming to *our* church."

Just prior to the benediction, Pastor Audrey said he had a huge surprise, then told the congregation that Bishop Colvin Culpepper and a portion of his choir would be worshipping with them next Sunday. While excited applause rained around her, Cassidy resisted fainting as a thread of hysteria tied itself to her heart.

"Didn't you used to be friends with Culpepper?"

Cassidy kept her pitch even. "We were in several classes together at Tilden."

Lena's eyes grew large. "Maybe you can introduce me to him." Her voice jumped to a higher level of glee. "Wouldn't it be outrageous if he could sing at my wedding? Oh, yeah, girl, you've got to get me up close and personal."

Cassidy sighed.

"What's your problem?" Lena asked.

"I need to ask you something about Dunbar."

"Yeah?"

Cassidy looked down at her wrist and touched her bracelet. "Have you ever noticed him looking at me?"

"Looking at you?"

"In a romantic sort of way."

"Girl, yeah, dozens of times."

Irritated with the world right now, Cassidy snapped, "Well, how come you never said anything?"

Lena gave her an "I know you better, get yourself together" look before answering, "I guess because it was Dunbar, and he just doesn't seem like the boyfriend type. He's more like a . . . "—she shrugged—"a pet. Why are you asking about him?"

"Trevor said something to me about him."

"Are you two okay?" Lena's voice resonated with worry. "I've noticed you guys don't seem to be all smiles and grins around each other like you were when you first got married."

Cassidy focused on the ladybug scaling the windshield. Poor little thing would take a few steps, then slide down to where it started. In spite of the pastor's teaching today and other times, Cassidy felt like that ladybug. Each time she worked up the nerve to tell Trevor why she was so afraid to get pregnant, she'd slip back into the isolated dimension of fear, shame, and guilt. "We've got some newlywed stuff to work through . . . like all couples." Too embarrassed to tell Lena about the vaginismus, Cassidy left it at that.

"You and Trevor have been going to the married couples' fellowships. Are they helpful?"

Cassidy nodded. "If nothing else, you learn that you're not the only ones trudging through a valley."

"Well, Hulk and I will be praying for you guys."

"Thanks. How are you two doing?"

Lena whipped on a smile. "It's rough, girl. We've got six more months of celibacy, and I can't even be on the phone with him without getting in the mood."

Cassidy smiled. "I made it. You'll make it through, too."

"It was easier for you. You had never been there, so you didn't know what you were missing."

Cassidy broke eye contact with Lena and watched the past.

"Come on," Minister urged, "we won't go all the way."

Cassidy had already been wooed from the living room to the bedroom. Now Minister wanted her to lie with him on the bed. They had never gone so far.

"Come on, baby, nothing's going to happen." He kissed her in between his pleas, and with every kiss, she was becoming more compliant.

"Okay," Cassidy finally panted, captivated by passion, yet still determined not to go all the way. She wanted to abide by the Bible and save herself for marriage. She had told Minister this many times before.

Once they were on the bed, he said, "You know I'm going to make you my wife one day."

She tingled with joy. "You are?"

"Yes. We're going to be together forever."

With that promise written on her heart, Cassidy allowed Minister beyond the boundary of her clothing.

"Will you marry me?" he groaned.

"Yes," she breathed, and suddenly, she didn't care what

the Bible said. She loved Minister, and he was going to be her husband.

"Well, I have to go." Lena opened the door. "Hulk and I are meeting his parents for brunch."

"I'll walk you over. I need to find Trevor."

"Are you feeling okay? You look kind of worn-out around the eyes."

Cassidy put on her sunglasses. "I haven't been getting enough sleep."

Lena formed a teasing grin as they walked ahead. "You and Trevor having those late-night parties, huh, girl?"

Cassidy did not correct her friend. They sauntered into the post-service crowd, and she hugged Lena and Hulk good-bye, congratulating them one more time. She strolled up the walkway toward the church, saying hello to members she knew and a few she didn't. Out of nowhere, someone stepped in front of her.

"What up?" Yaneesha hurled the greeting.

An internal warning beeped. "Hello, Yaneesha," Cassidy said, her salutation far from cheerful yet close enough to civil not to be considered impolite.

"Married life been good to you?"

"It's fine." Cassidy looked at the front doors of the church, hoping Trevor was coming through them.

"You lookin' for your *man?*"

Cassidy maintained a friendly facade. "Have you seen him?"

"I just got through talkin' to him. He's in the bookstore ordering this morning's message."

There was something mocking in Yaneesha's smile. Cassidy excused herself and stepped around the woman in her path.

"Trevor was at my place last night," Yaneesha called out.

Cassidy walked forward, meditating more on the scripture from today's sermon, not giving Yaneesha's mumbo jumbo a second thought.

⊘

"I'm coming," Cassidy shrieked. *"Hold on. Just hold on."*

Cassidy lifted her back from the mattress with a violent jerk. Drenched in sweat, she prayed into unsteady palms, "Oh, God, how much more of this can I take?"

Trevor sat up next to her. His hand covered her shoulder. "Did you have the dream about the little drowning boy?"

"Yes," she gasped. Within the last month, she'd had the dream four or five times a week. This was the first time she'd had it twice in the same night. She threw aside the sheet and crawled from the bed. Her legs felt like they'd been strapped with sandbags, and her sluggish steps to the bathroom were a reflection of the discomfort.

At the sink, Cassidy splashed her face with lukewarm water and reached for her towel. She held the thick cotton to her cheeks, then slowly pulled it away and faced the woman in the mirror with reservation. She looked bad. The fingers of broken sleep had painted dark and pronounced lines under her eyes.

Cassidy wasn't going to church today looking like this. She didn't want to go to church today, anyway—not with Colvin there. Cassidy imagined that the disappointment on Colvin's face would be as clear as it had been years ago.

"Who are you babysitting for?" Colvin asked, stepping into the living room of the apartment he shared with Minister. Colvin wasn't supposed to be back from his trip home to see his parents until the end of the week.

Cassidy looked from Minister to Colvin and back to Minister, waiting for Minister to say something.

"We're not babysitting," Minister slashed, peeking through the venetian blinds for the hundredth time.

Colvin dropped his duffel bag, and his face tightened with seriousness. "Then what's going on?"

"It's ours," Minister admitted, shocking Cassidy. Minister had been so adamant about no one finding out about the pregnancy. When he graduated in the spring, his daddy was making him the assistant pastor at one of the largest churches in Pittsburgh, and Minister didn't want a scandal that might jeopardize the position. Nor did Minister want to lose his financing. Minister's father would continue to pay for his education and his apartment as long as he maintained a GPA of 3.0 or better, didn't do anything illegal, and practiced abstinence.

Colvin inched to the couch and eased down next to Cassidy. "Yours?" he asked, disbelief glued to the word.

Cassidy nodded, and tears fell from her eyes. She rocked, but the baby continued to fuss.

Colvin placed his hand on her back. "You just had her?"

"It's a boy," Cassidy peeped.

Colvin sat dumbfounded for a moment. "Are you all right?"

Cassidy nodded that she was, realizing that Minister hadn't once asked how she was. "The delivery was easy. I *didn't have much pain. It felt like I had to go to the bath-room"*—she blushed—*"and then he was here."*

"Well, shouldn't you go to the hospital or something?"

"The hospital is exactly where we're going." Minister slapped his hands to his head like bookends and paced in front of them. *"Why can't you get it to be quiet?"*

Cassidy cringed every time Minister referred to the baby as *"it."* She silently questioned what kind of pastor Minister would be if he was this wired under pressure.

Using one finger, Colvin petted the baby's hand. *"He's so cute. What's his name?"*

Minister marched to the window again and looked through the blinds. *"We're not giving it a name because we're not keeping it."*

"What do you mean you're not keeping him?" Colvin's eyes zeroed in on Cassidy and examined her face for an answer.

Minister snapped at Colvin, stating their intentions. *"We're taking it to the hospital and dropping it off as soon as the crowd outside clears."* One of Minister's neighbors was in the middle of a late-night birthday party that had spilled onto the lawn.

"You're abandoning him?"

"We're not abandoning him. We're giving him a chance at a better life."

"You can't be serious, man. What could be better than this baby having his real parents?" Colvin asked her directly, *"You don't want to do this, do you, Cassidy?"*

"I don't know." She shivered with fear. *"I don't know what to do."*

Minister stormed toward them. *"Look, man, we don't need your input. We've already made our decision."* He plopped on the sofa on the other side of Cassidy. "Listen, baby, we've already discussed this. Giving it away is the best thing. I can't have a child in my life right now. I'm about to become a leader in the church. I'm on my way to grad school. I can't handle a kid right now. And you don't need one, either, if you're going to finish college."

"I could go back home and finish at a school in Philly."

Colvin interjected, "Lots of women go to school and raise kids at the same time."

Minister struck Cassidy where it hurt. "Are you going to ask your aging aunt to give you and a baby a home after all the sacrifices she's already made for you? And don't forget how crushed she'll be that you had a baby out of wedlock."

Colvin jumped up from the sofa. His eyes were ablaze. "Oh, man, don't even go there!"

Minister's voice was equally angry. "This is not your business, Colvin. Stay out of it!"

"Please, please don't fight about it," Cassidy begged. "You're scaring the baby." His cries were going through her, ripping her heart piece by piece.

"Don't do it, Cassidy." Colvin fell to his knees in front of her. "Don't give away your baby. You're going to regret it."

Minister put his arm around her waist and leaned in close. He balanced his voice a notch above a whisper. "Do you love our baby?"

She looked at Minister. His eyes were soft and his smile warm. This was the man she'd fallen in love with. "Of course, I love our baby."

"Then let's do the right thing . . . the unselfish thing. Let's give him a chance at a whole family—a mom and a dad. And I promise, we'll get married as soon as I get my master's and doctorate degrees. Then we'll make lots of babies and raise them together."

Cassidy peered at Colvin. His gaze was sad and pleading. "I didn't have a mom and dad," she said. She tried to make him understand. "I want my baby to have two parents."

"It's quiet outside. We should leave now," Minister said gently. He extended his arms.

Cassidy kissed the baby's forehead and placed his frail, writhing, towel-covered body in the cradle Minister made with his hands. She followed Minister to the door. Before she walked out, she turned and looked at Colvin. He was still on his knees, but he had curled over and buried his face in his hands.

chapter thirty-four

Cassidy put the wooden spoon on the counter and answered the ring of the phone. "Hello," she said into the handheld cordless.

"Hello," the female on the other end greeted her. "Is Cassidy Monroe in?"

"This is Cassidy."

"Cassidy, my name is . . ." Cassidy listened as the woman introduced herself and shared the reason for her call. "Sister Whittle gave me the names of people who might be interested in working with us, and your name was on the list . . ."

When the woman finished, Cassidy answered softly, "I haven't made up my mind yet."

"That's okay. We'd still like you to come to our next meeting. It's on . . ."

Cassidy reached for a pencil and jotted down the information on a napkin. The notepad on the kitchen desk was a more reliable place for recording information, but what did it matter? Cassidy didn't believe she'd be going to the next Sparrow Ministry meeting.

The woman chirped on like a sparrow, "We like for the members of our team to be properly trained so they can be effective servants. So many of the young women who come to us for help are in such an emotionally fragile state, harboring feelings of guilt and embarrassment as if pregnancy outside of marriage is a permanent barrier between them and God's grace. But we know that's not true, amen?"

Cassidy breathed deeply, unable to speak as she studied the scripture on the small chalkboard she'd hung on the wall. Writing the scriptures where she could read them often was a method of self-encouragement as well as a way to help Brittney and Brandi learn new verses.

"Amen?" the sister questioned again.

"Amen," Cassidy said with less force than what the woman was certainly expecting.

"Well," she said in the friendly voice she'd been using since the start of the conversation, "I hope to see you at the next meeting."

After closing the call, Cassidy restudied the verse on the wall. *The Lord is gracious, and full of compassion; slow to anger, and of great mercy.* She closed her eyes and said it several times, making the words a part of herself, although a part of herself still refused to accept that God was not infuriated with her for having premarital sex and then leaving her baby.

She returned to the stove and began stirring the contents of a large stainless-steel pot, making a dedicated effort to appear totally absorbed with the dinner prepa-

rations as Trevor walked through the deck-side entrance into the kitchen.

"Hi, Daddy," the girls chimed.

He strolled across the room to the table where the
sisters were seated. Cassidy glanced at him when she
was sure he wasn't looking at her. "Hi, angels," he said,
and stamped a kiss to two cheeks.

"Hi, Coach," the third smile said.

Trevor gave the same big, affectionate grin he'd
given the girls and pounded hands with Herbie.
"What's going on, little man?"

"We're creating." Brandi's zeal was as dazzling as the
sunshine beaming in from outside. "Cassidy said we
could make anything we want."

Trevor scanned the potpourri of arts and crafts supplies. Construction paper, crayons, cotton balls, pipe
cleaners, clay, glue sticks, scissors, and a dozen other
items covered the table from edge to edge. He carried his
gaze upward, and Cassidy briefly met his eyes. They were
round, clear, and fixed, as if he were trying to climb into
her head and decode her thoughts. She lowered her gaze
to the pot of vegetarian chili, a recipe she'd stumbled
across while surfing the Web. Solidly aware of Trevor as
he neared the stove, she gripped the spoon tighter, stirring the entire time, attempting to hide any clue of inner
misery.

"Cassidy," he acknowledged in a scratchy whisper,
stopping beside her.

She turned toward him, and the two kissed on the
mouth, a brief action, something one might see on a
1960s sitcom. Trevor laid his hand on Cassidy's back,

and her spine became a stiff line. "Dinner will be ready soon." She posted a smile, but it was taut with artificial joy.

The hand on her back remained as Trevor inched the front of his body against her side. He lowered his head, and his full warm lips pressed into her cheek as he caressed her with the tip of his tongue. She poked up her shoulder, insisting he stop. He got the message and dropped his hand from her back, although his feet stayed rooted. "Why are you acting like this?"

"The kids are here," she reminded him.

"It has nothing to do with the kids."

There was frustration inside his whisper. Cassidy glanced at the children to make sure they were involved with their art projects, then she returned her attention to the chili. "I need space right now." Her tone was hushed. "I told you that last night."

"What you *need* is deliverance." He paused, suddenly aware that his voice had taken a leap upward. They both glanced at the children before looking at each other. Cassidy couldn't sustain a mutual gaze for more than a breath and bowed her head. Trevor's hand was on the counter, a hardened fist, a reflection of the air engulfing them. "I can't take this," he continued, his tone returned to a strained whisper. "You're completely shutting me out."

Brandi unknowingly put a stop to an exchange that would have gone on longer. "Come look at what I'm making, Daddy."

Cassidy watched his fingers unfold, then looked up at him. Sadness, so raw it undoubtedly reached from his soul, filled his eyes. Cassidy shifted her gaze again, pain pushing her spirit lower. Trevor was right. She was shutting him out. He wanted to cuddle. He wanted to kiss. But cuddling and kissing usually led to something more. And something more usually took them to the bedroom. And it was there, in the bed, that her body reminded her time and time again that she could not perform all a wife should be able to. Not once during their most intimate moments had Trevor put pressure on her to do what she couldn't. Nor had he ever uttered a comment that made her feel inferior. Yet Cassidy knew her handicap had to be an excessive hardship for him. Married before, Trevor was a man used to experiencing more. So how could he be truly happy and satisfied with her, a woman unable to meet his needs the way they needed to be met?

"Guess what?" Brandi said.

"What's that, baby?" Trevor walked over, lifted her into his arms, kissed her chin, and she giggled.

"Cassidy's going to be Herbie's mommy just like she's me and Sis's mommy."

One . . . two . . . three . . .

Three full seconds crash-landed before Cassidy dared breathe and look Trevor in the eyes. Bewilderment followed by mistrust and disapproval were discernible on Trevor's face. He returned Brandi to the chair and shot another severe expression across the room. "Can I speak with you in our bedroom?" he said, and he pivoted, not waiting for an answer.

Cassidy snapped off the stove and thudded behind Trevor. The savory aroma of the chili, seasoned with herbs from her backyard garden, had drifted all the way up to their second-floor bedroom. She closed the door and kept her hands behind her, a grasp on the knob. "It's not what you think," she said.

He spun and faced her. Shoved his hands in his pockets and rocked once on his heels. "Did you tell Herbie we were going to adopt him?"

She shut her eyes and backed her head against the door. "No. I could never tell Herbie something like that unless I knew for sure."

Every seam of the room was stitched in silence. She surveyed Trevor, his face coffin-hard, his glare digging into her, his hands still buried. "Then why do the kids think you're going to be his mother?"

Cassidy repeated the conversation that had gone on between the children less than an hour ago. She'd been in the laundry room, out of sight, but in hearing range.

"I wish I could live here," Herbie said.

"Me, too," Brittney said.

"Me, three," came Brandi's vote. "My daddy could be your daddy, and Cassidy could be your mommy."

"Let's go ask Cassidy right now."

"Okay." The younger children squealed with exhilaration over Brittney's idea, and they all ran into the laundry room.

Brandi voiced the question that flamed in each child's eyes. "Can you be Herbie's mommy, too?"

"I didn't know what to say. I knew I couldn't say yes, but I couldn't bring myself to say no. I needed time to think, so I told them we'd talk about it later."

Trevor swirled, sighing through his nostrils, offering her his back, obviously dissatisfied with the way she'd handled the situation. He turned and glared some more. "I don't think it's a good idea for Herbie to be over here playing as much as he is. You and the girls are getting too attached."

Trevor had left himself out of the equation, but Cassidy knew with every bit of her heart that Trevor was crazy about Herbie, too. The phone rang, and Trevor marched over and swiped the ringing device from the cradle. He plopped and slouched in a suede recliner while he talked, massaging his forehead as if he had a headache. And maybe he did. The Herbie situation, her refusal to get counseling, her refusal to be intimate, it all was frustrating to him.

Well, she was suffering, too. Didn't he know how hard all of this was for her? She didn't ask to be cursed with vaginismus. At times, she wondered why God, in His omnipotence, wouldn't answer her prayers and heal her. Cassidy hurried into the bathroom and shut the door. She crossed her arms and chose pacing rather than throwing up her arms and frightening the children with a high-pitched scream. Walking more slowly, she clutched her head, covering her ears, trying to silence the voice that was telling her what she didn't want to hear.

You need to talk to Trevor. Tell him everything. With Me, you are strong enough to do it.

"But, God," she initiated protest, then stopped as the scripture she had quoted more than twenty years ago in a Sunday school play lined her memory. *Fear thou not; for I am with thee: be not dismayed; for I am thy God: I will strengthen thee; yea, I will help thee.*

❦

"How's the cake?"

Brittney grinned, a crumb of chocolate clinging to

one front tooth. "It's good, but I like yours better." She ate two more forks of dessert. This time when she smiled, the crumb on her tooth was gone, but a smudge of frosting colored her top lip.

Trevor smiled and let her enjoy her cake. She would clean up when she was done.

Their server for the evening breezed by their table but stopped on her way back. "More coffee, sir?"

"Yes, thank you." Trevor added cream and sugar to the dark brew. He put aside his spoon, then took a first sip and felt the heat roll from his throat to his belly. Brittney finished her soda, then wiped her mouth with the linen napkin, all signs of cake removed now. Their table was adjacent to a window, and the moonlight falling across the river flickered like diamonds. The shimmer in Brittney's eyes as she blinked at him was just as awesome, and it warmed his soul as much as the coffee had warmed his body.

"Can we come here next month?" she asked.

"If that's what you want." Ever since Cassidy suggested it, Trevor had taken the girls out, one at a time, on a date. Tonight was Brittney's turn, and she and Trevor had dressed in some of their best clothes and started the evening with a walk and a talk along Penn's Landing. As always, the time together was priceless. Brittney was growing up fast, her face losing much of its baby look, and subtle but solid nuances of maturity were settling in. Scary to consider that in less than ten years another gentleman would be sitting where he was now, drinking up Brittney's smiles.

"Daddy?" Her voice grasped his full attention, and he listened with his heart as much as his ears. "Are you and Cassidy going to stay married?"

Worry blurred the shine in Brittney's eyes. Trevor had hoped the problems in his marriage would not be noticed by his children, as he and Cassidy made every effort to keep their arguments behind the bedroom door.

Trevor stacked their dirty dishes and the floral centerpiece to one side of the cloth-covered table. "Put your hands up here," he said, stretching his arms forward, modeling what he wanted her to do. She stretched her arms on the table, and Trevor covered her hands with his. Unprepared for her pop quiz, he searched for the right words before speaking.

"You know how much I loved Mommy, right?" She bobbed her head. "I love Cassidy the same . . . and Cassidy loves me, but that doesn't mean there aren't going to be problems." He smiled in an attempt to diminish her anxiety. "Do you remember how much trouble you had with fractions?" She didn't answer, but her eyes were riveted to his, and he knew she was hanging on to every word. He continued, "You stayed after school for tutoring, and then you were fine."

"Yes," she whispered.

"Well, that's what Cassidy and I are going to do, baby. We need help with our marriage, and Pastor Audrey is going to be our tutor. He's going to help us."

This morning Pastor Audrey had stopped by Seconds and invited him and Cassidy to a marital counseling session. Because Cassidy was away, visiting Oliver Toby, Trevor hadn't discussed it with her yet, but he hoped she would see the importance of such a meeting and agree to go.

chapter thirty-five

I'm glad you came to see me."

"I'm having a good time." Cassidy smiled as she glanced out the front window at the layers of mountains in the distance.

"I never thought I'd say it, but I'm happy here with my son."

According to Oliver Toby, the father and son had grown closer now that they were living together again. Oliver Toby's son even attended church with him, and Oliver Toby believed it wouldn't be long before his son accepted Jesus Christ as his personal Savior.

Cassidy returned to the sofa and sat next to Oliver Toby. The afghan that his neighbor, Ramona Bucci, had crocheted for him draped his knees. Ramona, eleven years younger than Oliver Toby, still possessed some of her natural brunet hair and was in excellent health. The matriarch of a strong Italian family, Ramona, with something home-cooked in tow, stopped in to check on Oliver Toby each weekday while his son was at work. Cassidy thought Ramona was one of the sweetest women she'd ever met. In many ways, she reminded Cassidy of Odessa. Several times, Cassidy had teased Oliver Toby about how pretty Ramona was and what a cute couple he and Ramona would make. Humor flashed in Oliver Toby's eyes and through his voice as he assured her that he was too old for marriage and too young for death and that living with Ramona full-time would kill him.

Oliver Toby said gently, "Don't keep holding it inside, Cassidy."

She looked him in the eyes, then directed her surprised gaze toward the television, its volume set on low.

"Behind that smile you've perfected, there's pain. I've told you before, I can see it." Oliver Toby gave her consideration, a solemn but sensitive expression on his face. "Some memories need to stay just that—memories. But sometimes there are memories that can't be kept secret—especially if the memories are memories you can't handle on your own. And from time to time, life hands us things we can't handle on our own. We need God's help, and sometimes He sends that help in the form of others." With tear-framed eyes, Cassidy tenderly regarded her friend. He squeezed her hand with the strength his frail muscles allowed. "It's going to be okay, sweetheart," he said. "I've tried running from God a few times myself. Eventually, you get tired, though, and if you're smart, you stop and do things God's way."

❧

Trevor parked and hurried to the house, his heart racing with relentless dread. The door stood open, and he rushed inside. Trudy immediately jumped up from a chair that had part of its stuffing hanging out. Blood droppings had stained her shirt, and she clutched a homemade ice pack to her mouth. "Look at what Derek done did," she yelled. "I told you he ain't no good. Ain't never been no good."

"Where is he?" Trevor's question jabbed the air.

"What you worried 'bout *him* for?" Trudy snarled. "What about me? I'm the one bleedin' to death."

"Where is he?" Trevor insisted with more urgency.

"He upstairs. I told him he better stay up there 'cause if he come down here, I'm gon' call the cops on his no-good—"

"Derek!" Trevor shouted, and started up the wooden flight of stairs to the second floor as Trudy blurted cusswords.

"In here." The muffled response came from the end of the hall. Trevor twisted the knob and pushed open the door to Derek's room. He breathed a sigh of relief when he saw Derek was okay, at least physically. Trevor neared Derek, who was sitting on the edge of a bed without a headboard. Animosity raged in Derek's expression as he exhaled chopped breaths through his nostrils. "She kept callin' me names"—he shook his head—"and I just lost it and swung at her."

"Where are your little brothers?" Trevor asked, realizing how quiet the house was.

"Their father came and took 'em this morning. He ain't suppose to bring 'em back till tomorrow."

Trevor looked around the one-window room. A large dresser sat opposite the bed, the only two pieces of furniture. Several posters of professional athletes were taped to dingy walls. A closet door hung open. "Do you have a suitcase?"

"No."

"Start taking your clothes out and put them on the bed. I'll go down and get some trash bags from the kitchen. They'll have to do for now."

Trudy, seated at the kitchen table in front of an open bottle of liquor and an ashtray, tapped her cigarette and put it back to her bruised lip. After releasing a puff of smoke, she said, "Boy ain't got no respect. I shoulda called the cops. Let 'em put him in the same hole with his daddy."

"Where do you keep your trash bags, Miss Hines?" Trevor addressed Trudy with a dignity she had not earned.

She glared at him long and hard. She finally said in an unassertive voice, "Look in the cabinet 'neath the sink."

Trevor pulled three large bags out of a no-frills-brand box and faced Trudy. "I'd like to take Derek with me."

"Why?" Trudy leaned her head back and fogged the air with another cloud of smoke. "You ain't his daddy. Wish you were, but you ain't."

"But I care about your son, Miss Hines, and I don't think it's wise for the two of you to remain under the same roof. Either you or him are going to get hurt much worse if things continue like they are."

Trudy's harsh chuckle was followed by a ring of coughs, and it sounded like she had ash in her throat. "Didn't I tell you day was gon' come when you was gon' want me to do somethin' for you?" She muttered something unintelligible, and Trevor began to pray. It would take God to give him favor with Trudy. Before Trevor could end his private prayer, Trudy pushed her fingers through her uncombed hair. "Take him," she said flatly.

Trevor gave God a word of praise and then said to Trudy, "Thank you." He paused. "And thank you for calling me." She had been the one to call, screaming that Derek had attacked her and she was about to cut him with her butcher knife.

As Trevor helped Derek pack his belongings into the truck, he considered that Cassidy might find it unfair of him to ask her to take in Derek when he'd been so firm on his stance regarding Herbie. Trevor needed God to give him the sentences to say to Cassidy to convince her to let Derek stay with them, so Trevor began to pray again as he drove to the park. The court was empty. He strode around to the passenger side and opened the door. "A little b-ball always helps me unwind," he said to Derek. "Why don't we run a couple of games?"

Derek remained a statue on the seat, his fists clenched on his knees. "Trudy makes me so sick, always preachin' I'm going to prison."

"For I know the thoughts that I think toward you . . . thoughts of peace, and not of evil."

Derek turned his glare toward Trevor. "Shakespeare?"

"No. It's what God says in the book of Jeremiah. Now it's up to you whether you're going to choose God's blessing or your mother's curse."

Trevor and Derek studied each other. Some of the anger left Derek's face, but not the heartache. "It's all right to cry," Trevor said, and Derek's stiff jaw slackened a bit. "Being the man of the house at such a young age is a tough job," Trevor continued, remembering how tiring it had been, always trying to stay strong after his father died so that his mother wouldn't have the added burden of worrying about him. "But even tough guys hurt and feel pain."

"Don't tell the guys from the team." His watery eyes begged. His voice cracked under the weight of the tears. "Promise you won't tell."

"I promise," Trevor said, and Derek bowed his head to his knees and flushed his soul with sobs.

"I'm sorry, God," Derek wept. "I'm sorry I hit my mom." Soon Derek's cries softened, and he stuttered to Trevor, "Where . . . where I'm gonna live?"

"You'll stay with me until something else is worked out," Trevor said, knowing he had yet to discuss any of this with his wife.

"But," Derek started, then snorted and wiped his face with his shirt. No tissues in the vehicle, Trevor had to let Derek fend for himself. "But Mrs. Monroe," he finished, "she don't really like me."

"What makes you say that?"

"Just seem like she don't."

✒

"It will only be until I can find him another place." Trevor was explaining Derek's situation to Cassidy while Derek practiced his game on the court in the nearby park.

"It's fine," she said agreeably.

Trevor asked again just to make sure he wasn't dreaming.

"I don't mind," she said, and surprised him more by asking, "Has Derek had dinner?"

Trevor had eaten a late lunch, and a big one, so he hadn't thought about Derek being hungry. He checked his watch. It was after eight, two hours since they'd left Trudy. "He's probably starving by now."

"I'll prepare something," she said.

✑

Derek gobbled the turkey burger, mashed potatoes, and sautéed string beans Cassidy had fixed.

"I'll show you your room." Cassidy smiled and led Derek upstairs, Brittney and Brandi following.

Trevor cleaned up the kitchen, thinking it was nice of Cassidy to go to the trouble of cooking for him and Derek so late in the evening and on a night off. This morning Trevor had told her he wouldn't be home in time for dinner, and Cassidy's response had been that she wouldn't cook tonight but rather take the girls out for dinner.

Trevor encountered Cassidy in the second-floor hall on her way to the guest room, a pillow in her grasp. "Derek might want an extra one," she said. "Tomorrow I thought Derek and I might work out a tutoring schedule for the fall. He asked me to help him with his schoolwork last year and, well . . ." Her voice faded.

"Thank you for welcoming him into our home," Trevor said.

"Derek's a good kid, and I despise the way Trudy treats him. He doesn't deserve it. No child does."

"I told Derek he had you pegged wrong." Trevor smiled lightly. "The boy thought you didn't like him."

"I've always liked Derek"—Cassidy clutched the pillow lengthwise—"but I haven't done a very good job of showing it."

Trevor gazed into Cassidy's eyes, looking for explanation.

"Derek looks so much like Minister that I actually see Minister when I look at Derek. But that's my problem, not Derek's."

Trevor had heard the name "Minister" from Cassidy only once. He was somebody she'd met in college, a first serious boyfriend.

Now the instinct in Trevor's gut and the conflict in Cassidy's eyes suggested there were more chapters to the story about Minister. Trevor eased one of her hands from the pillow. "Would you like to talk about him?" he asked.

Cassidy clasped his fingers tighter, focused on his eyes, and parted her lips preparing to speak as Brandi let out a playful yelp. Trevor felt disappointment as what Cassidy was about to reveal sprinted back to the place where she kept her secrets. "I should get the girls out of Derek's room so he can relax," she said quietly, and walked away from Trevor and the question.

chapter thirty-six

Summer moved forward with sunny mornings, stormy afternoons, and humid nights. With Trudy's permission, Trevor had sent Derek on the church youth retreat, a two-week stint in the wilderness that would afford Derek a change of routine, the right to breathe something other than city air, a chance to make new friends, and an opportunity to grow deeper in God.

Gripping the newspaper, Trevor retired to the living room, which Cassidy had redecorated in contemporary style. He sank into one of two plush and spacious chenille-fabric chairs that matched the sofa, love seat, and a huge ottoman. Brittney perched on the wide chair arm and leaned against his shoulder, and he opened the newspaper to the sports page. Cassidy and Trevor's wedding portrait hung above the piano. Odessa's rocker, which Cassidy kept in the guest room, was the only other piece of furniture Cassidy had brought along from her old house. Everything else had been donated to a local mission.

Cassidy joined Brandi on the piano bench. Brandi swung her small feet, excited about her lesson. As Brandi mastered "Mary Had a Little Lamb," Trevor peeked over the edge of the open newspaper and regarded his wife. The majority of her braids were pinned up, but she'd left a few waterfalling along the side of her face. Her feet were bare, and she wore jeans and a short-sleeved shirt.

"Daddy, you're not paying attention." Brittney tapped him on the shoulder. They often took turns reading the paragraphs, and she reminded him, "Take your turn."

He kissed her cheek. "Sorry. Where are we?" he asked. He followed her finger to the printed spot, read his part, and returned his thoughts to Cassidy. Although she'd committed to attending the marital counseling session with him and the pastor tomorrow, she hadn't given any clues as to whether she'd changed her mind about seeing a therapist.

Trevor frowned as he worried about Cassidy. Most nights, she cooked the low-fat meals she preferred and he was growing accustomed to, yet she still wasn't eating enough, the kids having more on their plates than Cassidy had on hers. Trevor didn't know what Cassidy had eaten while in Denver, sure that if she ate there like she nibbled here, Oliver Toby had reprimanded her about it.

Brittney poked him with her elbow this time, and he took his turn, but if he'd been tested on his comprehension of the subject matter, he would have flunked. While Brittney read, Trevor clamped another glance on Cassidy and his younger daughter. From day one, Cassidy had loved and accepted the girls, referring to them as her daughters instead of her stepchildren. Cassidy's maternal instincts were as natural as her beauty, and Trevor couldn't think of anything more precious and holy than creating a child with her. During premarital counseling, she'd sanctioned the idea of having children with him. Now she was saying no to the prospect of pregnancy, and it left him feeling betrayed and rejected and worn-out with more questions. Why would Cassidy not want to have his baby? Was there something about him that led her to believe he was not a good father?

Brandi's lesson normally lasted thirty minutes, but this evening it was chopped to fifteen as someone leaned a finger on the doorbell.

"I wonder who that is." Brittney jumped down from the chair and sped to the front door.

"Do not open the door without looking out first," Trevor called behind her.

Brittney looked through the side window and grinned. "It's Auntie Kendall," she screamed, and Brandi squealed as high as her vocal cords would take her.

Trevor unlocked and opened the right half of a glossy black double door.

"Hello, hello, hello," Kendall McBride's voice trumpeted through the large foyer. Brittney and Brandi rushed into her arms, between the shopping bags dangling from her wrists. Trevor was speechless and only able to blink as their surprise guest blew through his doorway.

Kendall put down her bags, dropped to her knees,

and gave her godbabies kiss after kiss. When she was done, she stood up straight and stared at him. "Well, are you going to just stand there? Give me some of your love, too, gorgeous." Her naturally gritty voice flowed over him as she made a half-moon with her arms. Trevor grinned, the way only Kendall could influence him to grin whenever she called him gorgeous. Brenda used to tease him about it.

Trevor stepped into the crescent shape of Kendall's arms, sweeping her curvaceous, full figure into his, unable to ignore the striking scent of her perfume. He stepped back, and while Kendall smiled down at the children, he buried his hands in his pants pockets and gave her a discreet and rapid scan. Kendall's heels put her close to the same height as Cassidy in bare feet. She wore a simple pair of black pants, not overly tight, but form-fitting, and a matching sleeveless vest with a V-collar leading to her cleavage. Beaded jewelry dangled from her ears, hugged her neck, and circled both wrists. A modest application of makeup accented smooth skin the color of earth just after a good rain. And her dyed-blond hair was cut as short as his. It was a style not every woman could pull off. Kendall wore it to perfection.

As if she could feel his perusal, her large brown eyes, as spectacular as he remembered, lifted and nested with his, and for one crisp second, Trevor desired to hold her again. "So how've you been, Kendall?" he succeeded in asking with casual air.

She walked forward, moistened his cheek with a lingering kiss, and whispered, "I've been just fine," as the cabdriver appeared in the open doorway and cleared his throat. Trevor pulled a bill from his pants pocket and paid the man. "Thank you, gorgeous," Kendall rasped, leaned close, and kissed Trevor's other cheek.

Cassidy, who had taken the entire scene in from the living room, strolled into the foyer and halted near Trevor. She'd seen pictures of Kendall in the family album, so she'd known Kendall was an attractive woman. But pictures rarely captured the whole story, which was the case here. The living, breathing Kendall McBride was stunning.

"What's inside all these bags?" Brandi bubbled, peeping inside the largest one.

Kendall flashed a flawless smile. "Honey love, why don't you and your sis take them into the living room and find out?"

The girls joyfully obeyed, leaving the adults alone, and Trevor's long fingers gently snaked around Cassidy's elbow. "Kendall, I'm pleased to introduce you to my wife . . . Cassidy."

Cassidy narrowed the space between her and the other woman and extended her hand. "It's a pleasure to meet you. The children talk about you quite often."

Kendall took Cassidy's hand, but the shake was tepid and brief, on both their parts. "The pleasure's mine," Kendall said. She touched Trevor's hand and remarked, "She's lovely," before strutting off.

An immediate strong dislike for Kendall sharpened Cassidy's temper. She followed their visitor into the living room. "Would you like to sit down?" Cassidy asked courteously.

"Oh, no," Kendall said, kneeling on the plush carpet with the children. She had bought the girls a jewelry-making kit, a cosmetics-making kit, toy cell phones, CD Walkmans, and a stash of CDs. It was a bit extravagant, Cassidy assessed, but then again, Kendall was their godmother and Cassidy supposed godmothers splurged naturally, especially if they didn't have children of their own.

Cassidy rested in one of the chenille chairs and watched the children play with their gifts. Trevor lowered himself onto the ottoman. It wasn't long before Kendall got up off the floor and planted herself next to him, elbow-to-elbow, thigh-to-thigh.

"So what brings you to our half of the country?" Trevor asked as the girls quarreled over a CD.

"I came to see *you*," she said, then rolled her twinkling gaze toward Cassidy, "and your new wife." Kendall smiled at her, but Cassidy felt as if she'd been stabbed in the back. "On a serious note, though," Kendall went on, "Granddaddy figured it was his time again. A couple of days ago, he had chest pains and was admitted for observation, and overreacting, he had Aunt Wynona call all the family in so he could impart dying words of wisdom. By the time I got to the hospital this evening, he was sitting up in bed, flirting with the nurses, and demanding that the doctor release him. I'll be flying back to L.A. in the morning."

"How's Body Divine doing?"

"Wonderful. You know L.A. is America's beauty kingdom. You can never have too many spas. How's Seconds doing?" Before he could answer, she said, "I think the way you've decided to honor Brenda is fantastic."

Trevor smiled. After much soul-searching, he'd decided to open Parent Place. It was a room in the bakery, open on Saturdays from eleven to two. It was set up like a café, and moms or dads who'd lost their spouse to death could come and sit or read while having a cup of coffee. A grief counselor from the church volunteered his services, and he was there for up to two hours to help anyone who needed it. Cassidy thought Parent Place was a wonderful creation, and she'd praised Trevor for it on several occasions.

Brandi's eyes were happy and proud. "My daddy's making a cookbook."

"I'm thinking about it," Trevor said.

"You should do it, gorgeous."

Cassidy stiffened with resentment. That was the third time Kendall had called Trevor gorgeous. And the third time Trevor had strung that goofy-looking grin across his face.

"Thank Auntie Kendall for the presents," he told the children.

"Thank you," they chorused.

"I'd like to thank you for the crystal vase, Kendall. It's beautiful." Cassidy and Trevor had sent Kendall the traditional thank-you note following the wedding, but a bonus expression of appreciation seemed appropriate now that she was here.

"You're welcome. Thank you for the DVD of the ceremony. I'm sorry I missed it." Kendall ambled over to the wedding portrait.

"I'm glad you're feeling better."

"Yes. Much," she answered Cassidy. Kendall moved a little to the left and studied one of the new paintings

Cassidy had selected. "I see you've made quite a few changes to the living room." She gazed at Cassidy. Cassidy thought she might have been reading too much into Kendall's glance and comment, but it seemed as if Kendall wasn't happy about Cassidy making changes to the house. Well, Brenda was gone, and Kendall would have to accept that the house belonged to Cassidy now. Trevor and the children hadn't complained about any of the changes she had made to the rooms. And of course, Cassidy had been sensitive to Brandi's and Brittney's feelings and not altered their bedrooms, which Brenda had fixed up for them over the years.

"Can I get you something from the kitchen, Kendall?" Trevor asked.

"Now, there's no way I could travel all these miles and not indulge in one of your delicacies."

"Sweet potato pie, okay?"

Kendall showed her toothpaste-ad smile again. "Sounds delicious."

"I'll take care of it," Cassidy said, seeking escape from the room.

When Cassidy returned, she placed an elegant silver tray on the glass cocktail table, then she and Kendall took seats on the sofa. The girls knelt on the carpet, one at each end of the table. Trevor poured the hot tea, put the girls' milk-filled glasses on the coasters Cassidy had set out, and served the pie before sitting in one of the chairs facing the women.

Kendall steadied her eyesight on Cassidy. "Aren't you having any pie?"

Brandi swallowed the glob of pie in her mouth, making a gulping sound. "Cassidy doesn't eat sweet stuff."

Kendall reared back in amazement. "Girl, you mean you don't partake of this man's culinary creations? Tell me how you can stand not to."

Cassidy pulled her lips into a tight smile. "Somehow I manage."

"Cassidy don't eat french fries, either," Brandi chattered.

"Doesn't eat," Trevor corrected.

Brandi kept going, "And you hate pizza, right, Cassidy?"

"I don't care for pizza," Cassidy confirmed, passing Brandi the glass of milk her short arms couldn't quite reach.

"Well, I guess that's why you're so trim. My body's going to be at least five pounds heavier after eating this," said Kendall.

A white mustache hung like a rainbow over Brandi's top lip. "You've got big boobies like Mommy had."

"Brandi," Trevor cautioned, and Brittney giggled to the point of almost choking on her pie. Cassidy admonished both children with her eyes, and Brittney settled down.

"Would you like some more tea, Kendall?" Cassidy offered, surprised she was able to pump as much hospitality into her tone as she had.

"That would be lovely," Kendall said.

Cassidy refilled Kendall's cup as their guest had another bite of pie. Kendall smoothed her tongue over her top lip and rolled her eyes as if she had tiptoed into paradise. "Thank you," she said to Cassidy, then picked up her teacup and sipped.

Cassidy watched Trevor shift in his seat and glance

at the ceiling, trying to pretend he didn't notice every time Kendall leaned herself over, giving him a flash of her "big boobies."

"I used to tease Brenda," Kendall said to Cassidy, "about how fat she was going to get once she married this man." She looked at Trevor. "Do you remember how you used to bring those luscious desserts to Brenda's dorm room when we were in college? Banana puddings, peach cobblers, double-decker pound cakes with thick creamy fudge frosting." She glanced at Cassidy again. "Me and the other girls were so jealous of Brenda and her domesticated man."

"What's a domesticated man?"

"It's a man that knows how to do more than make the babies," Kendall answered Brittney.

"I thought the mommy made the babies." Brandi's eyes were bright with curiosity.

Kendall winked at the little girl. "Your parents will talk about it with you later."

"Thanks, Kendall," Trevor said lightheartedly.

Cassidy slid all the way back in her seat and crossed her arms. She stayed quiet mostly, listening as Kendall babbled about old times—memories that linked Kendall and Trevor. Before the first hour merged with the second, Cassidy had to admit she was envious of the camaraderie between Kendall and Trevor. She was thankful when Kendall finally announced she had to leave.

But more than an hour later, Kendall was still in the living room. "I can't believe that cab's not here." Kendall peered at the small crystal clock on the end table. "It's getting late, and I have an early flight tomorrow."

Trevor stood. "Why don't I take you back to the hotel?"

Cassidy stared at Trevor.

Kendall stared at him, too. "I don't want to be a bother."

"It's no bother. Let me get my keys."

"Okay." She smiled.

There was another smile beneath that smile. One that led Cassidy to suspect Kendall had lied about calling for a cab on her cell phone while in the powder room.

"Are you ready?" Trevor asked, returning with his car keys and wallet.

Kendall kissed the girls repeatedly, and Brittney asked, "Can we go with you to the hotel, Daddy?"

"No, you may not. You have to be at day camp by eight o'clock tomorrow, so you'll stay here and be in bed when I get back."

"Aw, man," Brittney mumbled.

"Our camp is going to a carnival tomorrow." Brandi blasted Kendall with the news.

"That sounds like fun, sweet feet. I wish I could go."

"We wish you could, too, Auntie Kendall." Brittney hugged Kendall good-bye.

Kendall hugged the younger Monroe child next. "Thanks for a lovely evening," she said to Cassidy moments later.

"It was nice having you," Cassidy said with manufactured enthusiasm.

After Trevor and Kendall pulled off, Cassidy helped the children prepare for bed. Then she came downstairs and loaded the soiled china dishes on the tray and carried everything to the kitchen. She filled the stainless-steel sink with warm water and squeezed in pink detergent. Cassidy washed one plate and let it glide back into the sink, her hands collapsing as her concern mounted. The concept of Trevor being intimate with another woman had never pervaded her mind until she'd seen how he acted around Kendall tonight and how quick he'd been to offer her limousine service. Cassidy had heard it prophesized more than once that a man will eat out when he's not getting fed at home. Last night, like so many nights before, Trevor had wanted to be close, but Cassidy had turned him away. So if her husband turned to Kendall, there was no one to blame but herself.

chapter thirty-seven

Trevor unlocked the door of Kendall's room, and the two stepped inside. He placed her hotel key card in her hand.

"Thank you," she said. "Come on in and make yourself comfortable." She dropped her purse to a round tabletop with a pole in the center that disappeared up under a shade. She kicked off her heels, strolled to the kitchenette, and grabbed a glass. "Water?" she asked.

"No, thank you," Trevor said from the middle of the living room quarters of the suite, his gaze shooting around. Everything was pale pink, including the upholstery of the chair she offered.

Kendall settled in a twin chair across from him and used the small coffee table as a footstool. She studied him as she sipped from her glass, and at moments he knew that she knew how turned on he was . . . here with her . . . in her room . . . just the two of them . . . alone.

He twiddled his thumbs. "So what time is your flight?"

"Seven a.m. That's why I opted to stay here instead of at Aunt Wynona's. That and the fact she never fails to work my nerves. I couldn't bear to listen to her yap about my marital status."

"Still the same old Kendall, you and marriage don't mix."

"My constitution wasn't designed for marriage. I get hives every time I think of being shackled to someone for life."

Trevor laughed. "I think you should have stayed with your Aunt Wynona so she could have yapped some sense into you."

Kendall shook her glass, and the ice tinkled clear notes. "Your new wife is a pretty girl. She has that clean and unpretentious appeal I've never been able to project." She smiled with a hint of sarcasm. "I guess I can see how such innocence might fascinate a man."

Trevor kept his face closed, barring Kendall access to his thoughts. His inappropriate thoughts. Thoughts of how different Cassidy and Kendall were.

Cassidy was reserved . . . Kendall was a rebel.

Cassidy was inhibited . . . Kendall was unfettered.

Cassidy could be so uptight . . . Kendall could be so upbeat.

Cassidy didn't want him. Kendall wanted him. He could almost smell the vibes she'd been putting out since arriving at his house. Silence continued between them, and they let it abide, Trevor dedicating the speech-free moments to additional musing about the woman across from him. He knew more about Kendall than she realized. Brenda had told him how Kendall had no qualms about sleeping with married men. She preferred them because they didn't want anything from her except a few hours of gratification and a sympathetic ear, and in this way, Kendall could come and go as she pleased.

She swirled the glass of ice cubes with one of her squared, manicured nails. "Coming to Philly was really hard. I haven't been back since Brenda's funeral. I really miss her, you know."

He had to give it to her. Kendall knew men well, and she knew he wasn't the kind you threw yourself at. She was slow-walking him, hunting for a vulnerable spot, the door to his heart.

"I remember how she used to smile all big whenever she was talking about the girls. The girls and you were the loves of her life," Kendall said, finding that door to his heart. Her eyes glistened with tears, and she vacated the chair, stepped around the coffee table, and sat on its polished wood surface, perching in front of him. She put a hand on his knee. "You must think of her all the time."

"Brenda was a huge part of my life." Trevor glanced at the hand on his leg. "I think about her every day." His gaze slid upward, languidly cruising over Kendall's cleavage and neck before parking on her face.

Kendall filled the next moment with a sigh. "You and Brenda had a beautiful marriage." She raised both eyebrows, but one arched higher than the other. "What about your new one? Is it good?"

Of course, Kendall, as perceptive as she was, had noticed the uneasy glances between him and Cassidy, felt the tension that hung between them. And the fact that he had only touched Cassidy that one time in the vestibule had probably been the true indicator that something was amiss. He was a hands-on man. He'd always had his hands somewhere on Brenda: her neck, her back, her leg, somewhere. Even after two kids, he and Brenda were hand-holders.

"I didn't expect to find the honeymoon over so soon. Or did I just happen to show up on a rare stormy night?" Kendall meddled more. "What's going on?"

Discussing the particulars of his marriage with another woman would be as smart as curling up in a pit of cobras. And letting Kendall keep her hand on his leg wasn't a good idea, either. But Trevor chose the passive alternative and permitted her hand to remain where it was. "My marriage," he said softly, "is not something I can talk about, Kendall." Her demeanor relayed that she was not offended as she smiled and rose to her feet. It was a good time for Trevor to stand and leave, yet he sat and studied the rhythmic bounce of Kendall's feminine attributes as she carried her glass to the kitchenette. When she turned to come back, he shifted his gaze away from her, while his conscience ticked like a bomb about to explode.

Kendall strolled to him and stopped between his knees. She tipped his chin and held his stare. "So if you don't want to talk, why are you here, gorgeous?"

After a pause that endured long enough for him to debate whether he should stay put or get out, he lied, "I don't know," sounding like a child, deciding he wouldn't be so quick to judge others who fell to the beasts of lust and adultery. Taming the beasts was harder than he had realized, and at the moment, he wasn't sure he wanted to tame them.

"You and I both know you didn't have to bring me back tonight." Kendall's fingers, a chiffon touch, slithered up and down his ear. "And you certainly didn't have to come up to my room."

Trevor's heart pounded triple time as Kendall's coconut-shell-brown eyes bored into his with a twinkle that put stars in his own eyes. She was right on both points. He could have let her call for another cab or even called for it himself. And when Kendall said she had a photograph up in her room that she'd like the girls to have, he could have waited for one of the hotel attendants to bring the picture down, as Kendall had suggested. But Trevor had been quick to say he could come up. And now, as she piloted a single finger across his left eyebrow, along his sideburn, over his Adam's apple to the top button of his shirt, he was in no hurry to go home. It felt good to be touched this way. Kendall's finger was cold from the glass, but he didn't mind. It was alive and exactly what a dying man needed. Soothed, he closed his eyes and continued to bask in Kendall's attention.

"Hey," she whispered, cupping his face between her hands. Trevor opened his eyes and rested his gaze on Kendall's painted lips. Lips he had not once considered kissing in all the years he'd known her. He considered it now as her hands clutched his shoulders. It was torture not to respond with a touch of his own, but he kept his hands nailed to the chair arms.

"Don't worry, gorgeous." Her words were insulated in soft seduction. "I know what you need."

Trevor was treading a thin-iced winter river and could not ignore the voice inside of him that warned him to stop and turn back.

But Cassidy's not meeting your needs, his flesh said. *She's not even trying anymore. That's a sin, too. A sin for a sin.*

Cassidy is the one you vowed to cherish, his spirit reminded him.

Kendall undid his shirt button.

Who knows how much longer it will be before Cassidy gets over the vaginismus? She might never get over it. How long are you supposed to wait?

If you love her, you'll wait as long as it takes, the answer came as Kendall undid another button and then another. She pulled his shirt open and laid her hands on his chest, and all of his skin reacted with heat.

Cassidy will never know about this, his flesh whispered.

The response was no louder. *But you'll know . . . and God will know.*

As their heads angled and their lips were about to seal an action that went against everything Trevor believed in, he let go of the chair and gently closed his hands around Kendall's wrists. "Stop," he croaked.

A self-assured and determined glow on her face, Kendall responded by kissing his forehead, the bridge of his nose, and almost his lips, but he stood suddenly, sending her backward. She would have fallen had his hold on her wrists not been firm. He made sure she was steady before letting go and brushing by her. His breathing erratic as the path of a tornado, he ran a hand across his head and down the back of his neck as if this would clear the black clouds shadowing his integrity. Kendall stepped behind him, surrounded his waist with her arms, and he felt her chin pressing between his shoulder blades. He gripped her hands and led them away from his body. "Kendall, it's best we end this."

She exhaled compliance, lowered her arms, and stepped away. Buttoning his shirt, livid at himself for coming to Kendall's room, and appalled at himself for allowing things to advance as far as they had, he barked, "I should go." He turned and started for the door.

"Wait," she hollered.

Trevor snapped around, his voice snapping, too. "What?"

"The photograph . . . I'll get it. It's an original black-and-white of Brenda and me when we were kids," she said, backing up, "and I want the girls to have it."

Kendall disappeared into what Trevor assumed was the bedroom. When she returned, he was calmer. "I'm sorry," he said to her, just as he had whispered to God seconds before.

She shrugged. "I was the aggressor. You really didn't do anything."

"I'm here, and I shouldn't be."

She shrugged again. "It's all good, Trevor." She handed him a white envelope. "The picture's inside."

As Trevor clasped the envelope, his nose began to tingle, and he felt as if he was reliving something. In a matter of seconds, realization slugged him with brute force, and he looked Kendall in the eye. "It was you," he charged. "You sent the info on the drunk-driving accident."

"Yes," she admitted directly.

Trevor gaped at the envelope, scented with something that watered his eyes.

"I sent it because I was concerned."

He frowned.

She explained, "Penny told me you'd taken Cassidy to some awards banquet. I was just being nosy at the time and started asking questions about her. I found out she was a Tilden student, like my little brother, Simon." Kendall folded her arms and leaned against the wall. "I called Simon and asked if he knew her. He said he remembered her. I asked if he had any dirt on her, and he told me she was clean. But a few days later, he faxed me the article. Considering how Brenda died, I thought you should know Cassidy's history before you got too involved with her. Apparently, her transgression didn't matter."

"No, it didn't. I shredded the article and never questioned Cassidy about it."

Kendall examined him with the concentration a scientist might commit to a slide under a microscope. "You really love her, don't you?"

"Yes, I do." Trevor started to turn but stopped. "You're like another mom to Brittney and Brandi, and it would hurt them not to have you in their lives. But I'm uncomfortable with what transpired here tonight." His eyes were unyielding. "It can *never* happen again."

Her feeble smile curved with sheepish remorse. "Been there, done that . . . it's over."

He turned away, then jerked back. "I need to make something else very clear to you. Although I think about Brenda every day—often more than once—not a day goes by that I don't fall on my knees and thank God for blessing me with Cassidy." Trevor opened the door and entered the hall. He looked at Kendall and said before stepping away, "The answer to your earlier concern is yes. Cassidy and I *are* in the midst of a storm. But I assure you, Kendall, there's no storm the God I know can't calm."

✑

Cassidy concentrated on the red numbers of the digital stove clock. It was 10:45, too late for visitors, so she decided the person ringing the bell a second time had to be Trevor. He kept his door keys on a separate ring from his car keys, so it was possible he'd forgotten to take the door keys with him. She hurried to the front of the house and took a moment to peek through the peephole in case she was wrong.

And wrong she was, but she opened the door, anyway. A bashful smile lifted the corners of Rave's lips. "Hi," Rave said.

Cassidy returned the greeting as ribbons of warm air entered the house. She ransacked her brain, scrambling to find something else to say. It wasn't as if she and Rave ever talked. And it was months since she'd seen Rave at church.

Rave seemed to be as disconcerted. "I realize it's late, but I saw the lights on . . . and, well . . ." Her gaze fell to the floor before returning to Cassidy. "My . . . um . . . mom lives a couple blocks from here now. I dropped by to see her, but she was busy, so I thought I'd say hello to you guys."

Rave's voice had a sincere note to it, and there was something about her that almost seemed human. Cassidy took a step back. "Would you like to come in?"

Rave nodded, and with a small smile, walked in, sandals clicking against the black and white tiles of the foyer. Cassidy glanced over the rest of Rave's attire. Her jeans didn't have that pasted-on look, and a roomy shirt hid her navel.

The women spent several awkward seconds beneath a high iron chandelier with pointed teardrop bulbs showering tranquil white light. Cassidy gestured stiffly. "Let's sit in the living room."

Rave strolled in first. "It's been a long time. How've you been?"

"I'm doing great," Cassidy lied with a dim smile, and joined Rave on the couch. "How are you?"

"Good." She stood unexpectedly and lifted her shirt. "*We're* doing good."

Cassidy stared at Rave's potbelly. "You're pregnant," she gasped.

"Four months," Rave said, and returned to the sofa. "Believe me, I went through all the stages of grief when I found out, but I'm okay with it now."

Rave anchored her hand on her stomach, and Cassidy wondered if the action was purposeful or instinctive. During her own pregnancy, Cassidy had often discovered her hand on her belly.

"I'm lucky that pregnant is all I am. I could have AIDS or some other STD."

Cassidy could appreciate the magnitude of that

statement. When she compromised her standards and carried out a sexual relationship with Minister that lasted for months, she had been reckless and failed to use protection most times.

Rave wore her hair parted down the middle, and a long braid hung on each side of her head. She fingered the end of one of the black cords before flinging it over her shoulder. "I was planning to tell my mom about the baby tonight. But she was entertaining one of her boyfriends and didn't have time to talk . . . the way it's been my whole life. I thought she'd be glad to see me, since we haven't seen each other for several months."

Cassidy heard the dismay in Rave's tone. "I'm sorry you didn't get to talk to your mom."

"It's no big deal," she murmured, but the tears in Rave's eyes said differently.

"I was about to have a glass of juice. Can I fix you one?"

"I didn't plan to stay long. Like my mom said, I should have called first."

"Well, Trevor's not here." He should've been back from taking Kendall to her hotel by now, and a ball of tension bounced in Cassidy's stomach, but she maintained a pleasant face. "And the girls are in bed, so you're welcome to stay and talk."

Rave took time to think. "If it's no trouble?"

"It's not," Cassidy reassured her.

Sixty seconds later, Rave sat at the kitchen table built for six. Cassidy poured two glasses of apple-cranberry juice. "Are you hungry?"

"Lately, I'm *always* hungry."

Cassidy smiled and pulled the remainder of the

sweet potato pie from a side-by-side stainless-steel refrigerator that matched a double dishwasher, an eight-
burner gas stove, and a trio of wall ovens. She put the
dessert on a stoneware plate.

Cassidy sat down, and Rave said softly, "I haven't
told anyone this, but I don't know who my baby's father
is." A forkload of pie disappeared inside Rave's mouth.
"I feel comfortable telling you. I guess it's because I
know you're not the kind to spread the stains of others
all through the church."

"Do you think the baby might be Kregg's? Kregg
would definitely want to be involved in the baby's life
if the baby is his."

"It's not Kregg's," Rave answered in a relaxed way.
"He always insisted we use a condom. Plus we stopped
sleeping together last winter. I wish it was Kregg's,
though. He's a good man. I didn't realize it when I was
with him." She licked a crumb of pie from her bottom
lip. "But he's moved on. I saw him with your sister-in-
law at the mall."

"They've been dating."

"I hope everything works out for them."

"I do, too. They've started coming to church, and
Trevor and I believe it won't be long before they'll decide to commit to Christ."

"I need to get back in church. I actually miss being
there."

Sorrow filled Rave's expression, and Cassidy felt the
Spirit of God nudging her to share His Word with
Rave. But with the problems going on in her own life,
Cassidy questioned if she was qualified. She thought for
a moment more. "Rave," she started slowly, "you've

been a church member, but have you ever given your heart to God?" No seeds of condemnation had been planted in the question.

Following a brief pause, Rave replied, "No. I've never asked Jesus into my life."

"It's easy to do."

"I know, all I have to do is believe. It's all there in John 3:16."

"And don't forget Romans 10:13. *Whosoever shall call upon the name of the Lord shall be saved.*"

"Yeah, but I've done so many ugly things, girl. Ugly," she emphasized.

"The Bible says all of us have sinned. That means no one's perfect. And that's why Jesus died for us."

"So that we *can* be perfect?" she said with some sarcasm.

"No, so that one day, we can live with Him for eternity, and so that while we're here on earth, we can commune with Him intimately, on a personal level. A lot of people think that being a Christian means you join a church or get baptized or take communion on first Sundays. But it's about so much more than that. It's about knowing God and striving to get closer to Him every day."

"How do you do that?"

"Well, in order to know someone, you have to fellowship with them, right?"

Rave nodded.

"In order to know God, you have to spend time with Him."

"Like praying?"

"Yes. And reading His Word."

Rave bit down on her bottom lip, and a shy blush stained her cheeks. "Do you really think He loves me?"

Tears formed in the corners of Cassidy's eyes. "He loves you, Rave."

"Will you help me talk to Him?"

"We'll say the prayer Pastor Audrey uses." She bowed her head. "Dear Jesus, I believe You died on the cross for my sins and rose from the dead."

Rave repeated each word.

Cassidy continued, "Forgive me for my sins and come into my heart," but Rave was silent this time. Cassidy waited, not wanting to rush her. The decision to accept Christ was one Rave had to make for herself. Some seconds later, Cassidy heard Rave sniffle and sigh, and she knew God was working on Rave's heart. Rave's voice trembled with emotion as she asked God for forgiveness.

Cassidy led the next part of the prayer. "Take complete control of my life, Lord. Make and mold me in Your image."

Rave voiced both sentences, then repeated the last line with profound conviction. "I will walk with You from this moment forward and love You with my heart, mind, and soul."

"Amen," Cassidy said.

A sparkle showed through the tears on Rave's face as she echoed, "Amen."

chapter thirty-eight

Typical of the day before the weekend, customers filed in and out of Seconds at a steady rate. Trevor lingered on the first floor, greeting the patrons. He carried a cake to the car of a young man on crutches, then went upstairs to his office to review a pile of applications. Before he could read through the first résumé, Grace rushed in. Visibly shaken, she met his gaze with troubled eyes, and in the same moment, they both remembered that *other time* she'd burst into his office this way.

Trevor pushed aside the paperwork and stood in a hurry, all of his pores spitting beads of clammy sweat. "Who?" was all he could push forth, accepting that someone he loved was in trouble.

Grace vented a labored breath and answered, "Cassidy."

At the hospital fifteen minutes later, Trevor blurted to the nurse at the station, "My wife is here."

She turned to a computer screen. "Her name?"

"Room 12, room 12," Trevor chanted, quickly passing cube-shaped rooms with peach-colored curtains for doors. His heart in a knot, he braced for the worst and shoved aside the curtain of room 12. A young doctor with red hair and freckles looked up from his metal stool seat. Cassidy, stretched on a gurney and dressed in a hospital gown, also met Trevor's gaze.

"Trevor," she said, her mouth easing into a smile.

Happy to see her, too, he let his hand come down over hers as his eyes searched for some visible injury. He didn't see blood, and she wasn't hooked up to any tubes, but he was only marginally relieved. "What happened?" he asked, fighting to keep his voice stable.

"I suddenly became tired, and everything started spinning . . ."

The doctor rose. His hand met Trevor's in the air above Cassidy's stomach. "I'm Dr. Falk. Are you the husband?"

"Yes," he answered, then questioned the doctor, looking at Cassidy the whole time. "Is Cassidy all right?"

"We did an EKG, and the results were normal. Your wife's lab results, however, show she has iron-deficiency anemia, which means a decrease in the number of red cells in the blood caused by insufficient iron. But overall, Mrs. Monroe appears to be in good physical health. As I've explained to her"—he looked at Cassidy, then at Trevor—"there could be a repeat of today's episode, or she could eventually develop serious health problems if she doesn't maintain a better diet. Food is to the body what gasoline is to a car. I've advised Mrs. Monroe that although she may feel stressed, she needs to eat." His gaze returned to Cassidy. "It might be wise for you to talk to someone. Before you leave, I'll give you the name of several doctors who deal with anxiety-related issues. How are you feeling now?"

"Better."

"I'll write you a prescription for oral iron supplements and give you that list of iron-rich foods." Cassidy's chart lay on the bed next to her, and the doctor picked it up. "The nurse will be back in to check your vital signs again. If all is well, you can be discharged."

As the doctor exited, Trevor sighed and kissed his wife's forehead. "I love you."

"I love you, too." Their grip remained intact, and she brought his hand to her lips. The sound of a baby crying filtered into the room, and somewhere a man shouted out, "Nurse, help me," every ten seconds or so. "I'm chilly," Cassidy said, and Trevor pulled the sheet over her feet and up to her chest.

They shared the next silent moments with feelings streaming between them twisted and tense, as this was the first conversation they'd had since Trevor had taken Kendall to the hotel last night. Cassidy was asleep when he got back, and this morning he overslept and had to rush out. He pondered if he should tell Cassidy what had happened with Kendall. He quickly decided against it. Cassidy wasn't feeling well, and he would not risk making her feel worse.

Cassidy's stomach growled, and they both smiled. He already knew the answer but asked, "Did you have breakfast?"

She wagged her head no.

"If I bring you something from the cafeteria, will you eat it?"

She wagged yes.

"I'll be right back," he promised. He walked through the corridor, turned right, and bumped into the shoulder of a man.

"Trevor," Dunbar said in greeting.

"Cassidy called you?" Trevor said right away with somber discontent in his tone.

"She was with me when she became ill. I'm the one who brought her here." Dunbar straightened his tie.

Grateful that Cassidy was in one piece, Trevor hadn't thought about where she'd been when she'd taken ill—Trevor glowered at Dunbar—or whom she'd been with. This wasn't the day Cassidy and Dunbar usually walked, and the image of them hanging out together just for fun forced a surge of blood to Trevor's head that pained his temples. Before they were married, he should have been honest and told Cassidy that he was uncomfortable with the relationship she shared with Dunbar. But he didn't think he had the right to ask her to give up a friend, because that's all Dunbar was—a friend. Now Trevor wondered if Dunbar had become more. Maybe Cassidy talked to Dunbar about the things she couldn't discuss with him. Maybe their relationship had deepened to a physical level. Trevor hated to think like this, but since Cassidy had been so cold toward him lately, he regarded such thoughts as legitimate.

"I'm on my way to get Cassidy something from the cafeteria." His voice was steel. "I'd appreciate it if you

weren't here when I returned." Trevor broke eye contact and assumed a brisk pace past Dunbar, ignoring the
inner menacing voice that coaxed him to punch the
man in the face.

✐

Cassidy and Trevor walked along a set of bricks that
snaked to the side of the parsonage. "I'm sorry I made
us late," she said. As soon as she arrived home from the
hospital, she'd climbed into bed. She slept into the
early evening without waking once. Cassidy told Trevor
he should have awakened her sooner, but he'd said she
needed the sleep, and they could reschedule this
evening's session with the pastor if she wanted to stay
home and rest.

Trevor slipped his hand around hers as they continued over the path. The warmth from Trevor's palm
felt better than a wool sweater on a cold day. She didn't
want to release him, but it was necessary, since the
stairwell leading down to the basement level was so
narrow. The first to reach the bottom, she turned to notice Trevor on the step behind her. His eyes talked to
her eyes, and her eyes talked, too, and they both perceived that being here was evidence that both of them
wanted something more for their marriage. When
Trevor first told her that the pastor wanted this
meeting, apprehension became her wall of defense. But
the pastor assured there would be no discussion of her
sexual dysfunction unless she mentioned it. This was to
be a general session, one he engaged in with married
couples from time to time. Most of the marriage coun-

seling at Charity Community had been delegated to a counseling staff, but Clement liked to stay in touch with couples in crisis, and Cassidy consented, more at ease with Clement than with anyone else.

Natasha answered the door. "Hi," the teen shouted. She had on a headset connected to a portable CD player. Cassidy couldn't tell what song was playing, but she could hear drums.

"Hi," Cassidy said along with Trevor, and Natasha invited them inside with another shout.

"My dad's in his office." She pulled off the headset, and her voice plunged to normal. "You can go on back."

"Thanks," Cassidy and Trevor spoke together again. Natasha returned the headset to her ears, tossed a bunch of the braided extensions that hung to her waist over her shoulders, and jogged to the other side of the room and up the stairs.

While waiting for Clement to respond to the knock on his office door, Cassidy stared from corner to corner of the spacious basement, taking in the sparkling white kitchenette, the glass dining table and four fabric chairs, the leather sofa that faced an on-the-wall plasma television, and a huge aquarium built in the wall and populated with brightly colored fish.

Clement smiled as soon as he saw them. "Come on in and have a seat. Would you like coffee, juice, water?" he said, gesturing toward a small bar.

"No, thank you." Cassidy and Trevor exchanged amused glances, having spoken in unison a third time. Cassidy thought that if she and her husband were always so in sync, there might not be a need for this meeting.

"Thank you for coming," Clement said. "Have a seat." Four armchairs were set in a square, and Cassidy and Trevor sat next to each other. The round coffee table in the middle held a Bible. Cassidy fiddled with her bracelet and for a moment thought of Dunbar.

Clement sat across from them. "As I told Trevor when I spoke with him on the phone, this meeting is informal. It's an opportunity to let you both know I'm praying for you, and I'm here to help in any way I can. The first year of marriage can be difficult." He smiled. "I remember well." Cassidy glanced at the wall. There was a wedding picture, the same pose but smaller than the version in the Audrey living room. Cassidy carried her vision back and forth across the wall, admiring the other family pictures. Most of them were taken when Natasha was still in patent-leather shoes and Vivaca's hair was longer, Clement's waist smaller.

Cassidy turned to Clement, already opening their session in prayer. She peeked at Trevor, positioned with his spine curled forward, his hands clasped and hanging between his knees. His eyes were closed, and his nose pointed to the carpet. Cassidy tightened her eyelids, too.

The prayer ended, and Clement asked, "Are you two praying together at home?"

Cassidy and Trevor linked stares. His eyes were a reflection of her thoughts. They rarely prayed together or read God's Word together.

"In my opinion," Clement started, "joint prayer is the deepest form of intimacy a couple can experience. It needs to be incorporated into your marriage daily. Vivaca and I pray together every day, even when one of us is out of town. No, it's not always easy to pray *with* her or *for* her when we've been arguing. But what I've found is, I can't talk to God and fight with Vivaca at the same time." Clement gave them several moments to meditate. "The devil, not each other, is your enemy. So pray together and pray the Word of God. It's the weapon that pulls down the barriers which keep us from fulfillment with Christ"—he paused to study them both—"and each other."

chapter thirty-nine

The next morning Cassidy brushed her teeth and tongue, eliminating the taste of the veggie omelet she had for breakfast. She'd eaten the whole thing. Had a glass of juice, a slice of toast, and a dish of honeydew, too. Another emergency room visit was the last thing she wanted, so hungry or not, no stress or stressed-out, she was going to eat. She'd already taken steaks out of the freezer for lunch.

A mint-flavored tingle in her mouth, she strolled from the bathroom and straightened the sheets, making the bed. The pillows in place and the bedding smooth, Cassidy ambled in front of the bureau mirror and untied the scarf she'd worn to prevent her braids from frizzing as she slept. She swept the cloth from her head and combed her fingers through the braids, gently lifting them and letting them swoop back to her shoulders. She'd showered before eating, and now she removed her robe and dressed in the white T-shirt and panty set Trevor had given her on their honeymoon. "A gag gift," he'd teased as they both remembered and laughed about the time he walked in on her in the bathroom.

A furry coat wrapped around Cassidy's ankle, and she glanced down. She still would not brand herself a cat person, but this one had found a place in her heart. She stooped and massaged Poopie between the ears. The cat purred appreciation and strutted out of the room.

Cassidy finished dressing, adding only a pair of checkered lounge pants to her ensemble. It was a stay-at-home-and-do-very-little Saturday. She had canceled out of the senior center for today. She needed the rest. She needed to meditate. She reached for her Bible. Last evening Clement had given her and Trevor a list of scriptures to study, independently and as a couple, and she thought she'd read over a few of them. It was the perfect morning to spend time with God. The house was empty. Trevor had gotten up early, taken the kids out for breakfast, and then he was driving them to the church to a special Kidpraise event before he went to Seconds.

Cassidy sat on the side of the bed and read from her Bible. She let the words sink into her heart, then closed the book and placed it next to her. She extended her arms, flattening her palms on the mattress. The sun entered through the windows and balcony door, laying tracks of light on the rug. From where Cassidy sat, she could see a piece of the sky, and in a matter-of-fact tone, she blurted, "So here I am, God." Cassidy relaxed her shoulders and grew still, more reverent, as her lids floated shut. "Okay, here it is, God. I'm scared. Trevor is a man who adores his children. So what will he think of a woman who turned her back on her baby? What will he think of a woman who kept such a terrible secret from him and who also let him believe she was a virgin when they married?" She swallowed emotion. "I've already lost so many people—my mother, my baby, Aunt Odessa." Cassidy didn't doubt she could survive on her own. But Trevor and the children were her loved ones now. She cherished them, and she couldn't imagine life without them. "I don't want to lose Trevor and the children, too. I don't want them to leave me."

I'll never leave you.

"I know that, God." She opened her eyes, focusing on His sky. "You've already proved it." The times in her life when she'd pulled away from God, God remained and waited for her return. "So what do I do now, Lord?"

Tell him. Tell Trevor everything. And trust Me to take care of the rest.

Cassidy sighed, tired of running from God's will and ready to do the right thing. "I choose to stand still and trust You," she surrendered as tears began to ease down her cheeks. "I don't understand all of Your ways, but I believe You want what's best for me. My hope is in You, and I know You're not through with me. There are things You want me to learn, things You want me to do. My life has a purpose . . ."

✥

Cassidy remained on her knees, slumped over the bed, as Trevor walked into the bedroom and knelt beside her. He laid his hand on her back. "Are you all right?" he asked, a ridiculous level of worry in his eyes.

And then she realized there was nothing ridiculous about it. Not when it was yesterday that he'd found her in the emergency room.

"I'm all right. I was talking to God. We had a lot to talk about, and I got all emotional." She glanced down at the crop of crumpled tissues on the bed, then snatched a fresh one from the box, also on the bed. She dabbed beneath her eyes. "I must look a mess."

His crooked grin was charming. "You look beautiful."

Trevor had on a black T-shirt and black jeans. He was scheduled to work this Saturday, and it now dawned on her that he would have dressed differently for work. "Why aren't you at Seconds?"

He clutched her hand. "I took the day off so I could spend it with you."

This is it, Cassidy. Tell him now.

Cassidy sucked in a sharp breath and let it out a bit at a time, the nervous pebbles in her stomach expanding into rocks.

Do not be afraid. I am here with you. I will help you.

She stared at Trevor. His head bowed, his eyes closed, his lips slightly moving, he prayed. She sensed right away his inaudible prayer was for her. "Trevor," she whispered.

"Yes," he answered without delay, as if he'd been expecting her call.

"I'm . . . I'm ready to talk to you."

Trevor squeezed her hand and nodded. "Whatever you tell me won't change how much I love you."

Cassidy had doubts, yet she began speaking. "I had . . ." She pointed her waterlogged vision toward the bed and a teardrop wet the bronze-colored bedspread as the confession came fast, breathless, on the wing of a whisper. "I had sex with Minister." The room was stiff with silence as if the walls were shocked and waiting for her to say it wasn't so. Too ashamed to pursue an eye-to-eye exchange with Trevor, she looked at their hands. The strength of Trevor's clasp had not weakened, and he began easing his thumb back and forth over her skin. "There was a baby," she panted through the heaviness pressing her chest. "Minister and I decided not to keep him . . . so . . . so we left him just inside the hospital entrance." The image zoomed from foggy to clear, and Cassidy could see her swaddled infant as he lay in the laundry basket. He had stopped crying, and he stared up at her as Minister grabbed her wrist and tugged her away from him.

Then the questions came, a pelting rain that poured on her each morning before she rolled out of bed and each time she passed a baby on the street or someone with a baby sat close-by. Each night as she closed her eyes, the same questions rained. *Is he safe? Is he happy? Is he loved?*

Cassidy clamped her teeth shut, confining the sob that wanted to free itself as one loud mournful wail. She pulled her hand from Trevor's and hugged herself as sorrow and shame, guilt and regret, gripped and strangled her harder than ever before. She flopped to her backside, drew her knees to her forehead, buried her face inside her folded arms, and finally, freely, wept aloud the grief she'd stored for too many silent years.

Trevor rose to his feet, and Cassidy accepted that one of her fears was about to come true. Trevor would not be able to love someone like her—a woman who'd rejected her own flesh and blood. Her husband would ask her to leave. He would forbid her to see the children. He would never want to look her in the face again. She was about to go into another "he would" when strong hands clamped over her shoulders and powerful fingers curled beneath her underarms, and he lifted her until she stood. Cassidy continued to shield her face, catching her sobs with her hands while Trevor sat on the bed's edge and pulled her down to sit on his leg, her legs between his thighs. Agony persisted, inflicting upon her stabs that sliced deep. She tied her arms around his neck and held on for support until her cries faded into a blend of gulps and pants that jerked her shoulders. Trevor reached behind his back and brought forward the tissue box. She pulled the last two and blew her nose. The tissues too damp to absorb more, she stuffed them into the empty box and began drying her face with her hands when Trevor clasped both of her hands with one of his, pulled them to her lap, and held them there as he continued the job of removing her tears with his lips. Kisses made of satin brushed against her cheeks and chin and the corners of her eyes.

She sniffled through a stuffy nose. "Why are you kissing me?"

"Because I love you," he whispered, and pressed his lips to her neck.

Instead of rebuking her, he was rewarding her. Instead of punishing, he was pleasing. While his kisses accumulated along her jaw, she slid her hands up the hard pack of his arms and gripped his shirt midchest. Her cheek against his, her concern quietly drifted into his ear. "I don't understand how you can still want me."

"You're the greatest woman in the world. Why wouldn't I want you?"

His voice was a whisper that intersected with her soul, and she flattened her hands over his ears, holding his head, halting his movements, observing him with all the amazement she felt inside. For several seconds, she was unable to see clearly through the new lakes of tears. "But didn't you hear what I told you?" She squeezed the words out, a hand still plastered to each side of his head.

A smile gleamed in the dark set of his eyes, and with gentle force, he seized her hands and carried them to his shoulders. He clasped her head as she had clasped his, and he tenderly kissed her mouth. Cassidy's chains of resistance loosened and melted, and she whispered his name between his lips as the kiss continued and he moved backward, pulling her with him. They lay sideways on the thick bedspread, within the sanctuary of each other's arms. Their deep kiss subsided into a delicate parting, and Cassidy opened her eyes, a small portion of her logic expecting to see some measure of repugnance, some crumb of judgment, in the eyes studying her so intently. But all she witnessed was the same love that had been there all the time.

His fingertip traced her ear to the earring-free lobe before dropping to her shoulder and caressing the length of her arm. "Your bracelet is missing."

"I removed it last night when we arrived home from the session with the pastor." Her arm felt strange, the jewelry no longer there. Cassidy braced on her elbow and leaned her head on her palm. She had come this far, and she was going all the way. It was time to tell the truth about Dunbar. "I felt sick yesterday morning, so I took the day off from ACES. Dunbar called and asked if I wanted to go to the park, so I went, just to get out. I thought it might be relaxing." Still congested, she sniffed. "That's why I was with him, and he was the one who drove me to the hospital."

Trevor's emotional withdrawal felt like the chill left behind when the sun suddenly disappeared behind a thick cloud and stayed hidden too long. Vulnerability showed in his eyes as he stared beyond her head, and Cassidy realized he wasn't merely jealous, he was hurt. She cradled her hand to his neck. "You were right about him. When we were at the park, Dunbar held my hand. Holding his hand was no big deal when I was single, but yesterday it didn't feel right. I asked him how he felt about me, and Dunbar admitted he had strong feelings. I told him we shouldn't hang out anymore, and I wouldn't be comfortable receiving any more presents."

"I owe Dunbar a big thank-you."

Cassidy lifted her brows in question.

"If Dunbar had told you how he felt before I married you, you'd be Mrs. Smith."

"I've never felt anything other than friendship for Dunbar," she said honestly. "I've never loved Dunbar the way I love you." Her hand glided to Trevor's chest, and he caught it. "This morning I read a few of the passages Pastor Audrey suggested. One of them was Ephesians, chapter 5. *Wives, submit yourselves unto your own husbands, as unto the Lord.* I apologize for how cold I've been in our bed." Residual moisture trickling down the back of her throat, she swallowed hard. "I was wrong."

"That chapter also says," Trevor responded, "*Husbands, love your wives, even as Christ also loved the church*. So I need to apologize, too, because I haven't been the man God wants me to be. Pastor Audrey was right. I should be praying with you every day. I've been married before, and I know what happens when joint prayer and Bible study get pushed out of the relationship." He paused under Cassidy's regard. "I almost lost Brenda because there was another woman in my life. Her name was Seconds. I spent a lot of time there because I loved it so much, but in the process, I neglected my wife. Whenever she asked me to study the Bible with her, I was too tired. And I really was. There was no balance to my life. So one day Brenda packed up the girls and they left. They were only gone for a week, but it was one of the longest weeks of my life. And the wake-up call I needed."

Cassidy lowered her head to the bed, continuing to face the man she loved as he lifted a handful of her thin braids, then laid them back on her shoulder. "What happened after you left the baby?" he asked.

It saddened Cassidy to remember, but Trevor had a right to know. "The report of an abandoned baby was on the late news that night. The reporter urged the mother to come forward. I thought about it, but the following day the news said dozens of families had expressed interest in the baby. I decided he should be with one of those families. Minister kept saying it was best for the baby, and at the time, I believed it, too. I loved Minister, and I thought he loved me. But now, as I look back, I can't recall him ever telling me he loved me."

"When did you break up with him?"

"He broke up with me," she admitted. "About two weeks after I gave birth, Minister called and said he needed a fresh start, and it didn't include me." A grudge invaded her voice, and she didn't care if Trevor heard it. "I soon realized the only reason Minister and I remained a couple throughout the pregnancy was because he wanted to make sure I didn't keep the baby . . . and no one would ever find out the baby was his."

There had been no formal face-to-face good-bye, no real closure between Cassidy and Minister, and there were moments she was positive Minister's decision to leave her was because she'd actually gone along with him and abandoned their child. It was possible he viewed her as pathetic, the way she viewed herself at the time.

Trevor said quietly, "I'm shocked Minister didn't try to talk you into an abortion."

"He suggested one. But when I found out I was pregnant, I was too far along for an abortion. Otherwise . . ." She was ashamed to say it, but if she'd found out earlier, she would have terminated the pregnancy if Minister had wanted her to. All she ever did was try to please him. Minister could have asked her to fly off the roof, and she would have tried it. She remembered the night Minister introduced her to alcohol. She had two beers before he asked her to go to the store for him. Halfway there, she couldn't remember what she was supposed to buy. But it didn't matter, since she never made it to the store. Instead, she crashed Minister's car into the mailbox of a local minister. He and his wife took her in for the night. In the morning, they said they had prayed, and the Lord had directed them to refrain from calling the police. Still, they wanted her to come and speak to the youth at the church as retribution.

"Minister's dead now," she said, and met Trevor's curious scrutiny. "He got involved with some preacher's wife. The preacher shot him in the head."

Trevor's voice remained soft. "Is the baby you had with Minister the reason you're afraid to have one with me?"

Cassidy was slow to speak, but she answered all that was in her heart. "Being pregnant would force me to feel the past, and I don't want to. I don't want to feel another baby growing inside me. I don't want to remember how it felt to give birth to my son and hold him. It hurts too much." Loads of women at church had given birth over the years, and while everyone else oohed and aahed and begged to cuddle up with one of the babies, Cassidy kept her distance. She avoided the church nursery and the diaper aisle in the grocery store and the baby section in department stores. "Honestly, I just want to forget that the whole thing with Minister and the baby ever happened."

He held one side of her face. "I wish I could get you through this on my own, but I don't know how. However, God's given every person a gift, and there are those He has called to help the emotionally broken. Baby, there's someone who can help you work through your issues and fears and bad memories." He lifted his head and placed a gentle kiss on her lips. "You can do this. I've seen how determined you are when it comes to those ACES kids. Now it's time for you to fight for you."

"Yes," she whispered, her trepidations about counseling already beginning to wane as her desire to please God increased.

"Heavenly Father," Trevor began, taking her hand, "we acknowledge You as our source. Therefore, we thank You in advance that Cassidy, as Your daughter, is equipped with Your strength, and she will not walk in fear, but in Your power. I thank You for her, Father. I thank You that she is a godly woman who loves You. Help both of us as we commit to live totally surrendered to You. Fill us with Your Spirit so that every part of our marriage will bring glory unto You. Help us as we attempt to raise our children according to Your Word so that they will grow up remembering Your principles and likewise they will one day teach their children Your way.

"Father, thank You for dying on the cross, so that not only can we know forgiveness, but healing, too. Your Word assures that You heal broken hearts and bind up wounds. Our wounds are too big for us to bear, but not too big for You to heal because nothing is too hard for You. So we lay our pain at Your feet, believing that we're already made whole and fully delivered." He kissed her hand and whispered, "Amen."

"Amen," she whispered in accord.

chapter forty

The flat heels of their sandals rapped the floor as Cassidy and Lena carried yellow plastic trays to a table. Saturday shoppers would soon pack the food court, but as of now, the closest people to Cassidy and Lena were three tables away. It had been a month since the friends had a day out together, and they'd spent the morning store-hopping from one end of the mall to the other and would spend the afternoon at the day spa.

"Hey," Lena said suddenly after chewing a bite of a thick cheeseburger. "I haven't given you proper congratulations for bringing home that spelling bee win." Lena stood, raised and lowered her arms in a dramatic representation of a bow.

"Girl, will you sit down," Cassidy said, shining a smile, tickled with Lena and with the fact that ACES had won the first-place trophy this summer.

Lena plugged Cassidy in on all of her latest wedding plans while they ate. "Hulk and I have decided to have the reception in the church hall. It'll be less expensive than the outside places we've investigated. We've selected a DJ, and she's going to play inspirational love songs. We want to have dancing. Do you think Pastor Audrey will allow it?"

"He might. You'll have to ask him." Cassidy poked a white fork into one of the strips of grilled chicken tossed throughout a garden of crisp mixed greens. When all the wedding talk came to a lull, Cassidy unveiled the part of her life Lena had not been knowledgeable about. Lena used a napkin to blot tears from her cheeks as Cassidy told her about the night she gave her son away.

"You could have confided in me." Lena blew her nose. "I would've been there for you."

"I'm in counseling for another matter as well," Cassidy explained a few minutes later, and Lena looked more stunned than when Cassidy had told her about the baby.

"You mean you and Trevor have never had . . ." Lena gulped the word rather than speak it.

"Intercourse," Cassidy helped her. "It's not a bad word, you can say it."

"What's the condition called again?"

"Vaginismus."

"Girl, I've never heard of anything like that before."

"It's not terminal or contagious," Cassidy said lightly, because Lena still looked so unsettled.

"And counseling has helped you cope with all this?"

"God is really using Dr. Tia to help me process everything." Sitting down and exposing her feelings had been easier than expected, although the first getting-to-know-you session had not been without some apprehension. But the therapist had an approachable smile, a gentle spirit, and a way of making Cassidy feel like everything she said was valid and nothing she said was stupid, and Cassidy had relaxed and opened up to Dr. Tia Morris within the hour. Now Cassidy looked forward to the sessions with Dr. Tia. As a Christian, she often pointed Cassidy to scriptures that edified and strengthened.

During this week's session, Cassidy exercised her emotional muscles and made Herbie a topic. In her heart, Cassidy still nursed wishes and dreams of becoming Herbie's mother. With Dr. Tia's assistance, Cassidy explored the possibility that she was trying to replace her son with Herbie. But with a clear conscience, Cassidy had been able to admit differently. She could never replace the precious baby she'd given birth to. And in turn, she could never put such a burden on Herbie. What she could do was give Herbie lots of love and a safe home. Trevor, however, had not mentioned the subject of adopting Herbie, and Cassidy had left it alone, too. For the time being, it was best to concentrate on herself, her marriage, and her daughters.

Recently, Brittney had started testing Cassidy's authority. Early on, Cassidy had thought Brittney's misbehavior was because Derek was in the house and she was showing off for his benefit. But with Trudy's brother and sister-in-law accepting guardianship of Derek, Derek had been gone for a week, and Brittney was still out of order. "Last night we had chicken for dinner, which I've fixed before and she's eaten with no problem. Yet this time she says with her face contorted,

'I don't like this chicken.' Then she whines, 'My *real* mom made better chicken than this.'"

"Ouch," Lena hissed. "That had to sting."

"More than a little," Cassidy confessed. "Of course, I didn't let the kids see the wound." Cassidy pushed her empty plate away, getting some of the leftover sesame-soy vinaigrette on her fingers. She wiped her hands on a napkin.

"So how did you handle the situation?"

"I told her calmly yet firmly she didn't have to eat the chicken, but she couldn't have any of the cake Trevor made, either. She agreed and helped me with the dishes without any complaint. That should've been a clue she was up to no good."

Lena listened attentively.

"When Trevor got in from work, Brittney ran to the door, jumped in his arms, and the first thing she asked him was, 'How was your day, Daddy?' They were both all kissy and giggly. Then the second thing she asked was . . ." Cassidy pointed to Lena.

"Can I have some cake?" Lena filled in the blank with no problem. Shaking her head, she said, "Kids will try you. So how did you and Trevor handle her?"

"Well, of course, she didn't have any cake. Trevor and I had a talk with her and then sent her to bed with no television, either."

Lena lifted the one french fry left on her plate and hacked it in half with her teeth. "It's good Trevor backs you up. I know parents who let their kids play those divide-and-conquer games, and all it does is cause more household confusion."

Cassidy and Lena placed their trays above the trash

receptacle on the ledge designated for dirty trays. Their spa appointment was scheduled to begin in fifteen minutes, and after a restroom stop, they hurried to the exit for parking lot D. "A massage is exactly what I need," Lena said, shopping bags hanging from both hands.

Cassidy smiled, depending on this massage, too. It would help her relax and feel more confident about the romantic surprise she had planned for Trevor.

chapter forty-one

A trail of long-stemmed red roses and the whisper of jazz lured Trevor to the master bedroom. He opened the door, a twine of excitement undulating through his body as he inhaled the fragrance of vanilla. He had no clue if it was the scent of the candles or something Cassidy had sprayed, but it was well pleasing.

He lingered in the open doorway, taking in the picture. All of the curtains were closed, shielding Trevor and Cassidy from any moonbeams, and one bedside lamp was turned on low. The dim room flickered with candleshine, and a small round table draped with a white tablecloth displayed a big bowl of fresh strawberries, a pair of flutes, and an ice bucket bearing a long green bottle of his preferred brand of sparkling cider. His wife adorned the center of the bed, reclining against a wall of pillows, looking lovely—and blue, dressed in the bathrobe he favored.

"Hello," she said in a low, musical voice.

Trevor feigned indifference for a few moments, and

then the smile he was stifling burst onto his lips. "Hello to you, too, Sky," he said. He reached to close the door behind him.

"You can leave it open. The kids are with Penny." She had arranged for a sleepover several days ago.

Trevor slowly crossed the room, removing his necktie as he walked closer to the silken voice. He stopped between the bed and the table Cassidy had prepared. Now he noticed the smaller bowl, filled with white powder.

"Powdered sugar," she said, gliding to her feet. Strawberries sheathed in powdered sugar were one of his favorite tastes, and he watched, fire spreading through his heart, as Cassidy selected one of the strawberries and rolled it in the soft dust. She raised the fruit to his mouth, and he opened so she could place the whole sweet prize on his tongue. She reached for a napkin, but Trevor wanted all of the sweetness, and starting with her pinkie, nibbled the excess sugar from each of Cassidy's plain, tapered nails, then tipped her chin and pressed his lips to hers, savoring every wonderful bit of the night's first kisses. Sighing in unison, they punctuated their kisses with an embrace, Trevor stroking the strip of spine between Cassidy's shoulder blades with tender admiration, absorbing the softness of her robe.

"No more waiting," she whispered.

Trevor pushed her braids out of the way and nuzzled her neck. "What do you mean?"

Her husky response tickled his ear. "You know what I mean."

Trevor worried that he did know. For a few moments, he hugged her tighter and hunted for words that would not wound or offend her. He looked into her face and said sincerely, "I think we should follow Dr. Tia's advice and let things happen slowly, without pressure."

Her eyes, so spirited when he'd first come home, became unsure. He was afraid she was taking his apprehension as rejection, whereas what fueled his hesitation was his concern that she was about to get in over her head.

"But I want us to have it all." She pushed to her toe tips and kissed his goatee. He realized his expression reflected his worry because she added, "I'm better. I know I'm better."

Trevor smiled into her eyes, although behind her loving gaze hung a shadow of something Trevor couldn't put into words, something Cassidy wasn't saying.

"Trust me, Trevor," she cooed up at him, and he allowed the silk-covered words to wiggle past his better judgment. A second later, he led her to the bed. A minute later, her robe sailed to the floor.

*

An hour later, the room lay netted in unspoken disappointment. Outfitted in jeans and a pullover shirt, Cassidy tied her sneaker laces with fast-moving fingers.

"Where are you going?" Trevor questioned, his tenor-tone tired as he sat up in the bed.

"I'm going for a drive." She spit her words as if she might otherwise choke on them. "I need to get out of here."

"Cassidy." He softened his voice more. "Don't walk away. Let's talk this out, pray through it—"

"I don't feel like praying," she snapped, and grabbed her car keys from the dresser. "I feel like screaming because I am so *sick* of having this condition."

"Honey, you're not *always* going to have it." He started to get out of bed, but she stepped back, a sign she needed space, and he abandoned the notion of going to her.

"All I wanted to do tonight was what a woman is supposed to be able to do." She swallowed what he could only think had to be a big ball of pain. "I want to be normal," she strained. "I want to be able to satisfy my husband."

He gave her the truth. "You do satisfy me."

She stared at him and then, right there, he saw it again—the same wave of "there's something I'm not saying" that he'd seen in her eyes earlier.

Cassidy marched to the door, the keys clinking in reply to her quick pace. Irritation and defeat and pride pressed Trevor to react with words, cold and mean, just so she would stay. Even if they were arguing, they would be communicating, and there was a chance they could fix things. But he held back, only saying, "Take my truck." The day was swiftly approaching when Hulk or any other mechanic wouldn't be able to do a thing for Cassidy's car, and Trevor didn't want his wife broken down on the road somewhere this time of night. "Or take Brenda's Maxima," he suggested.

Cassidy abruptly stopped and bristled like Poopie did whenever there was a sudden and loud noise. She walked out of the bedroom, and out of sight, but he heard her state clearly, "I'm not taking Brenda's Maxima."

Cassidy cruised into a spot in front of her old house. She thought about old times and the person she used to talk with at the kitchen table. "I miss you so much, Aunt Odessa."

There weren't any noises tonight, and not another human being in sight. Cassidy grasped the lever and let the seat of her car go all the way back. She closed her eyes and reflected on what happened in her bed, not this night, but the night before, and other recent nights. Trevor had called for Brenda. In his sleep, he pleaded for her. It left Cassidy pondering if he wanted Brenda back. If at moments Cassidy longed to hug Odessa, why wouldn't Trevor long to hug his first wife, his first love, the woman who had given him children and pleased him in bed in a way she still couldn't?

And then there was Kendall.

Cassidy laughed with sarcasm. Kendall had probably authored the manual on how to please a man. That could have very well been the reason Trevor had not come home until two in the morning the time he drove Kendall back to her hotel. Trevor thought she was sleeping when he slid in beside her, but Cassidy had only pretended to be asleep while choking on emotion as she examined the possibility that Trevor had given himself to Kendall. Why else would he not have come directly home or called and told her where he was or answered his cell phone when she called to find him?

And why to this day had he not offered any explanation?

Cassidy started the car and turned on the radio. Craving something other than classical music, she searched for a Christian station.

"I will praise God at all times," the woman preacher on the radio underscored with a strong, vibrant voice. "I will thank God if the table is full or if the table is empty. I will lift my mouth to Him with a blessing on sunny days and cloudy days." The audience in the background cheered, "Hallelujah."

Cassidy steered home, listening to the remainder of the message. "It doesn't matter how you feel," the preacher continued. "It doesn't matter how things look. God is to be praised. Peace comes through praise. Praise is the prelude to your breakthrough."

chapter forty-two

Cassidy rode in the passenger seat next to Trevor, the joy of the Lord mending her heart as she whispered silent praises to God all the way to church. When Cassidy arrived home last night, Trevor was gone, no note telling of his destination, and there had been no answer to her cell phone attempts to reach him. Anger, her first reaction, had been quickly quelled as she returned her focus to God and praised Him until she fell asleep sometime after one. This morning, when she came down for breakfast, she found Trevor stretched on the living room sofa in a deep sleep. She didn't think he was going to church today, but while she was dressing, he showered and dressed and was downstairs ready to go before she had decided which purse to take.

So far, neither had said much beyond good morning, although Cassidy had wanted to talk. Apologies needed to be made on both their parts, but the attempt she made to have a discussion before they pulled from the driveway had been met with a cool, firm "Not now, Cassidy." Cassidy believed her ongoing intimate praise party with the Lord was the main reason she had once again been able to put anger aside and respond with a respectful nod of acquiescence.

The second service was scheduled to start in five minutes, and Trevor veered into the last available parking slot as Lena scurried toward them.

"We've got to talk," Lena said as Cassidy stepped down from the SUV.

"What's wrong?" Cassidy asked. Lena's face was wearing the same expression it had worn several years back when she discovered that the new man in her life was living out of his car.

"I wanted to warn you, so I called you at home and on your cell phone, but you didn't pick up."

Cassidy hadn't felt like talking on the phone this morning, so she'd let the voice mail box for the home phone and her cell phone take all calls. "What's going on?" she asked, scanning the area. Some of the members had formed small groups, and they were looking at them and whispering.

Lena leaned her hand on the truck as if she needed support. "During the first service, Yaneesha said—" She grew silent as Trevor turned the meeting into a three-some.

His voice came down hard. "Yaneesha said *what?*"

Lena rolled her eyes up slowly, like it was hurting her eyes to look up that high. "Yaneesha says you and her are having an affair. She said you were with her last night. She said she was pregnant with your child, but had a miscarriage in the eighth week, and that you were happy that she had."

"Lena," Cassidy said, "we're really not in the mood for a practical joke this morning."

"I'm not joking." Under the weight of her seriousness, her expression became even more somber. "Somehow Yaneesha got past the ushers, wrestled the microphone out of the worship leader's hand, and in tears she confessed that she had sinned with you." Lena looked only at Trevor for a moment. "The congregation was so silent you could hear the dust falling, and I've never seen Pastor Audrey look so angry. You could see he was fighting to keep his cool as he snatched the microphone from Yaneesha, then told her to leave the pulpit and go to his study right away." Lena shook her head. "It was a *mess*."

The tips of Trevor's ears turned red, and his eyes were an inferno of outrage. He snapped a hand around Cassidy's and started marching toward the church. He was moving so quickly Cassidy almost came out of one of her heels. When they arrived at Pastor Audrey's office door, Trevor banged on the wood but didn't wait to be invited in. They stopped in the middle of the room, and he relinquished Cassidy's hand. She shook it because his grip had been firm enough to produce a small prickling of pain. "Where's Yaneesha?" Trevor demanded.

Clement observed them from his seat at his desk. He raised his big bones to a standing position and zippered his black preaching robe. His response was as calm as his presence. "I asked Yaneesha to go home for the day, and unless you compose yourself, I'll advise you to do the same."

Trevor stormed to the edge of the pastor's desk. "How composed should I be with a psycho running around spreading lies about me?"

Clement stared at Trevor through serious eyes.

Trevor responded with a look of disbelief. "Oh, I know you don't believe Yaneesha's crap." In his anger, his tone had become disrespectful, and Trevor had completely stepped over the line separating pastor from parishioner. He turned as if he was finished, then whirled back. "You know, maybe if you'd had better control over your pulpit, none of this would have happened in the first place."

Cassidy lost her breath, and her stare widened, her gaze whipping from Trevor to Clement and back. There was nothing in Trevor's expression that said he was sorry and nothing in Clement's that said he would accept an apology even if it was offered. Frankly, it looked as though if one man were to swing, the other would swing harder.

Cassidy edged forward, hoping that the slight disturbance caused by her movement might defrost the frowns on both faces and remind them of where they were. Cassidy breathed easier, singing internal hallelujahs when Clement finally breathed and Trevor dropped his shoulders a notch.

"I haven't had a chance to thoroughly talk with you or the other party, so I don't know what is or isn't 'crap,'" Clement said. "I'm meeting with Miss Polk this evening. Will you be available in the morning?"

Trevor folded his arms, and though he looked unhappy, he answered with a muffled "Yes." His gaze landed on Clement's desk, and he picked up a big black Bible. Trevor's full name, Trevor Jerome Monroe, imprinted in gold letters, decorated the bottom right corner of the soft leather cover. "I lost this Bible last summer. It never turned up in the Lost and Found, and I thought it was gone forever."

"Miss Polk brought it to church today," Clement revealed. "According to her recollection of the facts, you left it in her apartment."

Trevor chuckled. "That's ridiculous. I've never set foot in Yaneesha's . . ." Embarrassment robbed Trevor's face of any other emotion. He stared at Cassidy, and Cassidy's heartbeat picked up speed. Not for a moment had she believed Trevor had been involved with Yaneesha. Even though Clement needed to hear Yaneesha's side, Cassidy had believed her husband. However, her mind suddenly became colored with images, and they flashed one behind the other.

The Sunday Yaneesha walked up to her and said Trevor was at her apartment . . . the night Cassidy assumed he was with Kendall . . . last night . . . where was he last night?

Cassidy curled a hand over the back of a chair. The furniture would keep her from falling as Trevor confessed. One of Cassidy's coworkers had been in the middle of Thanksgiving dinner when her husband blurted out his infidelity. A sister at the church learned her husband was sleeping around when he stood up during service and put it in the form of a prayer request. So Cassidy knew this was how such news came. Quick. A sucker punch.

"Once." Trevor held the Bible in a rigid grip, down by his leg. "I was in Yaneesha's place *once*. One of my drivers had to take off early, and I had to pick up the slack like I do from time to time." His eyes never left Cassidy. "I made three deliveries that night, and one of them happened to be to Yaneesha. She asked me to come in and put her cake on the table, which I did. And left. It was so uneventful I never thought about it after that."

"I have a sermon to preach," Clement said quietly. "The two of you can stay in here and talk if you'd like, for as long as you need."

Trevor walked to the only window in the room. It offered a view of a miniature garden, planted in memory of Odessa and two other church mothers recently called to glory.

"Thank you, Pastor," Cassidy said. Pastor Audrey left the office, but not before looking back on them with concern. When the door shut, it felt as if she had been sealed in a jar with another insect that wanted to get out as much as she did. She studied the other insect. His hands were shoved in the pockets of olive-colored pants, and his back was a wall of tense muscle. The strain caused his shoulder blades to push against the cotton of an informal button-down shirt. Cassidy had on a jacket dress, and the linen brushed her fingertips as she hugged herself.

"Let's go." He pulled out his car keys and strode past her.

Cassidy walked quickly behind him, pleased with his request. She, too, would rather talk about this behind the closed door of their home. They departed the same way they had entered—through a side door, out of the scope of much of the crowd. In the truck, they fastened their seat belts, and Trevor started the ignition.

"I'll drop you off at home," he said as the engine hummed.

She stared at him and asked softly, "Where are you going?"

"No place special."

"But I thought we were going home to talk."

"Did *you* want to talk last night?"

"No," she whispered.

"Well, I don't want to talk now."

As they approached the end of the street, she said, "Pull over. I want to get out."

Her feet met the sidewalk, and it was Trevor's turn to ask, "Where are you going?"

Cassidy gently shut the door and glanced up the street. "I feel like I need to be in church." She set her eyes to convey how much she wanted him to come with her. She didn't care what people whispered about them. She wanted to worship, hear the Word with the man she loved by her side.

"I'll see you later," was all he said, and drove off.

Cassidy trudged up the street toward the church, old messages creeping into her spirit and stirring up fear. *I told you Trevor was molded from the same clay as Minister and Larenz. Trevor's going to hurt you, too.* Although tired, Cassidy fought back with the Word. "God has not given me the spirit of fear."

The negative messages continued to assault her.

Trevor slept with Yaneesha. Trevor slept with Kendall. You'll never be good in bed. You'll never be the wife, the lover, the mother Brenda was. Trevor doesn't love you. Brittney hates you. You're a failure, Cassidy.

Cassidy countered: "I am more than a conqueror."

"Amen to that," a familiar voice interrupted.

Cassidy jumped out of the meditation she'd been so deeply submerged in. "Oh my goodness, Sister Audrey, I didn't notice you."

❧

Some minutes later, Cassidy sat at the Audreys' kitchen table, heat rising from a cup of green tea. "Thank you for inviting me in," Cassidy said as Vivaca pulled out a chair and joined her.

"I'm just glad I listened to the Spirit's leading and came home early."

Cassidy nodded, also understanding it wasn't coincidence that had put them together. There was a greater force at work. "Trevor's angry. I thought he and your husband were going to fight right there in the church."

Vivaca gave up a chuckle. "That would have been a sight." Her alto sound was as smooth as the honey she'd put in her tea. "Have you and Trevor had a chance to talk about what happened during service this morning?"

"No," she answered disappointedly.

"Clement has told me that you and Trevor have had several sessions with him."

"Yes. They've helped us a lot, but . . ."

Vivaca raised her cup and took a sip, keeping her eyes on Cassidy the entire time. "But?" she prompted.

"I know Yaneesha is lying about being intimate with Trevor, but he may have been involved with someone else." Cassidy candidly voiced her thoughts about Kendall and Trevor.

"You and Trevor have to talk about something like that. A marriage without clear communication is destined for disaster."

"Disaster," she said quietly. "That defines last night."

Vivaca had a way of partially shutting her left eye when she lacked understanding.

"I still have vaginismus," Cassidy clarified.

"Since finding out you had the condition, I've done some reading, which I'm sure you have, too."

"Yes." She'd purchased a book and downloaded Internet information.

"Every case is different because every woman is different," Vivaca said. "Some women overcome the dysfunction quicker than others. You need to be patient and follow the procedures your therapist advises. And certainly, you as a Christian woman must keep standing on God's Word. Your healing is going to come, Cassidy."

Cassidy fiddled with the fringes of the place mat. "What if it doesn't? What if having this condition is the price I have to pay for something I did a long time ago?" Cassidy opened the door of her life wider, sharing with Vivaca about Minister and the baby. She waited in silence for Vivaca to reprimand her for her poor decisions. But like Trevor, Vivaca radiated compassion.

"God loves us even when we do things that displease Him. And when we go to Him for forgiveness, He doesn't have to think about it. He forgives and forgets the moment we ask."

"That's what I want to do. I want to forget that I was stupid enough to sleep with a man who didn't love me, and then give away my child."

Vivaca leaned forward and draped her hand over Cassidy's. "Sweetheart, forgivin' ain't forgettin'."

Cassidy stared at the pastor's wife. Vivaca smiled kindly and said, "The Bible says God forgives and forgets. But that's not how human beings are wired. Yes, the choice to forgive or not lies within us, but when it comes to our memories, we can't simply make them disappear because we want them to."

"But doesn't the Bible say we should forget those things which are behind us?"

"Baby, that scripture means that instead of sitting and dwelling on the mistakes of the past, we are to let go and move forward in spite of those mistakes. If we release the pain of our past to God, He will give us the strength to recall our past without experiencing the anger or depression that was once associated with it." She paused. "Do you understand?"

"You're saying I'll never forget."

"I'm saying you'll remember, but you'll have God's peace."

Cassidy nodded that she understood.

"As for your concern as to whether or not God is making you pay for your mistakes, trust me, Cassidy, I haven't been where you've been, however I've messed up, too. So I'm here to tell you, yes, while there are consequences for every action, good or bad, God is not inflicting pain on me or you because of mistakes we

made years ago or yesterday or even this morning. The
Word says the Lord takes pleasure in us. He rejoices and
sings over us.

"Over the years," Vivaca continued, "I've counseled
many women who've had abortions. One woman was
forty-two when she came to see me. For *twenty-one
years*, she'd lived behind the bars of self-condemnation.
And *you*, Cassidy, have self-imposed the same prison."
She made strong eye contact. "God's not punishing
you, but you've been punishing yourself. Now, I'm not
saying you're purposely causing the vaginismus, but
your body *is* reacting to what's going on in your mind.
And what I see is that you're not merely fearful of reliving another pregnancy, you don't think you're *worthy*
of another pregnancy. You don't believe you *deserve* to
have another baby."

Vivaca had discerned Cassidy's hidden truth, and
Cassidy dropped her gaze. Vivaca questioned gently,
"Isn't it time to revoke the life sentence you've given
yourself and love yourself as God loves you?"

Love herself. She had stopped loving herself the moment she stepped away from her son. Her eyes filled
with tears as she nodded, too choked up to speak.

"I want you to close your eyes and go back to the
night you abandoned the baby."

Cassidy tensed, shrinking from the instruction.

"You can do it. I'll walk with you." Sealing her
promise, Vivaca squeezed Cassidy's hand. Cassidy
closed her eyes. "Find the moment you returned from
the hospital," Vivaca said.

I can do this. Cassidy inhaled and exhaled. *I can do all
things through Christ*, she said to her fear, commanding
it to back away from her.

"Do you see yourself?" Vivaca asked.

"Yes."

"Where are you?"

"Sitting in my dorm room. Minister dropped me off there. He said he would be back soon. He had some stuff to do and—"

"No, Cassidy," Vivaca tenderly silenced her. "This particular moment is not about Minister. You're going to have to deal with how you feel about yourself before you can adequately deal with your feelings about Minister." Her directions were solid. "I want you to keep the focus on you."

Cassidy felt Vivaca come and stand behind her. Vivaca's hands covered Cassidy's shoulders, and Cassidy reached and clutched Vivaca's fingers, taking the support. "I'm sitting on my bed," Cassidy said.

"And how do you feel?"

"Sad." She sighed. "Scared, too. I want to go back to the hospital and get my baby, but I'm afraid."

"Go and sit with that frightened young woman," Vivaca directed. "Put your arms around her. Can you do that?"

"Yes."

"Now," Vivaca said softly, "tell her, 'I forgive you.'"

Cassidy stiffened, trying to hold herself together, but tears oozed out of her eyes and down her face. The few that didn't fall straight from her chin traveled under it, making their final home somewhere along her neck. "I forgive you," she managed to whisper.

"I release you of the guilt, the regret, and the shame," Vivaca said.

Cassidy swallowed hard and said it all.

Vivaca continued to guide with the voice of a caring shepherdess. "Tell her, 'God loves you and I love you.'"

"God loves you . . . and I love you."

chapter forty-three

A horn honked, a car pulled over to the curb, and Cassidy stopped walking. Dunbar got out of his Saturn and stepped up on the sidewalk. He had on a dark suit and a paisley tie. The cordiality in his eyes suggested he wanted to give her a hug, but he simply said, "Hi."

She smiled. "Hi."

"You okay?"

Dunbar had either been in the first service or heard what happened. Cassidy supposed the entire membership would know before the sun went down.

"Yes, I'm okay," she said, the pure truth.

"Good," he said. "Are you on your way home?"

She nodded.

"Can I give you a ride?"

A city transit bus rumbled past, and she waited until the gruff sound died. "I don't mind walking."

"You know, you once said you would always be my friend." He opened the passenger door. "And I'll always be yours. So come on and get in."

The shoes Cassidy had on weren't the best for the walk that lay ahead, and her feet had begun protesting three blocks ago. But even if Cassidy had been wearing sneakers, she would have accepted Dunbar's invitation.

He shifted the gears from park to drive. "How are your little girls?"

"They're fine. They're with their aunt today." Cassidy added, "Brittney's not too happy with me right now. She thinks I'm too hard on her."

"When she's older, she'll look back and she'll be glad you were hard. You just keep on being there for her and loving her and disciplining her when she needs it, and she'll be okay."

Cassidy nodded. "I know she will."

"Are you still walking for exercise?"

"Yes. Are you?"

"Yes, and I have a new partner." He paused. "Her name is Indiya."

Cassidy smiled. "Indiya Rovell? From the drama ministry?"

Dunbar's grin broadened. "Yeah."

"I've talked to her several times. She's a nice person."

"I think so. I'm taking her out next weekend."

Cassidy chuckled. "For real?"

"For real."

"That's great, Dunbar. I'm glad for you."

"Thanks."

Dunbar halted the car in front of her home. He came around and held the door open for her as she vacated the seat. His words froze her to the pavement. "Trevor loves you."

A long but gentle moment passed. "I love him, too."

"I'll be praying for the both of you. I want things to work out for you two."

Cassidy gazed into Dunbar's peaceful and sincere eyes. "Thank you," she said.

✐❦

The gravel shifted, its tiny teeth crunching under Cassidy's sneakers as she sauntered across the park toward Trevor. He was on the basketball court, thick into a game with a group of boys in their middle to upper teenage years. Trevor, hands poised, threw his strong shoulders left then right, stretched his long legs, and lifted his heels off the ground just before shooting the ball. His movements had been as fluid and as forceful as good music, and Cassidy understood why so many women found him attractive. But as handsome as Trevor was, it was still his heart Cassidy loved best.

Back at the other end of the court, Trevor reached into the air to block a shot and noticed Cassidy for the first time. He immediately lowered his arm, and the kid with the ball made the basket. "I'm taking a break," Cassidy heard her husband say.

The youngsters continued to play as Trevor walked to the sidelines. As soon as he stopped in front of her, Cassidy asked, "Do you know them?"

Somewhere between church and here, Trevor had changed clothes. He lifted the edge of his black T-shirt and wiped the sweat from his face, then looked back at the young men. "No, I don't know them. A couple of them were about to fight when I pulled up. I got them involved in a game to take their minds off of killing each other." He gave Cassidy a long stare. "How did you know I was here?"

When Cassidy stopped home to change into casual clothing, she had called Grace to find out if Trevor was with her and Houston. Then she drove to the gym where Trevor worked out and on to the bakery. With no sign of Trevor at either place, she had prayed, *Where is he, Lord?* The answer came as she was about to give up and go home. "I received some help from above," she answered, before sending a glance across the sun-toasted playground, the same playground where Trevor had proposed to her. "Can we talk, please?" Cassidy took in Trevor's face, an unreadable page.

"Over there," he said with a nod, and they moved toward the empty swings.

Cassidy sat on one of the black curved seats and rested her hands on her knees. She shoveled a patch of sand with the toe of her sneaker. Trevor had lowered himself to a seat, too. He looped his arms around the metal chains and hooked his hands together. He examined her, then looked elsewhere.

"So this is where you come to get away from me," she whispered.

"No. This is where I come to chill out and get my thoughts together."

She kept her voice low. "I don't understand why you don't pick up when I call."

"I usually leave my phone in the glove compartment when I'm playing ball." He paused. "But that's no excuse." His gaze held hers. "I know I was wrong not to respond to your calls. I know it was inconsiderate of me not to tell you where I was today and the other times. I'm sorry," he said.

"I forgive you," she said.

"I've never been with Yaneesha."

"I know."

"You're the only woman I want."

"Are you sure?" Seeing the confusion on his brow, she spoke frankly. "The night you took Kendall back to the hotel, you didn't come home right away. Did something happen between the two of you?"

Once again, he made sure they were locked into each other's gaze before talking. "I made a bad decision and accompanied Kendall to her hotel room. She came on to me, and initially, I didn't stop her because I didn't want to stop her. But I knew that if I didn't stop her, I was going to end up doing something foolish. So I walked away and never looked back."

His admission. It hurt. But to choose unforgiveness would hurt her, him, so much more. "Thank you for being honest," she croaked.

"Now it's your turn," he said, and she regarded him with surprise. "What was really going on inside of your head last night? Why were you so determined to go against the doctor's advice?"

Cassidy looked down at the sand again. "At the time, I thought you and Kendall might have been intimate, and I was blaming myself and wanting to prove to you and myself, too, that I'm just as much woman as she is."

Trevor pulled the chain of Cassidy's swing, turning her to him, bringing her closed knees between his open thighs. He spoke into her eyes. "Number one, if I had committed adultery with Kendall or anyone else, there's only one person that would've been to blame, and that's me. And number two, you don't ever need to prove anything to me because no woman in the world means more to me than you or makes me as happy as you do."

He continued, "When we said our marriage vows, and I promised to love you in sickness and in health, I never thought we'd be faced with something right away. I'm sure most people don't. But I meant my vows, Sky. So I will love you for as long as it takes you to get better, no matter how long."

Cassidy remembered last night. When she spoke of it today in Vivaca's kitchen, she said it had been a disaster. But the truth was that the early stages of her and Trevor's intimacy had been beautiful, and she cherished the closeness that came with it. Dr. Tia's advice to move slowly, though, had been wise. "I need more time," she admitted.

He nodded. "I will wait for you," he promised. "And during the waiting, I will remain devoted to you and only you." He held her chin, and his tone grew huskier. "You are my angel."

She smiled. "And you are mine," she said. She slowly leaned forward and tenderly kissed his lips. Sooner than she wanted, she put a period to the kiss, the teen boys nearby.

"When I go to see the pastor tomorrow, I would like for you to come with me."

"I'll be there," she said.

He looked to the car. "I see you drove the Maxima."

Cassidy wasn't sure why, but for once, Trevor didn't

refer to the car as "Brenda's Maxima." When she first
arrived today, she had thought she would tell him he'd
been chanting Brenda's name in his sleep, within his
dreams. But, she now realized, some things in life truly
didn't matter. Cassidy loved Trevor. Trevor loved her.
They both loved God. They had two healthy girls.
Derek was in a good home. Those were the things that
mattered. "My car wouldn't start. I don't think it can be
resuscitated," she said.

Trevor laughed and pushed off the swing. He stood
behind her. "Next weekend we'll go car-shopping."

"That won't be necessary." She stared over her
shoulder and up at Trevor. "I'd like to keep Max for a
while," she said, nicknaming the Maxima.

"Max?" he curiously questioned, pulling her swing
chains back toward him.

"Yes," she said as her feet left the ground. She
stretched her legs as the swing carried her forward.
"She's paid for, isn't she?"

Cassidy flowed backward, and Trevor gave her a
hearty push. "Yes," he answered.

"Well, there's no sense in making another monthly
bill right now." She smiled. She hadn't been on a swing
since childhood. The air swooshed by, caressing her face.
"Besides, I need time to think about what kind of make
and model I want to own. Eventually, I'll need something large enough for the girls . . . and the babies."

"Babies," he repeated, joy in his voice. "How many
babies are we talking about?"

"Three or four or *five*," she squealed as Trevor
pushed her firmly, sending her higher.

chapter forty-four

Cassidy advised herself not to freak out, but the foolishness Trevor had just served her was eating holes through her tolerance.

"Where are you?" she tried again. Trevor had come home from work at his usual time, but at a quarter past nine, he said he was going to run an errand. He kissed her and the children, said he loved them all, and now, an hour later, she was taking his call.

"I can't tell you," he said, his answer the same.

"When are you coming home?"

"In two days. Maybe more," he added after a pause.

"Trevor, I don't like this. Why can't you tell me where you are?"

"I'll tell you everything when I get back. Until then, you're going to have to trust me."

"This really isn't the best timing for this." It was only two days ago that they'd sat on the swings and he'd apologized for his previous disappearing acts. Now he was in the middle of another one.

"I need you to trust me." He sneezed. "Okay?"

"That's the second time you've sneezed."

"I know. I hope I'm not coming down with any-thing."

"If you were here, I could take care of you."

"Just take care of yourself and the girls. I'll keep my phone close, but I only want you to call if it's an emer-gency. I'll check in on you in the morning."

Trevor suggested they pray before he disconnected. Cassidy investigated every word of the prayer, deter-mined to expose the teeniest clue as to where Trevor might be. When he said, "Amen," she was no more in-formed than when he had opened with "Dear Jesus."

✍❤

"I'm coming," Cassidy shrieked. "Hold on." All she heard was the gurgle of the river. The child's cries were a memory. She made a frantic 360-degree turn. "Where are you?" she screamed.

"Here I am," a happy voice answered. "Look over here."

Cassidy faced the sound and found the boy. He was on the bank, and there was a woman with him. The woman smiled at Cassidy.

"She pulled me out," the boy said. "Don't worry, I'm okay."

Cassidy awakened in the dark bedroom. She wasn't sure what hour it was, but she knew it was late. She re-mained on her back, her hands turned down on the bed. She dug her nails into the soft sheets and sat up straight. "He's safe," she marveled as her eyes adjusted to her dark surroundings. She laughed openly. "He's safe," she said again, recognizing for the first time that the boy in the dream represented her son. Pressing her arms across her breasts in X-formation, she looked up. "Thank You," she whispered. She raised her hands to heaven. "Thank you, God," she cried louder and louder as water seeped from her eyes.

Cassidy praised the Lord for the rest of the night—sitting up, lying down, in and out of sleep, she praised Him.

As promised, Trevor called the next morning. Cassidy told him about the dream, and he said he was happy for her, then rushed off the phone. Ordinarily, a peppy good-bye like the one he'd flipped to her would have irritated her, but she was still up on her spiritual mountain, feeling too good to come down for any reason.

Brittney's long face didn't even get on her nerves today. And during prayer service that evening, when Yaneesha stood up and retracted everything she had said about Trevor, Cassidy didn't feel the anger she thought she would. What she felt was sorry for Yaneesha. People who did things to intentionally hurt others were people in pain. Yaneesha needed God's touch, and Cassidy would pray for her.

After the close of service, Cassidy walked downstairs to pick up Brandi and Brittney from Kidpraise. On the way to the large room, her path joined with Pastor Audrey's. "I know where God wants me," she said to him.

"I've known for a long time. My place is with the Sparrow Ministry."

"That's right," Clement said. "Your experiences have been painful, but the blessing is that those experiences will help you relate to someone else who has yet to overcome." His eyes gleamed. "You know, your aunt would be proud of the young woman you've become. I said I wasn't going to tell you this, but a few days before Mother Vale passed away, she told me about a vision she had. She said she saw you and Trevor exchanging wedding vows."

Cassidy felt her entire face smile. So her aunt had seen her wedding, after all.

"You should continue to be encouraged where your marriage is concerned," Clement said. "I imagine Mother Vale has formed a band of heavenly prayer warriors for you and Trevor." He waved at a parishioner on the other side of the room. "And speaking of your husband, have him call me when he gets back in town."

Cassidy pinned Clement with a questioning look.

"Uh-oh," Clement said.

She ground out each word. "You know where he is."

"Yes, but I can't tell you." Clement pulled an invisible zipper across his lips.

"Oh, all right," she finally relented, less concerned about Trevor now that she knew that the pastor was aware of his whereabouts.

As Cassidy strolled through the parking lot, she continued to feel carefree and joyous, and the surprise she received as she unlocked Max's door just made life sweeter. "I've been thinking," Brittney said, "I might want to call you Mom sometimes." She finished very businesslike, "I'll let you know."

"I'll let you know, too." Brandi climbed into the car, her smile rich with ecstasy.

"Why do you always have to copy me?" Brittney complained. "Cassidy, could you tell her to stop copying everything I do?"

"Stop copying everything she does," Cassidy responded lightly. She sat in the driver's seat and turned to look at the girls. She had never asked the children to call her Mom, but she and Trevor had assured them it was all right if they wanted to. Cassidy had said then what she said now. "You're both welcome to call me Mom. I would like that very much. But if you decide not to, that's okay, too." She smiled and the girls nodded. Once they were all buckled in, Cassidy pressed the button for the CD player. Bishop Colvin Culpepper sang about the goodness of God, and Cassidy and the children sang with him.

chapter forty-five

So ya'll come to see an old lady?" Almondetta stepped aside so Cassidy and the children could enter her apartment.

Cassidy kissed Almondetta on the cheek. "Hello, Mother Almondetta," she said, and the girls echoed the greeting. On the way over, Cassidy told the girls they were to take their shoes off when they arrived. All of them in socks now, Almondetta offered them seats in the living room. Cassidy and the children shared one half of a plastic-covered sofa. Almondetta sat across from them in a high-back wing chair. She spread her skirt and rested her arms on the chair. She looked like a storybook queen sitting on her throne.

"Where's your dog?" Brandi asked. Cassidy had also prepared the children for Delightful, nowhere in sight at the moment.

Almondetta's face showed a glimmer of happiness for the first time. "She's resting in my room. Would you girls like to go in and see her?"

The children waited for Cassidy's permission. Cassidy nodded yes. Minutes later, Almondetta returned to the living room without the children. "I put the television on. They're watching cartoons with Delightful." Almondetta sat back down in her chair. "Special Day ain't been the same since you quit," she snapped.

"Well, I—"

"No need to explain," Almondetta interrupted. "Yaneesha wasn't no help. Trifling girl was only in it for the money." Almondetta addressed Cassidy's confused eyes. "I'd forget and leave money in the pockets of my clothes that were in the hamper. Yaneesha was snooping around in there one day and found about forty dollars. After that, I knew Yaneesha was going to have to use the bathroom every time she came over. I left money in my clothes on purpose, to keep her coming back." Almondetta shrugged. "Can't be but so upset with her. Truth is, I wasn't no better than she was. I didn't care about the ministry as much as I cared about having some company." She closed her eyes. "Lord, help me some more," she prayed.

Cassidy crossed the room and sat on the footstool beside Almondetta's chair. "I'd like to visit you again, maybe next week"—Cassidy smiled and emphasized—"for free."

Almondetta cracked an eyelid. "Are you going to bring them sweet daughters with you?"

"If that's what you want."

"That's what I want," Almondetta answered, and patted Cassidy's shoulder.

"It's my turn," Brandi sang. She smacked a card on the growing pile, then looked at her big sister.

Brittney sighed. "I don't have anything." She picked up a card from the other pile, and both girls stared at Cassidy.

One of Cassidy's legs threatened to go numb, and she shifted for a more comfortable position. The family room needed a card table and chairs, and Cassidy recorded the items on her mental shopping list. As of now, the small room that sat off the kitchen contained only a sofa and a stocked entertainment center, so the hardwood floor served as their seats.

"Did you hear that?" Brittney's eyes widened.

Cassidy surveyed the line of cards in her hand, contemplating which card to throw down, while the smell of the spices baking into the chicken and broccoli casserole she'd prepared for dinner tiptoed into the room. "No, I didn't hear anything," she said.

"I hear something, too," Brandi said, her eyes big like her sister's.

Cassidy tilted her head. She heard something . . . no, someone . . . someone was in the back of the house.

"I bet you it's Daddy," Brittney yelled, and the three females instantly put their card game on hold and rushed through the kitchen to the back door.

"It's Daddy!" Brandi screamed.

The children ran down the deck steps to their father. Cassidy leaned over the rail and watched the show. One daughter at a time, Trevor lifted and hugged them.

"Did you bring us something?" Brandi asked with her head all the way back as she stared up at her superhero.

The superhero teased, "Could be something on the front steps."

Brittney dashed away.

"I hope it's a baby elephant," Brandi squealed, running behind her sister.

It grew quiet. Only the chirp of birds and the steady buzz of a neighbor's lawn mower sounded in the air. Trevor gazed upward, Cassidy downward. Her smile spoke the poem that was in her heart. *I love you and I missed you and I'm so glad you're home.*

Trevor smiled, too, as if he'd opened her heart and read every word. Cassidy trotted along the same path the children had, plastered against him, and their arms became locks. The embrace was broken only because he sneezed.

"Sorry, I didn't mean to spray you."

She smiled. "I guess I'll have that cold now, too."

"Come on," he said. He grabbed his duffel bag from the hood of the SUV and held her hand. "There's something you have to see." Moments later, in their bedroom, they took side-by-side seats on the bed. He unzipped the duffel bag and clasped two envelopes. "This one first," he said.

She opened the larger envelope and pulled out a sheet of paper. It was a letter, written by Trevor, and she read what it said.

"I have you to thank for that," he expressed when she finished. "I couldn't have written it without your example of obedience to God's Word." He changed his mind. "Well, I might have written it, but not this soon."

Although Minister was dead, as part of her therapy,

Cassidy had written a letter to him, telling him anything and everything she needed to say in order to release her anger, offer forgiveness, and experience
closure. And since her talk with Vivaca and the prayers
that followed, little by little it was becoming easier for
Cassidy to remember Minister, her pregnancy, and her
baby without attaching negative emotions to her memories. She continued to hold Trevor's letter: his words
to the man who had taken Brenda from him and the
girls. In precise and poignant language, Trevor had told
this man he forgave him and, most important, how
much Jesus loved him.

"I hadn't forgiven him," Trevor confessed. "I tried to
convince myself that I had, but each time I attempted
to pray for him, I couldn't. I can now. I've made him a
part of my prayers, and I'm going to send him this letter.
I want him to know Jesus the same way I do."

"Now we're both free," she said gently, and Trevor
knitted their fingers until they were palm-to-palm, as
she ogled the other envelope. "What's in that one?"

"The reason for my disappearance."

He passed the white envelope to her and unlaced
their fingers so she could extract the contents, which
she did, her pulse throbbing in anticipation of something she sensed would be a significant event.

A few minutes passed, and Cassidy was thankful
Trevor had allowed her to spend them in silence, giving
her room to ponder, and yearn, and memorize every
facet of her little boy's face. She knew it was her son in
the picture. A mother knew. "Where did you get this?"
Her voice was barely controlled as she gripped the

edges of the small photograph as though it might fly away if she were to apply less pressure.

"I drove upstate, and with a little amateur detective work, I came across an article at the library about families who have adopted. One of the families, the Walshes, adopted an abandoned baby. It was a long shot, but I tracked them down." He turned his face away and coughed. "The Walshes had a daughter, so I knew I was at the wrong house. Surprisingly, though, they gave me the name of the social worker they had dealt with. Turned out he no longer worked with the Social Services Department, and the person I did speak with said the files were confidential and that I should go home. And that's what I intended to do, believing it wasn't meant for me to find anything about your son." Trevor glanced at the bright-eyed boy in Cassidy's hands. "I returned to my motel room, packed up my stuff, and this morning I left. I stopped at this prehistoric-looking gas station a few miles from the turnpike, and this old black guy came out to pump the gas and clean the windows."

"Mr. Roy Roper," Cassidy said. "Everyone at Tilden knew him. I can't believe he's still alive."

"Mr. Roper started up a conversation, and I ended up telling him your story. Not fifteen minutes later, I was sitting in this poorly lit, smelly back room drinking coffee with Mr. Roper and a friend of his who he had asked to come over. His name was Mr. Johnny. Mr. Johnny has a daughter who adopted a little boy who was left at a hospital on the same night you gave birth."

"Mr. Johnny's daughter adopted my son?"

"Yes. She's married, and they all live in another state. Mr. Johnny assured me the child is happy and healthy."

Cassidy flipped the picture. There was nothing written on the back. "What's his name?"

"I don't know. I don't even know Mr. Johnny's last name, and that's the way he wanted it. He said it's always been his daughter's wish to remain anonymous, and I told him we would respect that."

Although her accepting that she most likely would not hold her son again was not without challenge, she nodded in agreement with Trevor.

"Mr. Johnny has cancer, and he believes his time is short. I believe that's why God led me to do this for you now."

"Thank you," she whispered. She leaned and kissed Trevor's cheek.

He squeezed her hand. "How are you doing behind all this?" he asked.

Furnished with a peace she recognized as God, she said, "I'm okay."

"Mr. Johnny thought you should have something of the child, so he sent along this picture. It was taken three years ago. Mr. Johnny also sent a message. He said some teenagers leave their newborns to die in Dumpsters and toilets, so he thanks you for leaving the baby in the hospital. Because you did, he has a grandson. His only one."

"Most states," she said, "give women the option of turning their unwanted newborns over to authorities with no questions asked. It's much safer for the baby to give him or her up that way instead of the way I chose to do it." Cassidy smiled at her son. He had her eyes and skin tone. "Pepperoni—that's what I nicknamed him while he was in my womb."

"Why would someone who detests pizza nickname their baby Pepperoni?"

"I haven't always detested it. When I was pregnant, I craved pepperoni pizza day and night. But ever since, just the smell of pizza makes me want to—"

"Throw up," he completed, smiling slightly.

"Yes." She smiled at him. The girls had come inside the house, and their laughter suggested they were thrilled with whatever Trevor had brought them.

"Are you still interested in making Herbie a part of our family?" he asked.

Cassidy knew that elation showed in her eyes. "Yes. I've never stopped asking the Lord to make a way for it to happen." They talked about Herbie for a few minutes, and then she reached up and rubbed the hard kinks in Trevor's neck. "You're tired."

"Some," he admitted.

"Would you like a cup of tea? It might help you get over that cold sooner."

"Yes," he said. "Thank you."

Cassidy walked across the room and rested her photograph on the dresser, against the mirror. Tomorrow she would go to the store and buy the perfect frame for it.

She cast a glance over her shoulder. Her husband had fallen back on the bed and laid his arm over his eyes. His breathing was even and heavy, a signal he was almost asleep, if not already sleeping. Cassidy knelt in front of his legs and untied his laces. She removed his sneakers and socks, then tenderly massaged each foot as rays of early evening sun spilled over her shoulders, washing Trevor's feet and her hands with warm light.

reading group guide

1. It isn't unusual for gossip to start surrounding a recently widowed (or divorced) person who resumes dating or even becomes engaged. Do you think there's an appropriate time lapse for a person to "mourn" a relationship before embarking on a new one? Why or why not? What reservations do you have about hooking up with someone who lost a former partner through death or divorce?

2. When depression threatens, Cassidy pulls out a memory verse to encourage herself. What scriptures do you keep on tap, so to speak, to lift your spirit?

3. To what degree are you content in the life God has given you—single or married? How do you relate to friends who are in different phases of life—or different degrees of contentment?

4. Cassidy knows her scripture, studies the Bible regularly, and truly believes the Word. However, she doesn't feel worthy of claiming the promise of God's peace and sustenance by surrendering her past to the Lord. What keeps you from laying hold of God's promises?

5. Considering that both Cassidy and Trevor are wrestling with issues of grief, their discussion about tears raises interesting questions. How do you grieve? How do you relate to others—men and women—who grieve differently? What does scripture say about grief?

6. Derek doesn't want Trevor to call Social Services or the police about his abusive and neglectful mother. At the same time, he struggles against hatred for her. How would you counsel youth like Derek?

7. What vibe do you get from the Special Day ministry meetings? Have you ever had a similar experience in a ministry—one that just didn't feel quite right? What was it about the ministry?

8. Like Brenda, Aunt Odessa dies without warning, giving no one opportunity to say good-bye. What comfort can we find when a loved one passes away suddenly?

9. While it is true Rave had ulterior motives for expressing concern about Trevor and Cassidy's living arrangements, Pastor Audrey seems to feel the concern is legitimate. Do you agree? Why or why not? How much effort do you expend in avoiding situations that might tempt you?

10. Do you believe in love at first sight? If so, how do you define it? What do you think of Oliver Toby's definition: "I'm saying that I only wanted good for Louise [from the first time he saw her]. She immediately became a part of my prayers . . . That's what true love is: wanting the best for the other person"?

11. Rave admits to herself that sex has become a drug for her. Does learning about her past experiences with sex (e.g., incest, rape, molestation) make it easier for you to sympathize with her and care about her? Why or why not?

12. Cassidy had Dunbar; Trevor had Kendall. Both struggled to accept the presence of the other's "friend" in their married life together. Is it possible for a married person to have a friend of the opposite sex without negatively affecting the marriage? Why or why not? How do you handle your spouse's (or boyfriend's or girlfriend's) friendships with a person of the opposite sex?

13. What was your response to Clement's advice about sex at the bachelor party? How do you apply Ephesians 5:28 to sexual intimacy? What experience have you had with power in a man's hands—for good or for evil?

14. Oliver Toby advises Cassidy that while some memories are just that and safely left in the past, other memories can't remain secret—because they can't be handled alone. How do you discern when you can safely put a memory to rest versus bringing it into the light?

15. Do you agree or disagree with this statement—and why? "Cassidy had turned him away. So if her husband turned to Kendall, there was no one to blame but herself."

16. Cassidy accepts pastoral counseling from Clement and Vivaca but strongly resists therapy. Why? What experience do you have with counseling or therapy? Were they Christian or non-Christian, positive or negative? Do you believe that seeking therapy (even from a nonbeliever) is beneficial? Why or why not?

17. What would you advise young women like Cassidy and Rave, who found themselves pregnant and without a supportive marriage partner? What options are available to such a woman? What seems good for her—and/or best for the child?

18. Second families—whether created through remarriage, foster care, or adoption—present complex politics, tensions, insecurities, and other challenges, for spouses and children alike. What experience do you have with such families? How have you navigated the challenges, and what sources of help have been available?

19. How has Cassidy's inability to love herself obstructed her abilities in other areas (e.g., marriage, parenting, ministry)? How does Cassidy's example shed new light on Jesus' selection of "Love your neighbor as yourself" as the second greatest commandment?

Reading Groups for African American
Christian Women Who Love God and Like to Read

BE A PART OF
GLORY GIRLS READING GROUPS!

THESE EXCITING BI-MONTHLY READING GROUPS ARE FOR THOSE SEEKING FELLOWSHIP WITH OTHER WOMEN WHO ALSO LOVE GOD AND ENJOY READING.

For more information about GLORY GIRLS, to connect with an established group in your area, or to become a group facilitator, go to our Web site at **www.glorygirlsread.net** or click on the Praising Sisters logo at **www.walkworthypress.net.**

WHO WE ARE

GLORY GIRLS is a national organization made up of primarily African American Christian women, yet it welcomes the participation of anyone who loves the God of the Bible and likes to read.

OUR PURPOSE IS SIMPLE

- To honor the Lord with <u>what we read</u>—and have a good time doing it!

- To provide an atmosphere where readers can seek fellowship with other book lovers while encouraging them in the choices they make in Godly reading materials.

- To offer readers fresh, contemporary, and entertaining yet scripturally sound fiction and nonfiction by talented Christian authors.

- To assist believers and nonbelievers in discovering the relevancy of the Bible in our contemporary, everyday lives.